"Who hasn't ~~dreamed of~~ joining the circus? Laura Lam's Micah does just that, discovering a world of clowns and acrobats, conmen and tricksters, corruption and incompetent doctors, and maybe more about himself. I look forward to more from this author."

Brian Katcher, author of Almost Perfect

"Welcome to a world of shills and showmen, fading tech and circus freaks, where nothing and no one is what it appears. An absorbing, accomplished debut."

Elspeth Cooper, author of the Wild Hunt *series*

"A lyrical, stunningly written debut novel, which set my heart racing with every lift of the trapeze. In Micah we have one of the most original – and likeable – protagonists I've read in a long time. An author to watch, without a doubt."

Amy McCulloch, author of The Oathbreaker's Shadow

"In *Pantomime*, Laura Lam has created a world which will take your breath away, and characters you will never want to leave. Enchanting."

Lou Morgan, author of Blood and Feathers

"Ancient myths, vintage tech and living wonders abound in the riotous carnival of fancy which is *Pantomime*. Lam .... rdust whil .... with subt ....

K

LAURA LAM

Pantomime

STRANGE CHEMISTRY

An Angry Robot imprint
and a member of the Osprey Group

Lace Market House
54-56 High Pavement
Nottingham NG1 1HW
UK

4301 21st Street, Suite 220B,
Long Island City,
NY 11101
USA

www.strangechemistrybooks.com
Strange Chemistry #7

A Strange Chemistry paperback original 2013

Cover by Tom Bagshaw.
Set in Sabon by THL Design.

Distributed in the United States by Random House, Inc., New York.

ISBN 978-1-908844-37-8
Ebook ISBN: 978-1-908844-38-5

Printed in the United States of America

9 8 7 6 5 4 3 2 1

For Craig,
who is always there
to catch me when I jump

1
SUMMER: AUDITION

"They say magic left the world with the Chimaera and the Alder. Whether they perished or abandoned us for the stars, the magic has leeched from the earth and left us only its scattered remnants. Its Vestige. They say perhaps if the Chimaera and the Alder ever return, magic will as well.
"I do not hold with such frivolity."

A HISTORY OF ELLADA AND ITS COLONIES,
Professor Caed Cedar, Royal
Snakewood University

"Well, *boy*," the ringmaster said. "What can you *do*?"

I swallowed. The clown who had found me eavesdropping tightened his grip on my shirt. "Pardon?" I asked.

He chuckled. "Don't tell me you're simple. What can you do? Are you a fire-eater? An acrobat? A freak?"

I was a freak, but I could not tell him so. I took a breath, smelling hay and sand. "I... I'm good at climbing, sir. Like a squirrel."

He raised his eyebrows and gave an amused look to the mirthful circus folk. "The boy can *climb*. Well, I've never come across someone with so rare and useful a skill. I'm afraid we've already got someone to take the glass globes up and down." He waved a hand toward the top of the tent and my eyes rested on the tightrope and the trapeze.

"It wouldn't take much time to turn me into an acrobat that can walk the rope and swing from the... swing." I pointed up at the trapeze, for I did not know what it was called.

"What's your name, boy?" the ringmaster asked, eyeing me up and down. What he thought of me was clear on his face: *scrawny runt.*

"Micah Grey, sir."

"Did Riley and Batheo's Circus of Mundanities send you?" He must have meant Riley & Batheo's Circus of Curiosities, the largest circus in Ellada.

"No, I have never seen Riley and Batheo." I took another breath, which was difficult with the white clown still holding onto the scruff of my neck. "I want to join your circus."

Everyone around me erupted into laughter. The greasepaint on the clowns' faces creased, looking cruel, almost goblin-like. The dwarf tapped the giant on the shin and asked to be put on his shoulder so he could have a better view.

"Well, little Micah, I'm sure you climb very well and all, but I think it's best you run along back to your parents."

I glanced at the two trapeze artists I had seen perform that night. The older man was grinning outright and the girl pressed four fingertips of her hand against her lips. When she saw me looking, she gave me a wink. It was enough.

"I'll prove it to you, sir," I said, and broke away from the clown and dashed toward the ladder to the tightrope. The circus folk jeered and catcalled. Their cries spurred me on. I clambered onto the small wooden platform and my head spun as I looked down, though I had climbed much higher than this in the past. I looked up at the trapeze and began to judge the distance.

"Hey, boy, come on, you've had your laugh, now come down!" the ringmaster called. "I don't feel like peeling your corpse from the ground and having to give your parents a pancake for a son!"

I ignored him and bent my legs.

"Arik! Aenea! Go bring him down before he kills himself." Far below, I saw the female aerialist, Aenea, run toward the rope and begin to climb.

As soon as I had seen the circus, I had known it would come to this. I had nowhere else to run to. The Policiers of the Constabulary were after me. There was no going back now.

I jumped.

2

SUMMER: LIGHTS AND SHADOWS

"Ladies and gentlemen! Boys and girls! Currs and skags! Step into the world as you've never seen it! Discover the skills, the mystery, and the magic of R.H. Ragona's Circus of Magic, the best circus in Ellada! There are the fabled felines of Linde and their fearless trainers! Men and women eat fire, stand upon a galloping horse, and contort into knots like rubber! Watch them fly through the air! This is the show you have always been waiting for, so step right up!"

Barker's cry of R.H. RAGONA'S CIRCUS OF MAGIC

Several hours earlier:

I spent my last few coins to get into the circus, counting the coppers in my palm. I knew it was stupid to do so, but I needed an escape from the real world. I also felt like I owed it to my brother. We had planned to sneak out of the apartments to see the circus when it was next in town or, even better, to see Riley & Batheo's Circus of Curiosities in the hippodrome in Imachara. Even Mother had once considered going when she heard that the Princess Royal had attended a show with the Two Child Queens of Byssia.

But my brother would not be here. Mother and Father would take out my disappearance on him, confining him to his rooms except for his lessons and visits to the courts with Father. He would not climb down scaffolding and come halfway across the city. He liked mischief as much as the next boy, but in the end he was a good sort. Unlike me.

I pushed past the men in bowler hats and the women in shawls to get a good seat near the front. The tent smelled of human sweat, old popping corn, and manure. Tinny music from a large gramophone lent the empty tent a festive air.

The tent had been constructed on a wide, flat slab of stone topped with sand and sawdust, with one large ring drawn onto the stage with white chalk. Above the audience rose a canopy of faded red and blue canvas, and a rope ladder led to the tightrope and the long, thin swings of the trapeze. Tiny glass globe lights dotted the ceiling like stars. I was surprised – the Vestige artefacts were not cheap and getting rarer each year. But I supposed they were cheaper than a fire in a circus tent.

People trickled in. Grubby little children grinned and pointed at the rings in the center of the stage. Courting and married pairs strolled, the men with their cravats and the ladies in their bonnets and bustles. Hawkers wasted no time and circled and weaved through the rows, calling out their wares.

"Peanuts! Popping corn! Sugar floss!" they cried. Most were young, fairly attractive women wearing skirts short enough to show their ankles. I desperately wanted to try some of the sugar floss that looked like clouds, but it cost nearly as much as the ticket. I settled into my seat, my stomach rumbling.

As I turned to watch the entering people, two Policiers came into the tent, their polished badges gleaming. They took off their helmets and tucked them under their elbows. I twisted toward the ring and slouched lower in my seat, forcing my breath to stay even. I hazarded another glance, my eyes following them as they made their way to the seats only three rows behind me. They were here for their own merriment – perhaps they had just gotten off a shift, and felt like seeing the circus on their way home. But they might have had my description. I tucked as much of my auburn hair as I could under my cap and pulled it lower over my forehead.

With a pang, I wished my brother was sitting next to me so I could poke him in the ribs with my elbow and share a grin. The large smelly man beside me would not have appreciated it, I was sure.

A man strolled out to the ring and the music faded. He was tall and burly, but had cultivated a paunch that threatened to burst his gold waistcoat. The quintessential ringmaster wore a crimson overcoat, a top hat, and sported a moustache waxed into curled points. He brandished a shiny teak cane.

"Welcome," he said, his voice booming, "to the greatest circus in Ellada, R.H. Ragona's Circus of Magic!" The audience applauded. He swept a bow, flourishing his white gloved hands and waving his cane.

"You are in for a treat tonight, my friends," Mr Ragona beamed. His voice had the lilt of some foreign country. I leaned forward in my seat.

"You are not in a canvas tent." He said, pausing for a few confused titters. "You are in a palace of magic. Men and women from every corner of the Archipelago have brought their secrets and powers to show you. Men and women fly through the air, and animals bow to their will. Here, nothing is impossible!" Cheers erupted again.

"We also offer more magic and more excitement than any other circus in Ellada. After the show, there is also a fun fair where you can see the animals close up – if you dare – or view our collection of human curiosities!" He beamed again. His teeth were very white.

"The show never ends with R.H. Ragona's Circus of Magic," he called. "But first, we must let it begin!" He threw up his hands and cane.

Fog rolled across the stage from each side of the ring. It filled the circus with the sweet scents of pine smoke and dried rose petals. The music faded into a silence that pressed against my skin. The crowd sat in a dark grey cloud, and not a cough or rustle could be heard.

A cymbal crashed, and lightning flashed in the tent. The audience yelled. Thunder rumbled and stars twinkled briefly in the fog before fading. The fog dissipated.

The music returned. Six golden-skinned shirtless men wearing loose pantaloons somersaulted on the rock slab of the stage with liquid grace. They paraded around the stage before forming a human pyramid in the center. They did not even appear to be out of breath.

But mine caught in my throat.

In the past life that was now lost to me, I had jumped through trees and scrambled up scaffolding, but it had never occurred to me to deliberately fall and flip. The men were beautiful, with rippling muscles, exotic, slanted features, and knowing smiles.

The man at the top of the pyramid stood and flipped to the floor, twirling in midair, and the others broke formation, moving like a pack of wolves towards backstage.

A man stumbled onto the stage. The music warbled to a stop.

The clown was tall and muscled, with incongruous white hair that looked like a dandelion standing out straight from his head in all directions. His face was painted milk-pale, with two spots of pale rouge on his cheekbones. His eyes were ringed in black and his lips cherry-red, with eyebrows painted high on his forehead. He wore clothes in a motley of cream and blanched pink save for a large orange flower on his breast.

A brass horn quavered. The clown cupped his hand to his ear, frowning. The horn chirruped again. The clown nodded vigorously and jumped forward.

He tumbled about in a parody of the acrobats that had just been on stage. With an odd, bumbling grace he somersaulted and stood on his head, kicking his feet. The audience laughed. He ran about the perimeter of the ring, pulling faces at the audience and sticking out his tongue.

Abruptly, he stopped, cupped his hand to his ear again, and continued his mute conversation with the horn. The horn urged him to do something, and the clown vigorously shook his head, holding palms out in front of him. The horn insisted. The clown crossed his arms across his chest and held his nose in the air. He stuck out his tongue and made a wet raspberry. The audience laughed.

The horn player blared, the sound startling everyone

in the tent. The clown jumped in the air and then crouched on his hands and knees in the middle of the ring. He sighed and shook his head, as if resigned to his fate, then whistled over his shoulder.

Other clowns somersaulted onto the stage. One was dressed in a blue motley, another in red and orange, one in shades of yellow, and another in shades of green. They cavorted on stage, linking arms and skipping. The white clown whistled again, impatient.

They formed into a human pyramid, but one far less graceful than the acrobats of earlier. They swayed to the right, and then they swayed to the left, looking as if they would fall at any moment. It must have been more difficult to do than the previous tumblers' pyramid. The white clown grinned at the audience in mischief, and then squirmed out of the bottom of the pyramid. The rest of the clowns tumbled and proceeded to chase the white clown around the ring and then offstage. I giggled with the rest of the audience.

I leaned forward in anticipation. Mr Ragona ambled back onto the stage and looked around, as if faintly surprised that we were all still here.

"Enjoying yourselves?" he called.

The audience hooted and hollered.

"Let me just say, girls and boys, ladies and gentlemen..." He held his hands out again. "You haven't seen anything yet."

A trick equestrian act performed. The man relied on brute strength, hanging from the side of the cantering horse. The woman looked as calm as she would if she were balancing on solid ground.

Between each act, Ragona made another announcement, or the white clown and his fellows mimed and parodied the previous act or told jokes. The pace of the circus never waned and each act only seemed to grow more daring and dangerous.

And between each act, much as I knew I should not, my gaze darted to the Policiers three rows behind me. They did not seem to notice me, but my heart still pattered in fear.

I had looked at a volume of exotic animals from around the world in father's library, but so many of them had looked like they could never be real. The illustrations came to life before me. Little furred creatures called otters trotted onto the stage after their trainer. Together, they stood on hind legs and danced, or tossed a ball from one to the other. They twined about their trainer, two perched on his shoulders and another twisted about his waist like a belt.

An elephant named Saitha balanced on its hind legs; larger than a hansom cab, with tusks longer than sabers. I wondered what the skin would feel like; it looked like grey tree bark.

Men ate and spat fire like human dragons. A solid slab of a man lifted barbells that were said to weigh more than three average men.

I peered at the empty ring, knowing that the finale was brewing. A child cried out and pointed. A man and a woman walked onto the stage, their costumes glittering in the light of the glass globes.

The slender woman wore green. With a long brown braid snaking down her back she looked like a forest elf out of legend. Her costume looked like the bodice of a woman's dress, but instead of skirts she wore pantaloons, thick tights and light slippers. The man in blue was older, his hair silvered at the temples. The woman curtseyed and the man bowed.

They walked away from each other and each climbed a rope ladder to the wooden platforms. I wondered what they thought, standing so high as they looked down into a sea of faces.

She picked up a lace parasol from the platform, pirouetting and opening it. She balanced on tiptoe, holding her other leg so high she could have kissed her knee.

The aerialist stepped onto the tightrope. The rope bent slightly under her weight and I held my breath, frightened she would fall.

But her feet were firm as she made her slow, steady crossing in midair. She looked so dainty and delicate as she walked, pointing her toes when she lifted a foot, holding the parasol aloft, as though she could bend her legs, propel herself upwards, and fly away. The light filtered through the lace, shadows dappling her skin. When she finally made it across, I let out the breath I had been holding and clapped as loudly as I could.

The man walked across next, and he was even more talented. He must have been an acrobat for decades since he did not hesitate as he stepped onto the thin rope to perform. He walked across it as naturally as though he were strolling through a park.

Once he crossed the tightrope, the man clutched the delicate wooden handle of the trapeze and pushed himself into midair. The woman grasped her trapeze and dived after him.

A flautist trilled a solo as they flew through the air

under the canopy of the tent, like sparrows in courtship, flittering close to each other only to coyly dart away again. At times it seemed certain that one would clip the other, but they never did.

The man shifted, hanging by the crook of his knees instead of his hands. The woman let go, somersaulted in midair, and clasped the man's hands above the wrist.

They swung together in a human chain. If the man's hands were to slip ever so slightly, the woman would plummet to her death.

The woman climbed up the man and stood on the top of the trapeze bar, her feet to either side of the man's knees. He changed position and again hung by his hands. They swung together, gaining momentum, and the woman flipped off the trapeze and rotated twice in midair. At the last second, she reached out a hand and grasped her trapeze.

The aerialists finished to wild applause as they shimmied down the ladder and bowed before exiting.

The circus ended with the entire cast reappearing. The elephant waved its trunk and clowns wove their way between the acrobats and the trainers, the strong men and the contortionists. All smiled and waved as they bowed.

The circus had been unlike anything I could ever have imagined and I could not walk away. I wanted to be a part of the magic; create it and wield it with such skill that it looked effortless. I wanted to fly.

It was the perfect way to lead a completely different life.

3
SUMMER: ON DISPLAY

"The circus and carnival grew in popularity starting in the late 107th century. Scattered funfairs with simple illusions and sideshows evolved into detailed worlds of entertainment, with trained acrobatics, animal shows, feats of human strength and strangeness, and Vestige artefacts to try and add a sense of wonder and magic.

"Of late, the human oddities have grown stranger and stranger. Are birth defects rising, or are the performers merely growing better at their disguises?"

A HISTORY OF ELLADA AND ITS COLONIES,
Professor Caed Cedar, Royal
Snakewood University

I jumped out of my seat and squeezed past the burly man and through the crowds before the Policiers had even stirred from their chairs. I was one of the first at the carnival outside, and I smelled sizzling meats and the burning fuel of the gas lanterns strung between poles. The carnival was a long alleyway, flanked with booths in lurid colors, and I was certain I recognized some of the sellers as merchants from the markets of Sicion.

I wandered amongst the booths, keeping an eye out for the pointed helmets of Policiers. Merchants in mismatched clothing sold jewelry and food. The women had daubed their eyes with kohl and tied their hair with scarves. Many of the merchants were foreign, for their eyes slanted or their skin was darker than Elladans'. They spoke with thick accents or called out to each other in exotic tongues. I started toward a jewelry stall run by a woman with skin as dark as the night and dressed all in scarlet.

"Come here, my boy," a voice behind me said, startling me from the scarlet-clad woman. It was not a Policier. The ancient man behind his counter motioned for me to come closer. The weathered wooden sign above the booth proclaimed him an "Alcymyst to Cure All Ills and Ails" in a wobbly script. His pale face was so wrinkled that it seemed to be slowly drawing in toward his shriveled, toothless mouth. He had a few stray white hairs bursting out of his head, ears, and nose.

"I can cure you," he said.

"Cure me of what?" I asked, skeptical.

"Of your... disorder."

My eyes narrowed but my stomach somersaulted like the tumblers I had just seen. Very few knew what was wrong with me. "And what disorder is that?"

He peered closer at me. "Child, are you a boy or a girl?"

I said nothing, but my palms began to sweat.

He picked up a vial of pale blue powder. "This will cure you."

I crossed my arms over my chest, trying to appear both confident and derisive. A couple of passersby paused in front of the stall. "Cure me of what, exactly?"

Others were standing about the booth now. "You don't want me to say in front of these people," the alchemist said.

I bit the inside of my cheek. I stepped closer. "Then whisper in my ear what my condition is, and then I'll decide whether or not I need your cure."

He smiled. "Of course, of course," he said with a magnanimous gesture toward the people gathered. "You will be my first satisfied patient of the evening." By patient, he meant customer. He was stressing his syllables oddly as if to sound foreign, but I suspected he was born and raised in Sicion.

I shuffled over to him. He tilted close to me, touched my arm, and drew me even closer. He smelled of musty clothes and soured milk.

"You have a serious condition. You have been to many to see to it. None have been able to help you." He did not lower his voice much. The people leaned in to hear him better.

My eyes widened. "How do you know this?"

He smirked and waved a hand. "I am both an alchemist and a psychic. Much of the mysteries and ways of the world make themselves known to me."

"Then why are you working in a booth in a carnival?" I asked. My voice was too loud and two women standing close to me giggled.

He slapped me lightly on the head. "Do not be impertinent, my young child. I am here because I choose to, not because I need to. I have healed the kings and queens of many colonies far across the sea. I have learned the ways of healing from the magic men of Kymri, the land of black sands, and they taught me all that they knew for many years. I help all – from the highest king to the lowest peasant! And for these wonders, *all* I ask for is a modest contribution for my help."

His words had their intended effect. I shivered. I leaned closer and whispered into his hairy ear, "Then what is my problem that no one will cure?"

He whispered into my ear, "You have warts on your nether regions."

I jerked my head back, looked into his solemn face, and began to laugh. I laughed until tears pricked my eyes and I could barely catch my breath. The crowd around me looked perplexed.

"Is his problem that he's mad?" someone asked.

I wiped my cheek. "Mister Alchemist, sir, I wish that was the worst of my problems." The crowd called jeers to the alchemist and he yelled obscenities at me as I walked away.

At the far end of the carnival a sign advertising "Freakshow" rose above a series of patched and faded tents. Another had a sign of an exotic woman with a snake wrapped around her and I shuddered. I did not much care for snakes. The show had already started, and the crowd of men seemed to be enjoying whatever the woman was doing with the snake. Cymbals pinged in time to Byssian music.

There was another tent further back, grubby and stained. There was little doubt as to what this tent held. Two beautiful women, painted in shades of blue, silver, and green gazed at me with half-lidded eyes. Families walked by the tent on the way to see the freakshow, but the parents hurried their children along.

"Care to see the dancing sylphs and undines of myth?" Compared to the other middle-aged and paunch-bellied men about, I must have screamed "young, lily virgin."

I shook my head and hurried on, even though a small part of me was curious. Very curious.

The same barker who had lured me into the circus was standing in front of the freakshow tent, and he had no qualms about shouting at the top of his lungs.

"Come and see the perfect show to end a fantastic evening at Mr Ragona's Circus of Magic!" he cried. "Come see the menagerie and the freakshow! Inside this tent are the strangest creatures ever seen by man. Animal and human, twisted in their nature. Animals from Byssia, Kymri, Temne, and Linde! Come and see, my good friends. Come and see things you've only seen in your dreams… or your nightmares."

I did not want to go into this tent, either. I feared they wouldn't be as freakish as I was.

But out of the corner of my eye I saw the shiny helmets of the two Policiers.

I turned my back to them and waited in line with the others, hiding behind a fat man as I had no money to give and ducking into the dark tent. It smelled musky, and the glass globes flickered over the cages and the animals inside. Most of the smell came from the large cats.

I had befriended small, feral felines in my youth, but creatures that looked sweet when they did not come up to my knee looked terrifying when they weighed twice as much as a man. There was a lion, almost comical with the gigantic ruff of tawny fur around his face. A tiger prowled the cage, displaying its orange, yellow, and white stripes. A cyrinx, a black cat that shined purple in the light, rubbed itself against the bars of its cage. It barely had enough room to turn around. I wanted to reach out and touch the fur, but a sign to the side read: "Do not touch if you value your hand."

The striped cat gnawed on a metal bar. He was fond of doing so judging by the scratched and dented iron, and his teeth were dull and worn. The sight of the cats behind bars twisted from exciting to saddening. I wanted to see them prowling through grass fields, not curled up within cages.

Saitha the elephant slurped water into her long nose before squirting it into her mouth. Her cage only barely contained her, the bars pressing against her flank. "Poor thing," I said, not realizing I had spoken aloud.

"She has her own cart on the circus train and she'll spend the day in the big top," the trainer said, his voice defensive. "She's not in this very long." He put his hand on the elephant's large leg. I nodded, though a cart of a train did not seem large enough for her, either, and continued through the maze of the tent.

Horses shied in their stalls, their nostrils flaring at the smell of the nearby predators and so many unwashed people. The star of the herd was from the plains of Kymri, its body a rich gold that darkened to reddish amber around the hooves, mane, tail, and nose.

As I moved deeper into the maze of cages and canvas, the animals shifted from the exotic to the strange and malformed. A turtle with two heads shared a tank with a fish with a strangely human face. A pig with two snouts stood in a pen, snuffling and hanging its heavy head close to the ground. A glass aquarium held an array of albino creatures – a frog, a water snake, and a few fish. One of the fish might have been dead. Another tank held a stunted albino alligator, its pink eyes gazing at us impassively, and its white tail lashing against the grimy glass.

A woman stood next to the covered entrance to the rear of the tent. She had unnaturally red hair, dusky skin, and wore large clunky jewelry wherever she could – earrings, five necklaces, jangling bangles, and a ring on every finger. Loose, multi-colored scarves were draped about her stout body.

After enough of a crowd had gathered, she spoke. "This is what you have entered to see, is it not?" she said in – of course – an affected, accented voice. "In here are people unlike you or I. In some way, these men and women are unique to any others. They come from all over the world just to show you their extraordinary bodies. Some you may find beautiful. Others you may find repulsive. Are they blessed? Are they cursed? You decide."

She held back the cloth door so that we could shuffle in. This section of the tent was darker, and somehow colder. It did not smell of animals, but dust and stale human sweat. I wrapped my arms about myself.

The woman snapped her fingers and the glass globes brightened. In a large circle men and women stood, or sat upon stools. Small plaques were hammered into the ground in front of them. Like the others, I gawked.

The middle-aged red-haired woman nearest to me looked like anyone's mother, aside from the fact that she had a bushy moustache and beard. She wore a long dress with a flowered print and an apron to heighten the oddness of her ginger beard. Her blue eyes crinkled at me and I averted my gaze. I raised a hand to my still-smooth cheek and wondered if I would ever sprout hair.

"Bethany here was a perfectly normal girl from the village of Rionan, but when she entered her blossoming time, she ended up growing a beard as well as breasts!" our gypsy guide said.

The strongman from the circus act had a pile of wooden planks, and he picked one up and snapped it as if it were sugar glass.

"Mr Karg here grew up in Girit on a farm. They used him instead of a plough-horse because he was stronger."

Next to him, to provide the utmost juxtaposition, was a tiny man who came up to my waist. His face was handsome, with swarthy skin and a furrowed brow underlined by thick black eyebrows.

"Mr Tin is the tiniest man in Ellada, but he has the biggest of tempers." The dwarf scowled at the gypsy woman and looked as if he would like nothing more than to kick her kneecaps.

A woman seated on a stool waved, and she seemed normal at first glance. She was perhaps thirty, with a handsome face and dark brown hair coiled into a bun, and she wore a maroon dress several years out of fashion. The woman held the taffeta skirt bunched in her lap so that we could see her pantalooned legs. Two of her legs were perfectly normal, finely-muscled legs in delicately-heeled black boots. But from her lower belly sprouted what looked like two child's legs, complete with shiny black children's shoes. She wiggled first her normal legs and then twitched her tiny legs. My mouth dropped open in shock and the four-legged woman laughed coyly.

"Madame Limond is one of the rarest women in the entire world. She has two pairs of fully functional legs and two working pelvises." She paused significantly, though at the time the allusion was lost on me.

A man wearing only a loincloth posed for us, covered head to toe in tattoos depicting all the myths I had heard growing up. The Lord of the Sun shone from the right side of the man's chest, his head crowned in sunrays, his hands aflame. The Lady of the Moon glimmered on the left side of his chest, her head haloed by a crescent moon. Female Chimaera were inked along his stomach and back – mermaids, centaurs, angels. Monsters twined about his calves – two hydra, two dragons, and a sea serpent. He flexed his muscles, causing the monsters and women to dance.

A man with the pimpled skin of a chicken bobbed his head and gazed at us over the beak of his nose, the slack skin of his neck wobbling. He wore a bobbled red cap and a yellow outfit. Our flame-haired narrator named him "Poussin." I half-expected him to squawk.

Next was the "Leopard Lady of Linde," though she looked as though she might have been from Byssia. Most of her skin and hair were bleached, like the white clown of the circus performance. Dark rosettes dotted her skin. Her eyes were ringed like a cat's. She was beautiful, her limbs long and graceful, as though she could sprint away at a moment's notice. Her skirt came to her knees, leaving her spotted legs shockingly bare. A man came too close for her liking. She hissed at him, flashing her pointed canines.

The last man was not a man at all, but "half-man, half-bull," the woman proclaimed. He was large and muscular and his body matted with hair. Though he was distinctly bullish in appearance, he was not the Minotaur out of legend. His face and head were still human, mostly. He had a heavily-boned face with slack muscles, a long nose with flared nostrils, and two horns growing from his head, though they were a bit lopsided. The flesh of his nose between his nostrils was pierced with a thick ring, like an ox, and he wore a leather collar. His wide, cow-like eyes did not appear to recognize us in any way.

"His is a sad tale," our guide said, holding her hand to her face in emphasis. "His mother was a beggar woman and heavily pregnant. A fearsome bull had escaped from the docks, where it had just arrived from Girit. The bull knocked his mother down and frightened her so much that when her babe was born, he was part bull. She herself died from childbirth and poor Tauro was left in an orphanage and grew up bullied by the others until he learned to fight. R.H. Ragona's Circus of Magic rescued him from the stocks so that you fine ladies and gentlemen could see him this evening." The bull-man only stared at us balefully in response.

The others chatted excitedly as we left the tent, but I was subdued and almost wished that I had not gone. First almost seeing the naked women in the tent, and now seeing the sadness of the menagerie and the freakshow had dimmed the vivacity of the circus. People wandered through the carnival, laughing and pointing out oddities. I watched a man juggle whatever the crowd passed him – bottles, trash, books, and a baby's doll – to the delight of the crowd. The fire-eater's dragon breath illuminated the funfair. Stalls sold hot drinking chocolate and roasted hazelnuts, popping corn and caramel apples.

I returned to the jewelry stall with the woman in the red headdress. The "alchemist" pointedly ignored me from across the lane. The woman's wares were lovely, polished black stones with silver wire swirling over their faces. A necklace looked as though a spider had woven a web over the stone, and another looked like plant tendrils had taken possession of it.

"Do you wish for a gift for a special lady?" the woman asked, her voice authentically exotic. She was from Byssia.

"I'm afraid I'm lacking in both coin and a lady," I said.

"Come to me when you have found both, will you not?"

I nodded and she smiled before turning her attention to a young pair new to love. The girl put a necklace to her neck and posed for the boy, tossing her head. His eyes glazed, and I knew he would buy it for her.

I stood on the stretch of sand that had once been a carnival and wondered what to do next. I sat underneath one of the nearby docks and watched as, little by little, people left and went their various ways. The merchants packed up their remaining wares or empty boxes and men came and lowered the front flaps of their tents and stalls. Circus workers led animals away and put them into large carts that were parked on the road overlooking the ocean. The carnival returned to being a stretch of beach with a few lingering tents, and more litter and footprints than before. I should leave, and find shelter to spend the night. But I had nowhere to go.

● ● ● ●

As the cold seeped into my bones and my teeth chattered, I saw the glass globes were still shining in the big circus tent, and I heard voices. A sign slung across the fastened entrance read "Circus closed."

I crept around the tent until I found a rent in the thick canvas. I crouched and peered in. I did not know what sparked me to do so. The memory of the magic of the circus, undimmed even by the darkness that undercut the carnival? The image of the trapeze artists flying through the air?

Mr Ragona stood to the side of the ring, beaming at those gathered around. The performers lounged in the stands, rubbing each other's muscles. The clowns sat in a rainbow of motley in the corner closest to me. Workers entered and left, stacking equipment into the corner of the tent.

"Excellent work, me lovelies," Mr Ragona boomed, his lilting false accent replaced by gravelly Imacharan vowels. He swung his cane lazily. "Excellent work. An extra round to all tonight."

The circus folk cheered.

"Now, to business." Mr Ragona rubbed his hands together. "We got a tight schedule coming up, with no room for mistakes. A show each night here for two months, and then a few weeks in Cowl, three months in Imachara, and then we're done for the season. If we keep filling the seats like we did tonight, then we'll all have a hefty bonus in our pockets for our troubles by the time the rains come." Smiles split the faces of those gathered, though their exchanged skeptical glances showed they had all heard the words before.

"But we can do better!" Mr Ragona said, pumping his fist for emphasis. "We can always push ourselves just that little bit more." He did not pronounce most of his "t"s. "We can add another flip to a routine, raise the tightrope, and teach them animals another trick. There's more seats to be filled, me lovelies."

"Yes, yes. So you say after every show, Bil. What a surprise to hear the words tonight," the bearded woman said with a smile, and peeled off her beard. The moustache remained. I gasped, for though the beard was fake, the moustache was apparently genuine. The white clown, who was sitting in the seats quite close to me, raised his head and looked around suspiciously. I held my breath and ducked away from the gap for a few moments before putting my eye to it again.

"And so I'm still waiting for a surprise of a full house, ain't I, my dear Bethany?" he said, winking at her. "I always like surprises." The white clown had gotten up and ambled toward my hiding place. I got up to retreat, but I tripped over a guide rope and landed heavily on my behind.

"Ah," I said in pain. The canvas lifted and I stared up into the pasty painted face of the white clown.

"Ah," I said again, for lack of something better. He grabbed me by the hand, lifted me up and dragged me into the tent.

"Well, I found a surprise for *you*, Bil."

4
SUMMER: THE TRAPEZE

"Find any retired aerialist and ask them what they miss the most. It is not the money, or the travel, the costumes, or even the show itself. It is the thrill of flying that they miss. The loss of flight is what haunts them until the end of their days."

from THE MEMOIRS OF THE SPARROW,
Aerialist Diane Albright

For a moment, I was weightless, and time almost stopped. My stomach dropped. It was like every other jump I had taken. I grabbed the smooth wooden bar of the trapeze and swooshed through the air. I let out a laugh so loud I knew they could hear it below. It felt so much like flying.

I used my momentum and swung back and forth across the top of the tent. I saw the girl, Aenea, on the platform, and so I swung the trapeze hard enough that I could land on the other. I jumped from the trapeze and crouched on the small wooden square. Aenea's mouth opened from across the rope.

"Come on, you," she called, nervous. "Come down from there."

"You climb down first," I said. "And I'll follow. I want to go down the ladder on your side."

"Are you mad?" she called. "It's one thing to swing around on a trapeze, but you've not the training to balance on a tightrope!"

"Who said anything about balancing?" I hooked my ankles and hands around the rope and worked my way slowly across. After travelling a third of the way, I let my legs drop. The girl screamed and the circus workers below cried out. I continued to work my way across using only my hands. The rope burned my hands and my shoulders protested.

"Start climbing down," I said when I was closer to her. She gave me an inscrutable look and climbed down the rope ladder.

I made it onto the wooden platform and stood up. People below clapped and cheered, and I bowed before climbing down to the ground. My face was burning crimson. What had come over me?

Mr Ragona did not look amused. "Well, that sure was stupid," he said.

"Perhaps, sir," I said.

Mr Ragona turned to the aerialists. "Could he be trained?"

"Easily," the man Arik said. Aenea hesitated, but nodded. "Yes."

He stroked his chin, shrewd. "Where are your parents?" he asked.

"Dead," I lied.

The ringmaster narrowed his eyes, considering. "All right. You can stay, for a time. But you'll have to earn your way up. You won't be going near a trapeze again for quite some time." He waved to his workers.

"Come on, get to your tasks."

As I followed the crowd out, I clasped my hands together to stop them from shaking.

The workers had made a giant bonfire on the beach. I stood in line by the clowns, unsure what exactly I was waiting for. The white clown looked over at me, his pale eyes unreadable.

"You have no idea what you're getting yourself into," the white clown said. The other clowns looked at him in disgust, clearly annoyed that he was speaking to an outsider, and a new one at that. His voice was educated.

"You could have let me be outside of the tent," I pointed out. "It wouldn't have occurred to me to walk in and try to join."

"That would not have been as fun. Worked in your favor, in any case."

"So it seems. Did you know what you were getting into, when you joined?" I asked.

"Not in the least."

He seemed serious and nothing like the carefree, bumbling clown I had so recently seen on stage. Now that he was not dragging me by his collar, I could see what he looked like. Up close, he was less ghostly. His thick white makeup had cracked about his eyes and mouth, the rouge and lip color garish. His hair was not naturally white – golden blonde roots sprung from his skull. The clown was younger than I thought. Twenty-two, twenty-four at the oldest.

"I'm Micah Grey," I said, holding out my hand.

He took my hand carefully, barely touching it, his fingers cold. "Drystan." He did not give his surname.

I prepared to introduce myself to the other clowns, but they turned toward the front of the queue. I had been snubbed.

The ghost of a smirk played around the edges of Drystan's mouth. The line inched forward and I took a step. The smell of chicken and vegetable soup reached us and my stomach clenched in hunger.

"Where did you learn to be a clown?" I asked, and winced at how clunky and awkward the words sounded.

He lifted an eyebrow at me. He had not expected me to continue the conversation. "I've always been a clown. A little funny, a little strange."

Drystan stared at me solemnly and then he grinned so wide that it looked like his face was about to split in two. His bulging blue eyes showed the whites, almost ready to pop from his head, and they vibrated in their sockets. I felt a strong urge to back away, and then run.

He relaxed into a good-natured grin and slapped me on the shoulder. The other clowns had turned to sneer at me.

"You reacted better than the last new member," he said. "Your eyes only went as big as saucers. The other one screamed and ran straight away and didn't talk to me for a week. Maybe you'll last a bit longer than him."

I laughed, relieved. I was tempted to ask what happened to "the other one," but I was smarter than to rise to that bait.

"There's no point in queuing," the white clown said. "The cook won't give you any food."

My stomach clenched in another hunger pang. "Why not?"

"You have to last the night, first. You'd be surprised how many say they wish to join just for the free meal. You'll get breakfast."

I swallowed and turned away from him, and I made sure to sit on the opposite side of the bonfire. The flames would part and I would catch glimpses of Drystan, his whiteness tinged orange and pink from the flames, laughing with his motley fellows.

No one else spoke to me. They milled and divided themselves into groups. The workers, with their grubby faces and much-patched clothing, congregated on the edge of the circle of firelight. The men were mainly in their thirties to forties, and beginning to redden in the face from their nightly drink. They did not even glance in my direction.

The performers, besides the clowns, also kept to themselves. The fire-eaters appeared to be quite friendly with the jugglers, lounging close to the fire and speaking with their mouths full. Everyone held rough mugs of beer, drawn from the large barrel by the food. The tanned acrobats talked to each other in foreign tongue so fast I could not tell where sentences began or ended. The male animal trainer had a particularly tame otter wrapped around his neck, the little whiskered face asleep beneath the man's chin as he spoke to the female trainer.

I assumed the woman with the snake twined around her neck was the snake woman from the tent. She said hello to the trainer, but kept her distance so the snake would not be too curious about the otter. She wandered over to two other young, pretty women. I knew immediately that they were the women from the other tent. One was impossibly blonde, and the other had hair of deepest black, both elaborately styled. They looked as alike as sisters and had bodies any male would want to see unclothed. They were smiling and jostling each other. Many of the men stopped and flirted with them, and the women flirted in return, throwing their heads back and laughing, obviously well-aware of the effect they had on the men.

The freaks formed another small nucleus near the clowns. The four-legged woman and the giant man chatted. The leopard lady read a book in the light of the fire, and Poussin the chicken man napped against a log. The bull-man, Tauro, sat with them, but focused only on his food.

I was startled when the two aerialists sat down beside me. They had changed from their costumes and were both clad in loose shirts tucked into trousers. The girl, Aenea, still managed to look feminine despite the male garb. The fire outlined her features and made her glow.

The man called Arik looked much older than he had on stage. His handsome, tanned face was lined, and he moved a little stiffly. His smile was warm, as was his hand when I clasped it in greeting.

"Arik," he said.

Aenea also took my hand in a strong grip. Her hands were rough and calloused. "Aenea."

"Micah." Following her lead, I did not give my last name. It was refreshing; surnames meant so much in my past.

"Here, I stole this for you," she said, passing me a roll filled with cheese and apple.

"Thank you," I said, taking it from her.

"Where did you learn to climb like that?" Aenea asked. Her voice had a working-class accent, but she spoke well.

"Here and there." I took a bite.

Aenea rolled her eyes. "Nice try, but you'll not get away with vagueness. You have the strength and balance, and you barely hesitated at all before you jumped, even though you were well over sixty feet off the ground."

I swallowed. "I climb a lot. And I have taken dance lessons since I was very young."

"What sort of dance? What did you climb?" Aenea asked, undeterred as a dog with a bit of rawhide. Arik smiled, obviously amused by her interrogation.

"I did different types of dance." I could not very well say ballet and court dancing. "I climb scaffolding. And trees," I added.

"Ah, rich boy," Aenea said, nodding, and I winced at my blunder. The only trees in the cities were in parks clustered in the rich sections of town, and the poor could never afford to travel into the countryside or former colonies.

"Merchant class," I said, quickly. "My parents live beyond their means."

"They 'live' beyond their means?" Aenea asked. "I thought you said they were dead." She was quick.

"Uh, they are. I am not used to... referring to them as gone." I endeavored to look morose.

Aenea winced. "Oh, I'm sorry! I'm cruel. I should not have pointed it out." She looked slightly disappointed,

as if it would be a better story were I a rich runaway.
I supposed it would be.

"How long have you been with Mr Ragona's circus?"
I asked.

She looked up as she calculated. "Six years."

"You must have started when you were young."

"I was eleven, yes."

Arik smiled. "Ah, the youth. You're how old, Micah?"

"Sixteen."

"I've been in circuses longer than both your ages added
together," Arik said. "I joined when I was ten."

"You've been travelling all this time?"

"Most of the time, yes. The winters I rent a room here
in Sicion from my good friend, but nearly every spring,
summer, and autumn I'm swinging from the trapeze.
There have been a handful of seasons I have not been able
to. Injuries, you know."

"What sorts of injuries?"

"Torn ligaments, sprains, a break or two."

"From falling?"

"No, I've never fallen," he said, drawing himself up in
pride. "And I never will. The break was from landing
badly, the others were done in the air." Landing badly was
not much different from falling in my mind, but I kept
silent.

"I won't fall," I blurted.

"Of course not," Aenea said. "We'll be training you."

"Really?" I said. "Mr Ragona wasn't just teasing me?
I'm not too old?"

"Really," she said. "You're older than most to start
training, but Bil has a keen business eye, or he wouldn't

have taken you on. You've the strength and the skill. But you need the patience. You will not be going up on that trapeze again until you're good and ready, and so don't even think about it until then."

"Of course," I said. *We'll see about that.* I was itching to fly again.

"Will we be a three-person act, then?" I asked. There were only two trapezes.

Aenea and Arik exchanged a glance.

"No," Arik said. "I'm slowing down and I'm tiring of the circus life. I'm going to finish this season, maybe next, and then I'm taking my savings and buying the little room I rent in Sicion in the off-season, and that's where I'll stay. I'm hoping having you trained and able to replace me will make Bil more willing to let me go. He must realize I won't stick around much longer, but all the same…" He had pitched his voice low so that it would not carry.

"He doesn't want you to leave?"

"He's not good at letting go of people he thinks are valuable. Not good at all."

The clown's words came back to me. What was I getting myself into?

The first night, I slept in Arik's cart. Arik lit a candle and set it on the clothes chest. He made a pallet for me and gave me his spare quilt. The cart was barely big enough for him and his belongings. With my pack and my pallet, the floor disappeared.

"We'll lay your pallet atop mine in the morning, so there's more room for dressing and whatnot," Arik said. I smiled at him in response.

Arik gave me a short candlelit tour of our shared abode. Despite the small size, the cart was immaculate. Floorboards swept and scrubbed, the pallet fresh, the bed linens laundered. Shelves on the wall displayed several tattered volumes of plays and a history of the circuses of Ellada and the Colonies. Arik picked up a collection of work by the famous playwright Godric Ash-Oak.

"I taught myself to read with this," he said, stroking the cover.

Not much else was on display. Clothes were tidied into a wardrobe, and all surfaces were bare and dusted. I worried about sharing a cart with him. I had never been the most tidy of people, even with a maid.

"I'll make room for your things," Arik said.

"Oh, no, I don't want to be any trouble," I said. "I can leave things in my pack here."

"Are you certain?"

"Of course. You've done more than enough."

Arik nodded and began to disrobe for bed. His body was lean and ropy. "You've had enough excitement for one day, young one. Practice starts early. Breakfast at dawn." He lay down and closed his eyes. I appreciated him not prying me with questions. He appeared to fall asleep immediately.

I was too restless to sleep. I had been away from home for almost a week, now. It felt like much, much longer. I had run from the authorities, feared for my life, and been hungrier and colder than I had ever been before. Though I might be safe for the moment, I knew nothing about what my new life would hold.

I shifted on the pallet, the straw ticking digging into

my back. I missed my down mattress at home and my warm duvet. I wanted to re-read an Ephram Finnes adventure and drink a hot mug of tea by gaslight, to joke with my brother as he reluctantly studied a law book, and feel safe and warm. I wanted to fall asleep with a cozy bedpan at my feet and Lia to wake me up with the same song she sang to me every morning. I missed my other friends, and wondered what they had thought of my disappearance and what my parents had told the others. I even missed my parents, despite all they had done to me. I wanted my old life back, but it was lost. My face was wet. I rubbed at my eyes, crying as silently as possible and settled down into my musty, uncomfortable pallet.

It was a long while before I fell asleep, and when I did, I dreamt of falling.

5
SPRING: JUMP

"A lady must remain dainty and demure at all times. Never should she raise a voice or a hand in anger or excitement. Never should she trot or run in the presence of gentlemen. She must always appear calm, collected, and effortlessly graceful."

A YOUNG ELLADAN LADY'S PRIMER,
Lady Elena Primrose

I crouched on the tree branch.

"Genie." My brother gazed up at me from the ground below. "Don't even consider it."

"I told you, Cyril, don't call me Genie. It's Gene!"

I jumped.

My arms and legs felt only air, and then I wrapped my arms around the next tree branch and hung from it, bare feet dangling. Cyril looked at me in disapproval. Thank the Lord and Lady that the bark was smooth or I would have shredded my palms. Oswin, Cyril's best friend, a boy with messy hair and a ready grin, jumped up and tickled my feet.

"Hey," I called, and kicked at him. He leapt away, laughing. I let go and landed lightly on the forest ground.

"I still don't know how you do it, Gene," Oswin said. "You're like a squirrel in the branches."

I swiped at the leaves tangled in my hair. "It's easy. I'm not a squirrel – you're merely a couple of timid mice."

Cyril glowered. "More like we actually have minds in our skulls. Yours is full of lint and daydreams."

"More interesting than what is inside your skull." I grinned up at my brother. He was a head taller than me, but I was catching up to him even though he was two years older. I was wearing an old pair of trousers and a tunic of his. I only had to roll up the legs and arms once now.

I sped down the path. "Race you boys to the pond!" I called over my shoulder. Their footfalls followed and I quickened my pace.

They nearly beat me. I jumped in and sank. Opening my eyes in the murky water, I watched Cyril and Oswin sink to the silt on the bottom of the pond. The chirping of the birds silenced and it was just us, the green water, the tadpoles and frogs.

I burst to the surface and gulped a lungful of air. The boys followed and we splashed about in the water. I was a better swimmer than either of them.

Afterwards, we sat on the riverbank and squished our toes into the mud. I sighed and lay down on my back, careless of the soil, tucking my arms behind my head and looking at the sky.

"I wish we could come to the countryside more often," I said.

"Me too," Cyril agreed. "A month or two a year in the Emerald Bowl is not enough time. It's a bit harder for you to jump off tree branches in the city, after all, isn't it, Gene?"

I chuckled at the sky. "There's always scaffolding."

"You haven't," he said, shocked.

I smirked.

"If mother ever saw you, she'd send you to finishing school quicker than a lager turns to piss."

I shrugged. "I don't do it that often. And I make sure no one's around and that I'm dressed like a mudlark. She'll never find out."

"She better not, little Miss Iphigenia Laurus."

I threw a handful of mud at his face. "Don't call me that." I had the most hideous name. My mother was a sadistic woman.

He laughed, his face and shoulder splattered with mud. Oswin opened his mouth.

"Don't you dare call me anything other than Gene," I warned, hefting another fistful of mud.

He put his hands up in mock surrender. "Of course not. Wouldn't dream of it, General Gene."

I threw the mud at him anyway. It landed with a satisfying splat full in his face. He squealed and a brief but violent mud fight ensued. Within a few minutes we looked like clay golems.

Cyril rubbed ineffectually at his face and looked up at the sky. "It's getting late. We have to get home before Mother and Father want us for supper."

Oswin made a face and looked down at his filthy clothing. "Me as well. I'm starved. Hope my brother and father caught something in the woods this afternoon when they went hunting." With reluctance, we took one last look at the surrounding forest and trudged up the path.

We almost got away with it. Oswin had turned off the road earlier and headed toward his estate. Cyril and I stopped at the wood's edge and rubbed away the worst of the mud with blades of long grass. We had just slipped into the bath chambers and closed the door behind us. We exchanged a relieved grin and began to strip off our clothes.

Creak. Our heads turned. Mother stood outlined in the doorway.

A short and squat woman, she always wore dark dresses that covered everything but her face and hands. The latter she covered with immaculate white gloves that I doubt she wore more than once. She strode into the room and slammed the bath chambers' door behind her, sending the long, jet beads she wore around her neck swinging.

We must have been quite a sight. We were both covered in mud aside from our pale torsos.

"Someday, you two are going to be too much for my heart and it will simply give out on me." My mother's voice was cultured and refined, but I knew it for the charade it was. Her father had been a luminary – a chandler and a gas light specialist – a fairly wealthy member of the merchant class with the thinnest tie to nobility. When she was *really* angry, she would forget herself and slip, dropping consonants and twanging her vowels. That was when I knew I would get a thrashing.

We looked down at the floor. "Sorry, Mother," we muttered.

"Cyril, I know you're at that age where you want to push boundaries, but the time is coming for you to grow up. When we return to Sicion, I am going to speak to your father about your attending council or court with him more often. You are seveneen and are almost of age. We have been lax in your preparations." Cyril nodded, still looking downward.

She sighed theatrically and turned to me. "And Iphigenia, I don't know what to do with you. The Couple knows I love you, but sometimes I think you were meant to be my trial in this lifetime. I give you everything you ask for. You're nearly of an age to enter society. Is a little respectability too much to ask for your poor mother?"

In fact, she gave me precisely everything I did not ask for. The best tailored dresses, fine powders and rouges appropriate for my age, delicate porcelain dolls from Imachara, fancy stationery, sewing and knitting lessons. The only things she provided for me that I actually enjoyed were the music and dance classes.

I wanted to learn to fence and shoot. When I asked if I could, over supper once, she held her hand to her heart as if I had stabbed her with the bread knife.

"Sorry, Mother," I said again, without much conviction.

"Cyril, please use the baths upstairs to ready yourself for supper," our mother said. Cyril gave me a sympathetic look as he left. She did not seem to care that sending him away meant that he would track mud upstairs as well. That was what the servants were for.

Mother clasped her hands together and gave me a speculative look. "Who were you with this afternoon?"

"Cyril and Oswin."

"And what did you do?"

"We climbed trees, raced, swam, enjoyed the fresh air like the young growing children that we are."

"Don't be cheeky. When you swam, did you remove any clothing?"

"Of course not," I said, indignant.

"I was merely being cautious. Oswin cannot have the slightest suspicion."

"I *know*, Mother. I'm not an idiot." I crossed my arms over my bare chest self-consciously and looked away. At sixteen, my breasts were just now starting to develop, though they were little more than swollen nipples.

"We're going to see another specialist when we return to the city next week," she said.

"Mother, no!" I had seen far too many doctors already, and none of them ever seemed to know quite what to make of me. They liked to exclaim, poke, prod, and then write articles in medical journals about me, calling me "Patient X" or some other dramatic letter. I could not face it again.

"There's a new specialist," she continued blithely. "Well, he's not new, quite. He's one of the best, apparently, but he stopped practicing for several years to focus exclusively on research out of the country. He's decided to open a surgical clinic again. He said your case sounds promising and he may be able to offer a solution."

My throat closed tight and a pain stabbed my stomach. I felt dread at the thought of more tests, but also a strange, guarded form of hope. No one had offered a solution before.

Even my oblivious mother could see that I was upset. She patted me with the tips of her gloved fingers on a mostly-clean shoulder. "Come now, darling, it'll all work out for the best. Now, wash up for dinner. Why don't you wear the purple dress tonight? We'll come back again to the estate in the summer. It's too early in spring for you both to be outside so much. It cannot be good for you. And you need your rest – there's the afternoon tea at the Hawthornes' tomorrow, remember?"

My mother called the servants in to run the bath. As the water swirled into the copper tank, I looked wistfully at the disappearing sun resting on the tips of the trees and wondered what the morrow would bring.

The purple dress was scratchy.

It was the lace at my throat. It kept tickling. I tugged at it.

"You never look quite right in a dress," Cyril said, toying with a silver fork.

"Why not?"

"You just don't. You look like you want to run but you can't because your skirts are too heavy."

"They are too heavy. You should try wearing a dress sometime. I'm sure you'd look very pretty."

He gave me a rude hand gesture just as our parents entered.

"Cyril!" Mother said, holding a hand to her breast.

"What did he do?" Father asked, his voice distant.

"Nothing, Stuart. Do not trouble yourself." They sat down. I scratched under my collar again.

"Iphigenia," Mother scolded. "Stop fidgeting."

"Sorry, Mother," I mumbled. Cyril kicked me under the table, and we exchanged smiles.

Father was staring off in the general direction of the centrepiece. When the servants set the food on the table, he seemed to return to our world.

"So your mother is urging me to take you to court more often, Cyril," Father said. "What do you think of this?"

Cyril looked taken aback. "I would like that very much, Father," he said. I didn't know if he was lying or not. Cyril would probably be good at law, which was lucky, I supposed, because he did not have much choice in the matter. Just as I did not have a choice except to hope that Mother could foist me off on some young innocent noble too naïve to notice my disfigurement.

The first course was potato soup. The food we ate in the countryside was made with less exotic foodstuffs than came from the markets of Sicion, but with fresher ingredients. It was thick and creamy, and I was hungry from our afternoon in the woods.

"Perhaps we can go next week and measure Iphigenia for her debutante gown. There's a new boutique opening on Jade Street."

I scowled into my soup. The threat of the ball had been hovering over my head for the last few months. Mother would ambush me with dress designs, ribbons and beads and flowers to plait into my hair. I might have been the only sixteen year-old girl of standing in Sicion completely uninterested in the debutante ball in a few weeks' time.

No mention was made of my impending doctor's visit.

It was never mentioned, except in private, where the servants could not hear. I took another sip of soup, keeping my head down.

6
SUMMER: PARIAH

"Cyrinx: A large feline, similar to the panther. Notable due to the dark purple sheen to its fur. Unseen in Byssia for hundreds of years, and believed extinct until 10766 when discovered by the esteemed explorer, Dr Redwood. Byssian legend states that the cyrinx has the intelligence of a man, and can shapeshift to human form at will. Dr Redwood began a conservation and breeding programme and they are now no longer considered near-extinct. No evidence of shapeshifting has been noted for certain, though many men and women in Byssia and abroad have claimed otherwise."

"Cyrinx", THE ARCHIPELAGO BESTIARY,
Royal Snakewood University

My new education began at breakfast.

Breakfast was an explosion of sound, sights, and smells. People pushed each other in the queue for food, quibbled with the cooks for another spoonful, and joked and insulted each other in the same breath. I found myself standing in front of the two dancers. I tried to avoid looking at them, but the dark-haired girl caught my furtive glance.

"My, my, Tila, look at the newest chit of the circus," she said, licking her lips and glancing at her friend. "Doesn't he just look good enough to eat?"

Tila laughed, looked me up and down. I squirmed under her gaze. "That he does, Sal. My, the poor lad's blushing! Look at how he looks at us. It's as if he's never tapped a pair of cupid's kettle drums before." She laughed and cupped her clothed chest. I swallowed hard.

"Dear, we're not that frightening, are we?" Sal said, running a finger along my arm. I startled at her touch.

"You eating or not?" the cook said. I had not noticed we had reached the front of the queue. Sal and Tila tittered again. My face could not possibly have been any redder.

I held out my bowl. The cook looked me up and down and gave me one solitary spoon of porridge and a lopsided fried egg. The others had received far more. I was too afraid to open my mouth. I could hear the cook chortling as I went to my seat by Arik and Aenea.

"You'll grow thin if you don't ask him to give you more food," Arik said by way of greeting. "And you've not much to spare. He does that to all of the new babies."

"Oh," I said, feeling stupid. I wondered if they had seen the two women teasing me.

"Your thin skin will have to thicken," Aenea warned.

"My skin isn't thin," I said, aware of how defensive I sounded.

She laughed. "We'll find out if you go home in the next month, I suppose."

"Don't have a home to go to," I said, trying not to sound too sullen.

"Then you'll go somewhere else."

"Why does my skin have to thicken?"

"We're a close-knit group in the circus," Arik said. "We're playing a joke on the world. Outsiders aren't in on the joke, and soon you'll start to see them differently, if you stay." The conditional hung in the air like an accusation.

"And so now, to the circus, you're still an outsider. You're still one of the 'normals'. You're going to have to prove yourself to all of them. Until then, they'll have nothing to do with you if they can avoid it. They may even be cruel to you. Don't take it personal, work hard, and you'll become one of us," Arik continued.

I looked around at the circus. A few people would glance at me every now and again and then pretend that they had not. They must all view me as a spoiled, skinny little rich boy who had run away. They all, even Aenea and Arik to some extent, expected me to return home. I ground my teeth together. I would prove them wrong.

"Tell me about the people of the circus, please," I said instead. "So that I don't make too much of a fool of myself."

Arik's eyes twinkled. "The workers will always hate you, and so I would not bother too much with them. Rag is the self-styled leader. He's the man over there with no teeth. His name describes him. He's, to be frank, a shitrag."

I was shocked into a laugh. "Noted."

"Workers don't mix with performers. This is part of your trouble. You're going to start out as a worker, so the performers will look down on you, but you're aiming to be a performer, and so the workers will hate you. You can't win, so don't try."

I nodded, my gut twisting with nerves and making my lone spoonful of porridge and egg look even more unappetizing.

Arik gestured to Aenea, and she took over. I had the feeling that they had gone through similar inductions with other new members of the circus. "Don't try with the Kymri tumblers, either. Most of them can barely speak a word or two of Elladan, and they prefer to interact with just each other, for the most part. Sayid there is an exception. He's a nice fellow and most of us can understand him." She pointed the man on the far right, who had a wide smile and thick black hair tied into a queue.

"In time, you'll probably become friendly with the contortionists, Dot and Mara. They're both sweet, though Mara loves the sound of her own voice, and Dot thinks it's charming to still speak like a child." Dot and Mara were both painfully thin, with pinched faces. Both had blonde hair – Mara's was long and coiled atop her head, and Dot's was short and spiky, almost like a man's. They had the same amount of food in their bowls as I did, I noted sourly.

"And them?" I asked, tilting my chin at the two women who had teased me in the breakfast queue.

Aenea's face tightened. "They're Sal and Tila. The *dancers*." They were two of the most animated of the circus that morning, joking and nudging each other with elbows as they ate. Sal caught my eye again. She winked and stuck out her tongue, wriggling the tip. They both erupted into chuckles.

"You should stay away from them, Micah," Aenea said. "They're nice enough girls, but they're bobtails and that's a fact. They've gotten many a circus member into trouble." She would not elaborate on what sort of trouble. "I'm sure you'll be able to find nicer girls." I was not sure if she was teasing me or flirting. Not sure how to respond, I smiled shyly, which I felt would soon be my trademark. I had never had a girl flirt with me, or many boys for that matter. And did I want a girl to flirt with me? My head wasn't sure.

"What of the clowns?" I asked, looking at the clowns, who had not yet changed into their motley, so I only recognized Drystan by his tousled near-white hair.

"The clowns are a mixed bag," Arik said. "I quite like Iano, Rian, and Drystan; they're the blue, green, and white. But the red and yellow, Jive and Fedir, are total tossers."

"So the earthy colors are alright, and the bright colors are not."

They both chuckled. "Yes. Should be easy to remember," Aenea said, nudging my shoulder. I blinked, focusing again on my plate.

"Who else to introduce?" Arik said.

"The freaks, animal trainers, and management."

"Oh yes," Arik continued "Madame Limond, the woman with the extra pair of legs, and Bethany, the quasi-bearded woman, are good folk. They'll probably warm to you fairly soon. Bethany especially hates the 'harrowing' of new recruits, as she calls it. You can call on her if you're in a pickle."

"Good to know."

"Nina, the snake charmer and sometimes our psychic, is good, though she can be a little…" Arik made a woozy face and twirled an index finger by his ear. "Juliet, the Leopard Lady, is lovely, but keeps to herself most of the time. Tauro, the bull man, is sweet but won't understand a word you're saying. Karg, the strongman, likes to read philosophy, which you wouldn't expect looking at him. Tin can be alright, but he suffers from being short – he'll be more aggressive than he needs to be, most times.

"Who else… Karla and Tym are the animal trainers. You'll work with them some, I expect. They're not too bad once you get to know them."

My head was swimming with names and professions. It would take me weeks before I'd be confident enough to address anyone by name.

"That leaves management. Always be beyond polite to Bil. He can be magnanimous when he wants, but you do *not* want to cross him. Same goes for his wife, Frit. She's not here, but if you see a scrawny woman who looks like she's just bitten into a sour plum, that'll be her. She runs the books and the circus would never have taken off the ground if not for her." Arik took the last bite of his breakfast.

"All right. I think I got that."

"We'll remind you if we have to. But of course, I'm the person in the circus you must fear the most," Aenea said, straight-faced.

"Oh?" I said.

"I'm the one you're going to curse each night before you go to bed and when you wake up each morning. I'm the taskmaster, and no animal trainer in this circus cracks a whip as cruel as mine!"

I pretended to cower and tug a forelock. "Please, have mercy."

She laughed. "No chance. Come along. Time to see what you're made of."

My own confusion only expanded as I pretended not to notice Arik's knowingly amused look at the both of us as we made our way to the big top.

Watching Aenea and Arik practice did not tempt me to sneak away from the tent and make my way home. It tempted me to run home. The morning passed slowly and painfully.

For over an hour, I stretched every muscle and ligament of my body, until I felt as if I were made of rubber. Next, I performed calisthenics, jumping in place until I was panting, squatting until my leg muscles were afire, and pressing myself to the floor until my arms shook. By the end of it, I was drenched in sweat and certain the trainers' animal tent smelled better.

Aenea and Arik could bend nearly as well as the contortionists. They stretched and flipped to warm up and, perhaps a little, to show off to me. Aenea always shot me a smug, triumphant smirk after landing from a flip or a cartwheel, chin high, arms held above her head. I would attempt to copy them, and usually fail. I would exert too little force and lose momentum mid-roll, or I would propel myself so hard that I would slide off the mat and across the rock swept free of sand, leaving my skin and my dignity shredded. I had the strength and balance to hold myself on my hands, but my legs waggled in the air like twigs in a breeze, while theirs pointed toward the top of the tent, unmoving as stone.

Their practice continued long after mine. Instead, I was handed over to the workers and given the most menial of tasks to prepare for the circus act that evening. I scrubbed stains from benches under the big top, holding my nose and trying not to think about what the foul crusts might be. The workers barked instructions at me, calling me "boy" and expecting me to know where the brooms and rags were as if I had been working there for years. By noon, I had stocked the entrance booth that Frit would man later on with rolls of tickets, and arranged the props for the show neatly in the backstage area.

At lunch, I asked the cook for a second helping of dry roast beef and vegetables. He laughed and motioned for me to move along. With hunger in my stomach and my limbs aching and trembling, I refused to move until he gave me another slice of beef. To me, it was a moment of triumph.

The relief was short-lived, however. Jive, the red clown, had been standing behind me in the queue, as I turned to leave, he stuck his foot out. I tripped and fell, my plate tumbling into the sand. I stood, wiping sand from my much-patched clothing. Jive leered at me. He was an ugly fellow, with eyes too small, mouth and teeth too big, and a crooked nose and sallow skin.

I took a deep breath and resisted a growing urge to reach out and strike him.

"Won't be much of a trapeze artist if you bumble about like that, will you, boy?" he asked.

I brushed more sand from my pants and shirt. A boy would hit him, and not even hesitate at the thought of a brawl. But the clown was much larger than me, and I had no confidence in my ability to throw a punch. He'd fight dirty. My only option was to lash out with a cutting, witty barb. But my tongue was blunt and thick in my mouth and nothing came to mind. Instead, I picked up my plate from the sand, dusted it off as well as I could, and held it out for more food. The cook gave me two helpings. Jive tried to trip me again, but I nimbly hopped over his foot, balancing the plate in my hand. His eyebrows rose and he cocked his head to the side. I nodded to him and sat down alone at table to eat my meal mostly free of sand, hoping that that would be the end of it.

After lunch, all I wanted to do was fall asleep. I had never been so exhausted, even after a day of playing in the forest with Cyril and Oswin or after an afternoon climbing scaffolding.

Instead, I was thrown to the lions.

Tym, the animal trainer, stood in front of the animal tent and said just enough to be understood.

"Karla's in town. Horse colic."

"Fetch water for Saitha."

"Bring food for the otters. Food's in the cook's tent."

I trekked to the other side of the circus, bringing back a dripping, squirming sack of frogs. I nearly dropped it more than once.

Feeding the otters quickly became one of the highlights of my day. Needle, Thimble, and Pin stayed in a shallow, collapsible metal pool. Platforms just above the water gave the otters a place to sprawl and sun themselves underneath a low-hanging glass globe. The area stank of fetid kelp, frogs, fish, and brackish seawater. The water needed changing, and I had a sinking feeling I knew just who would be doing it.

I overturned the sack and dumped the frogs into the water and watched the ensuing melee. The otters dove and twisted through the water. I was first horrified as I watched them dismember the live food. They chirped and squawked. Unable to frolic and swim in rivers and lakes or stretch and sun on riverbanks and beaches, their lives must have been boring and so unlike their wild kin, only having a brief taste of the wild at mealtime. Within moments, the pool had no more frogs, and the otters blinked contentedly at me.

When I returned for my next task, Tym was plucking pebbles out of the pads of Saitha's enormous feet. He said to her, "I tell Bil every year that this rock and sand is murderous for your feet and for the horses, but does he ever listen? No, Saitha, he doesn't." His voice was much softer and warmer than when he spoke to me.

I coughed and he glanced at me. "Meat for the cats is in the cook's tent," he said, turning back to Saitha.

I gaped at his turned back. I had just been to the cook's tent! Had he only told me that was my next task, I would not have been walking across the circus a second time for nothing.

"Will I be feeding any other animals this afternoon?" I asked, hoping the anger wasn't too clear.

"Maybe. Come back after."

And what nonsense would he have me do after that? But I knew fussing would earn me nothing, so I swallowed my pride and returned to the cook's tent and came away with a bag of almost rancid meat of indeterminable origin. I wondered if it was the same meat we had eaten at lunchtime, and my stomach churned.

During the day, the big cats were kept in the freakshow tent to keep them away from the otters and other potentially delicious meals. Several of the cats were asleep, curled together like gigantic kittens.

The cyrinx stretched, muscles uncoiling beneath her skin. The other cats looked at me with golden eyes. I tried not to make direct eye contact with any of them. I remembered reading somewhere that cats took it as a sign of aggression.

Then again, I had also heard that they waited for their quarry to look away before pouncing.

I opened the burlap sack and the rancid smell of the meat made me gag. I was standing too close to the cage; a dark purple paw dashed between the bars and grabbed the bag. Her claws grazed my shirtsleeve, ripping the cheap cloth. I cried out and jumped back. The cyrinx hissed and swiped at the other two cats, who growled but kept their distance. And the purple cat circled around her prize, glaring at me, before ripping through the bag with her claws and burying her muzzle into it to feed.

Shaking, I checked my arm to find it scratched but not bleeding. But she had taken all of the food. The others stared at me, clearly thinking that I would make a tastier snack than the rotten meat.

The cook must have been sick of the sight of me when I appeared in his tent for the third time that afternoon.

"Did Violet take it all?" Cook asked, nodding at my ripped shirt.

"Aye."

"Lemme see." He grabbed my sleeve and bared the skin. "Didn't get you. Come to me or Frit if Vi does take a piece of you. Her claws are dirty."

I thanked him.

"Keep this meat well back and throw it in. And here's the feed for everyone else. Tym will keep sending you back and forth to keep you busy." He briefly explained what type of food was for which creature. "I'm tired of seeing your face. Off you get." Though the words were harsh, his tone was not.

I smiled and nodded at him again, and made my way to the tent, burdened with bags and boxes. I fed every animal in the tent, lobbing the meat to the two unfed cats from across the corridor of pens. The freakish animals made my skin crawl. The two-snouted pig ate a bite with the first mouth, and then the second. The fish did not need to be fed at all, going by the tattered remains of skin and bones of the albino floating on the surface of the water. These were creatures on display only because they were malformed. Just as I would be put on display without a second's hesitation if I told the ringmaster what I was.

Tym only grunted when he told me to feed the rest and I said I already had. But as I turned away to discover who I had to help next, I thought I saw him hide a smile.

Because I had finished feeding the animals early, I went to watch the circus practice.

Dot and Mara balanced on their hands on the swept stone in front of the big top. In unison, they raised their legs so that the tops of their thighs rested on their heads. They stared straight ahead, strangely pensive in their impossible poses. Mara took a few steps forward on her hands. Spiky-haired Dot lowered her legs, stood up, and touched her toes, as if folding herself in half. Her hands lay flat on the ground. Smoothly, she stood and then bent in the opposite direction, again touching her hands to the ground behind her head. She did this several times, back and forth, like a broken doll.

"She's showing off," Aenea said, who had sidled up to me. "Most contortionists can't bend completely in both directions. Little Dot likes to boast to Mara, who can only bend forward completely."

Mara stuck out her tongue at Dot and lowered into a split.

Aenea wandered with me through the circus. She had a sheen of sweat on her brow, the small curls about her face matted to her skin, her cheeks flushed. I focused on the circus performers.

The fire-eater spat fire into the sand, wisps of smoke rising where the flames extinguished. The Kymri tumblers flipped across the sand, racing each other to see who could reach a boulder first. One of them flipped over the boulder, landing on his feet, arms above his head.

"It's different from what I'm used to," I said.

'Of course it is," she replied. "There's nothing like living in a circus. You'll love parts of it, and you'll hate other bits of it."

"What do you love about it?" I asked.

"The flying, of course," she said with a smile, tucking a stray strand of hair behind her ear and looking out at the sea. "The open mouths of the audience as they watch me. The clapping and the cheering. The glitter of the costumes under the glass globes. The smell of almost-burnt popcorn. It's marvelous."

"And what do you hate?"

She hesitated. "Sometimes moving from place to place is difficult. Living out of a trunk. Sometimes when you come across the normals outside the circus, they're a bit crude, because they have this idea that they know you because they've seen you on stage." She did not seem that upset by any of what she said.

"More good than bad?"

She patted my arm. The skin tingled where she had touched. "Yes, far more good than bad. It'll be interesting to see how you do. Don't let me down!" she teased.

I saluted, though I worried that I would fail her. "I'll do my best, ma'am."

She threw her head back and laughed – a full, rich laugh, her face split with glee; so unlike the dainty, lady-like laughs reserved for polite company. She flipped along the sand and I tried to follow. I managed a flip, though it was not as graceful as hers.

"Are you watching the show tonight?" Aenea asked as we walked toward the big top.

"Of course."

"I'll look for you in the crowd, then," she said. "I have to get ready."

I watched her saunter away, envying her easy confidence. She was so different from other girls I had known. She told you what she was thinking; she seemed to know who she was, and what she wanted from life. I was still figuring that out.

The afternoon had lengthened. The workers were erecting the tents that contained the smaller acts, calling out instructions to each other. In the big top, the clowns applied makeup, plastering each other in white and exaggerating features with their color of choice. The strongman tested his weights before setting them down with a clatter on the stone. Tauro the bull-man sat in the stands next to Juliet the Leopard Lady, rolling a ball idly between his large hands. Karla curried the amber and gold Kymri horse, speaking with Tym. She rested a hand on Tym's shoulder and kissed his cheek, and I realized that they were married, or close enough to it.

A woman with a solemn face was fiddling with a metal machine as big as a book in her hands. I craned toward her. This must be Frit – the ringmaster's wife. She saw me looking and gestured me over. She was the first person to actively seek my company aside from the aerialists and the white clown.

"Hello," I said, suddenly shy. I held out my hand. "I'm Micah."

She gave me a wan smile. Arik had said her face was sour, but to me she looked sad and tired. She had long, mousy hair tucked into a scarf. Small wrinkles outlined her eyes, and she wore no cosmetics. "The whole circus knows who you are, child. We don't get that many new members." Still, she took my hand and squeezed before letting go. "I'm Frit, as you probably know."

I nodded. "What is that?" I gestured to the bit of machinery in her hands. The square metal box was blue-black, covered with swirls and characters, with several knobs along the top. It was obviously Vestige –

leftover technology from the Alders, who disappeared centuries ago.

"It's the weather machine for the circus. It's acting a little strange," she said.

I felt disappointed. "So the lightning and the clouds weren't magic?"

She chuckled. "Depends on what you call magic, I suppose. I don't know how it was made, and I suspect you don't as well. Who's to say they didn't create it with magic?"

"Is it broken?"

She shook her head. "I don't think so." She pointed to a knob. "It's not turning properly, so sometimes the lightning doesn't go off. I think it just needs a bit of oil." She massaged some oil into the machine with a rag. The knob twisted easily in her hand. "Should we try it again?" she asked.

"I think so. Want to make sure it's working properly for the show, right?"

"Of course," she said knowingly. "It'd never be because a young lad wants to see a storm inside, now would it?"

"Of course not."

We shared smiles. I decided I liked her.

Frit stood up and clapped. "I have to test the weather machine!" she called.

The clowns, makeup intact, paused in their tumbling and bumbling and lounged against the stands. Karg set down his weights. Tauro ceased rolling his ball and Juliet the Leopard Lady crossed her arms over her chest, her dappled hair falling over one shoulder. Karla and Tym led the horse out of the tent, so the thunder would not frighten it.

Frit turned the knob on the left. The machine hissed
and fog emerged from a small hole in each side. Within
moments, the big top was lost in the sweet smoke. I could
barely see Frit as she twisted the knob on the right and
then the middle. Lightning flashed, blinding us, and the
same temporary stars glittered at us before dissipating
with the smoke. The clowns, the Leopard Lady, the Bull
Man, and the Strong Man all clapped, along with the
newest aerialists' apprentice.

We all ate dinner quickly, starving after our afternoon of
hard work.

I won three whole spoonfuls of stew from Cook, and
the stunted heel of a stale brown loaf. I even managed to
nab an apple for dessert. While it was still not as much
as I wanted, at least my stomach did not grumble after I
had finished.

Bil was in a good mood that evening. Earlier, he had
seemed moody and surly as he barked out orders to his
employees. He might have been drunk, judging by the
red eyes and the ever-full tankard by his plate. He spoke
loudly enough for the entire circus to hear his dinner
conversation.

"Frit, my love, light of my life, saved the circus for us,
today," he said, gesturing at her. Two spots of color appeared in Frit's cheeks, but she did not say anything.

"For what is our circus of magic without our perfect
opening of thunder and lightning, eh, I ask you?" he
paused. "Nothing, that's what!"

Some people exchanged dirty looks at this. "Oh aye,
we have the most talented performers in all of dear El-

lada," Bil recovered, "but the *magic*… the magic is what sets us apart from Riley & Batheo's Circus of Mundanities, for all the gold marks in their safe. It's wha' makes the children starry-eyed and begging their parents to come back the next day. The lightning is the key. It… transports 'em.

"And so I have my dear wife, Frit, to thank for bringing the magic back into the circus, as she brought it back into my life." He slapped his hand over his heart. Behind him, the yellow clown Fedir pantomimed puking. I hid a smile with my hand.

"A little applause, please, for my fair lady," Bil said, and the whole circus clapped. Bil clasped Frit's hand and made an elaborate bow before kissing her fingers. Frit smiled and acted bashful, playing the part for the audience. But it did not ring true. Her smile was tight, her eyes nervous, and she kept rolling her shoulder. Though it was billed as playful banter, there was more under the surface. Judging by Arik and Aenea's crinkled brows, I was not the only person who thought so.

Frit made eye contact with me, and my suspicions were confirmed. She looked trapped.

7

SUMMER: THE GHOST & THE SNAKE CHARMER

"The Lord of the Sun and the Lady of the Moon said: We brought human dreams to life for them. We named them 'Chimaera'."

from THE APHELION

I watched the circus again that night of the Penmoon.

I sat in the best stand in the house and felt as amazed as I had the previous night. After setting up the props, I knew the secrets to some of the tricks, but it did not matter. Though I had seen the weather machine in operation not an hour before, I still enjoyed seeing it again. Knowing that the fire eaters spat paraffin only made it all the more exciting and dangerous. I knew that when the tumblers first came on the stage they would soon make themselves into a human pyramid. I clapped, though an amused look from Aenea stilled my hands as she bowed at the end, the braid of her hair falling forward and the beads of her costume glinting in the light of the glass globes.

After the show, I wandered through the carnival again. This time I went to Nina the snake charmer's tent, and I did not have to pay at the door. The audience crowded each other in the tent, smelling of coal dust, grease, and human sweat. A worker switched on a cheap gramophone. Byssian music played – brass and nickel instruments, large drums, and twanging strings. It made me think of sunsets and yellow eyes and deep growls in dark jungles. Nina sidled onto the stage, swathed head to toe in scarves lined in painted wooden beads. I could only see her serpentine eyes, smudged with black and green.

Nina slid a scarf from her stomach and its wooden beads rattled together. Another scarf slipped, showing intricate henna tattoos along her left arm. Her fingers undulated, beckoning to people in the audience. Mostly men surrounded me, though I saw more women than I had thought I would. Another scarf fell to the floor. The other hennaed arm rippled into view, along with the tail of a bright green snake. The crowd gasped.

Nina slithered free from her scarves, revealing her face, stained with more tattoos, and black hair in thick braids to her waist. Her stomach was bare, but the rest of her was well-covered. Though erotic, the show was probably very different from what was on offer in Sal and Tila's tent. While over forty, Nina had a beauty that was wise and confident. With her darker skin and hair, I guessed she was half-Elladan and half-Kymri. Her gaze held secrets.

Her body moved in time with the music. The snake, as thick as a tree branch in its middle, curled about her neck and arms. I had never seen a snake like this before, even in books, and did not know whether or not it was poisonous. Men and women alike sat still and silent as she danced, mesmerized by her movements.

Nina untwined the snake from her neck and arms and slid it hand over hand into a wicker basket on the stage. Those in the front row backed away. From somewhere under her scarves, Nina pulled out a small wooden flute stylized to look like a snake and began to play. Her fingers danced along the rainbow of scaled reptilian keys. The snake poked its head up from the basket and swayed with the slow tempo she built. My own eyes grew heavy. Nina and her snake mirrored each other's movements as gracefully as any court dance.

The music stopped and I shook my head, taking a moment to remember just where I was. I wanted her to keep playing and the snake to keep dancing, to hypnotize me into forgetting my troubles. Nina bowed and passed a hat around. I would have given her some money, but I had none to offer.

I left the tent, the snake music still echoing in my mind. I found myself humming the tune as I explored the carnival. I came upon a tent that had escaped my notice the previous night: the Pavilion of Phantoms. The black canvas tent hunkered behind the others. Another Vestige fog machine or, more likely, the far more economical card-ice in water must have been spirited away inside it. Fog unfurled from the bottom of the dark tent, as though it had just been set aflame and then extinguished.

Again, I did not pay at the door. Fewer people attended this tent. The air felt colder inside, and another gramophone played echoing, ghostly music. Thin scraps of ragged grey veils fluttered in an unseen wind. I walked through ankle-deep fog. Haunting motifs in luminescent paint decorated the interior of the canvas, depicting pale ghosts with nothing but black holes where their eyes should have been. There were twisted trees, whose branches seemed to grasp the tattered clothes of the ghosts. A full moon with the hint of a sad face in its craters. Two solitary candles, set well within the middle of the tent and surrounded by small fences, were the only source of light, and their flickering flames made the ghosts painted on the walls appear to move.

Five others were with me in the tent – two coal miners, the soot forever stained into the grooves of their hands; a middle-aged couple who were probably merchants, judging by their tidy but unassuming dress; and an older man with a beard halfway down his chest who I could not quite place.

Another gust of wind caused the candles to sputter. The music grew more wailing, and then a disembodied voice began to speak. Though I knew it must be another bit of Vestige, it frightened me terribly – a high, thin voice that spoke in three tones at once, using a language that hardly anyone in the world knew how to speak anymore: Alder, the dead language of the Old Ones.

Fog swirled into a thin cyclone between the two candles. The voices grew louder, the different tones overlapping with each other until they did not even sound like they could be words anymore. The merchant's wife clutched the arm of her husband. The coal miners and the old man seemed unperturbed by events.

The fog cleared, and a ghost of a girl stood among us. Though not superstitious nor particularly religious, I whispered an incoherent prayer to the Lord and Lady, just in case. I nearly ran out of the tent, but I knew that the circus was all about illusion. This could not have been a ghost, as much as she looked like one.

I have seen false ghosts before. Mother once attended a séance at her friend's summer estate and forced me to come. The ghost that had appeared had obviously been made using an illusion. I researched it afterwards, and it involved mirrors and light, smoke and shadows.

But this girl did not look like an illusion; instead, she looked so alive, so *present*, aside from the fact that she was nothing but shades of white and blue and I could see through her. I looked about to see if there was any sort of projection, but if there was, it was too cleverly hidden. I could see every hair on her head and the down on her cheek. I wanted to reach out and touch her, to see if I would feel warm flesh, or only air.

She was not human. She was taller than I, and looked to be in her twenties. The proportions of her face were more Alder – larger eyes, higher cheekbones, elongated limbs. Strange tattoos dotted her hairline and traced the line of her neck. She wore a simple white gown that trailed the floor and disappeared. But she was not entirely Alder. She was a Chimaera. Behind her rose the giant, gossamer wings of a dragonfly. They were glistening and iridescent, and she flapped them soundlessly. She stared straight ahead, looking thoughtfully at something above our heads. The recorded voices lowered and disappeared.

A man dressed in a black hood and cape stepped out of the darkness. All five of us started and stepped back. He looked like Death.

"Friends of the afterlife," he intoned, and I recognized the gravelly voice of Wicket, a circus worker. I relaxed, despite my fear. This was nothing but another Vestige illusion. "I present to you the Phantom Damselfly. She was once a princess of the Chimaera, next in line to inherit the throne of the Dragonfly people. But she fell in love with the wrong man, the son of the rival family, and her parents would not condone the match. One night, the young prince flew into the castle of his lady love. But the king was waiting for him instead of his beloved. The king had a powerful temper, and challenged him to a duel.

"They fought across the room; the only sounds the clash of steel sword on steel, the panting of breath, and the stomp of their feet. The prince lost. The king cut off his wings and threw him from the tower, and the suitor perished.

"The princess never recovered from the tragedy. The night before her arranged wedding to another prince of her father's choosing, she tied her wings to her torso and jumped from a tall cliff, disappearing beneath the waves. But even death did not bring her solace, and her spirit wanders still, all these centuries later. She may never find peace."

I had no doubt that the story was a fiction but it was sad nonetheless. And she did look mournful. The hooded man retreated into the shadows.

The Damselfly shook her head, as though awakening. She paced in a slow circle, head bowed deep in thought, her wings flickering. One wing caught a candle flame, which did not waver. The other people in the tent backed away further from the ghost, their faces blank with wonder.

I stepped forward. I could not shake the feeling that she looked almost familiar.

"Oh, do be careful!" the merchant woman whispered

from behind me. "She could steal your soul. They say that dragonflies weigh the soul for the Darkness."

I ignored her and took another step.

The ghost stopped her pacing and her head snapped up, her eyes focusing on me. My mouth opened in shock. She was definitely looking at me, not in my general direction. She cocked her head. I shook like a leaf.

"My, but it has been a long time since a Kedi came to see me," she said, and I could not be sure if she was speaking Elladan or Alder. But I understood her. My breath came in gasps and I stumbled away from her. Her gaze followed me. She flicked her wings, once.

"I thought you might hear me," the ghost said.

"Did you hear that?" I asked the others.

They looked at me curiously. "Heard what, dear?" the merchant's wife asked.

"She... spoke. She said something to me. You didn't hear her?"

They shook their heads. "She... spoke to you?" the old man asked, his voice wavering. "Just now?"

"They won't hear me, little Kedi," the Chimaera ghost said. "Very few can hear me when I speak. You are the first in such a long, long time."

My breath left my lungs in a rush. I clapped my hands over my ears. "No!" I ran from the tent, leaving the ghost and the shocked customers behind.

I sprinted to Arik's cart, locking the door behind me and diving under the covers, shivering in abject fear. I almost expected her to follow me, to see the ghost shimmer in the cart. I tried to control my breathing, but it was a long time before I stopped gasping.

I must have imagined it. There was no possible way a Vestige ghost actually spoke to me. It was some sort of cruel prank from someone in the circus. She was a real woman in makeup and mechanical wings that had been projected into the tent with mirrors. But how would they ever have heard the term Kedi, the term I had so recently learned myself?

I rifled in my pack and took out the little soapstone figurine a man named Mister Illari had given me, not long before I joined the circus. He told me a story about a being that was worshipped as a minor god in the backwaters of Byssia. A being called a Kedi.

I ran a thumb over its crude features before tucking it back into the bottom of my pack.

Sleep would not come, and I lay awake with only my thoughts for company. I pretended to be asleep when Arik entered after the nightly bonfire. Near dawn, I finally drifted into a fitful doze. I dreamed of snakes twining about my arms and legs, hissing softly in time with Nina's music. But then the snakes tightened, strangling me, and I struggled to breathe. I tried to call for help. Help came, but not the kind I wanted. The ghost Damselfly from the Pavilion of Phantoms hovered above me.

"I know your secret, little Kedi. And I know what your future will bring. You poor thing."

Her ghostly finger touched my face, and then she was gone.

8

Spring: Afternoon Tea

"Under no circumstances should a gentleman and a lady be left unchaperoned. In the presence of a chaperone, a gentleman may kiss the back of a lady's hand. If he is very bold, he may kiss her cheek. Yet the young lady must take heed. No more is considered seemly, and no more may be allowed."

A Young Elladan Lady's Primer,
Lady Elena Primrose

The room was full of smiling, laughing people, and all I wanted to do was flee.

My mother's hand gripped mine like a claw as she steered me forward to our designated snow-white table. On my other side, Cyril wrapped his pinky with mine and squeezed. He winked, and I felt a little better, and better still when I saw Oswin at our table.

The Hawthornes always held the last social event of the spring season, and it was an afternoon tea, followed by outside games. It was exhausting, having carefully regimented and modulated amusement all day, always taking care to say and act just so, as many eyes were watching. It made me melancholy, as well, for it meant that soon we would be returning to Sicion and its sooty, sandy buildings and ever-present rain.

The Hawthornes prided themselves on their conservatory. It was large enough to easily host the twenty or so guests, with every wall paned in glass so clear that it would be easy to walk into it by mistake. The house perched on top of a low hill and the view was majestic. The dark conifer trees fell away toward a stream, and jagged snow-topped mountains cut into the sky.

I sat at our table, taking care to face the window. I felt woefully self-conscious – Mother had forced me to wear a horrible confection of a dress, with froths of white lace and a wide pale-pink sash high around my corseted waist. My auburn hair had been curled and artfully piled on top of my head, Mother had smeared my cheeks with a bit of rouge, and I wore white gloves. Cyril looked very smart in his light brown afternoon suit.

According to my ghostly reflection in one of the conservatory window panes, the overly feminine clothing emphasized the strong line of my jaw and my square temples. Mother rapped my knuckles when I stooped my shoulders and whispered in my ear to behave myself, disguising the words with a kiss on my cheek, before she went to the adults' table. I fought the urge to stick my tongue out at her retreating back.

Oswin grinned at me and elbowed me in the side. "You look like a right lady today, Iphigenia."

"I'd still whip you in a fight and you know it."

"Don't let your mummy hear you say that," he said,

holding his face primly in imitation.

I glowered at him. Lucy, Oswin's little sister, giggled, covering her face with her hands. A plump, happy girl who was always very taken with me and I with her, Lucy was four years younger than me and was still fond of her porcelain dolls. The other members of our table were Darla Hornbeam, a girl very concerned with her self-importance and close ties to royalty, and her younger brother Damien, whom I liked very much. We were an evenly-matched table of three brothers and three sisters. If I counted as a sister.

Oswin was spared a rude comment by the arrival of the tea. Each guest had his or her own little ceramic teapot, embossed with a certain type of flower. I had bluebells. Cyril had roses. We had to wait precisely three minutes for the tea to steep while Oswin's mother, Lady Hawthorne, gave a short speech thanking everyone for their attendance and hoping that we would have a pleasant afternoon. We all applauded softly, and then together we poured the tea.

Lady Hawthorne had spared no expense; it was a fine quality brew from Linde. I breathed in the steam. As we stirred in cold milk and sugar, the serving girls, graceful in their starched aprons and hats, set down the tiered plates of cakes and sandwiches. The plates looked fit to break under the weight of the food.

A string quartet played blandly appropriate music as we ate. The food was marvelous – sandwiches of the freshest white bread filled with various cheeses, cucumbers, crisp lettuce, salmon, smoked meats, and thinly sliced fruit. My favorite was one with a special ham and melon. All of the produce was grown right on the property. Lady Hawthorne spent as much time in the countryside as she could, though her children and husband spent most of their lives in Sicion and Imachara.

Snippets of adult conversation carried to our table over the clink of the cutlery. We listened with unabashed curiosity. We were at the age where adult matters shifted from dull to somewhat fascinating. My mother was speaking animatedly with Lady Oak about upcoming events in Sicion and mentioning her excitement at the boutique on Jade Street. My father was speaking to Oswin's father about law, of course. Father liked to speak about law and cigars at these events. It was all quite proper.

I ate my sandwiches and waited impatiently for everyone to finish and Lady Hawthorne to give her next speech so that we could start on the sweets. They were just sitting there, begging to be tasted, but it would be a breach of etiquette to do so before the speech. Chocolate creams, glacé cherries, caramelized imported bananas from Byssia, hazelnut mousse, cakes fluffy and soft as pillows, feather-light frosting... I could already imagine it melting on my tongue.

After what felt like an age, the adults had finished their sandwiches, Lady Hawthorne thanked us again for coming, and we were allowed to serve ourselves. I ate my way through half a dozen cakes before my stomach told me enough was enough. I felt a bit guilty when I noticed that Darla, who had not said a word during the tea, had one small candied cherry on her plate, but had not touched it. Too good for sugar. Stuck-up twit.

After a long hour, we were able to go outside for the games. The adults divided themselves into teams and began to play croquet. The elderly sat on lawn chairs, the women with fans and the men with cigars. Darla Hornbeam hustled over and joined the game, tired of being around us children. Lucy wandered over to her mother, sitting on the lawn and playing with her dolls.

I did not bother to watch. I cared little for a peel or a scatter shot, a rouquet or a rush. But the "children" had decided to play games of our own.

Cyril, Oswin, Damien, and I crept into the forest, hoping no one would notice our disappearance. They shouldn't; the adults were too busy with the croquet, and, besides, the sparkling wine had been opened.

I plucked a sprig of leaves from the tree as I walked, liking their texture. The bottom of my white dress was already specked with mud. Mother would be furious.

We settled into a clearing. It was an almost perfect circle within the trees, thick with loam and scattered green leaves. A small Penglass dome sprouted at the edge like an over-sized toadstool.

I walked over and ran my hand over the surface, so smooth it felt wet. I could see shadows and strange shapes through it, barely illuminated by the clearing's light. There were no openings, no cracks, no pits, and no dents. Sparks flashed off the surface in the sunlight, and I drew my hand away.

Penglass had always interested me, growing up. To my peers, it was like the crumbling ruins of old castles, or the bridge-like buildings over rivers. Something that was once used, but now is defunct, and had always been there. Another form of Vestige. But Penglass was different.

Penglass was not actually glass, but an unbreakable mystery. "Pen" meant *leader* in Alder, but my history tutor said it was named after the Peng, a mythical beast from Linde, which is a fish in the water and a bird in the sky, and whose wings were more radiant than the sun and firmament. Penglass was the deepest, purest shade of blue, bluer than sapphires or cobalt. Away from the major cities, there were only occasional small growths. But the cities were riddled with them, some taller than the highest buildings. Humans settled near the larger outcrops because they were by safe ports and provided good shelters from enemies. No one could shoot through Penglass. And nobody knew what was inside. This one or any of them.

A chill wind picked up in the forest, and I shivered. My heart pattered in my chest, though I was not sure why. We always snuck off after afternoon tea. Perhaps it was because we were all older, but this year I noticed Damien was rather handsome, with his strong jawline and half-lidded eyes.

Oswin reached into a pocket and produced four cigars, ostensibly nabbed from the adults' box. I widened my eyes. I had never smoked before. I did not expect anyone else in the group had, either.

"Aren't they going to notice they're missing?" Cyril asked, delightfully scandalized.

"They don't count," Oswin scoffed. It must be nice to have his parents. My mother would have counted.

He passed them around. I held mine gingerly. It looked

like the body of a dragonfly, and the smell reminded me of my father's study.

"Is the lady not wishing to smoke?" Oswin teased.

"Of course I will, you daftie."

"Genie isn't like the other girls," Damien said. I snuck a look at him and then stared intently at my cigar.

"Aye, it's almost as if she's one of the boys," Oswin said. Was that a jibe?

"Don't make me paint you with mud again, Oswin Hawthorne!" I joked to cover the flutter of nerves in my stomach.

Cyril laughed. "I hope you spirited away a light as well, Oswin."

"What do you take me for? An amateur?" He took a book of matches from his pocket. He bit the edge of his cigar and spat it onto the ground. We all followed suit. It tasted terrible, and I did not know if I had bitten off too much or too little.

Even Oswin did not like it. "I would have stolen a cigar cutter, but there's only two."

Oswin began to light the cigar, self-consciously puffing and rotating it into the flame. It was the first time he had tried, and he was aping his father. He passed the matches around and first Damien and then Cyril lit theirs. I did not want to smoke. It smelled awful, and I did not see the point. But I knew that if I declined, Oswin would tease me for being too feminine.

And so I lit the cigar. I had to try a couple of times, and I did not think I lit it properly. I inhaled and immediately began to choke. My eyes watered and my lungs were on fire.

"You're not meant to inhale, you silly girl!" Oswin

said. "You're just meant to hold the smoke in your mouth and then blow it out."

"What's... the... point... in... that?" I gasped in-between chokes.

Damien laughed and Cyril patted me on the arm.

When I recovered, we were all silent as we smoked. These were cigars of the finest quality, from Temne, Linde, or Byssia, but I still thought they tasted wretched. The tobacco was strong and overwhelming. I held the smallest amount of smoke in my mouth and blew it out quickly. Mostly I stared at the ember on the tip. It was beautiful, soft and orange as a coal in a fire.

When the cigars had burned down to stubs, we crushed them beneath our feet. I had the feeling that no one enjoyed them much, even Oswin. My head was swimming a bit from the fumes, and I felt dreadfully thirsty. The smoke seemed like it had permeated every pore and hair follicle. As soon as we returned, our parents would know exactly what we had been doing. We wandered further into the forest and drank water from the stream, lovely and sweet, far nicer than the medicinal taste of the water in the city.

Cyril decided that we should all play a game before the light dimmed beneath the trees and the adults wondered where their offspring were.

"Charades?" Damien suggested.

"We don't have pen and paper, idiot."

"Statues?" Cyril asked.

"I hate that game. I always lose," Oswin said.

"And I always win, which is why I suggested it," Cyril joked.

I was chosen to be the sculptor, and I posed them all in

funny shapes. I made Cyril hold an arm high above his head and stand on a foot, with the other hand posed to make him look as if he were about to pick his nose. In a fit of wickedness, I made Oswin put his head between his knees. His mouth worked furiously as he struggled not to laugh. Whoever laughed or moved first after they had been posed lost, and so I had to pose them very quickly so that there was not too much of a time lapse. I felt very nervous posing Damien. In the end, I made him rest an ear on his shoulder and stuck his arms and legs akimbo, with his feet facing in.

Oswin laughed first, of course. We played several more rounds and I lost more than half of the time, which was not fair because I wobbled easier due to my slippers, skirts, and corset. *Had I been dressed like a man, I would have won*, I comforted myself.

Next, Oswin suggested the game of sardines. Damien was chosen to be the first to hide, and we had to count to one hundred while he hid. I strained my ears and listened to him as he crashed through the undergrowth. I smiled slightly to myself as I counted in time with Cyril and Oswin. My sense of hearing was remarkably good, according to the doctors, along with my sense of smell, touch, and taste, and I rarely fell ill. They believed it was somehow linked with my birth disorder, though they had not come across it in other cases. One, Dr Birchswitch, published a thirty-page article about it, and went on a medical tour around Ellada and the former colonies. Thankfully my parents would not allow him to drag me along with him as his show monkey.

When we reached one hundred, I opened my eyes. I

started walking and Cyril followed me. He knew about my hearing. I raised an eyebrow at him and he reluctantly branched off. I moved as quietly as I could with my silly slippers, and held my skirt high off of the ground.

I did not know for sure if Damien had come this way. I paused and smiled when I saw a bit of movement: a branch of a bush quivered in front of a hollow tree. No one appeared to have followed me and I heard no other footsteps, and so I moved the bush branch back and grinned at Damien's shocked face.

"So quickly!" he whispered.

"You're not very good at hiding. Move over," I replied, and moved into the hollow tree. I crouched awkwardly, and Damien offered me his jacket to sit upon. I smiled at him, and noticed my heartbeat was echoing in my ears again.

"Do you think the others will find us soon?" he whispered.

"I don't know. We all went in separate directions."

"Hope they don't get lost."

"Oswin probably will. He'd get lost on a straight footpath through the forest."

Damien chuckled and gave me a considering look. "When did you grow up, Iphigenia?" He was one to talk. He was younger than Cyril, and only a year older than me.

I mock-scowled at him. "*Gene*. And I don't know if I would call myself grown."

"Gene." I liked the sound of my name on his tongue.

We sat in a tense silence. The hollowed tree smelled of

old smoke, damp wood and earth, and it muffled sounds from the outside. Water dripped, and animals occasionally rustled leaves. I breathed in deeply and closed my eyes.

"What are you thinking about?" Damien asked, still whispering.

"How much nicer the forest smells compared to the stench of the city."

"So much better. The air smells so *clean*. No soot, no coal smoke, no seeping sewage."

"Mm, can't wait to smell it all again in a few days!" I shocked him into laughter.

"You are different from other girls."

"I'm not easily scandalized," was all I could think to say in return.

Abruptly, he leaned forward and kissed me right on the mouth. I made a muffled squeak behind my closed lips. He broke the kiss, leaned away, and opened his mouth to apologise.

I did not give him a chance, and boldly kissed him. His lips were a little chapped from the sun, the skin on his chin just beginning to prickle.

Damien made a small sound in the back of his throat, almost a growl. He pressed himself closer to me and ran his hands over my torso. I could barely feel his hands through the layers of fabric. My stomach twisted. It felt nice, wonderful even, but I knew with certainty that I was not supposed to be doing this. A kiss or two was acceptable. My mother always spouted the virtues of playing difficult to catch, of stringing men along until they could not bear to be without you. She told me that playing difficult to catch was particularly vital for me.

I'll give it one more minute, and then push him away, I thought, a little woozy with all of the emotions swirling through my mind and body.

I did not get another minute. Quick as a snake, his hand worked its way beneath my petticoats and brushed between my legs. Every muscle in his body went still.

I scrambled away from him, to the opposite side of the tree, careless of the mud splattering my dress. It was too dim to see Damien's face.

"Please..." I whispered, hoarsely. "I was...born with–"

"A prick." His voice was flat, surprised and cruel.

My breath was ragged. "No, I'm a girl. That part, it just, it grew too big. I'm seeing a doctor soon. Please... please..."

He was utterly silent. I was panting in fear. If he told just one person, the entire secret would be something of the past. I would never find a man to marry me. All would shun me. I would be stuck with Mother forever.

"Please," I said again, my voice too low for a girl's, too frightened to even articulate the plea properly.

"I will not tell anyone," he said stiffly. "It was my own fault, for being too forward."

I smoothed my hair from my face, still shaking. "I had never even been kissed before."

He started. "My apologies." His voice still sounded flat. I realized that Damien had probably found his way beneath several skirts before this, with his social standing and pretty face. There were tavern wenches and he would have the money for tarts, but even some noble girls will kiss and pet, though most do not engage in anything that would result in a child. My friend Anna Yew had let a boy or two beneath her bodice. But Damien had never discovered anything quite like me, nor would he likely again.

Damien would recover from this. Someday, he'd barely remember what had happened this day in the woods. At least, I could only hope he would. But this was something I would never, could never forget. That the first person to discover what I was had recoiled in revulsion and would no longer look at me. I stared at the charred interior of the hollow tree, determined not to let him see me cry.

We sat in total silence until Cyril found us. It felt like hours had passed, but it had only been a couple of minutes. Damien did not look at me, the muscles in his jaws working furiously.

I disgusted him.

Cyril looked between the two of us but said nothing. When Oswin finally found us, we headed home as the light faded. I had a long streak of mud down the side of my skirt. I hid behind Cyril as we walked to the dwindling afternoon tea party, but there was no way to keep Mother from noticing. She admonished me the entire carriage ride home. At least she did not appear to have smelled the smoke.

She railed on about how no man would wish to marry a girl who runs along and plays with the boys, who cannot keep herself tidy. I said nothing, her words barely registering, and looked out the window at the trees streaming past, my knees pressed tightly together to stop them from shaking. I felt as though my mind and heart had been dragged through a thicket of rose bushes and caught on every little thorn. After all, no man would want me in any case. I was both man and woman. No one would marry a monster.

9
SUMMER: THE BURNING CHALK

"The Royal Snakewood family has ruled for over eight hundred years. Queen Nicolette Snakewood will come of age on an auspicious date – an eclipse that marks the date of the fortieth generation of Royalty. On that bright night, Ellada will have a celebration such as none have seen before."

THE SNAKEWOOD DYNASTY, Professor Caed Cedar, Royal Snakewood University

The tightrope shook violently under my feet as I made my way across it and I pinwheeled my arms to keep balance. I refused to fall.

"Focus!" Aenea said, poking me in the ankle. I bent my knees, gritting my teeth as I balanced.

"Don't do that!" I cried.

"Who's to say some unruly member of the audience won't throw something at you some night? You can't ever lose focus."

"Someone's going to hit me with something when I'm sixty feet in the air?"

"They might have a very strong arm."

"Then we can recruit them to the circus and replace the strongman. Did you know that his barbells are fake? Even I could lift them a bit!"

"Yes, it's true that he's more fat than muscle," she said as I continued walking across the rope, trying not to wobble and weave as much. "Bil's had plenty of men stronger who wished to join, but they weren't as big and Bil is all about appearances."

Aenea pulled a wisp of brown hair out of her face and furrowed her eyebrows. I itched to reach out and touch her hair. In our time practicing, she remained teasing but detached, aside from the odd flirtation, which left me flustered. I could not stop thinking about her, and frequently felt tongue-tied when she spoke to me. Did I like her, a girl? Was it wrong to like her? Did she like me?

"You look so ungraceful," she said.

"I'm trying," I said, slumping down in the middle of the rope and dangling my legs. "I haven't been sleeping well," I added, which was a gross understatement. Dreams of the Phantom Damselfly haunted me nightly, and I woke up covered in cold sweat, wondering what it meant and unable to go back to sleep. "Why are you being so hard on me? It almost makes me wish to give up."

"Would you give up that easily?"

"I said 'almost!' I don't plan to give up. This is the only thing I can see myself doing. But I'm trying as hard as I can."

She relaxed. "I can see that. And you're learning."

"Really?" I asked.

"Really. Last season, we took on another hopeful trapeze replacement for Arik. The boy showed great promise.

He had been trained in one of the smaller circuses. But weeks passed and he did not improve at all. The boy was as good as he was going to get, which is probably why he left the other circus. He was rather displeased when we let him go before we carried onto Cowl. Arik was devastated. He was hoping to retire last year. We were planning to try to steal another already trained trapeze artist from Imachara when we got there, but you would be far cheaper. Trained, very good artists cost a pretty penny."

I gazed at my feet in reply.

"I'm only hard on you because I want you to be a competent partner," she said.

"I understand. You're going to put your life in my hands and I'll put mine in yours."

She looked at her toes. "I'm sorry if it made you feel I disliked you." The words were frank, almost childlike.

"Thank you." She looked up, gave me a smile, and hopped up beside me, her side pressing against mine. I felt a stirring between my legs and crossed them quickly, mortified.

Arik padded over and sat on my other side. I felt a surge of kinship, yet sadness at how little I knew of their lives. All I knew of Aenea's parents were that they had also been performers, but I did not know if they still performed or even if they were still alive. Arik's parents had been merchants with a failing business, and he had run away early to support himself and lessen the burden on them, sending home what money he could. It did not help – their business still failed and they died a few years later.

"What if I don't improve more than I already have?" I asked.

"You're catching on quickly enough. It just takes time. For goodness sake, it's not even been a month yet," Arik said.

I pitched my voice lower, my eyes darting toward Frit up in the stands. Bathed in the sodium light of the gas globe, she scribbled in an open book in her lap. She returned my gaze. "How much longer are you planning on staying?"

Arik stared at a patch in the tent canvas. "I don't know. Depends on you," he said with a smile in my direction. "Let's get to practicing and find out, shall we?"

The days settled into a routine.

While most of the circus had seemed content to ignore me as much as possible, others were enraged that, two weeks later, I was still clinging on, stubborn as a limpet. I performed my chores, no matter how awful – and the circus folk could be quite creative – day after day without complaint. Though each muscle constantly pained me, I practiced my rudimentary tumbling, tightrope walking, and trapeze swinging, and I stretched on my pallet each night before bed. No one could accuse me of not working hard.

Those who did not like me made it known. The pranks were harmless enough – someone would slide a chair out from behind me as I tried to sit down and I'd land on my arse in the sand. Arik and Aenea dared not warn me of my impending victimization or they would lose face with their peers, but neither of them approved of the pranks that occurred at my expense. Others spoke to a space above my head or behind my shoulder, barely acknowledging my presence. Such jibes nevertheless left my

stomach twisting and my eyes burning. But my tormen-
tors never saw me cry.

When they failed to illicit a response, the pranks
worsened.

One breakfast, nearly three weeks after I joined the circus, I waited in the queue for porridge with everyone else.
Nothing unusual had happened in three days, and I was
torn between hoping they had given up and dreading
what may come.

The atmosphere of the circus that morning was quiet
but cut through with tension. A member of nobility was
supposedly visiting from Imachara and would be in the
audience that night. Aenea told me that rumors like this
circulated from time to time, but people always wished
and feared that the nobility would arrive.

"Think the Princess Royal herself is gonna be hiding
in the stands, boy? Gonna try to steal a kiss?" Fedir, the
yellow clown, asked when I was at the front of the queue.
I started, unused to being addressed directly.

"No," I said honestly, holding out my bowl for food.
Fedir tapped me on the shoulder.

"Yes?" I said, turning to look at him.

"Why not? Could be exciting for her, watching the
oiled, nearly naked tumblers, eh?"

"Were she to come to a circus, she'd probably go to
the Imacharan show," I said, annoyed at him and wishing
to return to my seat.

"Aye, well, when she does, I reckon she won't be able
to stay away from *this*," he gestured to his body which,
though well-muscled from his tumbling, was still somewhat gawky and gangly.

Fedir took his bowl of porridge and sauntered away, glancing over his shoulder at me as he did. As I walked to my seat near Aenea and Arik, I laughed at the thought of the Princess Royal in our roughened wooden stands, eating sugar floss and whooping with the other spectators. Our princess might have liked it.

The king and queen died four years ago, along with her brother, the prince. They were being flown across the sea to Byssia in a gyrocopter, but midway through the flight, the machine malfunctioned, and they crashed into the water.

At the age of two, the princess became the ruler of the land. But as she obviously was not yet able to rule, her uncle had assumed the role of steward, and did the job well enough, aside from watching the ranks of the impoverished grow. The princess was already receiving a vigorous education to help prepare her to take the throne as soon as possible. She probably had little to no time to play with dolls or see circuses.

I sat down and shook my head, breaking my reverie. Out of the corner of my eye, people stared at me. Snickers erupted and quieted. I sighed. What would it be this time?

Aenea's and Arik's faces were confused. Like me, they sensed the tension. I swallowed and set my bowl down.

"Hello," I said to them, determined to act normally.

They muttered suitable responses.

I stuck my spoon into my porridge and froze. Something was in it.

I fished out the remains of a decomposed rat. It stank of cooked oats and decay. Bile rose in my throat. I was no longer a stranger to foul smells, but to have it in my food was too much.

The callousness of the prank left me despondent; I felt as if I would never fit in and that I should leave at nightfall. Perhaps Master Illari would let me return and work for pennies and a simple roof over my head. I could hope the Policiers would not look for me there. I might even run back to my parents.

I would have failed.

Aenea ground her teeth in anger. Drystan's face was curious underneath his makeup, his head tilted to one side, wondering what I would do next. Nina rearranged some scarves around her waist, but I knew she was looking at me from the corner of her eye. Juliet the Leopard Lady blinked at me. Tym stared at the table, though he had stopped chewing his porridge.

I swallowed the bile in my throat and forced out a laugh. It came out high and girlish. I grabbed the rat by the remains of its tail and threw it into the sand some feet away from Sal and Tila. They squealed and laughed and the rest of the circus roared with laughter with them. At me.

I brought the remains of my porridge to the cook.

"Cook, I'd like a new bowl, please. Hold the rat."

The laughter grew louder and the chef snorted. I felt injured at this – he had helped me with the animal feed.

"Coming right up, boy," he said, straight-faced. He swapped my dish and gave me an extra scoop. I sifted my spoon through the porridge for a long time before I added my sugar. I could barely eat any of it. Visions of the rat swam in my vision every time I tried to take a bite. Under the breakfast table, Aenea rested her hand on the tip on my knee and squeezed. I took her hand, warm and calloused. When I looked up, she was smiling at me sadly. I returned the smile.

It was just a prank. I would not let them win.

I thought that the pranks could not get any worse. I was just as naïve as I had been my first night on the streets after running away.

The morning practice was going well. In addition to stretching, I could now perform simple tumbles, balance on a low beam, and swing on a lowered trapeze over old straw tick mats.

After warming up, I dusted chalk into my hands, slapping them together and looking forward to tackling a particularly difficult double twirl. The twirl I could do. The landing I could not.

I leapt onto the trapeze and swung, once, twice, three times as I readied myself to twirl. One last big swing, kicking my legs to drive me forward and my hands began to itch, and then to burn.

I cried out and slipped from the trapeze. My legs tangled in the rope, flipping me upside down and I banged my head on the pallet, hard. I hung there like an undignified puppet before slipping free and thumping onto the mattress. I rolled to my knees and rubbed my hands frantically across the hard rock, gasping and shouting.

"Micah! What is it?" Aenea rushed to my side.

"My hands…" I managed to gasp.

"Oh, son of a whore!" Arik exclaimed. "Some pox-ridden bastard switched your chalk for itching powder. I'll fetch medicine." He raced from the tent.

Other people were practicing in the tent. Most of the

Pantomime

clowns were there. Drystan wandered over for a closer look. The Kymri tumblers stopped their routines. Plenty of others had been drawn in by my cries. Heads appeared in gaps in the canvas of the tent.

I was blinded by anger so strong it finally loosened my tongue.

"If I ever find out who did this, I'll rip their balls out and give them to Violet for an appetizer! You hear me?"

I heard laughter and turned my head to see some of the clowns hiding smiles behind their hands. My pain swept away in a fit of anger, I rushed them, ramming the blue clown in the chest with my head and jabbing at others with my elbows. I could not use my hands. Blows rained down on me, and someone kicked me in the kidney. I went down, Jive's impish face leering above me. I reached my hands up, smearing itching powder into his eyes. I had time enough to smile before one good kick sent my head spinning and the tent grew dim, warm, and fuzzy.

I woke to find myself in our cart and Arik applying a cooling salve to my hands. "How long have I been here?"

"Most of the day."

I emerged that evening, bruised and shamed. That night, Bil stepped in.

"You may think you're clever clowns," Bil said after the show and carnival.

"I am a clever clown!" the green clown, Rian, called out.

"Shut it." Bil glowered. "But if anyone pulls a stunt that costs me any equipment, men, or money, then you're out. I don't give a tinker's damn who you are. You're out with no pay and no reference." He slapped his teak cane on the ground for emphasis. He did not look at me as he spoke.

But while his words stopped the pranks, they only heightened the resentment. And that night, my pack went missing.

I searched the cart, and it was not there. My heart pattered in my chest. I tried to keep my breathing steady and stay calm as I rifled through my bedclothes. It was not anywhere.

In my pack there was the Kedi figurine, a strange possession for a teenage boy. More importantly, there was also a dress, and a rambling letter to Cyril I had not sent because it was not in code, signed with "your loving sister, Gene." I bashed my fist on my pallet, angry at myself for being so foolish. My mouth felt dry.

My bandaged hands had stopped burning. I walked along the beach to gather my thoughts, barefoot in the sand as the afternoon lengthened to evening. I climbed a dune, the long blades of beach grass tickling my ankles in the wind. The air smelled of brine and smoke. The wind was chill and I shivered beneath my thin, patched coat. The sun disappeared over the sea.

I turned and looked toward the city. The ridge of Penglass had almost disappeared in the gloom. But as the darkness increased, the Penglass grew brighter, glowing first a dark midnight-blue, and then brightening to a luminous sapphire. Penglass only glowed on the night of the full moon. The light transformed the city of Sicion from a dreary, soot-stained sandstone city to something magical.

I stared at the glowing Penglass for a long time before climbing back down to the beach, my thoughts tumbling around in my mind. It felt as though I had only just joined the circus, but I would soon be heading home. Jive had probably taken my pack as a prank, and he would not hesitate to rifle through my belongings. Empty shells crunched beneath my feet. The sea foam of the dark water lapped around my ankles.

I wondered why I was letting them treat me this way, and why I did not simply take this as a sign that I was meant to return home. There, I did not practice tumbling and climbing until my hands were blistered and raw. I did not wake up from a clean, feather-down bed with my muscles feeling like they had been torn and sewn inexpertly together by a drunken surgeon. My life had not been perfect and had its own challenges, but I had so many who cared for me.

I missed Cyril with a sharp pang each and every day. I had written letters but there was no way for him to respond. Perhaps I should leave and return. Perhaps my running away would have proven to my parents that I would not allow them to change my life and they would leave me be.

Leave me be to be a spinster, tolerated in society but always just outside of it, pitied, and always under my parent's roof. And if they died before me, I would be a burden on Cyril. As a Laurus, I would have no way to support myself through employment, unless I became a governess or turned to writing or teaching, neither of which I thought would be my true calling. At least in the circus I had the freedom to be myself, even if most of the others did not seem to like me overmuch. I kicked a stone into the water.

I heard the padding of running feet and turned. Aenea

caught up with me. She had just bathed, and her hair hung in dark ropes against her skin. She wore a thin silken robe from Linde, printed with faded cranes and stylized clouds. She must have been cold, but she did not shiver.

"Micah. I went to your cart to see how you were," she said. "Arik said you'd gone for a walk."

I did not say anything, but I held my bandaged hands behind my back.

"It was a cruel prank that they did," she said.

"The chalk or my pack?" I asked.

A line appeared between her brows. "Your pack?"

"It's gone."

The line disappeared. "Ah. They do that sometimes. Don't worry – I know where they'll have hidden it. Follow me." We walked up the strand plain.

I pressed my lips together and looked out over the ocean. "Did this happen to you, when you joined the circus?"

"Yes, but not quite as badly."

"Why do you think it's worse for me?"

"Because you're merchant class. I think most of the others believe you think yourself better than us. Lofty, some of 'em call you."

I had tried to roughen my speech and not mention much of my past, but I suppose I still had not learned how to be convincing. "Do you think that of me?" I asked, fearful of the answer.

"No, I don't. You seem more... scared of us, almost. Like you always think you're going to say the wrong thing. Like you're weighing up all the different responses before you speak."

I caught myself considering all the different ways I could

respond, and smiled wryly. "I suppose I do. I don't know what to do. I feel like I'm always doing the wrong thing."

"I have a feeling it'll start to ease off, soon. Bil doesn't like that you won't be able to practice properly for a week at least."

Dread filled me. How would I spend my days? "I guess I'll work on my splits, or see if I can master that handless cartwheel you showed me the other day."

She laughed, and nudged me in the shoulder. "That's the spirit, Micah." I was grateful to the dark night that hid my blush.

We came upon a crevice in the rock of the cliffs. Aenea bent down, her arm disappearing into the darkness. I had the irrational worry that something terrible would be in the darkness and would hurt her. She had a rip in the seam of her robe at the shoulder. Her arm emerged unscathed, holding my sandy, damp pack. She threw it to me and I clutched it to my chest. My pack felt the same weight that it normally did, and I could feel the Kedi figurine through the canvas.

"Do... Do you think they've looked at it?" I asked, fearful.

She shrugged a shoulder. "It's possible. But if it was the clowns, you might be in luck. Drystan's the head of the clowns, so usually he goes through them first and decides if there's anything worth sharing in the group." She laughed. "One of the other circus hopefuls a few years ago was very surly. No one liked him at all. Drystan found a pair of his soiled undergarments in his pack and put them up in place of the flag of the big top. He left that night, without his drawers, and no one missed him."

I had a terrible image of my dress flying from the big top. I felt as though I might be sick.

We stared at the ink black ocean for several minutes, not speaking, but standing close enough to feel the warmth of each other's skin. We returned together, slowly, the glowing Penglass shading the sand with soft blue light. It would have been a good opportunity to take her hand, but with my injury I could not. At least that was my excuse.

I did not see the dress on top of the tent when I returned.

I lay on my pallet with my pack as my pillow. I had gone through it and everything was there and apparently undisturbed, even my letter to Cyril.

I supposed I stayed in the circus because I already knew what my previous life had been like and what my future would likely be if I returned. I would wait, and work, and see.

All that was certain in both lives was that I would always be keeping secrets.

"So how are you finding our humble circus, lad?" Bil asked me during a warm summer afternoon.

I started. I had just finished feeding the otters and was watching them wrestle and chase each other about as I emptied the water of their tank. It was far easier than filling it, for I only had to connect a pipe that led the fetid water far enough away from the circus and to sea. I would have to fill it bucket by bucket. The otters were very tame, and Needle had taken a particular liking to me, sniffing my hand and letting me stroke his smooth, wet back. Needle had darted to his fellows at Bil's approach.

"I... I like it very well, Mr Ragona" I said.

"Very well, eh?" he said, raising his brows. He swung his cane idly around. Bil was never without his beautiful teak cane, polished to a high shine. The curve at the top was carved into the head of a ram; details of the horns and face etched in silver, the eyes emeralds. Bil smelled strongly of aftershave, with perhaps an undercurrent of alcohol despite the early hour. His shirt was sweat-stained and his face shiny.

"There are obstacles," I said, staring at the cane as it swayed like a pendulum, "but nothing I cannot overcome, sir."

"Very good, my boy, very good. I was worried you would wish to call it a day, after what happened."

My hands itched in a phantom memory and my cheeks burned that he would bring up the chalk incident again. I also had the strange feeling that he was not asking out of worry for me, but to make sure I was not leaving. "I understand that it may be difficult for the circus to appreciate newcomers, sir. Arik called it 'hazing'."

"So it is. It is an unfortunate practice, sure enough, but there's a reason for it, lad. Many join without the stomach for it. A life in the circus is not easy. If you keep with us, then it will end, and you'll be the stronger for it and the others will respect you all the more." He patted me on the shoulder a bit too hard.

"I hope so. Thank you, Mr Ragona."

He swung the cane and gazed at the otters jumping about in the emptying pool. I thought he would have left.

"So, where did you say you came from, boy?"

I licked my lips. "I'm from Sicion."

"Aye, I'm not deaf. But where in the city did you live?"

"Um." My mind went blank. "Jade Street." I could not even remember if Jade Street had residential tenements.

"And what'd your parents sell?"

The interrogation was making me uncomfortable. I thought of my mother. "Gas lights and glass globes. Fancy scented candles and the like."

"Ah, luminaries. Did they teach you the trade then, boy?"

Oh, Lord and Lady. Was this some sort of trap? "Of course, sir. I was to take over the business one day from my father. Before… the accident."

He coughed. "Sorry to bring up the indelicate subject, boy. What kind o' accident, if I may ask? Naught with the glass globes, eh?"

He was testing me. That was a trick question, but so few had close experiences with glass globes. "Not many ways for a tragedy to happen with a glass globe, sir, unless you cut yourself on the broken glass. The light fuel in it is not flammable." Once, Cyril and I had accidentally broken a glass globe in the dining room. We had painted ourselves with the glowing liquid, pretending we were the fearful Nunda tribe of Byssia, and the light had faded from our skin after a few hours. Mother had been quite annoyed. Glass globes were expensive. "My parents were lost at sea, returning from Kymri, where they bought their glass and fuel for their lights."

He coughed again. "Course, my boy. Sorry to bring it up, as I said. Still, will be good to have a luminary apprentice in the circus, mind, in case our lights break."

I gave a quick, fervent prayer to the Lord and Lady that all the gas lights and glass globes stayed in working order.

Did the ringmaster know that my story was nothing but a lie?

"Arik says that you're training well," Bil said, changing the subject.

"Does he? That is very kind of him," I said, my voice too high.

"He's not kind in this, just factual. Keep up the hard work, my boy. It is not going unnoticed." He gave me one last nod and ambled away, whistling.

I could not help feeling like I had just been given a test and did not know if I had passed or not. In any case, the water-filled buckets I hauled to the otter tank grew no lighter with his praise.

10
SPRING: VISITATIONS IN SICION

"Patient X has proven to be one of the most interesting specimens of sexual development disorders we have discovered. It is unfortunate that a more detailed examination cannot be performed over the course of 'her' menarche and 'his' onset of puberty, due to the requests of the parents. I have kept a dialogue open with them, in the hopes they may change their mind. Patient X has such resilience to illness and infection that I wonder what secrets his/her blood may hold."

UNPUBLISHED MEDICAL NOTES, DR BIRCHSWITCH

The train ride to Sicion was a somber affair.

Father had left for the city immediately following the afternoon tea at the Hawthornes', taking the comfortable carriage. We had ridden to the station in the other hansom cab, and Mother complained about the outdated upholstery, muttering that she must convince Father to "transform" it. Cyril bought me a sherbet at the Emerald Station to cheer me up. The sour sugar fizzed on my tongue.

We had a compartment to ourselves on the train. Mother put a mask over her eyes and promptly fell asleep. Her mouth opened and she snored. I wished I had a camera obscura to take a photograph to capture the moment forever. It would be perfect for blackmail.

"Are you all right?" Cyril asked.

He always knew when I was upset. "No."

In hushed tones, I told him what had happened between Damien and me. Cyril's jaw muscles worked as he fought to keep down his rage.

"When I next see him I'll–"

"Do nothing," I finished. "It will solve nothing. He will not say anything. I will keep my distance from him. It will all pass over and eventually he may forget it ever happened."

Cyril held my hand for the rest of the train ride. I rested my head against his shoulder. Several hours later, Sicion appeared on the horizon, a dark smear backed by the grey of the sea. The bright cobalt of the ridge of Penglass that ran through the city center was muted in the fog of the early evening, and the sandstone buildings blurred about the edges. It looked thoroughly depressing after the lush green of the countryside.

Home.

As soon the door closed behind me in the claustrophobic examination room, my chest tightened and I wanted to flee.

Doctor Ambrose towered above me and was at least twice as wide as my father, and my father was not the smallest of men. He wore round, wire-rimmed glasses and had a bushy grey-tinged moustache and beard. Between that and his long, straggly hair, Doctor Ambrose appeared to have no face.

"Humph," Doctor Ambrose grunted through his facial hair. "You must be the young person I've read so much about."

I said nothing, but noted the gender-neutral word.

"Sit on the table, please."

I did. I gripped the edges of the table hard and gritted my teeth.

Doctor Ambrose put his fingers to my neck and shone a light in my eyes, as if it were a routine doctor's visit.

"Who else have you been seen by?"

I rattled off a list of names. There were about seven by now. I hated them all.

"What do you do?" he said, opening a tablet. His practice was successful, for him to afford a functioning one.

"Pardon me?"

"Your hobbies. Your interests. What are they?" He looked at me from under his bushy eyebrows, stylus still held at the ready over the tablet.

It was odd that he was not asking me about my physiology. I sensed a trap and was not sure if he would tell my mother or not. You can never trust doctors. "I enjoy dancing and music," I began cautiously. That was true. "And I like, um, sewing." A lie.

He scribbled. "Do you cavort more with male or females?"

I fought down a snigger. Cavort? "My best friend is Anna Yew." I did get on well enough with Anna, but my best friend was Cyril.

He scribbled again.

"Last menstrual period?"

I tried not to choke. Surely that information was somewhere in my medical file. "Never."

Another scribble.

He asked questions that seemed to have no correlation to each other or to anything relating to my condition – how many hours a day did I study? Or exercise? How often did I visit the toilets? How much had I grown last year? What size slippers did I wear? He took measurements of my head, my neck, my shoulders, my chest, my waist, my hips, my legs, my wrists, and my ankles. I kept my limbs lax, trying to think of other things as he prodded and peered at me.

He asked all of these questions from behind his beard, and always there was the scribble over the tablet. When he had finished a page, he would tap the stylus three times against the side.

"Right," he said after what seemed like hours, setting the tablet aside. He went to the door and called for the female nurse. "Please remove your clothing," he said. The nurse entered and stood in the corner, looking menacing – the guardian of my virtue.

I sighed and turned around so that the nurse could undo the line of buttons down my back. The doctor was like all the others after all, and once I presented myself for inspection, he would *hmm* and *hah*, write his article, have his name published in a prestigious medical journal, and then send me on my way without offering further assistance.

The afternoon at the doctor's left me feeling invaded and despondent. I did not want to face Cyril's sympathetic looks; the only other person who had any idea of what I was going through. So I went to visit Anna Yew.

I took the carriage to her apartments and told the coachman to tell my mother where I was. Mother was always delighted when I went to see Anna. Anna's elder brother was hopelessly dim, but he was a potential suitor in my mother's eyes.

Marrying George would be like taking a cat or some other sort of pet as a husband. He would be happy enough to sit in the corner and blink at you, smiling slightly and staring off into the distance. He would not know the first thing about female anatomy. He would do what he was told and no more. At least he was sweet, if not much else.

"Genie! So lovely for you to come calling," Anna said, taking my hand and leading me up the stairs to her room. "How was the countryside? Mother and Father haven't taken me yet and my eyes are starving to see green!"

"My eyes are already withering from all of the grey and brown," I said, laughing. "But it was lovely, yes. I wish we could spend more time there. I think I would happily spend all of my time there."

"Oh, I don't think I could go that far," Anna said. "I would miss the bustle of the city after a time."

Anna's room was very girlish. A garden of printed primroses grew on her bedding, twined up the curtains and dotted the circular rug that covered most of the hardwood floor. More flowers were etched into the vanity and the ornate framed mirror hanging over the fireplace. Even the wallpaper was flowery, though at least the pattern was subtle, in pinks only a few shades apart.

Anna, in many ways, was my opposite. She cared for propriety, for proper girlish things. Yet she had a wicked wit hidden under the lacy layers of femininity, though of late, it had not appeared as often. We did not used to be so different. She had once climbed trees.

We sat on the bed. Anna tucked her legs up and rested her chin on her knees. "Were any boys in the countryside when you went?" she asked.

"Oswin Hawthorne and Damien Hornbeam," I said.

"Damien Hornbeam!" Anna said. "He's so handsome. Those shoulders!"

"He is," I agreed.

"Would you marry him?" she asked. She was always talking about marriage of late. I supposed it made sense, since this year or next she would become betrothed.

I remembered the look on his face when his hand had brushed between my legs. How he had refused to glance at me the rest of the day. "No, he's not the one for me."

"You say that about *everyone*," Anna said, exasperated and not noticing the strained tone of my voice.

"And you would happily marry most of the boys in Sicion and Imachara, so we balance out," I said, more sharply than I intended.

She made an affronted squeak and blushed.

"Apologies, Anna," I said, rubbing between my eyes. "Mother's trying to matchmake again. It's setting me on edge."

She sighed. "I don't see why you're so against it. It has to happen at some point. Don't you dream of a wedding?"

"No."

"But you don't want to become a spinster in your parents' household. That would be awful."

I shuddered. "Yes, that would be awful." I shrugged. "Might not be anything for it. We all know I'm plainer than pudding. Who do you want to marry the most?" *For this week, this day, this second,* I added in my head, unkindly.

She looked up toward the ceiling and thought about it. Even the ceiling molding around the light fixture featured roses. "How about… your brother?" she grinned mischievously. "Then we could be sisters!"

I made a face. "Eurgh!"

She stuck her tongue out at me.

"Is being my sister such a terrible option?"

I stuck my tongue out at her in turn.

"It would be perfect. Your family's star is on the rise, my mother says. You've gone up two titles in the past ten years! It's rare for families to move so quickly after being at the same level for so long." I lifted an eyebrow at her crass assessment of my family, but she did not notice.

"And Cyril is handsome, and kind, athletic, and intelligent," she said, counting each quality on a finger as if she was ticking off a checklist. She probably did have checklists for every eligible boy in Ellada, balancing their strengths and weaknesses on an imaginary scale in her head. Sometimes Anna horrified me.

She continued, "He's going to be a solicitor as well as sit in on the councils, and that is a respectable, important position. Combined with those big blue eyes and broad shoulders, he's one of the best prospects in Sicion. Certainly you must have realized that?"

I made a face. "He's my brother. I'd never think of him in those terms. Would you ever think of George that way?"

Now it was her turn to make a face. "That's different. George is a catch for nobody."

For a moment, I was so tempted to tell her that Mother thought him a prospect for me, but it was too embarrassing.

"Are you looking forward to the debutante ball next month? Have you gotten your dress for it yet?" I asked instead, steering her away from the unsettling topic of marriage to the safer area of clothing.

Her face lit up. If there was one thing she liked more than marriage, it was clothes. Or best yet, it was the clothes she would wear when she married the boy of her dreams. The whole idea of a wedding to me seemed exhausting more than anything else.

"Not yet, but mother and I are going to go look for a dress tomorrow. But I did get this the other week." Anna went to the wardrobe, opened it, and brought out a dark blue taffeta gown. It would go well with the pink undertones of her skin and bring out the red in her strawberry blonde hair. I told her so and her face split into a wide, genuine grin.

"Why don't you try it on?" she said, eagerly. Anna loved to dress up.

And so I did, taking care to keep my petticoats on as I changed, turning away from her so she did not see my tiny breasts. Anna was well-endowed in that department already.

The dress looked silly on me. It was too short, as I was a head taller than Anna, the waist was too high, the bodice far too loose. Unsurprising, I supposed. The color was good for me, though.

"Are you looking forward to the debutante ball?" Anna asked, noticing my somber face in the mirror.

"Truthfully? No. But you know I'm not normally one for ball gowns and plaiting flowers in my hair."

She giggled. "That's true. The only time I saw you willingly with flowers in your hair was when you'd crawled through a forsythia bush!"

I smiled at the memory.

"But I suppose I always thought you'd outgrow it." My smile faded at her words.

"Maybe I'm just taking longer than most. I'll make an effort with the ball. Perhaps it won't be so bad."

We spent the afternoon being young noblewomen, dressing up and applying cosmetics, eating cakes and tea and discussing plans for the upcoming autumn season. I made more of an effort this time than I usually did, trying to fit myself into the role of a girl to see if I could ever make it work, instead of convincing Anna to play board games or go for a carriage ride through the city. But the act was like the dresses – ill-fitting and not quite right.

11
SUMMER: BELLS

"Once, you couldn't stick a spade in the ground without overturning a bit of Vestige – a square key, an arrow that always finds its mark, a light that never goes out. But now, only remnants are found – when was the last time a truly extraordinary artefact was recovered? With each passing year, keys never find the lock they were meant to open, the arrow begins to miss, the light dims. One day, there will be no more Vestige, and Ellada and its former colonies will be the poorer for it."

VESTIGE, Professor Caed Cedar,
Royal Snakewood University

Drystan continued to perplex me.

He would walk up to me, say or do something strange but not unkind, and then maintain his distance. I had no idea what he wanted or what he was doing. Was he taunting me? Was it some clownish game, or a bet among his fellows? I tried to return his banter and witticisms, but more often than not I was left tongue-tied and exasperated. Running underneath our exchanges was the niggling fear that he had gone through my pack when the clowns had taken it.

Without his strange makeup, he was quite striking. Fair in complexion and fair to look upon, the girl in me felt a strange surge of excitement when I looked up and found him watching me, though it was also tinged with dread.

Eventually, I decided that he was waiting for me to approach him. One morning, I found him shuffling a pack of cards by the blackened remains of the campfire.

He would be unimpressed with a standard greeting. "Tell me a joke," I said without preamble.

He raised an eyebrow, and scooted over ever so slightly on the log to make room for me. I perched on the edge.

"Asking me to perform off-duty? It'll cost you."

"What will it cost me?"

He pressed a long, thin finger to his lips. "You'll have to answer one question about yourself, and you'll have to answer truly."

"All right," I said easily, though I had no qualms with lying to him if he asked too pointed a question.

"I'll tell you a joke I've been banned from telling during the show." He set down the cards. "Novices of the monks of the Order of the Sun Lord and Lady of the Moon must test that they are beyond temptation before they can be declared full monks.

"Ten novices aiming to serve the Sun Lord stand in a line in the courtyard and are commanded to strip their robes and tie bells around their manly bits."

I kept my expression blank. "Right."

"A beautiful woman comes into the courtyard and dances in front of each novice in turn. She is glorious, naked as the day she was born, with full breasts like half globes, eyes of emeralds, hair like sunshine on a winter's morning, and all of that poetic balderdash. She dances past the first novice, undulating like an undine or a sylph. The bell is silent. She dances past the next novice, and the next, and the next, until she has danced in front of the first nine monks. All of the bells are silent. Finally, she dances in front of the last monk, and his bell jingles merrily. So merrily, in fact, that the bell falls off his tackle. Embarrassed and ashamed, he reaches down to retrieve the bell, and suddenly the bells of all the other monks behind him begin to tinkle!" His blue eyes glinted.

I thought a moment, trying to puzzle it out. "So they like the sight of him bent over?"

Drystan stared at me in astonishment and then laughed uproariously, slapping his knees. "Oh, Micah, you *have* been sheltered!" He shook his head, chuckling. I still looked at him blankly.

"It's been a long time since I've had to explain a joke to someone, oh my." He wiped his eyes. "The novices weren't tempted by the woman, Micah, because they had no desire of her. They preferred the close company of men."

I blinked and my blush deepened. "Oh." Cyril had told me about how children were made when I had asked him several years ago, but he had never mentioned this. "Does that happen often? Men preferring men to women?" I thought of my attraction to Aenea. Did I like her as a boy, or as a girl?

"More often than you would think."

"Are there any here in the circus?"

That sent Drystan into paroxysms of laughter again.

"They're all around you. The circus collects the outsiders like a flame tempts moths. Sal and Tila, for all their flirting with men, are devoted to each other. You really didn't realize that Arik prefers the company of men? Or that I do?"

My mouth fell open, and I snapped it shut. "Um, no." Drystan was looking at me very intently. "Do you... or they ever prefer both men and women?" I asked.

"Me?" he said, not letting me get away with my slip. "Sometimes, for a bit of variety. More sample both dishes than would probably admit to it." He looked at me slyly. "Why the fascination?"

"No reason," I said, quickly. "What do the Lord and Lady think of it?" I did not know if I believed in the Lord or Lady, but I was curious to know what they would think.

"They're completely silent on the subject. In none of the sacred writings is there a hint that it even exists. Some say that means that they consider it so terrible that it cannot even be spoken of. Others feel it means that it is a non-issue, that the Lord and Lady do not care, as long as those who love each other come together to be complete and to worship them. In ancient Alder, there were no different pronouns for gender. I think that in itself speaks volumes."

I glanced at him. Drystan used rather varied vocabulary. He toned it down around the others, like Arik and Aenea, but not around me. He knew we had more in common.

"What's your question then? As payment?"

Drystan leaned on his hands, languid as a cat. He looked at me, calculating. I was almost certain he was going to ask me whether I preferred men or women.

"Who do you miss the most, from your previous life?" he asked instead.

"My brother," I said without hesitating, relieved that I did not have to lie.

He nodded as if I was confirming something. "I miss mine as well. And my sister, though she was just born when I left."

I was surprised by his openness. Drystan picked up the cards again and shuffled, clacking them together with such force that it sounded like he was rattling wooden slates. We sat together in silence, watching the fire and thinking of our brothers.

"May I ask you a question?" I asked.

"You may, though it'll cost you another." His smile was benign.

I decided it was worth it. "My pack went missing not long ago."

An eyebrow rose. "Did it?"

"I found it."

"And was anything missing?"

"No, but I wondered if… anyone would have looked through it."

Drystan turned toward me, his expression unreadable but still dreamy. "One might have pretended to look through it, to placate one's peers."

A tightness eased in my chest. He did not seem to be lying, though with him it was difficult to tell.

"I see," I said. "Your question?"

"Hmm," he said. "So many I could ask."

"So there are," I said.

"What is your biggest fear?" he asked.

I was quiet, thinking. There were so many things I was frightened of. "Not being accepted or loved for what – who – I am."

Drystan again noticed the slip but did not comment. "Does no one accept you?"

"That's two questions. My brother does."

"What, are you lonely, Micah?"

His question took me aback. "Yes, sometimes. Aren't most people?"

"Hmm."

Drystan became less obtuse around me after that, shedding his persona of the odd, mystic fool and showing the human beneath. But when I looked up at him through lowered lashes and saw him watching me, I still felt a little thrill.

The after-show bonfires were strange but wonderful.

There was euphoria after each and every show, the emotions pent up needing a place to go. No one went straight to bed after a performance. There was always laughter, and more food, and a drink or two to unwind.

Some nights were wilder than others, with the Kymri tumblers and some of the workers playing their penny whistles, guitars, and little hand drums. Workers and performers would cross their divide: Wicket dancing with Juliet the Leopard Lady, or Dirik dancing with Bethany, whom he fancied, despite the moustache – or because of it?

Though few people spoke to me, I still had fun, clapping along to the music and nursing a mug of beer, chatting with Aenea and Arik, and sometimes Drystan or Frit. I still felt a part of the circus, more or less.

Bil was in a fine mood one particular night. He had disappeared into town during the afternoon, well before the show was due to begin. He did that, occasionally – leaving and returning with a mysterious package under one arm, stinking of booze.

"I got somethin' new for the circus today, me lovelies," he said. "Just to make us that much better." He swayed on his feet, and the bonfire behind him cast him in shadow. He fumbled in his pocket and took out a small Vestige figurine of a golden-haired monkey. It was a lovely little thing – the fur seemed to ruffle in the wind, though it was made of metal. Its little face looked like an echo of a human's, its dark eyes large.

"Now," he said. "I can only show you for a minute. Thing's almost outta power." I could barely understand his slurred words. He pressed a small button on the monkey's back.

The monkey shook its head and stood upon its bandy legs. It turned and looked up at Bil's face. I could see the little lever in its back. With jerky movements, the little monkey climbed up Bil's arm and perched on his shoulder, cocking its head at us. Bil chuckled and reached up and plucked the little monkey from his shoulder, holding it in his open palm. Bil pushed the lever and the monkey returned to its original pose.

"That is amazing," I breathed to Frit, who was sitting to my right.

"It is," she said, but her voice was tight.

"What's wrong?" I asked.

"Nothing," she said, pulling her shawl tighter about her, her shoulders hunched. "Never you mind, Micah."

I looked from her, to Bil, and back again. She looked as though she was mentally doing sums as she stared at the little golden monkey. "Vestige things are rather expensive, aren't they?" I asked.

She nodded her head once, her eyes on Bil as he laughed uproariously.

I understood.

She topped up my glass of ale and toasted me with her own. She drank, and so did I, though I did not like the taste.

12.

SPRING: PENGLASS

"There's poetry in glass and stone,
  in the old and the new.
  The sandstone hewn by human hands,
  stained with soot and time.
  Sounds drift into the street,
  laughter cruel and kind.
  The pristine glass looks like a shadow,
  a blue bubble about to burst.
  A memory of music not quite heard,
  The Alder dream, now cursed.
  Side by side they stand,
  Each with a treasure nursed.
  Never uttering a word.
  but which will crumble first?"

PENGLASS OF SICION, Anonymous

Cyril invited some of his friends to our house one afternoon.

I abandoned my woeful attempt at embroidery on my bed and casually walked past the door to Father's study, straining my neck to make sure that Damien was not there. He was not. I should have realized – Cyril was possibly even angrier with him than I was.

The sun streamed in from the diamond lead-paned windows and cast patterns on the thick rugs. Cyril, Oswin, and a genial boy named Rojer lounged on the leather sofas of the study, surrounded by my father's law books. Oswin saw me pass and gestured me in.

"Genie!" he said, grinning.

"Don't call me Genie," I said automatically, crossing into the room that was as masculine as it was possible for a room to be. The air smelled of musty books, the acrid tang of old smoke and the orange oil used to treat the furniture. Everything was maroon, hunter green, and brown.

I collapsed into a leather armchair without ceremony, sprawling across it as they did. My cream and pale blue lace contrasted with their dark city suits. And though I had often joined in when Cyril had his friends over, it felt different this time, much like when we had smoked cigars in the woods, as though they were all growing closer and I was only growing further apart. An invisible barrier of age and propriety had come between us.

"How are you boys?" I asked.

"Well and good, Iffygenial," Rojer said. He never, ever pronounced my name properly.

"For the hundredth thousandth time – I'm Gene," I said, as I always did. It was a game, though I grew tired of it. I never felt as though they took me seriously, if they could not even pronounce my name properly.

"What were you speaking about?" I asked.

"Dull political stuff," Cyril said wearily. "We're supposed to be studying for our exam tomorrow. We were doing all right until you interrupted us." He wrinkled his nose at me to show he was not truly upset.

"What sort of political stuff? Maybe I can help."

"What do you know of politics, Genie?" Oswin asked.

"Lord's teeth – it's Gene. More than you, I'm sure. I'd be very surprised if you've ever stayed awake through an entire lecture about Elladan history or politics."

"I'm sure I must have stayed awake through one. Possibly." Oswin thought. "Maybe not."

"I'm shocked."

"Come now, we should really study at least a little more," Cyril said, dragging the open book beside him on the sofa into his lap. "I'll ask you each a few more questions and then we can take a proper break."

"All right," Oswin sighed. Rojer settled into his chair, blinking as though he were already struggling to stay awake.

Cyril squinted at the book. "When will the Princess Royal come of age and become queen?"

"That's easy," Rojer said. "You should try a little harder to stump us. She will come of age when she is sixteen and have the full responsibilities of the monarchy," he intoned, as if from memory.

"How are decisions made now?" Cyril asked.

"Through the steward," Rojer said, bored.

"Only the steward?" Cyril pressed.

"Mainly, I think."

"Wrong!" Cyril said, gleeful. "Decisions are put to vote in the council, but the steward has the final say with the power to veto decisions."

"You're asking boring questions," I said. "Give me the book."

Cyril clutched it protectively. "I'm asking the questions."

"What? Afraid you'll be wrong if you're put to the test?"

"Give the book to Gene, Cyril. Let's see what you're made of."

I beamed at Oswin. He had called me Gene. Cyril gave me the book.

"So," I said. "What date, exactly, did the Colonies last secede from the empire?"

"The year?" Cyril asked.

"Exact date, I said. Are you deaf?"

"Easy," Rojer said. "The first day of autumn, 10822. Everyone knows that one."

"Not everyone. Oswin didn't. What were the reasons that Ellada became the head of the Archipelago Empire in 10353?"

"Lord and Lady, *boring*," Oswin said. "We had most of the Vestige weapons. The Colonies didn't have as many and the ones they had were often damaged by damp."

The history was more complicated than Oswin made it seem. Ellada constantly needed more water from the mountains. We would soon need more food than the farm island of Girit could provide. We needed nearly all of our fuel from Kymri, which kept creeping its prices higher. We needed more than the colonies wanted to give. Only the inflated prices we were willing to pay kept them selling.

For a long time, there had been too many people for the small amounts of land. Supposedly there had once been much more land, vast stretches where one could travel for months and still not reach the other end. Now as far as we knew there were a handful of islands still above the water's edge, and all else had been sunk, still below the waves. Explorers who set out to sail the world's circumference never returned. I would like to think that they found large, wonderful places to live, but they probably perished.

I had read a few books on economy, much to Mother's disapproval and Father's quiet sanction. Ellada had managed to gather so much power, not due to natural resources, but because there was a higher concentration of Vestige weapons.

Over the past centuries, we had fought countless wars that always resulted in the same cycle – we would conquer and use our opponents' lands for their resources, they would grow increasingly hostile to us stripping their lands free of crop and mineral, they would rebel and secede, we would conquer them again.

If I were actually an outside observer, I would find this period in history fascinating. For the past two centuries, Ellada had tried peaceful negotiations with Kymri, Linde, Northern and Southern Temne, and Byssia, spending the money to trade for goods rather than pouring the coin into the war effort. People had begun to immigrate and emigrate to and from different lands, mingling with the natives of each.

But relations as of late had become strained. If something did not change so that Ellada had what it needed, war would break out again, and it would be messy. Cyril and I recently had several impassioned discussions, naively proposing different solutions, convinced that we, young children, could solve the problems of the land that the men in wigs in the council could not.

"Next question, Gene," Cyril said, shocking me from my musings.

"Ah, right. What is the current political system of Temne?"

"That's a trick question," Cyril said. "Northern or Southern Temne?"

"Both."

"Northern Temne is a democracy and Southern Temne... um," Cyril faltered.

"Southern Temne is also a democracy, you nitwit, though their leader has more power than Northern Temne," Oswin cut in. "Remember what Professor Holly said? 'The south has power and pomp.'"

"Well done," I said, setting the book aside. "You're all set to pass. Now what?"

"I think we deserve cake," Cyril declared.

"I agree," I said. "I'll go ask the cook."

I scurried to the kitchen and asked Vach, the cook, for tea and any cake or biscuits that were lying around. He brought out most of a sponge cake that had been prepared for Mother's visitors the previous day, and filled the silver tea set.

"Lia will bring it up," Vach said. "Run along."

"Thank you, Vach," I said.

I returned to the study. Cyril, Oswin, and Rojer were discussing sports. Not terribly interesting, but I joined in where I could. I relaxed into my chair, the heavy book of history by my side. We laughed, and we joked, and we ate cakes and sipped our drinks. It was like a very informal afternoon tea.

Mother walked past the door and paused in the open doorway. Our laughter and chatter drifted to silence. She looked at my stocking-clad feet dangling over the arm of the leather chaise, the lace of the skirt hiked up enough to show my legs midway up the calf. She took in the empty tea cups and the crumbs on the table. I pushed my skirt down and scooted off of the chaise.

"What are you boys up to this afternoon?" Mother asked, smiling sweetly.

"Just studying, Mother," Cyril said. "Gene was testing us."

"Oh? And how did you fare?"

"They did very well," I said.

"That's wonderful. Oh, Iphigenia," she said, as if she had just remembered something. "How was that embroidery you were working on coming along? You did promise to show it to me this evening, did you not?"

"It's nearly done." I muttered, a faint blush creeping into my cheeks. Oswin was undoubtedly stifling a snigger behind me.

"Why don't you run along and finish, darling?"

My teeth squeaked together, I ground them so hard. "Of course, Mother," I said. "Good day, Oswin, Rojer," I gave them a little curtsey and left.

My embroidery lay on the bed where I had left it. I had tried stitching a dandelion, which had turned out rather lopsided. I spent the afternoon cutting each stitch out of the fabric, one by one.

"Let's go climbing," Cyril said to me that night.

"What? Now?"

"Yes. I need to get out and breathe, and you always say I should ask you to come along. This is me, asking."

"All right," I said, and we changed into the threadbare clothes we wore in the Emerald Bowl, where the family estates were. I tucked my long hair up into a cap.

We snuck past the servants and down the stairs. One of our neighbors, Lady Elm, was in the hallway as we passed, but did not really *see* us. We were just two scruffy kitchen hands, or not-too-sooty chimney sweeps. Beneath notice.

We slipped out of the servants' entrance. The night was warmer than it had been, but still a bit chilly. I gestured for Cyril to follow me as I navigated my way through the familiar streets.

I wanted to take Cyril to my favorite place to climb; a tenement in a nice part of the Gilt Quarter. The building had suffered structural damage and repairs had so far taken most of a year with no near end in sight. The tenement was right next to a large Penglass dome. Residences that faced the Penglass were especially dear, as, though the view of the Emerald Park was obscured, on a sunny day the rooms were bathed in swirling blue light.

I tried to climb as often as I could get away or as often as I felt the need to escape. Climbing made me feel in control. I could decide how high to climb and I was never afraid to look down. At the top of a building or a church spire, my day-to-day troubles felt insignificant. Below me stretched buildings and Penglass as far as the eye could see, and any people walking below were as small as ants. They never looked upward.

I climbed the scaffolding. The sun was setting, tingeing everything the pink and purple of growing dusk. The blue light of the Penglass shone against the sandy stone. I stopped and looked down. Cyril had hesitated at the bottom, but he grasped the metal and followed me, his face determined. I smiled and stopped at the fifth story.

The top of the Penglass dome was close enough that I could step across to it, and I did, very carefully. Penglass was notoriously slippery.

"What are you doing, Gene? That's so dangerous," Cyril called quietly, mindful of the curtained windows behind him. We were careful to not climb directly in front of any windows. A human-shaped shadow would frighten anyone inside terribly, and many inside carried firearms against intruders.

"Don't be a baby. Just be careful," I said. Cyril took a deep breath and stepped onto the Penglass dome, his fingers pressed white against the cerulean glass. He carefully navigated his way and sat beside me, just in time to see the sun disappear over the horizon. This was arguably the best view of the city. The Penglass dome crested a hill, and below us was the green island of the Emerald Park, the sooty buildings and the church spires falling away toward the open sea and the sunset. Clouds darkened to grey, like charcoal smudges on a watercolor painting.

The purple of dusk faded to the bright yet dark blue of early night. I sighed, content in the moment.

"Um, Gene?" Cyril asked.

"What is it?" I said, almost dreamily, still staring at the horizon and the half-moon.

"Look at your hands." His voice was frightened.

I looked down and was so startled I nearly fell off of the Penglass dome. Where my hands rested against the dome, the glass *glowed*.

I snatched my hands away from the glass. The outline

of my hands remained, in a white light tinged with blue, purple, and green. It looked incandescent, almost like when the sunlight hit a crystal or a dragonfly's wing. Cyril's hands did not change the glass at all.

"What is this?" I asked.

Cyril's wide eyes were my only response.

"Maybe we should go. What if it's going to explode?"

Cyril shook his head. "I don't think so." He trailed his fingers against the glass. Nothing. No light at all.

My handprints began to fade, the light dimming to dark blue.

"Try it again," Cyril urged.

I stretched my hand toward the glass, my fingertip hovering above the glass before I set it down. Light radiated from the single point. I glanced at the curtained windows of the tenements, afraid that someone would see.

"It's so beautiful," Cyril said.

"It is, but it's also damned terrifying," I said, taking my fingertip away. I had spent more time atop Penglass domes than most. I had watched countless sunsets and sunrises from them. Maybe that was why this one glowed at my touch. I spent more time on this Penglass dome than any others. Had it grown... used to me?

I told Cyril my theory.

"That must be it," he said, and I was relieved. I did not want to think of another reason why the Penglass should react to me and not Cyril. And why now? I had spent years touching Penglass, but this had never happened before.

I touched the dome again, mesmerized. I trailed my fingertip along the glass, and a trail of light followed. Cyril and I both laughed in pure delight and amazement. I swirled my fingertips, creating beautiful glowing spirals, like the aurora borealis.

"Can I try?" Cyril asked, reaching for my hand.

He held my index finger and wrote "MAGIC," with stars surrounding it. He let my hand fall.

"It is magic, isn't it?" my brother asked.

I took my hands away from the glass again, watching the light slowly fade. "I don't know. It might be. Alder magic."

"Maybe you could open the domes," Cyril said, excited. "Imagine if you did. You'd be famous and you'd go down in the history books forever. The girl who solved the mystery of Penglass."

My eyes widened with the daydream. I tried knocking on the Penglass, half-expecting a little door to open to let us inside. But I heard nothing but the dull tap of a fist on glass. "What do you think would be inside?"

"I always imagined they were the home of the Alders," Cyril said. "So maybe they would be filled with tons of Vestige. We'd be rich beyond imagining!"

I licked my lips. "There could be dangerous things in there as well. Maybe the domes are prisons, filled with monsters."

His smile wavered. "Maybe it's filled with Chimaera."

I gulped, wondering what was inside what we were sitting on. I lay down and pressed my ear to the glass, but I heard no scrabbling of claws from within. The imprint of half my face and my ear remained when I sat up.

In a fit of silliness I wrote "GENE'S PENGLASS. NO TRESPASSING." The light of the day was well and truly gone, and my name glowed like a beacon. I swiped my open palm over the words in a swathe of light.

"I've never seen anything like this," Cyril said.

"We shouldn't tell anyone," I said, watching the last of the light fade from the Penglass.

"Why not?"

"Because it means more tests. I've had enough tests, don't you think?"

He swallowed. "Of course." He peered at me. "You think this might have something to do with how you were born, don't you?"

"No," I said, my voice sharp as a knife. "It's only because I've touched this dome so much. I bet if I touched another nothing would happen. It has nothing to do with me."

"We should head back," Cyril said, wisely changing the subject. "Before someone sees us." He glanced over his shoulder at the curtained windows. He stood. "I also have that damned exam tomorrow, but I've no idea how I'll sleep tonight after this."

"You and me both–" I started.

Cyril teetered on the smooth Penglass. He half-smiled as he reached out for me to steady himself. But the act of reaching unbalanced him and his feet slipped out from under him. My hand snatched out, but I only caught the cuff of his coat. My brother slipped from my fingers.

And he fell.

Without thinking, I followed him, sliding down the blue Penglass, cold and smooth beneath my hands. I controlled the slide, whereas Cyril scrabbled as he fell, his clutching hands not slowing his tumble at all. I could only watch in horror as he headed directly toward a tree in the Emerald Park. At the last moment, he managed to swerve, but he still hit an outstretched branch with a sickening crack before landing in a bush.

I landed on the grass in a crouch and rushed toward him. *Please don't be hurt*, I prayed. *Please, please, please.*

"Cyril?" I asked, barely able to breathe.

He groaned.

I went to his side, afraid to touch him. "Cyril, are you all right?"

He breathed hard. "My shoulder. And – my arm," he managed. Even within his coat I could tell the arm was bending in a way it should not.

"Can you walk? We're not far from home? Should I call the Constabulary? Oh, Cyril, I'm so sorry."

I heard muffled shouting from up above. Several people in the scaffolded tenement and the building across from it had opened their windows. They were gaping at the two long swathes of light left by my hands as I slid down the Penglass. Oh, Styx.

"Cyril, I don't think the Constabulary is an option anymore," I said. "We have to get out of here."

My brother sat upright and gasped with pain. I put his good arm around my shoulders and hauled him upright, thankful that I was stronger than I looked. We hobbled home, Cyril grunting in pain. At one point, he staggered, and I fell against another Penglass dome.

I knew before I pulled my hand away that it would be glowing beneath my touch.

13
SUMMER:
THE GIRL IN THE NEWSPAPER

"The prognosis for Miss Laurus is difficult, but my plan of action is the correct one. She has not yet reached menarche, and may not be able to do so. Yet according to her parents, her behavior and appearance has been growing steadily more male. I have received confirmation of this treatment from several other esteemed doctors, including a doctor who has already treated her, Dr Birchswitch, and even a foreign correspondence with the Royal Physician himself."

UNPUBLISHED MEDICAL NOTES, DR LEONARD AMBROSE

"I feel like I'm going to be sick," I said, bowed over my breakfast.

"How much did you drink last night, Micah?" Arik asked, poking me in the shoulder.

"I don't remember," I said, covering my eyes with my hands. I barely recalled the bonfire.

"I've had more than my fair share of sore heads the next morning. You should eat something, drink plenty of water, and go into town and have a beer or two," Arik said. "Works every time."

My stomach clenched at the thought. "Maybe some water," I said. I drank a glass of water, managed one spoonful of porridge, and staggered to my cart to lie in darkness until practice began.

I dozed, dreaming of nothing, for once. I woke at noon, groaning and blinking. I promised myself I would never drink another drop of alcohol as long as I lived.

I struggled into my clothes and stumbled to the cook's tent. I was starved and ate the cold cut sandwiches with glee, not caring that the bread was stale and the ham dry. The food turned to sawdust in my mouth, mid-chew, as I saw the open newspaper on the table. I swallowed with effort and moved my plate on the front page hurriedly, hoping that Arik and Aenea had not seen my face staring out from the ink.

Arik discussed his plans for our training after lunch. I could not hear him, my heart thudded so loudly in my skull.

"Are you all right?" Aenea asked, laying her hand on my shoulder.

"I think… I think I'm going to be sick," I muttered, and I thought I would be.

Arik and Aenea looked alarmed. My face must have been ashen. I clutched the newspaper and my plate and staggered away, nearly throwing the plate to the cook as I made my way back to my cart to read the news article that might end my new life in the circus.

I held the newspaper with trembling hands.

SCANDAL! YOUNG NOBLEWOMAN OFFICIALLY DECLARED MISSING

Words by correspondent Charles Hodsworth

Authorities are questioning the Laurus family of Sicion after it has been revealed that their daughter, Miss Iphigenia Laurus, had gone missing several weeks ago and the parents had not reported her disappearance to the Policiers. Friends and acquaintances, when inquiring after Iphigenia, were told that she had been sent to Primrose, a remote finishing school in the Emerald Bowl for a semester. But when a concerned family friend sent a missive to the school and discovered that Iphigenia was not an enrolled pupil, the friend alerted authorities. The Constabulary had already begun a covert search for the missing Laurus daughter.

The Laurus family declined to state why they had not felt the need to announce the disappearance of their only daughter, though they did state they had also hired a Shadow to discover her whereabouts directly after her disappearance. They claimed to have several leads, which they have now shared with the Policiers. The Laurus family insisted they love and miss their daughter very much and had reasons for keeping her disappearance out of the public eye.

Iphigenia Laurus is sixteen years of age, tall and slim with auburn hair and hazel eyes. She vanished from her home in Sicion on the night of 17th of Eral. Foul play may have transpired. Information leading to the discovery of Miss Iphigenia Laurus will result in a substantial reward.

Please contact your local Policier station if you know anything to help authorities find young Iphigenia.

"Oh no," I breathed, my head suddenly all too clear. Bile rose to my mouth. Crumpling the newspaper in my hands, I struggled to keep hold of my lunch, my thoughts scurrying about my head.

I already knew that the Constabulary was looking for me, but my eyes kept returning to the phrase "hired a Shadow." A Shadow worked outside the law. They did not need probable cause. A Shadow could whisk me away from the circus and deposit me back home.

I looked again at my face, trying to be rational. The photo had been taken a year ago. My face was fuller, surlier. My long hair had been curled about my face, with flowers and ribbons plaited into it. I wore a high-necked lace gown and rouge and cosmetics Mother had forced me to wear. I looked uncomfortable in my skin. In the tarnished mirror of the cart, a very different face gazed at me now. My face was thinner, and my body taller and more muscular. Looking at the photo, someone would see my hair and the lace, and not necessarily *me*.

But if someone looked close enough, they would be able to tell. And plenty of people would hazard a guess for the chance of gold or silver. Everyone knew I could read and that I came from money. The people I worked with were uneducated, not stupid. Eventually, someone might remember that I joined the circus at the end of Eral, that I never visited the bathing cart.

Someone might notice a little too much.

• • • •

That night, I had a bad belly and did not go to the after-show bonfire. I lay on my pallet, cursing the cramps that radiated through my lower stomach. A bad meal and I had missed an entire day's practice and had to find some-one else to cover for my animal-caring duties. Even more humiliating had been begging others, bowed over in pain, to cover for me. I asked half of the circus before I found Drystan and he offered to help.

"Are you all right, Micah?" he asked me.

"Fine," I managed. "Ate something bad, I think."

His brow furrowed. "That's odd. I feel all right, and we ate the same lunch."

"Maybe Jive smuggled something in my food that he shouldn't have. I wouldn't put it past him."

Drystan narrowed his eyes at me. "Perhaps. I'm sure it's nothing serious."

From the way he said it, I wondered if he knew more than me. But he only smiled at my puzzled glance.

"I'll take care of the animals, Micah, don't worry about it. Go rest."

The cook gave me a piece of ginger root to chew, telling me it would ease a sour stomach. It did not help.

Throughout the afternoon I had slept, fitfully, dreaming of distorted circus folk chasing me through the freakshow tent, ripping my clothes from me, putting me into a cage and feeding me Saitha's peanuts before my parents finally came to take me away to Doctor Ambrose. I woke up drenched in a cold sweat.

The pain became too much to bear and I dragged myself from the pallet. Mid-crouch, I paused, aghast. There was a small bloodstain on the pallet. I looked down and saw the stain echoed on the crotch of my trousers.

"No," I whispered. I put a shaky hand between my legs. My fingers came away blushed with blood. My breath was shallow. This was not supposed to happen.

Anna Yew had told me about moon blood. My mother never spoke to me of things like that. Anna loved to complain about how pained she was by the "woman's trial," taking to bed the first day of her cycle with a damp cloth against her forehead and a bladder of hot water against her stomach, a box of chocolates at the ready on her bedside table.

She had looked sympathetic when I said that mine had not started, putting her hand on my arm and saying that some girls started later than others. Anna had started very young.

I had grown to doubt such a thing would happen to me. I had thought that I was not woman enough. As time passed, I only seemed to grow more male. My voice had lowered, occasionally cracking when I spoke. A small layer of down sprouted on my cheeks.

I stood there, blood on my hands, more scared than I had ever been. I did not know what to do next, and I had no one to turn to. I fought back a sob. Did it mean I would be able to bear a child someday, if I so desired? The thought was terrifying.

Snatching my discarded trousers and the thin sheet I put over my pallet, I stuffed them into a bag. Thank the Lord and Lady the blood had not soaked through to the straw ticking. I wiped my hands on an old rag and stuffed it between my legs and pulled on my only other pair of trousers. Holding the sack close to me, I snuck out of the cart and down to the water's edge.

I walked far enough down the beach that no one from the circus would be likely to see me. I shivered as I scrubbed my trousers and the sheet with sand. The cold water removed all traces of blood.

I went to the laundry cart to wash the salt from the cloth. Mara entered with an armful of washing just after I had thrown my sheet and clothes into the tub. She did not look at me and hummed under her breath as she worked.

I rubbed lye into the trousers and scrubbed them as hard as I could against the washing board.

"You're going to wear holes in them like that."

I looked down. My knuckles were bright red from the lye and the cold.

"Sorry," I said, unsure what else to say.

She gave an amused sound, something between a cough and a snort, and fished out a blue and black costume and worked it against the board.

I hung the washing on the door of my cart and more cramps ripped through my abdomen. I crouched down and gasped with the pain, wondering how women could bear it.

Crossing my arms over my stomach, I staggered to Bil's carts hoping he was still at the bonfire. Bil aligned two carts with a corridor of canvas to make three rooms: a "reception room" with two worn wooden seats in the middle, an office, and his sleeping quarters. I stood in the reception area at the door to his office, my hand resting on the doorknob. I was not sure if Bil would be there, but I thought the door would be locked.

The doorknob turned, to my surprise. Not the best security. A cramp clutched my belly and I opened the door. The cart was dark and smoky. Opulent rugs covered the wooden floor in front of me, sand ground into the swirling designs. I took one step to find Frit in front of the open safe, a hand full of gold coins, and the other holding the Vestige golden monkey. She had a little open chest by her feet filled with more coins. I froze.

She started in surprise, throwing the coins back into the safe – which was emptier than I would have expected – and knocking closed the lid of the chest. "What do you want?" she asked. She still clutched the golden monkey.

"I, um, need something from the medicine cabinet," I said.

She swallowed and gestured toward the cabinet. "Help yourself."

I walked to the small chest and picked up bottles, squinting to read their labels and until I found the one for pain. I could feel Frit's eyes on me and gooseflesh rose on my arms. I choked a spoonful of the medicine, making a face at the horrible taste.

I turned to leave, but something stopped me. Curiosity, perhaps. Frit looked so guilty, but her gaze was hungry. The Vestige monkey sat like a little human on her lap, its face turned towards mine. I felt inexplicably drawn to it.

"Can… I see the figurine?" I asked, gesturing to the golden monkey, as if finding her with her hand in the safe had never happened.

She passed it to me. "Don't turn it on, please." she said. "The power's nearly out." Once the power was out, it would likely never move again. Extra power packs were rare and dear.

It felt light in my hands. The detail was exquisite, from each carved strand of fur to the little pores on its nose. I passed it to her. Frit gave me a wavering smile as she tucked it into the safe. Aside from the coins, I noticed the smoke machine and a few other Vestige circus props. She took out a flat disc of metal that glowed like a rainbow in the gaslight.

"Do you know what this is?" she asked.

I shook my head. She held it out to me.

"It's the Phantom Damselfly."

I jerked my hand away. "The ghost?"

She made a sound that was almost a laugh. "It's no ghost, except a memory of the past. Probably just an illusion or a parlor trick for the Alders. I convinced Bil to stop the haunted tent. It wasn't making enough to justify the expense, and eventually someone would have realized what it was and stolen it." She turned the disc around in her hands. It had a small button in the middle.

"It never speaks, does it?" I asked.

She shook her head, setting the disc back into the safe. "No, of course not. It's just a projection. Why?"

"No reason." We lapsed into silence. Frit rubbed her fingers together. The awkwardness grew. "Thank you for the pain medicine."

"What did you need it for?"

"My head aches terribly."

"What you took doesn't help too well with that, I'm afraid. It's better for body pains." She fastened the door of the safe and stood. "I'll get you some tablets." She went to the medicine cabinet and shook out a few pills from a bottle, which she set down on top of a newspaper. I swallowed. It was yesterday's newspaper. Frit's gaze fell onto the photograph of my former self. She stared at it for a long moment, and then met my gaze. Her eyes flicked to the newspaper and to my face. She passed me the tablets. I clutched them in a sweaty palm.

She knew.

When she spoke, she kept her voice carefully neutral. "You didn't see me here tonight. You'll speak of this to no one."

"I won't," I promised, my hand on the doorknob again. "It's nothing to do with me." But it was to do with me. My wages were in that little chest. And whatever Frit wanted those coins for, I knew it was not for the circus.

"You can't judge me," she said. I twisted toward her. "I'm not."

"You are. But you can't judge me. You don't know."

"What don't I know?" I asked.

Frit pulled back the shoulder of her dress. A mottled bruise was there, just beginning to yellow at the edges. In the dim light of the tent, she slumped forward, as if the act of sitting up was too much. She looked both older and younger than she was.

"He seems to always treat you like a queen," I said, remembering Bil doting on Frit, bringing her flowers, dancing with her at the after-hours parties.

"Some of the time, he does."

And the rest of the time, he does not. The words floated through the air between us.

"You can't judge me," she said again, a waver in her voice.

"Believe me, I do not."

She smiled at me, and it was the first genuine smile I had ever seen from her. "We're all entitled to our secrets. Aren't we... Micah?" It was not a threat. Not quite.

"We are," I said. The door clicked shut behind me.

14
SUMMER: STRAW HOUSE

"Moonstone gin is only one small step from Moonshine."
WELL-KNOWN ELLADAN SAYING

One night, our circus sold out. Every seat was filled, and some sat in the aisles or on the hard rock at the edges of the ring.

This was a rare occasion for our circus; there was no room for that many seats to begin with. Most of the poor could not afford tickets. Many of the rich found it too low-brow an entertainment to trouble themselves with. The middle class were too tired after their ten hours of work that day.

But today, it was full. The local schools had just released their pupils for four weeks of freedom, and many children had been taken by their parents to celebrate, or they had snuck out to go on their own.

More people were in Imachara as well for the week of the international market. It brought larger numbers to the city center, the beach, and therefore the circus. For these few weeks, everyone ate food fresh off the boat from Byssia and the other colonies, rather than nearby Girit.

In keeping with the spirit, many men wore imported silk cravats and women dressed in jewel-toned robes and wore headdresses of bright plumage. Balls were held in Imachara and Sicion with international themes. I went to one last year at my mother's insistence and wore a violet dress and a mask made of gold, purple, and blue feathers and flowers in my hair. When the market left, things returned to normal, save for a few lingering feathers.

Usually when I watched the shows in the evening, I would steal an unused seat. Often, I could be in the best area of the audience because people could not afford the tickets. The merchants who had paid premium price were sometimes a bit miffed at this, though I was always quiet and wore my unpatched clothing. But that night I had to hide behind the stage and peek out. It meant I saw the show from a different perspective. I saw the performers' faces right before they entered the stage. They would pat their hair self-consciously, rubbing their hands and pressing their lips together to steady their nerves despite the fact that they did this most every night. From this angle, I could not see the faces they put on for the audience.

And so, for this show, I watched the audience. Their faces were small from this distance. Children sat on the rocks at the front, nudging each other and pointing, mouths agape. I marveled that it had been only a few weeks ago that I had been among them, staring so starry-eyed up at the magic of the circus. I felt so much older already.

The rest of the crowd was little changed from other nights. Old men and women who had been married for decades. Lovers with wandering hands who sat in the back rows. Gaggles of young men and women. Lonely people who came because they had nothing better to do and a spare coin in their pocket. And all of them looked skyward during the trapeze act. It was impossible not to be impressed by Arik and Aenea.

The applause at the end of the show was extraordinarily loud in the crowded big top. The performers came out and bowed, a funny sight when I was behind them as opposed to in front of them. I remembered Drystan's joke and laughed.

Most of the performers waited in the tent or returned to their carts as the fun fair outside continued, though some enjoyed going to the carnival. Afterwards, the workers and I would snake through the stalls to pick up the detritus left behind. The carnival was lasting longer than usual because there were so many more clientele willing to part with hard-won coins. I snuck out of the tent and scrounged a meal from the food cart.

I found Drystan lounging against my cart door, already out of his costume and his face freshly-scrubbed. He would not be recognizable in the carnival with his naked face and shabby coat.

"Good evening, Micah."

"Hullo, Drystan. What are you doing here?" I asked.

"Same as you. Going to the carnival. I go at least once a week. It's fun to walk among them, without them ever knowing I was the clown they were laughing at earlier in the evening."

"How did you know I would go tonight? I haven't really gone since the night I joined the circus," I said.

"Because it's an exciting pastime for a young man." He paused and smirked slightly. "And you told Arik that you were thinking of doing so, meaning that everyone now knows."

I laughed.

"Why haven't you gone before this?" he asked.

"Because I don't have the money to buy anything, I see the same acts in the circus anyway, and the freaks make me nervous."

He nodded. "But the fake freaks are stranger than the real ones."

"Exactly. I don't know why, though."

"Constantly pretending to be odd has an effect on you. I should know. Come along, then."

We walked toward the lights on the beach, the air still warm and stifling. The seaweed stank from its day under the sun, and shells crunched under our feet into the sand.

The fair was an endless stream of people swirling past each other or caught in front of the stalls. Some stopped in the middle of the thoroughfare for no discernible reason, leaving others to grit their teeth and flow around them, mumbling and cursing to themselves.

There were twice as many people as the last time I visited.

"We won't stay long," Drystan whispered into my ear. "Bil will want to prance around and exult in front of everyone in the tent."

The alchemist was at his usual booth in the carnival. He glared at me. I gave him a two-fingered salute and he turned from me and spat in the sand. I snorted. Charlatan.

"Friend of yours?"

"Not in the least."

I briefly told him the tale of the alchemist and the strange affliction I did not have.

Drystan cackled. "Genital warts was the best he could do? I'm amazed he earns any coins here."

Drystan stopped in front of a stall. It was a game where if you threw a ball into the basket on the far wall, you won a few coins or a small prize, like a doll or soldier to give to a child. Most were trying for the coins to spend in the beachfront pubs.

Drystan made a show of giving a coin to the circus worker manning the stall. I thought his name was Slar or Sar or something similar. He passed Drystan three small, wooden balls from beneath the stand.

"All right," Slar or Sar said. "Whatcha do is you throw the balls inta the basket. You get one in and you get a coin or a wooden horse." He held up a small, rudely carved horse about as large as a hand. "You get two in, you get two coins, or a toy soldier," he demonstrated. "You get all three and you get ten coins or you can get this," he held up a small porcelain doll. A few murmured appreciatively. It was not anywhere near as fine as the ones from Imachara I had hidden under my bed in my old room, but it was still something any little girl would cherish.

Drystan cradled the wooden spheres in his long-fingered hands. He balanced the first one delicately on his fingertips, contemplating it. The ball was painted a bright orange with a white star painted on either side. He stared at the wall, at least ten feet away. The wicker basket tacked in the center looked barely large enough to fit the ball into.

He took a deep breath and closed his eyes. A few passersby had stopped to watch him.

Drystan opened his eyes and lobbed the ball and it landed delicately into the basket on the first try. A few people clapped.

Drystan held up the next ball, this one blue with an orange sun design. It too landed in the wicker basket. The cheers grew louder.

"He's the first to get two baskets this night!" Slar or Sar called.

The last ball was green, with a simple stripe around its diameter. Into the basket it went. Drystan made a great show of acting abashed as people clapped him on the shoulder.

"Now, now," Slar or Sar called, quieting them down. "Which do you want, the coins or the doll?"

Drystan paused, scrutinizing both prizes, as if he were torn. I half-expected him to choose the porcelain doll. "Coins, please," Drystan said eventually with a small smile. The coins chinked in his palm and disappeared into one of the many pockets in his coat.

We weaved our way out of the throng. Many more people were passing coins to Slar or Sar to have their turn at the baskets.

"It was a trick, wasn't it?" I asked.

Drystan put his hand over his heart and looked injured. "I'll have you know I have excellent aim. Comes from years of juggling." He grinned. "It worked and got more playing, did it not? And I won enough to buy us some drink before the carnival ends and our meeting begins."

"But what if someone else also has really good aim?"

I asked as we walked toward the line of pubs on the beachfront.

"If anyone else gets two, most of the time someone standing behind the wall will slide a ball into the bottom of the basket so that the third one bounces out."

"But that's cheating!"

"Why yes, Micah, that's cheating."

"Does it happen with other games?"

"Oh plenty. There's usually one of us out here per night, giving the marks a taste of what it's like to win. We swindle with a swagger," he said, demonstrating his swagger.

"Hmm, which is the seediest gin shop?" he asked as we wandered down the promenade. They all looked seedy to me, dimly lit with grimy windows. The promenade was far from deserted at this time of night. Some were circus-goers who could not be bothered with the funfair but did not want to socialize with the others in the tent, or other residents of Sicion who came here most every night, circus or no circus. Most of the pubs were incredibly full, people spilling from the entry way and drinking openly on makeshift driftwood benches.

"Wait here," Drystan said, tucking up his sleeves. "I'm going in."

I watched as he maneuvered his way between drunken men and women and disappeared into the dark confines of the pub. I waited outside, my eyes darting nervously at the faces of the people passing me, their features harsh in the lights of the gas lamps.

Drystan returned, a green bottle held in his hand.

"Let's go down by the docks and celebrate a straw house at the circus and fatter coffers for Bil," he said.

We wandered down the promenade and onto a dock, our feet clacking against the boards. The briny breeze teased my hair and slipped under the seams of my coat. We sat at the end of the docks and looked out over the dark expanse of the sea.

Drystan twisted over the bottle, took a swig, and passed it to me. I took a small sip and tried not to gag. It tasted how wet paint smelled, with an aftertaste of juniper berries.

"Gin," Drystan said. "Cheap, horrible gin. I had to grossly overpay to convince him to let me leave with it."

I nodded, eyes watering.

I did not know what to say to him, so I said nothing.

"Do you think Tauro is actually a Minotaur?" he asked after another gulp of the burning liquor.

"What?" I furrowed my brows. "There's no such thing as Minotaurs. You might as well say there are mermaids in the ocean and harpies in the sky." *Or a Kedi walking about town.*

"Every culture has the same myths. From the east to the west, there are tales of dragons, of mermaids, of harpies, and Minotaurs."

"And are you a scholar of world mythology?" I asked.

He smiled, more to himself than at me, and passed the bottle. I took another sip and managed not to cough.

"Tauro doesn't seem quite human though, does he?" Drystan asked. "It's not only how he looks. It's the eyes."

"I think he's a little slower and hairier than most. That's all." My head was light and I no longer felt the cold.

"He's the one of the closest things we have to a real freak," Drystan said.

I shifted a little uncomfortably.

"There's Poussin and Juliet," I said.

"Skin disorders, no more."

"Even Juliet's fangs?"

That gave him pause. "Most likely surgical alterations."

I did not think they were, but I decided to leave it be.

"There's Tin and Karg, the midget and the giant–" I started, but Drystan shook his head.

"You see polarization of size in all cultures..." he started but trailed off when I looked at him, an eyebrow raised.

"What?" he asked.

"Well," I said, "you don't make much of an effort, do you?" I said, dropping the roughened voice that had become almost second nature and using my former, posher voice. "When did you go to university?"

He laughed. "The others all know that I come from a lofty background. You're the one that insists on hiding yours, though you don't do it very well. And yes, I went to the Royal Snakewood University in Imachara, and nearly finished as well. I studied philosophy. It opened my eyes and so I became a fool."

"Were you originally from Imachara?" I asked.

"No, I was raised in Sicion," he said. His voice was slightly slurred. I wondered if he would be answering so frankly were it not for the gin. The bottle was half-empty.

"What was your family name?" I asked, pressing.

He looked at me, sizing me up, his eyes slightly unfocused. "My, but it's been a long time since I've said it. Hornbeam." He almost sighed the last word.

I gasped. "You're from one of the noblest families in Imachara… and you're a *clown* in a *circus*?"

And not only were the Hornbeams the strength behind the crown, but it meant that Drystan was related to Damien and Darla.

He drew himself up. "I'll have you know, *boy*, that I would have been a clown back in Imachara but in fancier motley!" His voice had hardened.

I took another sip of gin. My head spun. "Sorry," I muttered.

We drank in silence, listening to the crashing of the waves.

The silence begged to be filled. "Are you Darla and Damien's brother, then?" Memories were coming back to me, tales of the eldest Hornbeam boy who had been cast out of the family tree, raising Damien to the status of heir.

He blinked at me. "Yes."

My, but our world was that small. Damien was the brother that Drystan missed. I tried to remember, but a decade ago we did not have a house in the Emerald Bowl, and so I would not have seen him at the afternoon teas.

He made a noncommittal sound and swigged more gin. "Your turn," he said. "Your family name."

I opened my mouth but hesitated. I wanted so badly to tell someone, anyone. "Can I trust you?"

He leaned close. His breath reeked of gin. For a moment, I wondered if he was going to kiss me. "I trusted you, didn't I, *Iphigenia*?"

My breath caught in my throat.

"You already know," I whispered.

He leaned back, closed his eyes. "Laurus of Sicion." His eyes opened. "They had their child go missing not long ago."

"They did."

"I read about it in the paper. They still have their son. Your brother."

"So they do," I said. I was shaking.

He looked at me, and I knew he was trying to see the woman in me. "You're a brave little thing. I'll give you that," he said, but his voice was cool, almost disappointed.

"Are you... going to tell anyone?" I forced the words from my throat.

He looked out to sea. "We're all entitled to our secrets. I'll not say a word about yours, and you'll not say a word about mine."

A little tension left my body. "How'd you guess? About me?"

"The dress in your pack was quite the hint. And your letter."

I pushed him in the shoulder. "You *did* search it." My cheeks burned with embarrassment. I had been quite frank in that letter, unleashing all of my uncertainty. At least I hadn't spoken about any members of the circus specifically. Like Aenea. Or Drystan.

"Of course I did. But I was the only one, I'll promise you that."

He hauled himself to his feet and tossed the bottle into the sea. How much of that bottle had I drunk? The world would not focus. Drystan had to help me up, and I nearly fell. I giggled.

"I, Master Hornbeam, would like to take Miss Iphigenia Laurus's arm, if it is not too forward." He gave a courtly bow.

I laughed again and gave my best curtsey, holding out imaginary skirts. Something in my chest felt lighter. Someone knew, though like everyone else, he did not know the whole truth. I was good at keeping a certain secret. "Of course, Master Hornbeam. As long as you never, ever call me Iphigenia again. It's the most hideous name. Before I ran away, I called myself Gene."

"Yes, it is rather horrific, Gene." And we, two nobles living secret lives, weaved and tilted our way back to our circus.

Bil was so pleased with himself he looked as if he were about to burst. He strutted in front of us, his grin wide and yellow, tugging on his coat until the gilt buttons threatened to pop.

He was proud; a specific sort of pride that I did not think anyone could possess unless they had started something from nothing. Arik had told me that Bil had grown up desperately poor – his mother was a widow who worked in the laundry to keep Bil and his sister clothed and fed. He had gone to see the circus whenever it was in town and decided that he would start one. And so he did.

The circus used to be a sham, with every member an alcoholic or delirious on Lerium. The acts were pathetic, and the entire circus had a seedy air, far more burlesque and boudoir than carnival. The main draw had been buxom ladies in scanty costumes that showed more than a little ankle or leg.

After seeing Riley & Batheo, he began to transform the circus, and now, though it was still far seedier than the other "Circus of Curiosities," it was far more professional than any other small circus in Ellada.

And Bil was not yet satisfied, dreaming of showing his circus in the fixed amphitheaters in the metropolises of Ellada. He yearned to perform before royalty. Bil was a man who would never be content until the next goal had been met, and then he would promptly set another. I admired this trait, but also felt sad for him, that he would forever be striving and never content.

"That was beautiful, my circus, just beautiful," Bil said, standing with his legs apart before us, pointing his cane to each of us in turn. "Never have so many people gathered round our humble tent to see our performances. This is a milestone for our circus. Who knows, my lovelies – we may need to invest in a bigger tent once we arrive in Imachara!"

We clapped, whistled, and stamped our feet. I was sitting in between Arik and Aenea, and the world was still not quite focusing, though the sensation was fading and my head ached. Arik and Aenea had not commented on the smell of gin about me, though I was sure they noticed. It would have been hard for them not to.

"Things are going well, indeed they are, my fools and friends," Bil said, beaming. "Tonight, we celebrate! Two extra casks of ale cracked!" We cheered, but not quite as loudly.

"That is what Bil considers a bonus," Aenea whispered in my ear.

"I've heard him mention bonuses before," I murmured.

"That's all he does, is mention them. He conveniently forgets or says the money has already been spent by the time the season comes to an end."

I remembered the open safe in Bil's tent, the clink of gold in Frit's long, thin fingers. Frit remembered this as well. When I looked at her, her dark eyes were already boring into mine from her drawn face. She shook her head ever so slightly.

Bil noticed the lack of enthusiasm. "Why the long faces? This is a night to celebrate."

There was a pause, but then: "Our pockets do not celebrate," the young contortionist, Mara, said loudly. I was a bit surprised. From what I had gathered from watching her, she was a young girl who frequently spoke but often did not have much of import to say. She stood.

"Pardon me, Miss Mara?" Bil said with exaggerated politeness. "Perhaps I misheard you?"

"I've spent years in the circus, now," Mara said, dragging a toe over the sandy rock. "You promise bonuses, but you never give 'em. I understood the first year – I was new, and we was still a small circus. Sometimes the seats was over half empty... but this year, it's different. The circus is doing better than ever. I'm happy for you and for every member of the circus. We all worked so hard... shouldn't we all be rewarded?" It was an obviously rehearsed speech, and Mara glanced over her shoulder at other contortionists and acrobats, who nodded encouragingly.

Bil laughed, and it appeared warm and genuine. "This circus is doing well just now, m'dear Mara, but what happens when we're practicing for the new acts for Imachara in Cowl next month?" He hitched his thumbs under his suspenders and leaned forward. "I'll be honest with all of you. Who pays for the great expense of packing and unpacking the circus, of the train that takes us from town to town? We put on shows up the coast, most of which are empty because the entire population of the town could fit in the tent with room to spare. I pay for it because it's practice, valuable practice, whether an audience is there or not.

"And I have accrued such debts from the years when this circus did poorly, and the creditors howl and scratch like cats if I cannot pay. I paid you when I could not pay myself. It was a struggle to support my wife. You have no idea, little Mara, the true costs of running a circus. It is more than you could possibly imagine." He had kept the small smile on his face and earnest set of his eyebrows, which, while he wore his full Ringmaster regalia, made him look like a possessed nutcracker.

It was a convincing speech and I looked around to see a scattering of heads nodding. The circus was nearly on the brink of financial ruin, but I knew why – it was because Bil bought Vestige, and because Frit was skimming off the top. I could still feel her gaze on me.

Mara's slight shoulders sagged, her shoulder blades jutting against her thin costume. She was so small, especially next to Bil. But she drew herself up and tilted her chin up at Bil. "That may be so, but the numbers still don't make no sense. If everyone who comes to see the circus pays enough to get in and then buys food and games at the carnival..."

She trailed off as Bil began to slowly shake his head from side to side and chuckle. His chuckle grew into a laugh that echoed deep within his chest.

"You're an uneducated girl from Niral, Mara, and you and your little friends have no idea of the true costs of a circus. None. I will pay bonuses, and I will pay them when I can. Would you rather have bonuses and no job next season?" The performers exchanged glances, looked away from little Mara. She was on her own now.

She saw her fellow performers' subtle rebuff and her nostrils flared. "Then I quit!" she said. "There are other circuses and I won't be treated unfair."

Bil snapped. "Treated *unfair?*" he sputtered. "You're treated a hell of a lot better than you would be in any other circus in Ellada, you ungrateful little wretch. You could barely do the splits when I took you on. I let you train under my best contortionists; I took you on when there were dozens of other little nymphs who liked to bend before the men in the audience." He stepped close to Mara, and to her credit she did not cower. She stared stonily into his blotched face. For the briefest of moments, it seemed he was about to strike her.

"You're not quitting, little Mara," he spat. "I'm throwing you out. You go and try to get another circus job. No one will take you on. You'll have to make your living how you would always have if I had not let you into my circus. On your back." Mara blanched. Everyone was very silent, especially Tila and Sal.

He gave a contemptuous look at the performers. "No ale at all tonight. If anyone else feels as Mara does, you can leave with her in the morning." Bil pointed toward the flap of the tent.

Mara fled, hunched, her hand over her mouth. After a moment's hesitation, Frit followed, probably to offer comfort. Bil did not like that. His fists clenched at his sides and his jaw was tight.

"Styx," Aenea swore quietly under her breath.

"Styx," I agreed.

15
SPRING: DEBUTANTE

"One must memorize the Twelve Trees of Nobility: Ash, Balsa, Cedar, Cyprus, Ebony, Elm, Hornbeam, Oak, Poplar, Redwood, and Walnut. And, of course, Snakewood. This forest shelters Ellada, bringing it life.

Levels of bowing and curtseying vary depending on your ring of nobility compared to the Twelve Trees. Please see the next page for more detailed diagrams.

Failure of correct royal etiquette is one of the most egregious offenses one can make."

A YOUNG ELLADAN LADY'S PRIMER,
Lady Elena Primrose

"Where did you and Cyril go last night?" my mother demanded as soon as she had closed the door to Cyril's room. She grabbed my upper arm and frog-marched me into the study. Father was still at work.

"N… nowhere," I stammered. I knew for a fact Cyril had not told Mother where we had been, no matter how much pain he had been in. It had been terrible to see him lying on the sick bed, his arm wrapped in plaster, a bandage on his head. He was the very picture of a sick bed patient, from his sweat-matted hair and clammy skin to glazed eyes from the laudanum Doctor Walnut had given him.

"Though I know you may feel differently, Iphigenia, I am not stupid." Her anger slipped and I could see that she was worried about Cyril.

I found a way to modify the truth. "We couldn't sleep, so we went for a walk. We went to the Emerald Park, and I convinced Cyril to climb a tree with me to watch the sun set. He lost his grip and fell. That's all." I would never have told her we climbed Penglass. I would not be allowed to leave the house for a month or more, but for the ever-looming debutante ball.

My mother shook her head in dismay. "Iphigenia, the time has come for all of this to stop."

"For all of what to stop?"

"Just as Cyril must accept his future responsibilities, so must you." Her gloved hands worried with the beads of her long necklace.

"Aren't I?" I asked, puzzled. "I'm studying all that is asked of me, and I'm going to the debutante ball next week."

"I've no complaints about that, aside from your terrible embroidery." She said it with a smile, as though to lessen the blow. My stomach was still in knots. I braided a section of my hair, concentrating on the weaving of the strands so that I did not have to look at her.

"Iphigenia," my mother said, and I paused in my plaiting and met her gaze. "You need to grow up and accept what is to come. You do as you're asked, but I am not blind. I know you enjoy none of it, and that you prefer to at times pursue… boyish pastimes. But you are a woman and must accept a woman's responsibilities."

"Do you mean marrying and birthing and mothering? We do not even know if that is possible for me, Mother. And you know as well as I do the possible reason for my occasional interest in 'boyish' pursuits."

Mother cleared her throat delicately. "I mean that despite your condition, you have been raised as female and you are female. With the name Laurus comes a future of privilege, and you will be presented to society next week as a young woman of consequence. I think you might be happier if you try a little harder to behave as a young lady should." Her voice was rather tender, but the words cut to the quick.

"I'll try, Mother," was all I could say in response.

"I know, Iphigenia." She took my hand and squeezed. Her hands were cold through the gloves. "I must be off as I've promised to visit Lady Candlewood this afternoon. She's just returned from her lecture tour around Southern Temne, and I'm sure she'll have wonderful stories to tell."

I nodded, and she swept from the room.

I felt the sudden urge to weep. It felt as though I was being pulled along a certain road and I was not sure it would lead me to the right place. I rubbed a hand over my face, squeezing my eyes shut so they would not fill with tears.

"Miss?"

I raised my face from my hands.

Gale, our butler, hovered in the doorway. "Yes, Gale?"

"Cyril has asked for you."

"Oh. Of course. Thank you, Gale."

He hesitated. "Are you all right, miss?"

"I'm fine, Gale, thank you for asking. I'm just fatigued."
He nodded and left.

Cyril clutched a newspaper to his chest. He looked scared.

"What is it, Cyril?" I asked, my stomach dropping.

Wordlessly, he passed me the newspaper. The front page had an image of a Penglass dome with two streaks of light. The Penglass from the night before. Another, smaller photograph showed the glowing outline of a hand. My handprint. Did Mother suspect?

I read the article, which was from a less-reputable paper, the *Sicion Searcher*. It stated that a strange light from the Penglass had awoken the inhabitants of the tenement on the corner of Emerald and Silver Streets. They saw the light for only a few minutes before it mysteriously disappeared. An inhabitant of the tenement managed to take a photograph just before the light vanished. The constables had been alerted and scientists conducted tests on the dome this morning to ensure it was safe. The Constabulary had no official theories, but the *Sicion Searcher* had plenty. The Penglass Dome was an Alder vessel and had awoken to travel back to the stars. The Penglass around the city had finally grown unstable with time and could explode at any moment. The person or monster that had left the handprint and the streaks of light had set in motion events beyond the average citizen's control.

"Styx Cyril," I said, crumpling the newspaper in my lap. "Styx."

"They don't seem to have any leads."

"I think Mother will suspect, if she sees this. I told her we were in the Emerald Park last night."

"Why did you do that?"

"Well, I didn't bloody well know it'd be in the papers, now did I?"

"Keep your voice down," Cyril hissed.

My eyes darted toward the door. "What do we do?"

Cyril shrugged, and then winced in pain. "I don't know. Just try not to draw attention to ourselves. Hope Mother doesn't see this newspaper. And I'm afraid you probably shouldn't touch any more Penglass," he said regretfully.

"I know," I said, but my heart sank. Creating those trailing swirls of light had been one of the most amazing moments of my life. It had been frightening, but it had also felt almost *right*. Like I had been doing something I was always meant to do.

Cyril's features twisted in pain again. "Do you need more medicine?" I asked.

He nodded. I measured out a small spoonful of laudanum. Cyril grimaced as he drank it, despite the honey in its mixture. Soon his face relaxed. I sat with him, holding his unbroken hand, until he fell asleep.

I burned the newspaper in the fireplace.

"I am deathly ill. Terribly, dreadfully ill."

"Poppycock," my maid, Lia, said, hitting me on the head with a pillow. "Get yourself up."

"But I am… *dying!*" I had been reading in bed that afternoon and fallen asleep, the book open on my chest. The warm bed enveloped me; I did not want to leave it to go to the debutante ball.

I half-fell out of the bed onto the carpet, clutching my stomach. "I cannot move for the pain. Tell my brother I love him," I said, reaching out to her, my legs hopelessly tangled in the covers. Lia tugged the quilt so that I fell to the floor.

"Lo, I have perished," I said, my cheek resting against the rug.

"You should join the theatre, miss," Lia said. "What with all your carryings on."

I sat up, pushing my tangled hair out of my face. "Mother would *love* that. But please, tell Mother I am an inch away from death and I cannot possibly go to the ball tonight. I'll be sick all over the guests. That should do the trick."

"Don't be daft, Miss Iphigenia."

"Gene," I corrected her. Cyril seemed to be the only person in my life who actually called me by the name I liked.

"Do you realize what a thrashing I would get if any-one heard me calling you Gene, miss?" she said, as she always did.

I made a face at her and got out of bed. "Fine, but call me Gene in here."

"Of course, miss," she said with a small smile. "Come on, love. Your bath is ready."

"Please tell Mother I'm unwell," I begged, tossing my dressing robe and nightgown onto the bed. Lia was one of the few to know what I was. There was no way she could avoid doing so – she dressed me every day, and when I was little she used to bathe me. She was paid a handsome wage and swore never to tell anyone, not even the other household staff. She was fifteen years older than me and had always been kind.

"To what point and purpose, little miss?" Lia countered. "You've been preparing for this for weeks, and it'll be quite the embarrassment for your mother if you do not go at the last minute. And this will only be delaying the inevitable, miss – if not this ball, then the next. You might as well get it over with now."

I sighed. "You're right. I'm being childish."

She smiled. "Only a little. Go, and try to enjoy yourself. Your dress is beautiful and all your friends will be there. There will be food and dancing and flirting. It need not be so bad. I would have given my eye teeth to go to such a ball at your age." She winked. "I wouldn't say no to going now, neither!"

I laughed. "All right, then, we can swap. You can wear my dress and I'll stay at home."

"Nice try, love," she said, and gave me a quick kiss on the cheek. "It won't be so terrible, just you wait and see."

I hoped she was right.

And so I bathed and brushed and shaved and scented myself. All the while, I tried to stifle the feeling that it was like a holy animal from the rural parts of Byssia being pampered and perfumed before slaughter to the Chimaera demi-gods. I may have been feeling a little melodramatic.

Lia had laid all of my clothing on the bed and helped me into my petticoats and undershirt and slid the corset around my torso.

Lia grunted slightly as she pulled the stays. My ribs constricted and I clutched the bedpost.

I felt caged in a corset. The device did give me a bit of an illusion of a waist, I thought, looking at my body in the mirror of my dressing table. Lia slipped the dress over my head and it fell about me in a wave of blue fabric so pale it was almost white. I twisted my hips and the fabric settled into place and Lia fastened the dozens of tiny buttons on the back. The dress was lovely, with simple lines, the only decoration pink satin ribbons about the waist and the high neckline and the hem of the skirt. Mother and I had disagreed on every other dress I had tried on, but as soon as I had come out of the dressing room in the shop on Jade Street, we had both agreed it a success.

Lia plaited my hair into a crown about my head with more ribbon and tiny sprays of baby's breath. She left little curls about my face and another at the nape of my neck. I sat patiently as she powdered and painted my face in such a way that it did not look as though I was wearing cosmetics at all, which I did not see the point in. I stepped into heeled pink dancing slippers. A little strand of pearls about the neck and elbow-length gloves and a feather fan completed the look.

All dolled up to look like a girl and the illusion was fairly convincing.

I chewed the inside of my cheek as I waited to enter the ballroom. I kept clutching at the fabric of my skirt and fiddling with the ringlets of my hair. I felt like an imposter – like I was not meant to be here, about to parade in front of Sicion's highest society and declare myself ready for offers of marriage.

"This is so exciting," Anna Yew said next to me, smoothing down her dress. She looked pretty and tempting as a cupcake, and all eyes would slide past me and land on her and stay. That was fine by me. She flipped open a little mirror from her handbag and scrutinized her reflection, plucking an errant eyelash from her cheek and freshening her lip stain. I had not thought to bring a mirror, so I borrowed hers. I looked nervous.

The music started. In the past, all debutante balls took place in Imachara and young ladies were presented before the king or queen, who would kiss the young women on the forehead, blessing their new lives as women as opposed to girls. But as the current Princess Royal was only six years of age and the Steward, her uncle Ira Snakewood, had no interest in performing such a duty, smaller debutante balls were held in the larger cities – Imachara, Sicion, and Niral. I was glad for it – I did not think I would be able to handle a debutante ball three or four times the size of this. The murmur and chatter of the guests downstairs in the ballroom floated up to us: hundreds of lords and ladies and their sons and daughters, waiting for us.

The girls left the hallway one by one, their names called as they floated down the staircase to the music. When these girls had previously been announced at balls and other functions, they had been referred to as "miss." Now, they were "ladies."

"Lady Darla Hornbeam." Applause sounded as Darla descended the stairs in her pale golden dress.

"Lady Winifred Poplar."

"Lady Tara Cypress."

Name after name, pale dress after pale dress descended, until it was our turn. My stomach felt as though it would explode with nerves, the trapped birds and butterflies escaping from my stomach and fluttering about the room. I swallowed and pasted a smile on my face.

"Lady Anna Yew."

Anna flashed me a smile over her shoulder and gathered her pink skirts, holding her head high as she glided down the stairs.

"Lady Iphigenia Laurus." I straightened my shoulders and stepped into the bright light of the ballroom, making my way down the wide, marble stairs. The stone was slippery, and I feared falling. That would make quite an impression, and I imagined myself tumbling head over heels down the stairs, landing in an ungraceful heap of chiffon, ribbon, and lace. The smile that curled my mouth widened.

The lights of the golden glass globes blinded me from the upturned faces of the nobility below me. I reached the bottom of the stairs without mishap, and the matrons of each of the Twelve Trees of Nobility waited for me at the bottom to kiss my forehead and seal my new life as a woman: Lady Oak, Lady Hornbeam, Lady Cyprus, Lady Poplar, Lady Elm, Lady Ebony, Lady Balsa, Lady Redwood, Lady Ash, Lady Walnut, and Lady Cedar. Lady Snakewood, the queen's aunt, was not able to attend. Their kisses were as light as dried leaves whispering across my forehead. Everyone, including me, was solemn and grave as the fifteen sixteen-year-old daughters of their nobility marked their way into womanhood.

The girls gathered in an outward-facing circle toward the guests ringing the Beach Ballroom. In unison, we curtsied, and the nobility applauded. The glass globes brightened and the ball began.

Immediately, I gravitated toward the wall out of the way, wanting to people-watch before speaking to anyone. I still felt the echoes of the ceremony moments before. I knew it was only a ritual, but it had left me pensive. Was I now a woman? I still felt more like a boyish girl in a dress, out of place no matter how many jewels and silks I wore.

I had not been to the Beach Ballroom since last year. The building was extraordinary – octagonal in shape, with diamond-paned glass windows staring out at the ocean in full sunset, the stars just beginning to twinkle into existence. The wooden floor was polished to a glistening shine, though showed evidence of long use. The ballroom was built on stilts to keep it well above the fluctuating tides near an outcropping of Penglass. Some of the domes were too high, but the architects decided to work with the Penglass rather than trying to find a different spot, as the view was too perfect. And so around the edges of the dance floor, the tops of Penglass domes peeked. Dancers were already lounging against the smooth blue glass, looking like pixies visiting their fairy rings. A lavish buffet of delicacies lined one wall, and the small orchestra was in the opposite corner, the musicians hunched over their instruments as they played classical music. A massive chandelier made of tiny glass globes hung suspended from the ceiling, each globe colored with an element to make them shine in blue, pink, purple, and a dark orange to mirror the sunset.

Anna Yew was already flanked by two boys – Evan Redwood and Anthony Cedar. She laughed at something young Lord Cedar said, the diamonds in her ears flashing in the light, bringing attention to the column of her throat. I did not know when Anna had learned to enchant men so easily. I wondered if someone had taught her, or if it was simply something instinctual, some female part I had been born without.

Winifred Poplar and Tara Cypress meanwhile flirted with Cyril. Cyril responded just as easily to their talk, smiling down at them in a way that must have caused the girls' hearts to quicken. Anna had not been lying when she had told me that Cyril would be a good catch – others seemed to feel the same way. But Cyril politely extricated himself from their clutches when he spied Elizabeth Rowan, his intended. The Lord and Lady Rowan had already spoken to my parents – it was all but decided, and Cyril seemed besotted. He bowed low over Elizabeth's hand and led her to the buffet table, fetching her a glass of wine. I smiled to see their courtship.

Oswin sidled up next to me with a plate piled high with food.

"Heya, Genie," he said, mid-chew. "You hungry?"

"Hi, Oswin," I replied, eyeing the plate. "Absolutely starved." I stabbed a cheese-stuffed olive from his platter with a toothpick and ate it, the saltiness of the olives and sharpness of the cheese a delight. We made short work of the plate, using the toothpicks to skewer the small delicacies – salmon en croûte, roasted and pickled vegetables, rare and expensive sausages and cheeses, deviled eggs – so as not to dirty our gloved hands. When we finished, a servant came immediately to take the plate away. I felt better and more grounded with food in me, though now my stomach pressed even more unpleasantly against my corset.

Oswin tugged at his cravat, which might have been almost as uncomfortable as my corset. "So are you searching for a wife tonight, young Lord Hawthorne?" I teased, leaning against a Penglass dome, mindful of my gloves so that the surface did not touch my bare skin. Being near it calmed me.

"No, though I bet my parents are," he said. "What about you – out to catch a husband?"

"Not likely," I laughed. I was glad Oswin had come to speak with me so that I did not stand awkwardly on my own. I had always felt comfortable around him.

The first dance had begun, and young future Lords and Ladies partnered off and twirled about the dance floor, the current Lords and Ladies looking on. "Look at Bart," Oswin said, pointing at Bartholomew Fir, a spoiled little rich boy I had never liked, and chuckling to himself. Bart missed every other step, swaying from side to side like some sort of dancing duck. His partner, Darla Hornbeam, was unamused. I giggled behind my gloved hand.

"They're perfectly matched, aren't they?"

"Aye, they're both insufferable," Oswin said. The first dance came to a close.

"Hey, you want to dance?" Oswin asked. My head whipped around to face him. *That* was the last thing I had expected him to say.

"Of... of course," I stammered.

Oswin coughed, as if embarrassed by his outburst, and then bowed elaborately, his nose to his knees and held out his hand. "I meant to say: would Lady Iphigenia Laurus of the House of Laurus care for a short dance with the Lord Oswin Hawthorne?" he asked, in a voice uncannily like Rojer Cyprus's plummy tones.

"She would be most delighted, Master Hawthorne," I said, inclining my head. He hesitated before putting his hand on my waist. This was very strange. Oswin had always been Cyril's friend and the boy I teased and who teased me in turn. This dance changed the dynamic.

We swept cautiously onto the dance floor. Both of us had received copious dance lessons from our parents over the past few years, and so we knew the dances and the steps well enough, though neither of us performed with any sort of finesse. We twirled when we were supposed to and our feet followed the patterns, but our arms and legs were stiff and nervous. Oswin kept pulling faces to lighten the mood. I tried to stay very serious, but soon I found myself laughing. Our movements loosened and we were merely two people having fun, tapping our feet against the floor planks, my skirt swirling like a bell behind me along with all the other dancing girls in the room.

Oswin and I danced for four pieces in a row, before the music stopped so the Lady Hornbeam could give a brief speech, as she was the Lady with the highest social standing. Oswin and I were a little breathless and beamed at each other. I patted my hair, tucking the bits that had escaped into the plaited crown. Across the ballroom, I could see Mother watching us intently. My excitement faded as I read the blatant thoughts flickering across her face. *A Hawthorne,* she must be thinking. *A Hawthorne boy would be a most valuable match. Would raise us another title…*

We switched partners, making our way in a circle to each other. I danced with my brother, and with Rojer, who could not dance at all.

And then I found myself face to face with Damien.

He started to smile, but it froze on his face. He refused

to touch my hand. He would not meet my gaze, and in the middle of the dance he left the floor to the refreshments table. Luckily, the music ended, for the dance could not continue with one partner missing.

I swallowed, turning my head away from Damien. People were exchanging looks between us, wondering what had happened. Gossip and rumors would fly faster than a gyrocopter. I pressed a hand tight against my nauseous, sore belly before I realized it might make people think I was with child. An impossibility, I was sure.

Somehow, I made my way to my spot of wall. Oswin came with me, his brow puzzled. I ignored the questions he wanted to ask. I refused to let the tears fall. Damien did not matter to me. His look of revulsion should not matter. But it did.

Perhaps sensing the lurch in the party, Lady Hornbeam *ting*ed a glass with a fork, delicately. She told us the well-known fable of the Lady of the Moon falling in love for the first time with the Lord of the Sun.

"In the time before, all was the Darkness and there was nothing. The Sun and the Moon were separated from this darkness by the Styx, a river of blackness that no light could penetrate. But one day, the Lady of the Moon was so sad and so lonely that she began to cry. Each tear tumbled from her lovely face and became a shining star. The stars fell into the river Styx and one made its way to the Lord of the Sun, whose flames had dimmed in loneliness.

"He cupped the star in his hand and walked upstream of the river, until he came to a spot where it was short enough to cross. There, he found the weeping Lady of the Moon. As soon as they saw each other, their light reflected off one another. The Sun's flames burst into radiance, and his light lit the Lady of the Moon. The forgotten tears scattered into the sky, only seen at night. And the Lord of the Sun and the Lady of the Moon began a dance that has lasted for millennia, dancing and circling around each other. Their light drove away most of the darkness of Styx, though death and darkness still take their toll, and their light warmed the world in which we now live.

"Their dance continues. And tonight, several young boys and girls here today may begin a dance that lasts a lifetime."

Polite applause erupted about the ballroom. Oswin pretended to puke, and I smiled, but I thought the story sweet. And sad. Even with their love, the Lord and Lady were still a world apart in that fable.

And though I spoke with my friends and several other boys, time and time again Oswin and I found ourselves dancing together.

Oswin and I grew overheated from the dancing and went outside to the balcony, drinking more cool wine and staring out at the ink-black sea. My head spun from the wine and the dance.

"Having a good time?" I asked, leaning on the wooden bannister.

"I am. Lots more fun than I thought I would."

I half-smiled. Of the boys here tonight, if I had to marry one, I would choose Oswin. He could be thick and sometimes a little crude, but he was jovial and I found him favorable to look upon, with the freckles on his nose and his bright green eyes. Part of me wondered if, perhaps, I could one day fit into this life, if I had a companion like Oswin who made me laugh. But, as ever, I wondered what Oswin would think of me, if he knew the whole truth. He might very well react as Damien had, which made me feel as though someone had punched me in the stomach. I sipped my wine again, and pushed the thought from my mind.

"What got Damien's panties in a twist, do you know?"

The small smile fled my face. "I don't know. I just don't think he likes me."

"Well, I guess that's his loss," he said, nudging me in the shoulder again. "You're a good 'un, Genie." He grinned and downed the rest of his wine.

"Come," I said, taking him by the hand. "I think it's time for more dancing."

16
SUMMER: MICA IN GRANITE

"The branches of the Twelve Trees cast the trunk and the roots in shadow. For centuries they have been our monarchs, the successive ruler chosen through divine right rather than by the people and for the people. The nobility have sunshine and greenery in the Emerald Bowl, more wealth spent on one article of Vestige than many of us will make through the course of our entire lives. For us, they leave little more than dirt and foul humors. Sign the petition. Join the movement. Become a Forester."

LEAFLET FOR THE FORESTER PARTY

"Let's go into the city today, Micah," Aenea said to me over breakfast one morning.

"What about practice?" I asked, my mouth half-full of porridge. My mother would be appalled.

"You deserve a day off after yesterday," she said. I had mastered a double back flip.

"Where will we go?"

"I don't know, we'll wander. It is our last day in Sicion, after all," she said. "We should say our goodbyes."

Last day in Sicion. So far, I had only been thinking of going to Imachara, rather than thinking of leaving Sicion. I had been to Imachara before, for fringe court functions we could garner with our name, but it had mainly been to go to stuffy operas, plays, and balls where I was expected to dance with men of a suitable age and background. I had not actually explored the city.

I wondered if I would return to Sicion during the next circus season, if I were still a member. No longer would I be close enough to my brother and my parents to return home within an hour if I changed my mind.

Would I ever return? There were no guarantees I would be with Bil's circus a year from now. I had given so little thought to my future over the past few weeks, trying to avoid thinking of my family to avoid the pain of leaving them. I planned only until the next moment, the next meal to be eaten, the next flip to be mastered, and the show each night. I focused on Aenea's face.

"Yes," I said. "Let's go."

We brought our platters to the cook and raced each other to the carts to gather our belongings. Arik was inside, lounging on his bunk and reading. He looked over the battered book at us as I grabbed my coin purse from the dregs of my pack and re-laced my shoes.

"What are you children up to?" he asked.

"Micah deserves a day off, and I think our muscles could use the extra rest as well," Aenea said.

Arik nodded. He had not said anything, but there was a stiffness to his movements lately. "We're going into the city, to say our goodbyes to Sicion."

Arik closed the book. "You'll bid your farewells as I welcome it as home. That is fitting."

"What?" we asked at nearly the same moment.

"I'm resigning tonight. While you're gone, I'm going to tell Bil that I won't be going on to Cowl or Imachara."

"With no warning?"

"The way he treated Mara last night, a night's notice is all he deserves."

"He might hold your last few weeks' pay," Aenea warned.

Arik shrugged. "So be it. I still have enough for my little room. That's all I need."

Aenea had told me that the room he was buying was in a flat owned by his longtime lover, who he only saw in the winters and never mentioned. It seemed everybody had their secrets.

"But what about the trapeze act?" I asked.

Aenea smiled a little sadly. "I've done solo acts before."

I was quiet. Our triad was fracturing after it had just found its balance. That uncertain future opened its jaws wider.

"Don't think of me today," Arik said. "Go out and enjoy yourselves. I'll see you before I go."

It was easier said than done. Aenea and I trudged up the beach and toward the promenade. The bright sun warmed our shoulders and the backs of our heads. The sand shifted beneath our feet, but the wind off the ocean was cool and bitter.

I glanced at Aenea every now and then. Her hair, usually tied up and out of the way in elaborate buns or braids, flowed freely over her shoulders. She wore a simple dress of pale green linen that trailed against the sandy promenade, tied with a pink sash about the waist.

My shoddy clothes embarrassed me in comparison. What I wore was a step above the shabby garb a boy named Calum had given me, but my wages were meager and I could only afford simple shirts and my trousers had a patch in one knee. I never thought I would miss dresses and skirts after being forced to wear them my entire life. Aenea looked so lovely in her dress, so much better in a dress than I ever did. It was a very strange sensation, to be both attracted to her and envious of her looks. I adjusted the cap on my head self-consciously.

"So where are we going?" I asked.

She shrugged. "Anywhere. You're from here – where are the nice places in Sicion?"

I thought about it. "The Emerald Park is really lovely. It's been a while since I've seen trees and greenery."

She laughed. "True. We can go climb the trees."

I laughed. "In your dress? Climbing in dresses is difficult."

"And how would you know?" she teased. "You've never had to climb in a dress."

My smile faltered. "I imagine it would be difficult."

"That it is. Breakfast was small this morning, and you're always hungry, so let's find something to eat."

"Of course," I said, my stomach fluttering, but not from hunger. Both of us together all day, eating a meal, going to a park. Was it friendship, or something more? The girl next to me haunted my thoughts when I was alone in the cart at night. I sifted through her words for hidden meanings, unsure if she felt anything more for me, or if it was wrong for me to have these feelings for her.

We went to a pub not far from the beach, the Tipsy Pig. It was not the nicest of establishments – the walls were tobacco-stained and the clientele mainly older men who looked curiously at us, the young, unescorted couple by the window.

"What do you do on the circus off-season?" I asked, realizing I'd never asked her before.

"This and that," she said. "Once I travelled. I went to Linde. So hot and humid, but so much green! It was a nice way to spend the winter, though I haven't been able to afford to do it since. Usually I go to my parents' place, in a little village not too far outside of Imachara."

"They're still alive then? No longer performers?"

"Yes, still alive, and no, no longer swinging about above the ground. They gave it up not long after I joined the circus as a performer. It's funny, because I feel like they felt guilty for raising me in the circus. They settled down to give me the option not to go into it."

"So why did you?"

"You've been on the trapeze. You know what it's like," she said with a smile. "If that's what you love to do, then living in the same tiny room in the same little village, feet always on the ground – it feels like prison."

"There's always scaffolding."

She laughed. "You can be fined for that, you know. If you're caught."

"I know. I've had Policiers yell at me a time or two. It's pretty easy to get away from them, though."

"Too fat to climb!"

We giggled over our food. I insisted on buying her meal and drink, feeling like a gentleman.

She curtseyed. "M'lord is so gallant."

I bowed. "Anything for my fair lady." Emboldened by our banter, I took her arm as we left, and she let me.

The park was fairly empty despite the fine, mid-summer weather.

The homeless had been shooed away by Policiers, and most of the poor and middle class were working their long shifts, so only the fairly well-to-do were about, the women bonneted, gloved, and wielding parasols against the sun; the men in suits and cravats.

It had been so long since I had spent a day at leisure. In my prior life, I would have lessons in the morning from private tutors, but the afternoons were always mine to do with as I saw fit, as long as I spent them becoming "accomplished," by mastering musical instruments, painting and drawing, dancing, embroidering and sewing for my dowry, and studying selected "relevant" subjects like the history of art.

However, my tutors quickly grew to dislike me, for I never practiced anything other than dance and music, and I never studied the subjects they wanted me to. Instead, if I was not out dressed in rags and climbing, I had buried myself in medical books, especially ones on birth disorders. Mother once tried to convince Father to lock up his books so I could not get to them, but he refused and sent her into a sulk. I smiled a bit at the memory.

Aenea tapped me on the shoulder, bringing me to the present.

"You were miles away," she said. "Penny for your thoughts?"

"I was just thinking about how I didn't end up at all like my parents expected me to. I almost can't imagine how scandalized my mother and father would be if they knew what I was doing with myself these days," I said.

"How did they die?" she asked.

I hesitated, and then decided to tell the truth. "I think my parents are dead, but I don't truly know. I was adopted, and I ran away from those who raised me when I found out they had lied to me all of my life." Near enough to the truth.

She said nothing for a time. We sat on a bench and she clasped my hand. "I'm sorry."

"It's fine," I said. "I'm having much more fun in the circus with you than I was having in my old life."

That might have been a lie. I thought of the tea parties I used to have with Anna Yew, of swimming in the pond and pranks played with Cyril. Of dancing with Oswin at the debutante ball. Was it truly better to train until I felt ready to drop, to being ignored or slighted by most of the other circus folk?

But it was still better than what my parents had planned for me.

Aenea's eyes met mine and she leaned against me. Her warm arm pressed against my coat sleeve, and she smelled of rosewater and almond soap.

We walked to the granite fountain in the center of the park. A few leaves, green and edged in brown with the promise of the coming autumn, had fallen and settled into its pool. The fountain was the statue of a mermaid. She was looking upwards, as though underwater and yearning for the surface. Water ran from the top of her head all the way down her body, running off her outstretched hands and the tips of her fins. We ran our fingers through the cool water in the pool.

"Is your name really Aenea?" I asked.

She looked surprised. "Yes. Aenea Harper. Why?"

"Aenea Harper," I said, rolling the name on my tongue. "I don't know. It sounds so ethereal and goes so well with Arik that I thought perhaps it was a stage name."

A little line appeared between her brows. "What does e-theer-eal mean?" she asked, pronouncing the word slightly wrong.

"Ethereal," I corrected automatically. "Oh. Um, otherworldly."

"Ethereal," she said, slowly, memorizing the word. "I suppose it does. My parents were performers. They made sure to give me a name that would sound good on the stage. Arik's name is fake, but his real name is Regar Bupnik, poor man, so it's understandable that he changed it decades ago. I suppose Arik and Aenea do sound good together." She paused. "Micah Grey isn't your real name, is it?"

"No, it's not. I chose a new name when I ran away."

"What's your real name?"

I licked my lips. "Gene."

"Gene," she repeated, cocking her head and looking at me with slightly narrowed eyes, trying to match the new face to the name. "What's your second name?"

My mind blanked. "It, ah, doesn't matter," I said. "It was never really my surname, as they weren't my parents."

She opened her mouth, as if to ask more, but she let it pass. "How did you choose Micah Grey?"

I half-smiled. "I chose it when I came here, actually, the morning after I ran away. I had no idea what to do or where to go." I took her hand and led her to the other side of the fountain. "I stood right here and I stared at the water trickling over the mermaid. The light caught the water and the flecks of mica in the stone. And so that was the name I gave when I joined." I felt silly telling the story now. I could have chosen any stage name, a name with great meaning. Instead, I had liked the sparkle of light on stone and taken my new name from that.

"I like that," she said, her smile brighter than the reflection of the sunlight on the water of the fountain. "Micah Grey. It's fun to say. Mi-cah Grey." She rolled the syllables on her tongue. "It's a good stage name, though I like Gene as well. Has a ring to it. It'd look good on a poster too, I imagine."

I remembered that I had a circus poster folded up in my pocket. I had stolen it because I liked to look at it in my tent in the evenings sometimes. Posters just like it were plastered around Sicion. I brought it out and spread it on my lap. "Perhaps one day it will be on this."

"What does it say?" Aenea asked. "I always wondered. The picture is pretty."

She could not read. I had already lectured her on the meaning of "ethereal." I didn't want to feel like I was showing off my learning.

"Go on," she said. "I've felt too silly to ask anyone, really. I don't know who else in the circus can read anyway, other than Drystan, and I would not ask him."

"Why not?"

"Drystan thinks very highly of himself" was all she

would say, and thinking back, I had never seen them speak often to each other. Had they quarreled?

I knew it would gnaw at me, so I ventured, "Were you two once close?"

She laughed. "No. We merely never had anything in common, and his manner grates on me at times. He is a good clown and a good performer, but I would not count him among my friends or enemies."

Relieved, I returned my attention to the poster.

"The lettering at the top reads 'R.H. Ragona's Circus of Magic' and the smaller part below reads 'The Most Magical Circus of Ellada'." My fingers traced the illustration that took up the middle of the poster. It was well-rendered, with a svelte Bil in full ringmaster regalia, smiling and gesturing at the equestrians, the elephant, the trainer with the whip, the fire eaters, clowns, and the two aerialists swinging far above. "Below it is only a list of the acts. It calls your act 'Arik and Aenea, the fairies of the trapeze'. Not much else, really."

She giggled. "'Fairies of the trapeze?' Bil's having a laugh."

"Makes sense. You're both slight, graceful, and lovely."

She looked at me, eyebrows raised in amusement. "So you think Arik is lovely?"

My blush deepened. "Well, I mean, I meant…"

She leaned close to me. "I know what you meant," she whispered.

Her lips moved toward mine, and for a moment panic thrummed through me. Every bit of me wanted to kiss her, but would I be a girl kissing her, or a boy? And it was dishonest to let her kiss me, without telling her what I was. But just as I was about to closed my eyes and lean in, I saw a group of young men were on the path leading toward us over her shoulder.

I jerked away.

"Oh no," I whispered. Aenea's face fell, hurt by my reaction before she noticed I was staring at people behind her. Her head whipped back, the long swing of brown hair obscuring her face from me. I cursed fate for the timing, yet felt the smallest stirring of relief.

Cyril and his friends walked toward us. And, Sun and Moon, Damien and Oswin were with them. Though this was the closest park to my apartments, they were meant to be studying for the last of their exams. It had been very silly of me to expect they would do so on such a lovely day. I pulled my hat even lower on my forehead, tucking the stray hairs underneath. My hands shook. I could only hope they would not recognize me.

"What?" Aenea asked.

"Nothing," I said, my gaze glued to my brother. I wanted to run to Cyril and throw my arms around him and hug him close, to kiss him on the cheek and tell him how much I missed him and loved him. I had not seen him in two months. He looked much the same. *Keep calm.*

My eyes rose and met Cyril's. His eyes slid away from mine. My shoulders slumped in disappointment and relief. He didn't recognize me.

Rojer Cyprus took a second look at Aenea.

"Why, I say," he exclaimed. "Aren't you the trapeze girl from that circus on the beach?" Rojer always had an extraordinary memory for faces. Names were another matter. I stopped myself from self-consciously smoothing the front of my shirt. *He won't look for what he does not expect to see. He won't see me if my brother doesn't – will he?*

She started, her hand tightening in mine. "Yes," she said guardedly.

"You were brilliant! What's it like, to be in a circus?" he asked, enthusiastic as a puppy.

She relaxed her grip in mine. "It's difficult, but there's nothing better." She smiled at him.

"Have you all been to see the circus, then?" I asked, glancing at Cyril. He looked lost in thought, staring off to the other side of the park. I wanted to hit him over the head and grab his attention, to force him to look at me and *see* me.

Oswin likewise did not seem interested in our conversation. His gaze lingered on Aenea's face. He had danced with me but a few months ago, and played with me countless times over the years, and he did not know me now. He was the boy who might have become my husband. My two lives had collided. I had tested most of these boys on history not long ago, laughed and joked with them as another person. A girl. A great wave of sadness passed over me, as though the old Gene was well and truly gone.

Damien looked interested, but his eyes were only for Aenea. He did not even glance in my direction. The appreciative glance he gave her made my blood boil. I refused to remember our awkward fumblings in the hollowed tree a lifetime ago. I could see Drystan's features echoed in Damien's, now that I knew to look for them.

"Just me and my friends Bart and Damien here so far,"

Rojer said. "I've been trying to convince the others to go, but they're afraid of their mummies and daddies finding out. Are you in the circus too?" he asked. Rojer had always had a frank, open way of speaking. Not good, considering his father was a politician.

I took a deep breath. "Of a sort. I'm new and training on the trapeze as well, but I have not performed yet," I said in tones a little closer to my normal voice. It was enough. Cyril's head whipped around. I met his eyes again and smiled and they widened in shock.

"Tonight is our last performance in Sicion," I said, still looking directly at him. "You should come and see it before we move on."

"Where will you be going next?" Cyril asked.

"Up to Imachara," I said. "Stopping at a village called Cowl along the way to work on our newest acts."

"I will definitely go, if only to see this one in her trapeze costume again," Bartholomew Fir interjected. "What lovely hams!" He looked her up and down. Damien smirked.

"Bart," Cyril admonished. "There's no call."

"You watch your mouth," I said without thinking.

"I think you should watch yours when speaking to a gentleman," Bart said, straightening his waistcoat, which probably cost the equivalent of three months of a miner's wages.

"And a gentleman should be kinder to a lady, sir," I said. He didn't scare me. I had known him since he was a little boy. I had made him cry once, when we were younger. He tried to order me to be the servant in a game, and I had refused and punched him in the nose. Bart had cried for hours and run to his mother, who had declined to invite Cyril and myself over again for several months. He looked like he was about to punch me in the nose this time. I braced myself for the blow.

"You don't have to speak for me, Micah," Aenea said. It was damned lucky she had used my new name and not called me Gene.

Aenea looked straight at Bart, holding herself tall. "As long as you pay the coin to see the show, I don't care if you look at my legs. Look all you like, for it's not as if you'll ever touch them."

My mouth dropped open in shock. The boys whooped and Bart's face colored in anger. "Give it up Bart," Rojer said. "You've Elizabeth Rowan to look forward to."

I looked at Cyril in sympathy. Evidently the courting had not gone according to plan. I fished in my pocket for the poster.

"Here," I said, holding it out in the direction of Cyril, Rojer, and Oswin, the only ones I could stand to look at. "You don't want to miss the most magical circus in El-lada."

"That I don't," Cyril said, taking it, his fingers brushing mine. "I'll come see it tonight."

I looked at him. "Thank you. You won't regret it." I took Aenea's hand in mine again. Cyril's eyes lingered on our intertwined fingers. I supposed for all he knew of me, he had not quite expected me to court a girl.

"Let's go," I said to Aenea.

"With pleasure," she said, tossing the hair from her face.

I fought the urge to look over my shoulder one last

time at Cyril before we left. I let out a shaky breath. None of them seemed to have recognized me except for Cyril. So strange, that my childhood friends could not see past a bit of grime and a patched shirt.

But as we left them behind, Aenea turned on me. "You know those horrible people?"

"Only Bart and Damien are horrible," I said without thinking and pressed my lips together.

"So you do know them."

"I do."

"You know a group of nobles. By first name." Her voice was flat. "Who the Styx are you?"

"I'm Micah Grey now. It doesn't matter who I was before."

"It does matter."

Nerves gnawed at my stomach. "I only knew them because they came to my father's shop. He was a luminary," I said, the lie coming far too easily to my lips. "He sold glass globes like the ones in the circus tent, but more sophisticated. Some of the rarer globes have been shaped, like flowers and dragons and the like. They're very popular with the nobility."

"So why do you know them by first names?"

"When we were younger, our differences in social standing did not matter so much. We would play together sometimes, when their parents came to the shop. Sometimes they'd leave their children there while they did their other shopping, knowing that my mother would keep an eye on them."

She looked away from me. I did not know if she believed me or not. I hated lying to her. I had been lying to her every day, and as we grew closer I could not help feeling that she did not know me at all. How could I know she'd accept who and what I really was? Was I willing to risk losing her? I needed to tell her everything. And soon. But how?

"Let's go. We might be late for practice," she said. I sighed, letting the questions drift away for now.

My hand was still in hers. I did not pull away. "I'm sorry for what he said. You were brilliant though, to stand up to him. He's all talk and bluster. His father's a politician."

She relaxed into my embrace. "That explains a lot."

I laughed. "And besides, it's true, you do have nice legs," I said, shocked at my boldness. I wondered if I was being too forward, but she laughed in surprise and slapped me on the arm. "Come on," I said.

We returned to the circus, hand in hand.

17
SPRING: THE CRACKED TEACUP

"Once, a wolf girl fell in love with a human. She wished and wished that they could be together, and she wished so hard that the Lady of the Moon let three stars fall from the sky and onto the wolf girl's fur. Even though the moon was little more than a scimitar in the sky rather than a full moon, she transformed into a beautiful woman. The Lady cautioned her that she must leave her beastly nature behind and remain a woman, and the former wolf girl promised. She wore three diamonds around her neck.

The man she fell in love with loved her in turn, and they married beneath the light of the full Penmoon, with the girl's pack watching from between the trees.

Their marriage was a happy one, until one night a man crept into their home, aiming to steal all they had. The robber grabbed the diamonds from her neck, and she turned back into a wolf and fell upon the man like the beast that she was. Her husband, though grateful that she saved him, could no longer be with her, and she escaped into the forest, realizing that she was *happier there. Much as one wishes, one cannot escape one's nature."*

"The Man and the Jeweled Wolf," HESTIA'S FABLES

A few nights after the debutante ball, I woke up hungry. I was always hungry during that time of my life. Every morsel of food seemed to go toward helping me grow taller rather than fuller. I crept downstairs to the pantry and made myself a sandwich from the leftover roast from dinner and had a bowl of spiced plums and cream, gulping the food down. I made myself a cup of mint tea to take to my room with me before I fell back asleep. When I was nearly to the servants' staircase, I heard voices from the parlor. I recognized my parents' voices, raised in anger. They must have been there as I passed earlier, but had not been shouting. I thought I heard my name.

I pressed my ear to the crack in the door.

"Of course this is what must be done," Mother said, her voice firm.

"None of the others suggested such a radical course."

"That's because all of the specialists we have seen are useless and have recommended nothing at all!"

"Nothing like this has been done before. We don't know the risks. What if it makes things worse?"

"How can it be worse than it is now? As time passes, she is growing more masculine. I see her changing right before my eyes. The Hawthornes have made an offer for Iphigenia's hand for Oswin. This is our only chance to make things right. For Iphigenia to marry as a woman."

My stomach tightened.

"Perhaps things are already right. Perhaps Iphigenia is

meant to be masculine rather than feminine, or somewhere in the middle," Father said. "Perhaps we are being too hasty in marrying her off to the first family to make an offer, even with their good standing. You're so quick to see the worst in everything. This is how Iphigenia was made. I believe it is the will of the Couple."

"Yes, yes," Mother said, and her dress swished as she paced the room. "I know you think Iphigenia is special how she is, and that is why you agreed to take her into our household without my consent, merely because some doctor came into your office and begged."

My tea cup fell to the plush carpet, bounced, and the mint tea bled over the Arrasian hall rug.

Father sighed. I could just imagine his round form reclining on the settee, a hand stroking his whiskers, the other holding the pipe he was never without in the evenings. A short glass of brandy would be on the bedside table. He was up late every night in that study, reading a book of law or history. I had always found it amusing that he conformed in nearly every way to the stereotype of what a lawyer and minor nobleman was meant to be like. Perhaps he cultivated that image, like Mother did with the inflections of her voice.

"He hardly begged," the man I had thought to be my father said. "He reasoned, very logically. You could not have a second child. You were elated until you discovered her... condition."

"An' you were mighty grateful for the money he threw at you for her," Mother said, her cultured tones roughening about the edges.

"As I recall, you were far more interested in that than

me. You were so proud about that extra title, for the possibility of an estate in the Emerald Bowl."

I could not even blink.

"I am grateful for that money. And I'm grateful for Iphigenia. You know that. But I'm not grateful that as soon as we discovered what she was, this Doctor Pozzi was suddenly nowhere to be found. Yes, it is a condition. A condition that now has a cure."

"I'm still not convinced this is a cure."

"Iphigenia can become a girl. Only a girl. Doctor Ambrose is positive that the surgery would be successful. She'd have a bit of scarring, but he says it will be minimal. Between that and some daily medication, she would be female."

"I don't think Gene could ever be wholly female, considering how fond she is of boyish things, especially as of late. Besides, wouldn't removing... half... affect her in some way?"

"It may result in her not enjoying the marital bed as much as another woman..." She cleared her throat, embarrassed at mentioning such an indelicate subject. "But at least she would have a chance at a marital bed!"

I could not breathe. My vision swam and I slumped against the wood paneling of the hallway. I cupped my hands between my legs and shuddered. I did not like what I was, but I liked this proposed cure even less. Deep down, I had known that one day it might have come to this.

"You do have a point," Father said grudgingly. "No man will want her as she is." Tears pricked my eyes as I thought of Damien. He had not wanted me.

"We are financially secure as of now, but if we have to keep Iphigenia on as a spinster her whole life, she will be a drain."

My breath caught in a muffled sob. I pressed my fingers so hard against my lips the edges of my teeth almost cut my mouth.

"That still won't begin to negate the money we were given. I don't like this. What if we were not meant to do this to Iphigenia?"

"Then he would have said something to you about it. Iphigenia was probably a child he fathered on a woman he was not meant to, and the Couple created her like this as a punishment, and the man decided to make her our burden to bear."

A hot tear slid down my cheek.

She sighed. "You don't have to like it, Stuart. You just have to realize it is the best thing for Iphigenia. You want what's best for her, don't you?" Her voice became sly and wheedling, and I knew my fate was sealed. With enough effort, Mother could get Father to agree to anything.

I darted up the stairs, not caring that I had left the teacup on the floor.

I awoke far too early the next morning, hoping that it had all been a dream. I lay in bed, curled into a small ball beneath the covers, convinced that it had been a horrible nightmare. The husband and wife downstairs breaking their fast together were the man and woman who had born me. Cyril was my brother. The doctor did not have a cure.

I slid out of the warm cocoon of my bed and tiptoed

down the hall. I pressed my ear to the crack in Cyril's door and heard his soft snoring. It was just dawn.

My worst fears were confirmed. The teacup was still on the floor. It had rolled into the corner of the hallway, which was lucky. If it had not, Mother and Father would have seen it when they left the study. The mint tea had not left a stain on the rug – another stroke of luck.

I picked up the teacup. A crack ran along its side. Cradling it in my hand, I took it to my room and sat on my bed. This innocuous little teacup proved that my entire family was not my family, that I was a strange unwanted freak born to an unknown man and an unknown woman. That whether I stayed or whether I left, my life was about to change.

The sun continued to rise and stream through the windows of my room. I looked around with new eyes. How many of my possessions had been bought with the doctor's money? My desk with its delicately carved legs and large, etched mirror? The little pots of cosmetics that I never touched? The large bed and its canopy, the blue damask curtains? The wardrobe filled with uncomfortable, stiff dresses?

Anna's words came to me, her voice echoing in my head: *You've gone up two titles in the past ten years! It's rare for families to move so quickly after being at the same level for so long.*

And why did a doctor give me away? With a sudden twist of dread, I wondered: was I nothing more than an experiment?

"Iphigenia!" Lia called through the door, startling me from my thoughts.

"Gene," I corrected her. I hid the broken teacup under a pillow.

"Good morning, love. I awoke a little later than usual today. I will have to dress you quickly."

Lia opened the wardrobe and took out a brown linen dress with dark blue velvet piping. I smiled; it was my favorite.

"Not too tight today," I said as she laced my corset. "My stomach has been upset."

"I thought you seemed a little unwell this morning," Lia said.

"Just a bit of a sore belly," I said. "I'll be fine."

As Lia brushed my waist-length hair, I fingered my pots of cosmetics until I came across the flesh-colored one for "hiding imperfections." I dabbed some beneath my eyes and smoothed it with my fingertips until I looked a little more human.

Lia did not say anything, seeming to realize that I was not myself. She plaited my hair into a plain queue. When she was finished, she gave my shoulders a squeeze, a quick kiss on the cheek, and left to do her other morning chores.

My family was all silent at the breakfast table. I did not know what to call them in my head anymore. They were not my mother, my father, or my brother. What were they? Calling them Stuart and Veronica sounded wrong. I gave up. Mother and Father snuck looks at me in between bites of porridge. Cyril noticed the tension, perplexed, but focused on his food. With the cast on his right arm, it was harder for him to eat.

I barely touched my porridge and left the table as soon

as I could. During my lessons, I did not pay attention and doodled instead, drawing crude renditions of my parents with coins for eyes looking at a baby, a dark man in shadow behind them.

That afternoon, Father returned from work early and came to see me in the drawing room. I was half-heartedly playing a song on the piano, but the piano was out-of-tune and my tempo uneven. The song trailed off when he entered.

"Hello, Iphigenia," he said and paused. I looked at him, wondering what he wanted.

"Hello, Father."

"I had the afternoon off and thought I would come home to see you. Would you like to go have an ice cream, like we used to?"

Going for an ice cream was a fond childhood memory. There was a parlor not far from where we lived and we had gone every week after church, just me and him and Cyril, if he did not go somewhere else with his friends. It had been over five years since we had last gone.

"Of course, Father," I said, but my stomach sank in dread.

Father already had the carriage ready. I put on my bonnet, my gloves, and my cloak and climbed into the carriage. Father sat across from me, hands folded across his bulbous stomach. He cleared his throat a couple of times as if he were about to speak, but in the end remained silent. I stared out of the window, swaying with the motion of the carriage.

We walked into the ice cream parlor. A few young suitors were there, the nobles with a guardian pretending not to notice the way the lovers' fingers intertwined under the table. Three children were happily eating sundaes in the corner with either their mother or a nanny, though more of the ice cream had managed to splatter their faces than reach their stomachs.

The young waitress came over and father ordered two dishes of ice cream with caramel and chocolate sauce, sprinkled with walnuts and dried cherries. I was touched that he remembered what we used to order five years ago, but I no longer liked walnuts.

I ate a couple of spoonfuls of my ice cream when it came and I ate the walnuts anyway, though their bitterness ruined the dish. Father ate most of his before setting down the spoon.

"We have not been able to talk much as of late, you and I," he said, his moustache twitching. "All of a sudden you have grown so much. You are almost an adult, now."

"Not quite yet," I said. The knot was returning to my stomach, and I wish I had not had the ice cream. The cloying sweetness lingered on the roof of my mouth.

"You are almost of an age to be betrothed," my father said.

"We both know that may be a little difficult to achieve," I said, forcing my voice to stay even.

"It may not be so difficult as that," he said. "You have had an offer or two already."

Yes. Oswin Hawthorne. I could not believe their family had already made an offer. Had Oswin asked them to? The night at the debutante ball with him had been enjoyable, but not particularly romantic. Not yet. But the Hawthornes were of a higher social standing than ours...

I looked closely at my father. Just how much money had Father received for taking me into his home? And how had they done so without the entire nobility finding out? There had been rumors of my mother disappearing from society for several months and returning with me. People had been surprised; she had not looked pregnant when she left.

"Who has made an offer?" I asked.

"Now, now, they have not been acted upon quite yet, as we thought it too early," he said, interrupting my thoughts. "But next year, I think, will be soon enough," he continued. "In the meantime, you must fill your dowry chest. Your mother tells me you have fallen behind in your embroidery."

"I have been practicing music and sketching more, Father." I managed to say. My fingers gripped the edges of the table until my nails blanched.

"Well and good, my dear. Well and good."

I toyed with my spoon. My hands were shaking. I used to yearn for a close relationship with my father, but I had given up on the dream long ago. We were different creatures.

"Your mother and I will both take you to your appointment tomorrow," Father said, taking another bite of ice cream.

Dread rose within me. "Why?"

"To support you. I feel I have not been involved enough with… those proceedings." He was very good at dancing around a subject without saying what it was directly. I supposed that was why he won many cases despite seeming out of touch with reality most of the time.

"What will my appointment entail?" I asked, determined to be more direct.

"It's just another appointment. A consultation, if you
will," he said, smiling and shrugging, the spoon in one hand.

He was lying. I looked into his face, his seemingly can-
did eyes. He was a good liar, but I could tell.

"Can I visit Anna Yew after the appointment tomorrow?" I asked.

"You may be a little tired after the appointment. It would
be best if you came straight home with us," he said, benign.

I felt so sick to my stomach that, had I been standing,
I would have doubled over.

They were going to operate on me tomorrow, and they
were not planning on telling me.

"Cyril!" I said, shaking him awake.

"Hnngh," he groaned, and turned over.

"Cyril! Wake up!" I said, my voice girlishly high.

"What is it?"

"You… you have to help me run away." Tears were
streaming down my face and dripping onto the covers. I
had managed to keep myself together during the day – in
the carriage returning from the ice cream parlor, during
tea time, as Lia undressed me for the night – but my control had collapsed.

"What?" he sat up and rubbed at his face, and when he
saw me, he started. "Gene? What happened? What's the
matter?"

"I… I… I have to get away. Tonight. Now. Right now!"
I sat on the bed and wrapped my arms around my legs,
desperate to hold in the tears, but failing.

"Gene," he said, gripping my shoulders. "Gene, look at me." I did, and the concern in his eyes undid me over again and I began to sob. He shook me. "Tell me what happened so I can help."

I took a deep breath, focused, and tried to bring the tattered edges of myself together. "Last night, I woke up, and I was hungry, so I went downstairs to have something to eat. On the way back, I heard Mother and Father arguing. It was about me. Cyril, they're not my parents. Some doctor called Pozzi gave me to them when I was a baby. He gave them a lot of money. I'm not your sister, or your brother, or any sort of sibling." My voice cracked.

"Oh, Gene," he said, stroking my head. "I'm so sorry." I did not think he knew, but he might have suspected.

Looking at him, I wondered why I had never questioned my heritage before. Cyril has both fair hair and skin, and light blue eyes. He was bulky and strong. I had auburn hair and hazel eyes. I turned golden with the slightest bit of sun, and I was whippet-thin. Cyril's features echoed Father's, whereas I looked little like either parent.

"You're still my sibling," he said, and folded me into his arms. I buried my head into his shoulder. "That's no reason to run away," he told me.

"It gets worse," I whispered into his neck. "They were arguing about the doctor I went to see the other day. Evidently Doctor Ambrose thinks he knows how to... fix me."

"Fix you?" Cyril echoed.

"They're going to turn me into a girl. A *complete* girl."

"But how can they do that?"

"They want to… cut the male part off."

Cyril winced and hugged me closer. He breathed a shaky sigh. "You don't have to do it, though. They wouldn't force you."

"They would."

"Can you think about this for a bit, first? They won't do this tomorrow."

"No, they will."

"What?"

"Father took me to the ice cream parlor today."

"He hasn't done that in ages!" His eyes widened.

"I know. They've had an offer from… a family." I could not tell him that it was for his best friend. "Father said both he and Mother would bring me to the appointment with Doctor Ambrose tomorrow. He said it was a consultation. I think he was lying. No, I am sure that he was lying. The operation is tomorrow, and they do not plan on telling me before I go."

Gently, he pushed me away and left the bed and began to rummage through the drawers of his desk. Mother had recently bought him a large, manly one of laurel wood.

"What are you doing?"

Cyril took out a small bag that clinked. "Pocket money from the past six months. I was saving up to get Elizabeth Rowan a locket as a courting gift. Here."

"Cyril, you don't have to… I have a little money."

"Gene, you have no concept of money in the outside world. Our pocket money combined will only last you a month or two at most, and we're lucky we have that."

Dread grew within me. "Cyril, what am I going to do? Where am I going to go?" My voice wavered.

His shoulders slumped. "I have no idea. Please, Gene. Are you sure you should go?"

I shuddered. "I'd rather go and make my own way than have it decided for me."

"It would be easier to stay." He did not want to let me go.

"It would not be easier to go through my entire life as a girl. I do not feel like a girl. Or a boy."

He gave me another hug. "I know. I like you how you are." Cyril rummaged in his wardrobe and brought out a box of old clothes. "These fit me last year. They should fit you well enough now." I pulled my nightgown over my head and pulled on a plain tunic, trousers, and a long woolen coat. As I changed, Cyril saw me naked. I did not turn away from him. He did not say a word and I did not know what he was thinking.

We would soon be of a similar height, but the clothes were still too big in the shoulders and the waist. Cyril found me a belt.

I dashed into my own room across the hall and put on my own stockings and leather boots. I started throwing things into a leather satchel – a plain dress in case I needed to be female, my own small bag of coins, some jewelry that might be worth something, my diary, and a small knife. Next, I went to the bathing room and gathered soap, a hairbrush, and a toothbrush.

Cyril was gone when I returned to his room to pack a spare set of male clothing. He entered a moment later, his arms full of hastily-wrapped parcels of food. And, somehow, he managed to stuff them into my already-brimming satchel. I slipped his coin purse into my pocket, spied scissors on his desk and picked them up. I held them out to him.

"My hair," I said. "No boy has hair to his waist. But leave it as long as you can. Just in case." I turned around.

Hair fell around me, slithering in waves down my arms and hands.

Once he was done, I looked into his small shaving mirror as Cyril tidied up the mass of hair on the floor. Cyril had made a horrific mess. My hair hung, lank and jagged. I took the scissors and evened it some, and then I pulled it into a tail at the nape of my neck. I put on a cap.

I turned out to be a better boy than I thought I would. I looked like a very young sixteen year-old. I slid the satchel onto my shoulders and gave the clothing a last brush of stray hairs. Cyril turned me around and looked at me, his hands still resting on my shoulders.

"Be careful, Gene."

"Don't worry about me, Cyril. I'll find my way." I smiled and hoped that I looked brave. "I'll write as Elizabeth Rowan's cousin, Euan. He'd never actually write and they will think it's him passing on courting news. I'll disguise my handwriting."

His eyes softened. "I'll be fine. This is better. Thank you, brother." I wrapped my arms around his neck and hugged him tight, wondering when I would see him again.

"I love you, Gene. Don't you ever forget that. If you need me to come for you, if you need help, or money, or anything – write to me."

I nodded. "I will."

Cyril ran his fingers through his hair. Both of our eyes were misty. "Won't the servants hear the front door?" he said, trying to smile. It fell a little short.

"Remember the construction at the Elm residence below?"

Cyril squinted and frowned. "The scaffolding?"

I gave him an impish smile in return.

"Gene!" Cyril said, his frown turning to a smile and he laughed in spite of himself.

I went to the window and opened it. I turned and said, "Goodbye for now, Cyril. You will see me again. I promise."

I climbed out the window and started down the scaffolding and into the cool morning mist. Cyril put his head out after me, gave me a little wave, and watched, but remained silent. When I was at the bottom, I looked up, but Cyril was lost in the fog. I waved back, unsure if he could see me, and I set off on my own.

18
SUMMER: THE NEWEST PERFORMER

"I think, even at the tail end of my career, I still had that last, heady rush before I stepped out onto the stage. The quiet just before you begin a performance. Trusting your body to move exactly as it should. It's like the same rush as a dark cloud of Lerium smoke. It curls about you and works its way deep into your lungs. I still suffer withdrawals, and I think I will until I die."

from THE MEMOIRS OF THE SPARROW,
Aerialist Diane Albright

We found Arik packing his bags when we returned to the cart.

Aenea's face fell. She had been hoping that Arik would change his mind. My stomach sank as well. The trapeze act was easily the most impressive part of the circus, and while I could now do basic tricks and balancing, it would take years before I was anywhere near as talented as Arik, even with age slowing him down.

"Have you told him, then?" Aenea asked.

"Yes, I told him."

He moved stiffly and I noticed a bandage around his knee. "You're hurt!"

He smiled. "No more so than usual."

Aenea and I exchanged glances.

"I ended up being too afraid to tell Bil to stick his tyrannical ways right up his ever-expanding behind."

We giggled. "So why the bandage?" I asked.

"I've pled that I suffered an injury last night that has tragically cut short my dwindling career." He placed the back of his hand against his forehead in mock distress.

"And Bil believed you?"

Arik laughed, showing his yellowing teeth. "I enlisted some outside help. Dr Hollybranch agreed to affirm my condition for only a small parting of coin." Dr Hollybranch was the resident physician for the circus when we were in Sicion. He was the illegitimate half-brother of the current Lord Holly, but he did well enough for himself, though the family had probably paid for his medical training.

I smiled back despite my sadness at him leaving.

Aenea returned to her cart and I changed in mine – turning away from Arik and leaving my undershirt on – and walked toward the big top for practice. Arik stayed to "rest his leg" and finish packing, but he promised to say a final farewell before he made his way to his little room in Sicion.

Boldly, I clasped Aenea's hand and we walked into the circus together. There were a couple of raised eyebrows in our direction at this – Drystan's among them – but no one said a word or looked particularly astonished.

Bil was red in the face, which meant that he was drunk

and angry, but not at anyone in particular. It was when his face went purple that someone was going to be in trouble.

"As you all have probably heard by now, you useless bunch of gossips," he said, pointing his cane accusingly at his audience, "there's a major hiccup in tonight's plans. The last circus in a city is meant to be the best. But now half of our final act cannot perform."

Eyes fell on Aenea and me. "I can perform just fine on my own," Aenea said. "I've done solo acts before."

"The poster says that there are two performers! Two performers flying over my head in the illustration! There must, therefore, be two bloody performers!"

He sounded like a child in a tantrum, but a very large, very hairy child. I half-expected him to stamp his foot and start wailing.

"These things happen in circuses," Aenea said, keeping her voice even.

"Not in my circus! I let you take on this whelp and train him up because I knew Arik was wearing at the seams."

"Micah's only been with us two months," Aenea protested.

"I saw you both the other day. He's learned quickly."

"Not quickly enough that I would trust him to catch me sixty feet off the ground!"

I felt a little hurt at this. I would not drop her.

"This seems unwise," Drystan said, standing up from the gaggle of clowns. "Micah has made amazing progress in so few months, but it would be bad form if we ended our last circus with an… accident." He let the words hang in the air.

Bil's face reddened, dangerously close to purple.

Drystan endeavored to salvage the situation. "Why don't we have Aenea and Micah perform the final act this afternoon in practice, on the trapeze and with nets? If they perform without mishap, then they perform tonight. Without nets."

Bil's face lightened a bit, and he brought a hand up to his chin. He liked a wager. Mentally, I applauded how well Drystan was able to manipulate Bil to his own desires. I smiled at him gratefully, and the white clown stuck his tongue out at me in response.

"Aye, I like this bet," Bil said. "Do you both agree with the stakes?"

"Yes," I said immediately. "Yes, yes, yes."

Aenea hesitated, and I looked at her, pleadingly. "Aenea, I can do this."

In her eyes, I saw a flicker of doubt. "Let's see how you do at practice," she said, and she gave me her hand. "Holding my hand here in the bleachers is one thing, but sixty feet above the circus floor is another."

The platform at the top of the trapeze felt twice as high and the platform under my feet felt like it had shrunk in half. It had only been two months ago that I had been so foolish, to jump and catch a trapeze with no training.

Aenea was tiny on her platform at the far side of the big tent, a small, pale face and a smudge of brown hair. The nets spread out below us like a web. I had practiced until my muscles ached and trembled and withstood the circus ignoring me, all for this. For another chance to fly.

"Combination one," Aenea called across to me.

"On three!" I called back, clutching the trapeze bar.

"I'll count!"

"If you wish!"

"One... two... three!"

We jumped.

It was better than I had remembered. The warm, stale air of the circus tent whooshed past my face. My legs held rigid and my toes pointed down toward the tiny circus performers below. I swung.

I kicked and pulled myself into a sitting position on the bar. I had grown much stronger over the past few months. I had not turned bulky, but my muscles were well-defined and the little bit of fat I had around my stomach and thighs was long gone.

Aenea and I swept past each other, both of us balancing on one leg. I flipped backward so that I hung inverted by the crook of my knees. I reached the peak of my arc, held there weightless in the air for a glorious moment, and swung down, picking up speed with the wind whistling in my ears. Aenea swung down from the far side. I reached out–

This was a test of trust. If Aenea hesitated, if she was not sure I could catch her, then our act would not work if there was ever a shred of doubt. We had practiced this routine plenty of times, ten to fifteen feet off of the floor on lowered trapezes. At this point, I could almost do it blindfolded. But she needed to trust me, not at ten feet, but at sixty feet.

Aenea leapt, stretched, and reached. Her hands caught my wrists and mine hers. We flew through the air. I grinned down at her and she beamed just as widely. I could feel her pulse thumping in my palms.

We performed a simple routine, child's play compared to Aenea and Arik's former acts. A catch, a few twirls on the trapeze bar, and hanging from the arms and the knees. Nothing fancy. No mid-air twirls and somersaults by me on my trapeze.

It felt ten times better to be six times higher off the ground. We swung onto our respective platforms on either side of the tightrope and bowed. The performers applauded below. On a whim, I began to make my way across the tightrope, trying to walk as naturally as if I were on the ground.

Aenea shifted to make room for me as I joined her on her platform. "You have a flair for the dramatic, don't you?" she whispered.

I wasn't sure if she was angry at me or not. She relaxed and smiled at me. "Good job, Micah."

"I had good teachers."

She turned and began to climb down the ladder. I followed, my spirits as high as we had been as we flew together on the trapeze.

Bil slapped us on the backs when we reached the ground again.

"You've been busy, my little starlings!" he said. "Looks like we have a final act."

I looked ridiculous in my costume.

It was one of Arik's. We were of a similar height but his shoulders were wider than mine and his shirt hung on me like a cape. Frit helped take in the seams, but it still did not look quite right.

"What are these?" she said, touching the bandages

around my chest, though she knew. The bandages were not visible, but she could feel them. I pulled away from her touch.

"Violet grazed me the other week," I said. "I didn't want anyone to think me clumsy, so I didn't tell anyone."

"Is that why you needed something for the pain?" she asked. Her eyes were as just as shrewd and calculating as they had been on that night when I caught her with her hand deep in the circus safe. She did not like that I knew her secret. I did not like that she knew mine, or a portion of it.

"Partly yes," I said. My heart was hammering beneath the bandages. Over the past two months, my breasts had grown enough that I could never get away without strapping them down. I had to wake up before Arik every morning, hunching in the darkest corner of the cart and hoping he would not wake as I adjusted the strips of cloth. They were uncomfortable, the skin beneath chafed and red.

"You should let me take a look at them. Cat scratches can become easily infected, and it must have gotten you badly to need so many bandages."

"It's almost healed now. I can probably take off the bandages within the next couple of days," I said. "Please don't worry about it. But thank you."

"Hmm," she said, and threaded the needle. She paused before stitching, as if she were about to ask me something else. But she did not. She left as soon as she had finished. I let out the breath I did not know I had been holding.

Aenea entered and looked me up and down. "You look the part. How do you feel?"

"I'm nervous. And excited. It feels the same. And I look like an idiot."

She took my hands in hers. "You don't have to do this if you don't feel ready. And you don't look like an idiot, either."

I squeezed her hands. "Aenea, I'm ready. I've been climbing high off the ground since I was ten. You've taught me well. We'll be fine."

She took a deep breath. "Let me paint your face."

"Why do you two do that? It's not like anyone can see your faces, that high up."

"They see our faces when we walk onto the stage and when we come down. It adds to the overall effect. Come now, it won't offend your manly sensibilities, will it?"

I watched her face as she applied the paint. She was so trusting and so open with me, and I had repaid her with lies. Nausea roiled in my stomach. My eyes focused on her lips. I wanted to kiss them. Desperately. But I was too frightened.

"Done," she said, setting the brush aside. "You have rather delicate features for a man."

The queasiness grew worse. To cover it, I stuck my tongue out at her. "So I look like a woman, you're saying?"

She stuck hers back at me. "No, but you're pretty rather than ruggedly handsome. I like it, don't fret."

I reached for her hand. She squeezed my palm, the calluses rough and hard. "I have to paint myself. I'll see you during the act."

"Do you trust me?" I asked. "On the trapeze?"

"Yes, of course," she said. She turned away and left, and I hoped she was not lying to put me at ease.

• • • •

It was such a strange feeling, to be behind the stage about to go on.

The other performers treated me differently now that I was one of them. They looked at me rather than through me. Some told me to "break a bone," and a Kymri tumbler even clapped me on the shoulder. It was a bit unnerving to so quickly become noticed again.

My unease grew as each act came on. Not only was I finally having the chance to perform on the trapeze, but Cyril was in the audience, watching. I peeked out of the tent flap and saw him sitting in the expensive seats. I stretched and tried to keep my breathing even.

I wish we could have talked on our own. There was so much I wanted to say. I had sent a few letters, but they were all in heavy code and signed as Euan Rowan. We'd have to find a better way to communicate. I had started countless other letters to him, both in code and not, but they were still half-finished in my pack. I kept putting off finishing them, telling myself I would finish the next day, afraid that he would judge me, or that Mother and Father would open his mail. What must he have thought happened to me, with only my infrequent, cryptic letters as clues?

I took a deep breath. *He knows well enough now*, I thought. *Focus on the present.*

Aenea was next to me the entire time. We did not speak, but we had our arms around each other. Aenea ran her fingers along my arm when she noticed how badly I was shaking. Unfortunately, that only made me shiver more.

Finally, it was our turn. "Here we go," Aenea said as we dusted chalk onto our hands.

We walked onto the stage hand in hand. People cheered and I felt a heady rush. My mind seemed to float away, but my body knew what to do. Aenea and I climbed our respective ladders toward the platforms. The gramophone played its cheery, brassy tunes. I looked down toward Cyril, but he was merely another pale dot in the crowd. I grabbed my trapeze. Aenea nodded at me from across the big tent and we swung from our platforms.

The wooden bar of the trapeze was smooth beneath my chalked fingers. My eyes caught the glare of the bright glass globes. There was a rushing in my ears. I reached the peak of my swing, flipped upside down on my bar, and began the long swing down. It was the first time I had looked at the floor far below from the perch of my trapeze and not through a net. A touch of vertigo spun away in my chest. I reached for Aenea.

Aenea flipped off of her trapeze and I caught her. She climbed atop of me and we swung on the trapeze, back and forth, back and forth, before she jumped to her own swing, flipping around the wooden bar and distracting the audience from the fact that I could not do much except catch.

After the trapeze act was finished, Aenea crossed the tightrope. I hung from my trapeze from one knee, arms and leg posed. I still both hated and loved to watch her do it. She looked so delicate, like a strong gust of wind could blow her away. She met my gaze and lost her balance slightly, wavering on the rope. I gasped, powerless on my trapeze. She was right in the middle of the tightrope.

The parasol danced toward the ground. Aenea was flapping her arms, nowhere near graceful, desperately trying to keep her balance. She fell. I cried out. The audience below gasped.

But one strong hand caught the rope. She hung, feet dangling. Sweat had melted her makeup into white rivulets. Her other hand reached up and grasped the rope. She hung there, panting. Cheers erupted beneath her. Most of them probably thought it was part of the act.

"Aenea!" I swung onto one of the wooden platforms. "Do you need me to come help you?" My throat was tight.

"No, no, I'm all right," she said, her voice faint. She folded her body up and wrapped her legs around the rope and made her way awkwardly to my platform, much like I had made my way across the tightrope when I auditioned for the circus. When she was close enough I helped her off of the tightrope and hugged her close. More applause sounded from below. I cupped her face in my hands.

"Are you alright? What happened?" She was shaking, and so was I.

"I don't know. I just slipped. It's fine. It's happened from time to time. I always catch myself. It makes the show more interesting." Her smile quavered. "Let's get down from here."

"You first." She nodded and began to make her way down the ladder, and I followed behind.

She held her hands up and bowed when she reached the ground, and the circus audience yelled and stamped their feet, startling the elephant in the animal tent into a trumpet. I followed and bowed as well, though I wanted to get off of the stage as quickly as possible. When I returned to the stage for the grand finale bow, Cyril was beaming at me. I was proud of what I had done, but the entire performance was soured by what had almost been.

I left the big top as soon as I could, my patched coat thrown over my costume. I still wore my smudged face paint. Aenea had left quicker than I had, and I ambled about the carnival – attracting odd looks – not expecting to find her. She would be in her cart, and she wanted to be alone.

The loud music of the funfair, and the chatter and press of the people made me feel claustrophobic. A man in a bowler hat almost tripped me with his cane as he hurried past. The juggler nearly hit me with the dolls he tossed about for three little girls with ribbons in their hair. I staggered from the crowd and fled to the relative quiet of the beach.

With my sharp hearing, I could tell someone was following me from a long way off. From the stride, I also guessed who it was. I waited in the damp sand for my brother to catch up with me.

Cyril, his broken arm long healed, swept me into a tight hug, not caring that I smelled of sweat and that he was getting greasepaint all over his cheek and the neck of his coat. I hugged him just as hard, tears streaming down my face and blurring the cosmetics further. My brother was here. My brother.

"Cyril," I murmured. "I've missed you so."

He released me and looked down at me, though he did not have to look down much. We were almost of a height.

"You look so different, and yet just the same," he said, tousling my hair.

"You look just the same," I said, and he did. His golden locks curled about his face, and his cheeks were rosy with the salty breeze.

"Are the others here?" I asked him, meaning Oswin and his other friends.

"No, none of them were actually brave enough to sneak out."

"How'd you manage?" I asked.

"I used a trick of my sister's and used the scaffolding." He half-smiled.

"You're not too afraid to climb anymore? After what happened?"

He shook his head. "I reckon I won't climb on Penglass again anytime soon, but normal scaffolding is just fine."

I hugged him again, breathing in Cyril's comforting smell and the lavender soap that the servants used to wash our clothes. The one person I didn't have to pretend with about anything. My truest, closest friend.

"How have you been, Gene? It was such a shock to see you in the park today, and I couldn't think of anything to say in front of the others that wouldn't give it all away. And seeing you tonight... wow, Gene. Just wow. You were incredible."

"I'm fine, Cyril, really," I said, and I told him of my time in the circus, glossing over the crueler of the pranks and my fear that Frit knew who I was. "It's wonderful, here, truly. And being an aerialist – it feels like what I was always meant to do. I'm not sitting about, waiting for decisions to be made about me. I'm out there, doing them."

Cyril's smile faded. "That's great, Gene. But... do you know what it's been like for us, since you left?"

I grew unnaturally still. "No," I whispered. I imagined that both parents would be angry at my leaving and scared for my well-being, and that perhaps they missed me... but Cyril's voice sounded as though it were more than that.

"Mother and Father are in a spot of trouble with the law. You saw the newspaper article, didn't you?"

I nodded.

"Well, the Constabulary still thinks it's rather suspicious that they didn't report your disappearance for a few days. I'm not sure why they didn't, either. I suppose they thought you would come back. That's – that's what I thought would happen."

My stomach twisted with guilt.

"They've been fined quite a lot. And Mother has been beside herself with worry."

I blinked at him in surprise.

"She can be tough on us, Gene, but she's barely left her bed since you left, and she's developed a cough that won't go away. She finished off the laudanum for my arm. She ranted at me once, when she was on it. Mother blames herself for driving you away. She's moved into the old nursery and doesn't sleep in the same bed as Father anymore. She seems unwell, Gene."

I felt as though someone had punched me in the gut. Mother had often been so cold, I almost expected her to be relieved that I was gone. No longer did she have to worry about me shaming the family by doing something too boyish, or worry about finding me a suitable husband and avoiding scandal. So stupid of me – a daughter running away was scandal enough. But a traitorous thought twisted through my mind.

"Are you sure she's worried, or is she frightened?"

"What do you mean?"

"A doctor gave them a lot of money for me. What if he's mad that they were going to cut me, and that I ran away?"

A sudden thought occurred to me: had the doctor been planning to come for me? I pressed the back of my hand against my mouth, fearful that I would puke.

He considered. "Maybe she's a little frightened. But I don't think it's only that, Gene. I think she misses you, and regrets how she handled things."

I did not know what to say to that. "And Father?"

Cyril shrugged. "He seems much the same as he always is, but he drinks more in the evenings. He's sharp as ever in court when I go with him, but otherwise it feels as though he's going through the motions."

I squeezed my eyes shut and bowed my head.

"I think you should come home, Gene."

I felt torn in twain. Realistically, I knew that I probably should. It was the life I always thought I was going to lead. When I left, I had not wanted to hurt anyone, and yet my whole family missed me as much as I missed them. They were in trouble because of me. But when I tried to imagine actually going back to life as Iphigenia Laurus, I could not. I was a different person now.

"I'm not Gene anymore," I whispered.

"What?"

"I'm Micah Grey. I'm not Gene Laurus, and I'm not sure if I could be her again, Cyril."

He looked away from me. "You could try," he said, as if ashamed to utter the words.

"I could try, but then I'd lose all that I gained here. If I left the circus just after I've become a performer, they'll hire someone else. Someone with more experience as an aerialist." I stepped away from him and ran a hand over my face. "I don't know what the right choice is. It feels selfish to stay, but at the same time, I don't feel I should have to sacrifice all I have gained to return to a life where I don't belong. I wasn't happy as Iphigenia, Cyril. I mean, I love you and many people from my old life, and I mourn not seeing them every day. But… it never felt right. And I feel that this new life is right more and more each day. Can you understand?"

Cyril's shoulders slumped. "It's what I thought you would say. But I had to try. I wish you would come back, though I understand why you don't want to. For me…" He trailed off and stared at the sea. "I feel trapped, sometimes, like you did. But not enough that I would consider leaving. Maybe I'm just not brave enough."

I laid my hand on his shoulder, and remembered a proverb. "We all have different paths to follow. No matter which fork we take, it's going to be difficult."

"You'll still write to me, won't you?"

"Of course," I said. "As much as I can, though I'll have to write in a certain code and leave many things out. But I'll find a way to always let you know where I am and what I'm doing. And whenever I'm in Sicion, I'll come visit you, and if you're in Imachara any time this summer, you should come visit me as well. All right?"

"It's a promise," he said.

I took his hand and squeezed. "And don't worry about me, Cyril. I always land on my feet."

He stayed a while longer and we talked of lighter subjects. But when he left and I saw his wide back disappearing up the beach, it was all I could do not to run after him and say I would return, despite the difficulty, just to be with my brother again.

19
SPRING: A MUDLARK'S SICION

"Good morn, Good morn.
  The Sun Lord peeks his head,
  bidding 'good morn, good morn'.

Good bye, Good bye,
The Moon Lady waves her hand,
bidding, 'good bye, good bye'.

Good day, good day,
Bid the clouds and the stars
As they pass overhead.
exclaiming, 'What a good, new day'."

GOOD MORNING, LIA'S SONG FOR
LADY IPHIGENIA LAURUS

I wandered alone through the city of Sicion, fascinated by previously forbidden streets and sights I had only seen from behind carriage windows. It was an hour before dawn and I explored alleys choked with homeless men and women, through dark parks with rustling bushes, and along pungent docks. Not once did I reach for the small knife in my pocket. Knowing what I do now, I would never have walked through that area of town without a weapon in my hand.

I had walked in the city dressed as a boy before when I went climbing, but it felt utterly different now. This time, I would most likely stay this way, introduce myself to others, and have to be convincing. On the streets, I observed the way the men walked and attempted to emulate them. Stiff, straight legs, shoulders back, head high, hands in pockets. In my head, I tried to imagine how my voice would sound as a male. Rougher, lower, more direct. I was terrified that I would not be good enough at pretending to be a boy. How could I hope to unlearn sixteen years as a female?

Before long, I was lost in a maze of crumbling buildings and alleyways. There were no street signs, the roads were more dirt than cobblestones, and the gas lamps were almost all unlit or sputtering. Between the dim light and the fog, my world had shrunk to a tiny sphere. The fear caught up with me. My breath came faster. There were no landmarks by which to ground myself. I was hemmed in by limestone on all sides.

I turned, and out of the darkness three young men appeared. They were perhaps two or three years older than me, and they had obviously been drinking. Immediately, I sensed danger, backing away, hoping that they would not notice me and carry on. The fog hid me, and I watched as they drunkenly sang off-key. One fubbed a line of the lyrics and another took offense. Before long, they were tussling, and then brawling. The thump of fists on flesh, the grunts of anger.

Keeping to the darkest parts of the shadows, I edged my way around them until my back was against an exposed gutter pipe. I dared not breathe. Eventually, the other two left, leaving the third on the ground. The bad singer had not won the brawl. I hoped he was only unconscious. I crept closer to him, until I saw blood, black in the moonlight. He groaned and rolled over, and I darted back to my hiding place.

I climbed away from the scene. The pipe was cold and slippery with damp, but I found purchase on the bolts and did not look down. I clambered onto the roof and stayed there, despite the cold. The past few hours did not seem real. I almost felt as if I were dreaming – that soon I would awake in my bed, Lia would bring me tea and sing me the song she sang every morning as she combed my hair, and my old life would continue to march along.

The sun rose and thinned the fog to a pink and orange mist before burning through it and illuminating Sicion. I could see to each horizon and the view was breathtaking. Twin limestone spires of the churches of the Lord and Lady of the Sun and Moon reached toward the sky. The light filtered through the cobalt-blue Penglass domes that threaded their way through the city like the backbone of some gigantic beast, illuminating the black veins of the glass and the murky shapes within. In this light they looked delicate, like dragonfly wings.

The sun rose over Sicion, and the first day where I was no longer Miss Iphigenia Laurus.

As I was about to climb down from the roof, I peered through the window of the attic. The flat had been long since abandoned, with the roof in poor repair. I managed to open a window and shimmied in. Slivers of early morning light peeked through holes in the roof, and dust rose in a cloud about my feet, the motes golden in the light of dawn, and I sneezed.

Sheets stained with damp and mold covered irregular lumps of furniture. Nothing covered the walls but cobwebs.

I wondered who used to live here and what their jobs were. I could almost feel their ghosts lingering like the layers of dust. Families gathered about the battered dining table passing food, laughing or arguing. Children huddled together like puppies against the cold on the sagging spring bed. Generations of entire families surely lived here, as many as eight to ten people in the cramped quarters. I wondered why they left and where they went.

The families would have been as different from mine as night and day. This was a hovel – an abandoned flat in a poor part of town. These families may never have had quite enough food or ever fully chased the cold from their bones. But they had left furniture. With a start, I hoped this was not a plague house. I rubbed my hands along my arms, trying to warm them against the early morning chill.

I spent the morning clearing a corner of the worst of the dust with an old broom I found. After a failed attempt to nap, I ate some of the food in my pack, and decided the place seemed safe enough to leave my belongings hidden under one of the musty sheets. I filled my pockets with my coins and more of my food. And I climbed down the gutter pipe and back into the Sicion I had not seen before.

• • • •

The day passed in a haze of fatigue. I did not know where to go and simply went where my feet took me. Before long, I was hopelessly disoriented in the twisting streets of the darker side of Sicion. Here, the streets had missing cobblestones, and refuse gathered in the gutters. The air smelled of coal smoke and garbage. The streets were lined with pubs and second-hand clothing stores. More beggars than I had ever seen slumped on the streets, some performing off-key music, others not bothering with pretense and holding a battered tin for spare coins.

I held a hand over the bag of coins in my trousers, wary of pickpockets. In the cold light of day, running away seemed a silly idea indeed. I ate the last of the food I had packed, but it did little to fill my belly. Perhaps I should simply go home and admit my mistake before I became a beggar on the streets.

I didn't want to be like the men slumped on the pavement, reeking of gin, their stained smiles more gaps than teeth.

After tentatively asking a washerwoman for directions, I found my way to the merchant quarter. Here would be a good place to stay and eke out a new life for myself. I peered in the shop windows of flower shops, grocers and bakers, bookshops and jeweler's and illuminary shops. The latter advertised a "help wanted" sign in the window. I walked past the shop thrice, striving for nonchalance. I gathered my courage and stepped into the shop.

Crystal glittered and glass globes of all different sizes hung high on the ceiling, burning in all colors. I was the only person in the shop but the owner.

"Can I help you, sir?" the man behind the counter asked, looking over his half-moon glasses at me. His face was decidedly unfriendly.

"I saw… the sign in the window…" I began, hesitantly.

He took in my frayed clothing, and his gaze lingered on my face in such a way that I wondered if I had a smudge of dirt on it.

"Have you worked in an illuminary's before, boy?" he asked.

I shook my head.

"We're looking for someone with experience. Thank you for your interest." He looked beyond me, to the door, clearly signaling for me to leave.

And I did, the bell clinking shut behind me. I saw other signs on Jade Street asking for assistants, and I asked at each one. I told them I could read, that I could count, that I would work hard. But they couldn't look beneath the patched clothes and the smear of dirt on my face, and I received the same reply at all of them, with varying degrees of contempt.

In late afternoon, I found my way to the Emerald Park. The sunshine warmed my shoulders, and the green of the grass and the trees calmed me. I sat on the barrier for the mermaid statue in the middle of the park, trailing my fingers in the water, staring at the Penglass dome that Cyril had fallen down only scant days before. Home was but a few short steps away and it was risky to be here, but I wanted to be among familiar surroundings. If only it could be easy to return, to climb the scaffolding covering the Elm residence and slip through my window. My parents would be angry but relieved I had returned.

But I did not know if they would cancel their plan to operate. I did not think I could forgive them for being willing to operate without giving me a choice. I rubbed my nose, so close and so far from my old life.

I needed a new name. I couldn't call myself Iphigenia – not like I would want to. And though Gene could be a boy's name, it'd link me to my former life. I wanted to shed my old life. Try on a new one and see how it fit.

Water trickled down the mermaid's face as she reached above her for something that seemed just out of reach. The mica flecks of the grey granite caught the sun. I smiled. I had a new name.

Micah Grey.

I liked it. It was short, it was different from my real name, and it had a nice ring to it. Micah Grey. It would do.

The light of the day faded. I left the park, drawing my cap low on my forehead. I felt exhausted and could not wait to fall asleep, even if it was in a cold, abandoned flat.

I was also too tired to be aware of my surroundings. A moonshade, one of the ladies of the night, crept close to me and grabbed my shirtsleeve when I was nearly "home."

"How are you today, sir? Fancy a night on the town?" she asked.

I shook my head, trying to shake her off my shirt. "No thanks, Madame."

She laughed, showing her yellowed teeth. One of her canines was dark with decay. "Madame, he calls me. Ain't that sweet. Come along, young thing, you'll enjoy yourself, I promise."

I tugged harder, reclaiming my shirtsleeve. "No, but thank you for the offer. I'd best be getting back."

She steered me toward an alley. "We needn't go out and about. Just here would suit us fine."

I was shocked by her audacity. "I really must be getting home. My parents are expecting me."

"What's a few minutes?" she asked, backing me into an alley. She glanced over my shoulder, and I knew someone was behind me. I twirled, and the club aiming for my head missed and hit where my neck met my shoulder. I cried out as pain radiated across my torso. Another moonshade dragged me to the floor, and the first straddled my lower legs.

"Hurry, Mattie," the first hissed. Mattie rummaged in my pockets. I struggled to throw her off, but they were strong and the pain blinded me. Mattie found the coins in my pocket. All of my coins.

I opened my mouth to plead, but Mattie pressed her hand over my mouth. She smelled of cheap perfume and a body not recently washed. "You hush your mouth, young sir, and be grateful we're letting you go." She shook the bag, the coins clinking. "My, my. What's a little scamp like you doing with all this dosh?"

She tossed the bag behind her, and I heard the first woman catch it.

And then Mattie drew her fist back and hit me, hard. Pain exploded in my head and the night darkened further.

I awoke in squelching filth in the dark of night. My face felt as though it had been broken, and I could barely move my neck. I groaned. I struggled onto my elbows. I was alone.

Painfully, I pulled myself upright and hobbled to the gutter pipe that led to my new little nest. I rested my head against the cool metal, trying to find the will to climb. I did, eventually, and made my slow ascent. My pack was still where I left it, at least. I searched through it. No coins. I had not a copper to my name.

I had a small mirror in my pack. A black eye had bloomed on my face. I pressed my fingers gently against it and cried. I missed Cyril, and even the parents who were not truly my parents. I missed Anna Yew, and Oswin, and everyone.

But I cried even more, because without any sort of money or any way to gain employment, it felt like I was going to have to slink home within a few days, and take up life as Iphigenia Laurus once again, before I could even find out who Micah Grey could be.

The next day, I felt as though I had shed all emotion along with my tears. I had no more food, and my stomach ached in hunger. Judging by the looks people were giving me on the street, I was quite the sight. I wandered Sicion's merchant quarter again, hoping to see more help wanted signs but not going in, knowing that my black eye would immediately disqualify me. But I needed employment. I needed to eat, and to sleep somewhere where the wind did not whistle through the crumbling walls.

I passed a bakery. Fresh brown rolls lay on a ledge, topped with an egg glaze and toasted oats. I stared at them, my eyes large as dinner plates. My stomach was too hungry to even rumble at the sight. Before I knew what I was doing, I had picked one up. The fresh, yeasty smell made my mouth water.

"Hey, boy," the baker said, sticking his head out of the shop. "You going to pay for that?"

I gulped. What had I been thinking? I had nothing to pay, and nothing to trade. We stared at each other in an impasse. The baker had a clean-shaven face and rosy cheeks, his hair receding on his forehead. My face must have been smudged with dirt, the skin underneath pale but for the lurid bruise. His eyebrows were furrowed in annoyance.

"I'm sorry," I said, and then I ran.

"Hey!" the baker cried after me. "Thief!"

I clutched the roll to my chest, dodging the people strolling down the street. The baker thundered after me. Several people tried to grab me, but I evaded them, their fingers only just grasping my clothes. The baker soon gave up the chase before returning to his shop in defeat.

I held my prize of a now sadly dented roll. I bit into it in a shadowed alley, and closed my eyes in ecstasy. It was the most delicious thing I had ever eaten, though I felt terrible not paying for it.

I could not do this much longer.

20

SUMMER: FAREWELL TO SICION

"Searchers find what they seek through the regulations of the Constabulary, working closely with Policiers. Shadows appear on their heels almost immediately, sneaking and spying around the law as much as they are able. While sometimes, it must be said, their methods are fruitful and aid existing investigations, many others believe they steal money from Ellada's citizens and lessen the implicit trust in the law of the land."

A HISTORY OF ELLADA AND ITS COLONIES,
Professor Caed Cedar, Royal
Snakewood University

A man in a dark suit strode up the beach.

He stood out as I gathered my lunch dishes to take to the cook's tent. On such a lovely summer's day, the beach was busy. A small gaggle of children made sandcastles nearby, openly gawking at the circus folk. People strolled along, pausing to pick up seashells or take in the view of the sea. The man walked with a purpose, his legs stiff, hands in his pocket, chin tilted upwards beneath the wide brim of his hat. No one else seemed to notice him. I brought my dishes to the cook and then loitered, watching. The man in the dark suit surveyed the circus, taking a notebook from his pocket and jotting something down. He didn't look like a Policier. I licked my lips.

I waited with bated breath. The man took a last long look at the circus, taking in each member. His face lingered in my direction for a moment, or maybe I imagined it. He tucked the notebook in his pocket and strode down the beach.

Surely he couldn't be the Shadow?

The man in the dark suit lingered on my mind, even as Aenea and I bid farewell to Arik before we left for Sicion.

We both hugged him close. Aenea was openly crying, and I only barely stopped the tears.

"Now, now, don't cry, little one," he said, stroking her hair. He clasped hands with me and kissed me on the cheek. "This is a happy day."

"You've been like a father to me," Aenea said, voice thick.

"And you're the daughter I never had. And like father and daughter, we'll part ways but still see each other. You come to Sicion every year. And every year, I'll be here. Come see me. You know where I stay."

"I will," she said, wiping her eyes.

"And you too, Micah. We may not have known each other long, but I've become quite fond of you."

"I've become quite fond of you too, Regar Bupnik."

Arik sputtered. "Aenea! You promised never to tell anyone else my name!"

"Oh come on, old man, Micah doesn't count, surely?"

"I should spank you for your impertinence," Arik said, lifting his palm threateningly with a smile.

She gave a watery laugh. We all hugged each other one last time. Arik shouldered his bag and made his way along the beach, making sure to limp for appearances.

"He can rest, now," Aenea said.

I put my arm around her, feeling chivalrous. "He's gotten what he wanted. Time for us to pack as well."

We left Sicion.

Everyone, worker or performer, had to work together to dismantle a circus. We all scurried about as quickly as we could, but it took all day and long into the evening to pack up possessions, to link the carts together into a caravan, to dismantle the tents. Bil hired several mudlarks to pick up the garbage, and they scuttled about, throwing anything flammable into the fire and leaving a long trail of smoke. Just as the smoke would eventually dissipate and leave no trace in the sky, we would leave no trace on the ground.

A half-dismantled circus is a pathetic sight. The horses of the carousel were piled into a cart with no ceremony. The collapsed tents looked wilted upon the sand, and there was no trace of magic left. Everything was broken down and stored away.

After the last bonfire on a Sicion beach, we slept in our carts, crowded amongst our possessions. The next morning, the workers ensured there was enough fuel in each cart and we drove them. Behind us, the site of the circus was nothing more than another part of the beach, nothing left behind but footprints and tracks.

We drove our carts to the train station, rattling through the cobbled streets. Bil, ever the entrepreneur, turned it into a parade. On the sides of all the carts were simple but colorful painted circus scenes. I had two clowns dancing on the side of mine, with kernels of popped corn clustered around the edges. A few balloons floated from the tops of each cart, and bells jingled on the wheels. Saitha, the elephant, strolled through the streets, occasionally trumpeting along with the musicians. People gathered and waved at us as we passed.

They would not miss us for long. The Riley & Batheo's Circus of Curiosities would be coming soon to the small hippodrome in the city center, with their three-ringed circus and twice as many acts and animals. We were the taster circus, and it rankled Bil no end. The ringmaster's rival circus would not stay long in Sicion and would be performing in Imachara soon after we arrived, and when it did, business would drop off sharply even if we cut prices, and the crowd would become rougher.

At the train station, Bil the ringmaster turned into Bil the train master. The locomotive was already there, steaming, the sides of the train cars painted in similar scenes to those on our carts. The animals were loaded in the first two cars behind the engine, where the ride was the smoothest, one car for the prey and one for the predators. The animals growled and squawked as they were loaded – the cats howled and Violet even swiped at Tym and was duly reprimanded with a crack of a whip. I did not mind no longer working with the animals.

Everyone strained to load an entire circus into a train that seemed far too small for a procession of our size. Bags and boxes were stacked floor to ceiling, tied haphazardly with rope. Without the room to sprawl along the beach, I realized just how many things a circus required – animal feed alone needed a substantial amount of space. Costumes, props, the tents, the trapeze, high rope, balance beams, practice mats, the personal wagons, the various equipment that I had no idea what its purpose was, or how everything could hope to fit.

The sun was bidding us farewell over the horizon by the time we had finished loading everything. We would set out at dawn the next morning. We unloaded enough provisions to have a cold meal, and everyone ate in the last two cars of the trains. Snug on a bench next to Aenea, I found it odd that Arik was not among us. Dinner was a quiet affair.

Afterwards, I climbed into my cart with some difficulty and tried to sleep. Once we arrived at Cowl, someone else would take over Arik's empty bed. I was not looking forward to the prospect. Arik never commented on the secretive way I dressed and cleaned myself, and I had trusted him not to rifle through my bag. There were not many in this circus that I trusted.

Far too early the next morning, we crammed into the passenger cars and left Sicion behind. We started at a slow roll, but quickly gathered steam. Excitement and nerves bloomed in my belly as the buildings, mainly old warehouses and ramshackle apartments, began to blur as we sped past.

Next to us, Madame Limond and Bethany chatted about the places they would go once they reached Imachara. I pretended to be asleep and listened.

"I'm ever so glad we'll have our next pay by then," Madame said. "All of my dresses are beginning to fray at the seams, but you cannot find decent dresses in Sicion." She must spend the majority of her income on clothing. My notion of money from my old life was hazy, as I rarely had to physically handle it, but even Mother and Father only allotted me one dress every three months due to the cost, though I supposed I was growing quickly.

"I couldn't give two huffs about dresses – I cannot wait to go to proper pubs and restaurants. And," Bethany said, lowering her voice, "I heard that a new circus and vaudeville has started up in Imachara and means to be based there year-round. Headed by that Alan Nickelby fellow."

"No," Madame gasped. "Has Bil heard yet?"

"I'm sure he has, if I know," Beth said.

"How did you become privy to such information?" Madame asked.

"The gentleman friend that I will be dining all over Imachara with wrote me a letter. He says I should join, so that I can be nearer to him more often."

"I hope you don't find this rude, but... this gentleman, he doesn't mind the moustache?"

Bethany laughed. "No, actually, not at all. He's quite partial to it, really. His wife is a mealy, thin little thing, so pale she looks as though she has no eyebrows or eyelashes. Perhaps that is why he began courting me last year."

"Mistress Bethany!" Madame Limond exclaimed, happily scandalized.

Bethany batted her eyes from behind her fan. She was an attractive woman, despite the moustache, in a vivacious, curvy way. She was a lot of woman. It must be strange, though, to dine with a man that was another woman's husband.

"What do you think Bil will do?" Madame asked.

Bethany shrugged. I peeked and she flicked her eyes toward Aenea and me and the others who were all studiously pretending they could not hear what the two women were saying. "Bil has plans for new acts, so he says. I suppose we'll all have to work even longer hours to ensure that we are better than this new circus. Or, we jump ship and join the new one." She stroked her moustache thoughtfully.

"Would you really do that?" Madame asked. "You've been in this circus since it began. You were the first of the freaks! If this circus is trying for nobility and that, I don't think we freaks have a chance. The big circuses, they don't have folk like us. We're not classy enough. Not like those trapeze artists and that." Madame pitched her voice louder. I opened my eyes, stuck my tongue out at her, and pretended to return to sleep. Madame and Bethany chuckled.

"Hnngh," Tauro said behind me. Aenea and I turned around. He appeared even less human than usual, the early morning light picking up the downy hair of his face, the pits and crevices of his skin. His nostrils flared as he breathed, and his eyes were a deep golden brown. If the circus failed, he would have nowhere to go except the work shelters. But what would happen to all of us? I reached over and clasped Tauro's warm hand. He squeezed it and settled into his seat, closing his eyes with a snuffle. Not for the first time, I wondered how much of the world around him he actually understood.

The Leopard Lady of Linde and Poussin the human chicken likewise looked nervous. They whispered amongst themselves, casting furtive glances at the others in the cart.

I turned and settled into my own seat. I chewed my lip. I should probably attempt to join the Imacharan circus. Sicion was risky, as running into Cyril and his friends had proved. And the Shadow. Few knew me in Imachara.

Aenea settled against my shoulder again, her breath warm against my neck. I rested my lips against the top of her head, our hands intertwined, smelling the warm, almost spicy scent of her hair. I still wasn't quite sure what was going on between Aenea and I. I wanted more, and I feared it.

As Aenea slept against me, I watched Sicion disappear though the window. In the poorer parts of town, Penglass domes were painted with malformed animals and scrawled rude words. Within a week or so, the paint would flake off and leave the surface pristine. Occasionally the sun would backlight the odd glass, illuminating the train car with a soft, blue glow. If I squinted at the structures, I thought I could see odd shapes lurking within.

The train topped a rise and the center of Sicion lay below us. The dual spires of the cathedrals of the churches of the Sun and Moon grasped toward the sky, one painted light and the other dark. Far off in the distance, I saw my old apartment building, and even the window of my old room. I felt another pang of homesickness, of regret, and then we passed a bend and my old life was lost to me.

We were leaving Sicion. Buildings were far between now. To my right was the endless plate of iron-grey sea, and to my left were the brown and grey hills and rocky mountains of the Kithaereon Range. Golden grasses mingled with the twisted, stubborn trees that crouched in bits of soil scattered among the rocks. Few visited the coastline of Ellada for the scenery.

Drystan grew restless, pacing up and down the train, peering out of the window. He perched on the back of the seats in front of Aenea and me. Aenea cracked open her eyes.

"What the Styx are you doing? If there's a lurch in the train, you're going to fall on us."

"Maybe that's what I've a mind to do," he said, winking. "Want to play cards?" He shuffled a pack that appeared out of thin air. I pressed my lips together. Aenea looked at him coolly, and Drystan only batted his eyelashes in response. I felt distinctly caught in the middle.

We played cards and Drystan summarily beat us every time, aside from an occasional fit of pity. Aenea and I learned to play the relatively simple "beggar my neighbor," and "the oldest hag," and dusted our skills at rummy. Aenea was better than me. She won a hand or two, and I had the feeling they were hard-won and that she really wanted to beat him. And Drystan might have let her.

I lost each and every game.

"You're both cheating," I said, churlishly.

They smirked in response, confirming my suspicions.

"Teach me how!"

Eyebrows rose. Drystan reshuffled the pack and taught the basics of how to count cards, how to slip a valuable one up your sleeve if you suspected you would need it the next round, how to distract your opponent. My head spun from trying to take it in.

"How did you learn this?" I asked Aenea, who hid and produced cards as if by magic.

"I grew up in the circus," she said by way of answer, shrugging a shoulder.

"Oh."

The sun rose higher into the sky as the train followed the coast toward the little village of Cowl. The landscape outside our window changed very little. We grew tired of cards, and I grew tired of losing, though Drystan did not leave and instead squeezed in between us. He fell asleep, his head resting against my shoulder. Aenea rolled her eyes at me as I shifted uncomfortably.

"Sorry," I said, softly. "I seem to be everyone's pillow today, though I wouldn't have thought myself very comfortable."

"It's sweet, really, I suppose. He rarely takes such a liking to anyone." But her voice was too light.

"Mm," I said, neglecting to mention that he may have taken a bit too much of a liking for me. She already knew.

After a time, Aenea fell asleep against Drystan, and I had the weight of both of them against my left shoulder.

Usually when I took the train, I would have a book to pass the time, but it had been months since I had such a luxury. I rifled through my pack, trying not to disturb them, and took out the little figurine Mister Illari had given me what felt like years ago, though it had only been a few months. I ran a finger over the smooth contours of the carved stone as I stared out of the window.

"What's that?" Aenea asked softly.

I clasped my hands about the statue, startled. "I didn't realize you had awakened." I had the sneaking suspicion that Drystan was awake as well, and merely pretending to snooze.

She shifted until she was sitting upright. "Come on, let me see."

I passed it to her, feeling shy and as if she had caught me doing something a little naughty. She ran her fingers over the statue's crude face. "What is it?"

"It's a statue a friend of mine gave me. It's a Kedi, a mythical creature from um, Byssia, I believe."

"Hmm," she said, tilting it in her hands.

"A Kedi is both male and female," I said, choosing my words carefully. "The Byssians believe that it is the only creature that is ever complete."

Aenea frowned slightly. "So they worshipped them? Bizarre."

"Not that bizarre," I said, defensive.

She turned to me. "I suppose it's an interesting idea. Does the Kedi have any magical powers? Like a siren and her song?"

"Well, according to the man who gave it to me, the Kedi were supposed to be stronger than a human. They never became ill. And they learned very quickly. So yes, they ended up being worshipped by the Byssians as gods, like the other Chimaera."

"And were they? Gods, I mean?"

"I don't know. The Byssians worshipped a lot of creatures as gods. I remember from a history lesson that they believed that divine humans were mixed with other animals, like fish to become mermaids and humans with wings. But this one was considered the strongest of all, which is a bit hard to believe. It's still human."

"We have those stories of Chimaera as well."

"Yes, we do, but they weren't worshipped, I don't think. More feared." They were viewed as monsters or tricksters, most of which had to be outsmarted or defeated.

She settled into her seat. "So you think that maybe they were real?"

"Maybe." I hesitated, and then said, "Every island has myths about them. What if they are still around, but in hiding?" Perhaps there were others like me.

She giggled. "You mean humans that bundle their wings under coats and hide horns with top hats? That there are people around us that are both male and female? I've seen my fair share of strange folk in the circus, but none like that."

I sighed, took the figurine from her, and returned it to my pack. It would have been nice if she had been intrigued by the Kedi, considering she was possibly courting one.

A circus is far easier to disassemble than erect.

We would all have to help with the manual labor tomorrow. I would sweep the black slabs of stone to make room for the tents and carnival, and carry box after box.

We unloaded the carts so that we had a place to sleep and extracted enough food and supplies to cook a hasty meal. It was incredible how tired I felt even though I had been sitting down for most of the day. Aenea still instructed me to stretch and flip a few somersaults along the beach as we waited for the food to cook. She walked along the damp sand on her hands.

"Have you ever been to Cowl before?" I asked her as she did one last flip and we made our way back to camp. The sand was darker here, almost black. From the beach, the entire village was visible, consisting of several ramshackle buildings gathered around a small, cobbled square that contained a statue of a man with scaled skin and the grim face of a lizard. The buildings were thatched rather than slated, with badly patched cracks in the granite and oilskin for windows. I had not realized that such dilapidated, old-fashioned houses could still be lived in. It was as if I had stepped into the past.

"We stop through here every season," Aenea explained. "It's a good village to practice our new acts for Imachara. It has a few hundred people, and they're insular folk, difficult to please. If we make them laugh and clap, then we know that Imachara will like it."

"Why are they difficult to please?" I asked.

"They have hard lives. No land to grow anything, no natural resources anymore. Used to be a mining village. Most make their livelihood trying to take things that are broken from the bigger cities and fix them to sell at a higher price. Many are not very good at it."

"Ah." We reached camp, loaded our trenchers with a slop of lentils, carrots, peas, and bits of ham, and settled ourselves close to the fire to ward off the chill from the night air.

Bil did not make his usual late-night pep talk, welcoming us to the town of Cowl. Candlelight glowed from his tent, but as I went to my cart to sleep, I thought

I could hear hushed, angry voices. Frit had seemed upset the last few weeks and moved stiffly from more concealed bruises. She was always kind to me when I interacted with her, but I avoided her. She hadn't reported me, though she suspected who I was, but she could at any time. Marriage trouble could be one reason why Bil had lost his temper so at Mara, though that did not excuse it.

I had the cart to myself that night. It was a rare freedom to undress without fear of someone seeing me. I took off the sweat-stained bandages around my chest and soaked them in water with a lump of lye soap. I scrubbed them, rinsed them, and then hung them haphazardly about the cart. I cleaned myself next. The skin on my chest stung horribly. I needed to stop tying the bandages so tightly.

Hesitantly, I touched my chest. My breasts just fit into the palm of my hand now, warm and surprisingly heavy. Small by anyone's standards, but there was no mistaking what they were. They moved uncomfortably as I stretched and twisted, trying to see the rest of my body. I wanted a full-length mirror.

My body, though still lean, had developed slight hips. My waist tapered inwards a bit, though the muscles of my abdomen were well-defined like a man's. Hair had sprouted underneath my arms and in a faint line on my stomach, leading to my nether regions. I investigated the oddest parts of me, trying not to feel uncomfortable. This was my body. I would have to get used to it. It was un-likely to change and I had already run away from a chance to change it, for better or worse. With a sigh, I rubbed some lotion onto the skin of my chest. I had finally bought new bandages, and I wrapped them around me, wincing. It was so tempting to leave myself unbound for a night.

I tormented myself with questions. What would I have looked like, if I had allowed the surgery to go through? Would I actually have looked like a girl? What did Aenea look like without clothes? I entertained myself with the thought for a moment. I had only seen her in her performance clothes, but that was enough to spur my imagination.

"Micah?" a voice called from outside. I started and swore softly under my breath. Aenea. Of course. Impeccable timing.

"Just… Just a moment!" I grabbed a long linen shirt and put it on and jumped into a pair of breeches, thinking of Bethany's moustache to attempt to snuff my desire. I grabbed my half-dry bandages and looked around in a panic before stuffing them underneath Arik's old pallet.

"Yes, Aenea? What is it? Is anything the matter?" I was nervous and my words came out curter than I meant.

"Can I come in?" she sounded hesitant.

"Y… yes," I said, heart hammering.

She pushed open the door and ducked her head to enter. She had just washed and her hair fell about her face in half-dry ringlets. She took off her coat and wore night-clothes and a dressing gown underneath. She sighed and sat down on my pallet.

"Are you all right, Aenea? It's late."

"Well, yes. I could not sleep, so I bathed and took a walk along the beach. I saw your light." She smiled, though her eyes were shadowed. "Should I leave?"

I swallowed. "No, of course not."

I sat next to her, the straw of the pallet crunching beneath my weight. My stomach fluttered and I did not know what to do with my hands.

"Is it strange, being in the cart on your own now?" she asked.

"I miss Arik. Though I don't miss his snoring."

She laughed. "Be kind. He broke his nose thrice."

"True," I said.

We lapsed into silence. I listened to her breathing, and the faint sound of the wind and waves outside.

"I shouldn't let it get to me anymore," Aenea said, staring at the light of the gas flame on the trunk.

I paused, waiting for her to elaborate. "Shouldn't let what get to you?" I asked, when she remained silent.

"Almost falling," she whispered.

I tried to block out the image of the parasol trailing to the ground, of the sight of her tumbling from the tightrope and her hand clasping it at the last minute. I could not.

"I was so frightened for you," I said.

She leaned against me, slightly. "I know. And the past few days, I felt all right. I thought it was nothing – just another almost-accident. Moving distracted me, and I was so tired at the end of the day that I fell into bed. But tonight, when I tried to sleep – I couldn't. I kept remembering it." She shuddered.

I put my arm around her, worried that she would pull away. But she leaned into me, resting her cheek on my collarbone. I could feel the ridges of her strong shoulder muscles through the thin fabric of her dressing gown. I felt her breathing and heard her heartbeat, just as quick and nervous as my own. She tilted her head up toward mine–

Her lips were warm and wet and soft. I sat there stiffly, my heart hammering in my ears. My own lips pursed hesitantly. Kissing a girl was very different from my awkward kiss with Damien. Aenea's arm wrapped around my neck and pulled me closer and her other hand rested on my ribcage, right below the bandages around my chest. I felt a stirring between my legs, and a hardening of my nipples. I tensed. She broke the kiss.

"What's wrong?" she asked. "Should I not have…?" She chewed on the corner of her lip in a most distracting way.

I shook my head. "I've… I've not done this much. I'm doing it wrong, aren't I?"

She laughed softly, still close to me. "Not bad. Care to try again?"

As she pulled me toward her again I briefly wondered who else she had kissed, and decided I did not care. Her lips were on mine again. I rested a hand on her cheek, silken and downy. Her hair cascaded forward and covered our faces. Dizzy with the scent of her skin, I moved forward and bumped teeth with her. She giggled, the sound echoing in my mouth. I cradled her face with my hands. Aenea twined a hand in my hair, the other resting on the back of my neck. I was surrounded by her smell – sea salt and sweet almond soap.

The kiss lasted a moment, an age. We broke apart, and I smiled at her, dazed. Aenea laughed again at my expression. I blushed. I took her strong, calloused hand in my own, which was now nearly as rough as hers. I no longer had a lady's hands.

"I'm rather new at all of this."

The corners of her lips curled and she pulled away to look at me, sensing how overwhelmed I felt.

"You've never had a female… companion?"

"No." *Nor a male.*

"I find that surprising."

I laughed softly, remembering how Mother dismayed at ever finding a match for me. "Why would you say so?"

She leaned back on the pallet, drawing me down with her. She leaned her head on my shoulder and twined her fingers with mine.

My face warmed. "Never thought I was much to look at." *As a woman*, I finished. It was not lying if I finished in my head.

"You caught my eye when I first saw you."

A warm glow kindled in my stomach. "When I was a bedraggled urchin spying on the circus and jumped into the air sixty feet above ground like an idiot?"

"Yes. Especially when you were an idiot. You were very brave, to do such a foolhardy feat. I knew it meant you truly wanted to be here."

"I do. I feel as if I belong here far more than I did in my old life. I can be more like myself, rather than the person my parents wanted me to be."

She leaned on an elbow and looked down at me, her damp hair curling about her face.

"May I ask you something?" I asked.

"You already have." I made a face. She smiled. "But yes, you may ask me something else."

"Have you had many male suitors?" I said, trying to be delicate.

She raised an eyebrow. "Are you asking me if I'm some sort of trollop?"

I sputtered. "N... no! You seem much more comfortable with all of this, so I thought maybe–"

She held up a hand. "That's enough, that's enough! I take pity on you. I've had two other suitors in the past."

Her mirth fled her face, and I realized I had brought up a very stupid topic of conversation. Moments after our first kiss and I was already quizzing her about past lovers. So stupid.

"Only two, and neither of them were in the circus. The first was a boy from Niral named Petyr. I was only thirteen. We held hands and we snuck a kiss or two underneath the docks. He was sweet."

"I never had that sort of childhood romance," I said. "I was far too shy to approach the girls, and they were likewise too shy to approach me."

"That's a shame. The other one... well. I'll tell you of him another time." Her face closed but for the secrets swimming in her eyes.

"I'm sorry," I said, feeling even more like a goof. Here I was, hoping to comfort and help her forget about nearly falling, and I only reminded her of more pain. "I shouldn't have brought it up."

"It's nothing," she said, though she was feigning nonchalance. "Come here."

My stomach roiled uncomfortably. I shifted closer. She pressed her lips to mine again and I responded. Our bodies did not touch, but I sensed the warmth of her skin, just an inch or two away. We remained like that for some time, trailing fingertips across faces and along necks, shivering. And then we curled together on the pallet and talked, the conversation meandering across many topics, learning more about each other, with me spinning still more lies but trying to weave in the truth as much as I could. Before our conversation trailed away and we fell asleep, I let hope flare within me that one day, there might not be a need for lies.

21
SPRING: THE SPICE MERCHANT'S TALE

"They say the spices of each island of the Archipelago echo their country of origin. The cassia and clove of Kymri mirror its rich, hot sands. The chillies of Southern Temne showcase its citizens' quickness to temper, while the mace and nutmeg illustrate the complexity of Northern Temnian culture. Linde is known for its five-spice, for it was long the hub of the spice trade. And Ellada grows few spices and borrows from all the others."

SPICES OF THE ARCHIPELAGO, Chef Siam Oakley

I thought I would faint at any moment.

I staggered through the crowded main square of Sicion. It was market day. The merchants had set up their wares early and the first customers started to trickle through. It was so busy that I thought I'd be able to steal some food without being noticed. Nothing had passed my lips but rainwater from the gutter for well over a day.

Even though it was not the largest city in Ellada, like Imachara, Sicion was still crowded. There was no room for a large market square. Instead, the market was vertical.

Ten stalls could fit on each level, and a wide but rickety wooden staircase zigzagged up its side.

Each level had a theme. The bottom layer had stalls of fruits and vegetables, mainly from nearby Girit, a once-lovely island whose emerald forests had been cleared for crops and orchards. The only way to emigrate to Girit was to promise its governor that your future was in farming. I had never been to Girit and, seeing how I killed every plant I came across, doubted I ever would.

The second level was filled with meats from animals shipped from various colonies, like Byssia and Linde, and some of the smaller isles of the Archipelago. Fresh meat was expensive, as a lot of animals did not survive the journey across the sea; many of the animals therefore arrived pre-slaughtered and salted. The third level was full of spices, and smelled of tarragon, cinnamon, clove, thyme, and countless others. I sneezed.

On the fourth level were the bakers. I could not resist the sweet, yeasty smells and stole a warm meat-filled pasty. I was more successful this time, pretending to peruse another stall's wares and reaching behind me when the baker was distracted with an order. I sauntered off and ate my prize as I explored. I could have eaten ten more just like it.

The next level held clothes and jewelry from various countries, gorgeous things wrought from precious gems and metals mined in the far corners of the world. I fingered a long, airy green dress made of a fabric that was soft and cool to the touch. Why had my mother never bought me a dress like this? I would have actually liked to have worn it.

It was all so overwhelming. My eyes feasted on fruits and vegetables of all colors, lingered on unfamiliar dead animals lying prostrate on wooden tables, and yearned for the brightly dyed clothing and intricate jewelry. My nose imbibed the odors of alluring and pungent spices, fresh meat and the acrid tang of blood, the yeast of fresh bread, and cloth dye. My ears rang at the cries of merchants, customers, and livestock.

I found an unoccupied corner of the market and tucked myself into it, wedging my pack behind me, wondering what I should do next. I knew no one. No one knew me. It was a feeling both freeing and terrifying.

Since I had nothing else to do, I spent the rest of that morning in the corner. It was a perfect vantage point to study people. I would watch them shop, haggle, argue, and exclaim over a bauble that caught their gaze. People of all ages, shapes and sizes passed by, barely sparing me a glance. If I turned around, then I could watch the shoppers on the bottom level scurrying to stalls or leaving. They looked so small and inconsequential.

Someone tapped me on the shoulder and I started. Hovering above me was a tall thin Policier with a bushy black moustache that constantly twitched. His eyes were small and beady, but not unkind.

"Are you finished with your purchases?" he asked with a raised eyebrow. I had the feeling he had been watching me for some time and found me amusing.

"Aye, sir, I'm finished," I said, trying to pitch my voice deeper and rougher, well aware that I had no bags of shopping.

"Folk are going to start dismantling their stalls soon, and you'll be underfoot. Although," he said while looking at me up and down, "are you looking for work?"

Hope must have been stark on my face. "Yes, please, sir," I said, trying not to look too eager.

The Policier pointed to a stall on the opposite side of the level. "Mister Illari, the spice merchant, would probably give you a coin or two if you help him. Tell him Policier Mattos sent you. He's getting up there in years and I don't see his boy around today. You strike me as a good sort and haven't nicked anything in the past hour, but I'll not have you stealing from him."

"I would do no such thing!" I said, though guilt gnawed at my stomach, keeping company with my stolen bun.

The man's moustache twitched again. "You're still speaking too posh to pass as a street rat, young 'un. You should work on that while you're out slumming the streets. Just make sure you don't speak rough to your parents at teatime."

I must have looked comically dismayed as I watched him go. Was I that obvious, even saying so few words? But I thought of Policier Mattos' voice. I could tell that he was from a working-class background; he could have worn all the silks and gems in the world and it would not have been enough to disguise that.

Mister Illari was shuffling slowly across his stall, gathering a few remaining bottles and putting them in chests that looked far too heavy for him to lift. I rubbed at my grubby face self-consciously, mindful of my fading black eye.

"Scuse me... Mister Illari?" I asked, timidly.

He turned a face so wrinkled that it looked like it had cracked and was about to shatter. "Eh?" he asked.

"Policier Mattos sent me. Said you need help packin' up." I was sure I still didn't sound like a street rat, but hopefully Mister Illari was too old to notice or care.

Mister Illari nodded. "He's a good man," he said in a surprisingly strong voice. "Usually finds some undernourished thing like you to help an old codger like me." He gave a phlegmy laugh. "The tent's rented, so we can just leave it and they'll take it down and store them until next week. Thank the Couple, because they're bloody heavy. Start with those chests there." He pointed at a cart on the other side of the square. "Put them there and then come up for the rest of it. I'll relax up here with the money box. Mattos is usually good at spotting the honest ones, but I'm old, not stupid."

I smiled. I liked him already.

Mister Illari laughed again. He only had a handful of teeth left. "Though you're such a scrawny thing, you don't look like you could lift a feather duster."

I frowned at him. "I'm stronger than I look!"

"Prove it and grab them, then, off you get." He sighed and linked his arms behind his head.

I hoisted both of the spice chests with a little difficulty and weaved my way to the staircase. I glanced over my shoulder at Mister Illari. One watery eye was open. "You *are* stronger than you look."

Shrugging as best as I could, I hurried down the stairs. The chests were awkward to carry, and I was panting when I finally reached ground level and my arms burned.

I made my way to the sturdy pony and wooden cart tied up in front of a pub called the *Bronze Cockerel*. A barmaid stuck her head out of the front of the pub while I was rummaging to put the chests in.

"Oi! Whatcha doing, lad?"

"I'm 'elpin' Mister Illari put 'is spices back." I might have been trying too hard with the accent.

She looked me up and down, judging my worth. Whatever she saw, it made her nod. "Alright, then." She returned to her clientele.

I ran up and down the stairs, carrying chests and bags and twists of spices. Their dust found a way into my lungs and I wheezed. When I finished, Master Illari tottered down the stairs with his money box, ambled up to the window of the pub and gave the barmaid a coin.

"Thanks again, love," he said.

"See you next week, Mister Illari," the girl said flatly, pocketing the coin and turning away.

Mister Illari clambered ungracefully into the cart and picked up the reins. I wondered whether it would be rude to hold out my hands for the promised coin.

"Well, don't just stand there, boy, hop on," he said.

"Pardon?"

"I'll need help unloading as well. I've got a boy back at my place, but he's not as strong as you on the best of days and he's been hurling up his guts for the last three. And just because that's not enough, it looks like rain."

I hesitated. "Come on, come on," he said, gesturing to the cart. "I don't have all day, look at the sky!"

The sky was full of bruised clouds. I clambered into the rear of the cart, hunched under the canvas covering, and sat on a sack of what smelled like ground thyme.

"All right back there?" he called.

"Yes, thank you," I responded. I sneezed.

"Pungent, I know," he said. "By now I can't smell them

at all. Too old! I've been doing this so long I can still tell when the herbs are good by their color, and my boy Calum's got a good nose on him."

"How long have you been in the spice trade?"

"Nearly thirty-five years now."

More than twice as long as I had been alive. I could not wrap my head around such a concept.

"I travelled a lot in my youth. Joined the Royal Navy and saw the entire Archipelago. The travel bug bit me after that, and so I went into spices. Good money in spices. I may only sell at the town market square in Sicion, but I've had a comfortable life, and that's all anyone really needs, don't let them tell you no different."

Through a gap in the canvas, I watched him settle himself deeper into the driver's seat, wince, and sigh.

"If it was so comfortable," I asked, "why are you still working at your age?" I only realized how rude it sounded once the words were out of my mouth. "Sorry," I said belatedly.

"It's fine, my boy," Mister Illari said, laughing. "It's my own damn fault. See, I didn't realize I only wanted a comfortable life until I was in my forties. Before then, I was determined to be the richest man in Ellada. I invested in businesses that crumbled, I gambled, I hired men that swindled me. I'd be wrapped up in some big set of apartments right now if I wouldn't already be dead from boredom."

We stopped in front of a tenement of apartments that looked like all the others in Sicion – a tall building made of limestone and streaked liberally with soot. This one had a bit more filigree stonework about the edges than most, and thick double doors inset with stained glass.

Mister Illari clambered down from the cart and gave two short, loud whistle bursts. A window three floors up opened and a boy a few years younger than me popped his head out. His brown hair was unkempt.

"Back already?" he called.

"Yes, you lazy good for nothing!" Mister Illari called up at him. "Feel any better today?"

"A little," the boy returned. "I haven't been sick yet this morning!"

"If you puke just now, make sure you aim away from us and the cart! But it's nearly afternoon, Calum my boy, so I think you're on the mend! Feel like lifting chests of spices?"

"No way, old man! Looks to me like you found yourself another helper and don't need my poor starved muscles."

Mister Illari gestured in my direction. "This is... Sorry, boy, what was your name?"

"Oh. Um. Micah."

"This is Micah. I found him in the market. I think he's a runaway!" he yelled.

I winced and looked up and down the street to see how far his voice had carried. Fortunately, not a head in the crowd had turned my way. "Am I really not a convincing street boy?" I asked him.

"No, not at all. As an extra payment for helping me today, I'll give you some tips."

"So... you're not going to make me go back?"

"Nah, I'm not a busybody. Why you ran away is your own business. Why, are you valuable?" He winked.

"No, not really." My gaze fell to the pavement.

"Good. Then let's put that wretchedly thin back of yours to work and have you carry that chest of marigold up the stairs."

I half-smiled and set to work. Mister Illari and the small boy watched as I brought chests and heavy bags of spices up to their rooms. The apartments were small but comfortable, richly furnished with trappings originating from the same colonies as Mister Illari's spices. The floors were carpeted with rugs of intricate, circular patterns. Tapestries lined each wall, with panels of plants, people hunting wild game, and fantastical beasts long disappeared into legend. One of a winged horse about to trample a man with a bow and arrow caught my eye and, each time I passed, I slowed down to absorb some more of its details.

After I carried up the chests of spices, I lingered in a warm drawing room. Figurines of more mythical creatures cluttered its shelves and table space, all of them coated in a thin layer of dust. Brass-scaled monkeys, serpentine dragons, a giant octopus and a squid with long tentacles that dangled over the edges of its table, a ship perilously balanced on one raised limb. A large shelf next to the fireplace held humans blended with all kinds of animals – feathered, scaled, and furred.

A tiny figurine to the right of the shelf caught my eye. It was a smiling person carved from grey stone, its arms raised parallel to the ground. A hand had broken off. It was naked, with full, pointed breasts, a rounded stomach, and oversized male parts between the legs. I carefully picked it up and cradled it in my hands; it was crudely made and rough to the touch.

Mister Illari shuffled into the room, and Calum followed, carrying a tea tray which he set on an empty space on the table in the middle of the room.

"Where did you get this, Mister Illari, if I may ask?" I asked the merchant, holding it up to him.

Mister Illari squinted at it. "Hmm, where did I get that old thing… must be Byssia. Yes. They have excellent cardamom on that isle. I picked it up from an old man who carved them from soapstone and sold them at the market. You can keep it, if you like. I have far too much stuff cluttering these shelves."

"Thank you," I said, moved. "I haven't really come across any, um, two-gendered people in tales from here. Is it common in other places?"

He raised an eyebrow. "A young scholar of mythology, are we?"

I said nothing.

"It's popped up a few places, as I recall." He paused and thought, his eyebrows drawing together into a line. "Oh yes, I remember the story, more or less."

Calum and I sat on the sofa and poured ourselves what turned out not to be tea, but strong coffee reminiscent of gasoline. I took a sip, made a face, put in a lump of sugar, took a sip, made another face, tried it all once more, and then gave up and put the cup back on its saucer.

"It's foul stuff, innit?" Calum whispered loudly to me. I nodded and we shared a smile.

"You upstarts have unrefined palates. Try it again in twenty years and then tell me what you think, if this sack of skin and bones is still moving about. This is probably all that keeps me going now." He took a sip with obvious relish.

"The myth you mentioned, Mister Illari?" I reminded him.

"Ah, all right, all right." Mister Illari sighed. "I heard this story a long time ago, mind you.

"Long ago, before anything had been written down in Byssia, creatures of myth and legend still walked the Earth. Humans like us were far from the only intelligent creatures around. Human and sometimes Alder folk were just as likely to be half-fish, or half-serpent, or any of these other bits and bobs I have all over this room. They created weapons far deadlier than any we could hope to make now, but no one ever grew ill or frail. When they wished to die, they went to sleep and did not awaken again. They lived in houses, castles, caves, and boats of dark blue glass."

"Like the Penglass all about the city?" Calum exclaimed. "But why are there only domes and spires around the city, now, though? Where are the boats? I want a Penglass boat."

"Don't interrupt, Calum. Any that still remain are probably at the bottom of the ocean. Or maybe they never existed in the first place and are only myth. Or the Chimaera sailed into the far reaches of the world on them never to return. Who knows? But yes, they were made of Penglass. It's all over. On every island I've visited, there's always been at least one sealed-off mountain of Penglass. It's very troublesome when they almost form a mountain range across a whole island. They're so slippery they are impossible to climb. In Temne, the mountain bottlenecks the island and you have to sail out to sea to get around the blasted thing!

That's why the people are so different in the north and south of that isle. They were separated for hundreds of years.

"But in Byssia," Mister Illari continued, "the human or Alder and animal mixtures were revered. The Chimaera were much stronger than full humans. They were more agile and were wickedly intelligent. Historians believe they were the ones who invented the weapons, the Penglass, and all of the other artefacts they left behind. And it was this combination that allowed most of them to rise to power, which is probably where the religious worship started. Royalty is almost always tied to divinity, you know. But none of the Chimaera were revered as much as your new pocket ornament there." He nodded at the stone sculpture in my hands.

I looked at it again.

"They called it a Kedi. It's still worshipped in some backwaters of Byssia. This creature was their god and considered perfect. To its worshippers, a man is incomplete and a woman is incomplete. Whether or not they were crossed with some other creature, they were not whole. But this being was not. It did not need another man or another woman. It was complete within itself.

"Men and woman would try to be like this god, see, by coming together. Only when a man and a woman mated–" Calum giggled, his hand covering his face. "Shush up, Calum. As I was saying, when a man and a woman mated, then they were like the Kedi. They are complete and they are one.

"I suppose the Couple is a bit like that idea. You can't have the Sun Lord without the Lady of the Moon, and they form a complete whole. Two differing sides of the same coin."

"Are you a philosopher, Mister Illari?"

He snorted "Hardly. I've just seen a lot of different places and a lot of different things. You start to notice how similar they are, after a time."

"So if there was a creature like this Kedi, would it be content to be alone all its life? Were there other Kedi for it, or just the one?" I asked.

Calum piped in. "It seems to me like it'd have the best of both – it could rut itself!"

"Calum," Mister Illari warned. "Don't be crude. I don't know, Micah. I think there were only one or two. Doesn't matter much, eh? It's only stories."

"Yes," I said, my fingers gripping the stone figure tightly. "Only stories."

22
SUMMER: PLAY ACTING

"Gather around all ye young and ye old
To hear a tale of love richer than gold.
Between a young princess virtuous and fair,
And a kind prince who saves her from her lair.

A king's wicked greed: the young lovers' doom.
The Lord and Lady's grace spares them from gloom.
Rejoined at last, they swear never to part.
So ready or not, the show will now start!"

LEANDER & IONA, Godric Ash-Oak

"No, you're absolutely terrible!" Bil cried.

Aenea scowled at him and planted her hands on her hips. "I told you I was no good at play acting, Bil Ragona! You refused to believe me."

"You're all performers! How is it that every comely, bendy young woman I have reads lines like a stiff wooden board?" he grasped two handfuls of his hair, trying for comical dismay, but true frustration was under his own performance.

I was sitting next to the other contortionists and acrobats in the stands.

"Your girl Aenea was better than I was, Micah, though not by much," Dot, the youngest contortionist now that Mara was gone, said cheerfully.

The pantomime planned for Imachara was a retelling of the classic romance *Leander & Iona,* one of those stories where the young man and woman must overcome the obstacles blocking their love.

"How does the story go again?" Dot asked.

"You'll be sick to death of it by the end of the season, but the short of it is that Leander, the foreign princely hero and narrator, must rescue Iona, who has been locked in a Penglass tower by her cruel father, King Zimri, and is guarded by a minotaur. The Fool, the king's most trusted servant, attacks Leander along the way in the form of various beasts and monsters. So there'll be magic and fighting and changing scenes and danger. But, of course, love will win the war." I held up an arm in triumph, though *Leander & Iona* was not my favorite of Godric Ash-Oak's plays. The princess was passive for much of the play, waiting to be rescued by her prince.

"Romantic, isn't it?" Dot asked.

"Mm-hmm," I said, leaning back in the bleachers.

The entire circus had been forced to sit and watch the auditions for the various parts. Bil had been planning to put on a pantomime in Imachara, but he did not want to waste money on actual trained actors, and so he was determined to find the brilliant actors hiding within his midst.

Pantomime

The problem was that most of the circus had never acted, except to smile and bow at a crowd, and nearly everyone was wretched at it.

Drystan had been chosen as Leander, Fedir the yellow clown as the king, and Jive as the Fool. Tauro would, naturally, be the Minotaur to guard the princess. More circus folk were willing to be monsters, which required no speaking but for an occasional grunt or roar.

"Maybe if you practice until we reach Imachara?" Bil wheedled Aenea.

"No!" Aenea stomped her foot. "I perform well on the trapeze and tightrope and nowhere else. I'm sure there's someone who could do better." She strode off to the stands and slumped next to me, crossing her arms across her chest.

"Fine, but you'll play the Lady of the Moon in the finale," he called after her.

"What? I will not!"

"She doesn't have any bloody lines! You just have to wear a gown and look pretty. You'll manage that well enough."

She rolled her eyes. "Fine, as long as I don't have to speak."

"So who's our leading lady, then?" Rian asked.

"Frit?" Bil asked, helpless and more desperate.

"I'm too old to play a leading lady in a romance," she said.

Bil clenched his jaw, the tendons in his cheeks jutting. "I do not understand. This is a circus, full of creative and talented minds. You lot were decent," he pointed to the clowns. "Why don't one of you play the female lead? Iano?"

Iano guffawed. "I am not playing a woman. Not if you threatened to cut off my balls and give them to Violet for a meal!" Behind Iano, Jive looked at me and smirked, and I knew he was remembering my screams after the itching powder incident. I glowered at him and he raised his eyebrows, as if perplexed by my annoyance.

"More like a small snack," Rian said loudly.

Iano responded with a rude hand gesture, Rian made an even ruder one, and they began to tussle in a blue and green blur. The other clowns and several of the performers and workers called out encouragements or began to take bets on who would win.

"Halt!" Bil roared. They climbed off each other, brushing sand from their costumes.

I was biting my lip in the stands. Growing up, acting had been a favorite pastime. Mother had encouraged it, upon seeing how much I enjoyed playing "dressing up" with Anna, Cyril, and George. I never let Mother see when I played male parts. I would not say I was talented, but I did enjoy it, and I would probably be better at a female role, given that I had several years' experience pretending to be one.

Bil had not asked me to read lines. The male parts had all been filled by the clowns and Bil stopped asking the rest of us from reciting the same dull passage.

I wanted to open my mouth and say the words that would bring all eyes on me again. I was confident I had a place on the stage. But too many eyes meant too many chances to see something not quite right. My gaze flicked to Frit before I hunched my shoulders and looked at the sand-encrusted floor of our temporary circus.

"Those of you who have not read lines, queue up, then," Bil said, sighing. "We're finding our heroine tonight if it is the last thing I do. No breaks, no food, and no ale until this is sorted."

While everybody moaned, I fought to keep a smile from my face. The choice had been taken from me. It would not be up to me. It was up to the ringmaster.

Bil clasped his hands together. "Next!"

Tauro stepped forward and looked at Bil balefully. He opened his mouth.

"Argh, Tauro, you're all right – you know full well you already have a part. Sit down," Bil said.

"What, you're not going to let him try out for the heroine?" Jive snickered.

"Do not test my patience today, Jive. You will not like the result. Tauro, sit."

Tauro shuffled to the stands. He looked a little disappointed.

A Kymri tumbler was next. He was one of the twin brothers. Zahn?

"Oh, moon and stars, lord and lady on high –
*Shine your light on a…wretch whose end is…*neigh? Nigh?"

We all winced. Though Zahn had made headway in learning our tongue, it was clear he did not know the meaning of half of the lines, and his accent was thick. The audience would never understand him, and he was too handsome and muscular. Bil ushered him to the stands as well.

I was next.

"You'd make a decent woman, Micah," Bil said, a little hopefully, eyeing me up and down. "Do you need the lines said aloud to you?" he asked wearily.

"No, Bil, I think I have them memorized by now." Bil nodded and waved at me to begin.

I slid into the role. It was a dismal scene of the play, at a point where all seemed lost. The Fool turns into a human and tells Leander that Iona has married another at her father's behest, and he believes the falsehood. Iona was heartbroken, certain that her life was over. She contemplates suicide.

I sat down on the floor and gathered imaginary skirts about myself and looked up, as if out of a window at the top of my cell. I wiped an imaginary tear from my cheek.

"*Oh, moon and stars, lord and lady on high –*
Shine your light on a wretch whose end is nigh.
Leander, my love, is in danger so true.
My cheek's petals are now heavy with dew."

I looked down at my clasped hands.

"*Please, moon and stars, lord and lady, free me*
From this life full of lonesome agony
If no more my lips will his fingers trace
I'll trade him for sable death's sweet embrace."

The play was not particularly delicate or subtle, but it evoked the emotions needed from the audience. There were a few half-hearted claps from the stands. Bil's eyebrows snaked up his forehead.

"He's not bad, let's have him as the woman and open some ale!" Rian called. A bruise bloomed on his cheekbone.

"Try the second set of lines, Micah, where Iona first meets and falls in love with Leander," Bil said. He read the lines from the page before him, furrowing his brows and stumbling over the meter.

I stood up, dusting my trousers. "Can I see the paper?"

He passed it to me and I scanned the lines a few times.

"Doesn't surprise me much that you can read," Bil said, digging. I ignored him.

"Oh yeah – Drystan, your lines are first," Bil said before I began.

Drystan came from the stands and was given his own lines to read. Unlike me, he did not hide who he had been outright, though he had neglected to tell them he was one small step removed from royalty. He stepped forward, clasped my calloused hands and gazed into my eyes, his face relaxing into an adoring smile. It was an effort not to look away in embarrassment.

"Never have I seen a lady so fair,
How I long to touch your long, flaxen hair
A mere man like me – I'm in awe of you.
With a brow so noble and eyes so blue.

"How is it that I dare to speak to thee?
Some spirit of love has o'er taken me
Oh, strike me, stone me, good Lady and Lord
I am too base to call her my adored."

Drystan must have taken theatre training as a child or at university. He embraced the clunky lines, making them seem like natural speech, earnest and sincere. When mentioning my flaxen hair, he had nearly stroked my head, but his fingers had danced away at the last second, as if he did not dare. He drew me closer, pressing me against his chest. I felt a stir a little too similar to how I felt when I had been alone with Aenea. It was easy to act bashful, to gaze down at the floor and turn my face away from his.

> *"Oh sir, you waste the coin of your rich words*
> *My face is not fair, though I come from lords*
> *My looks and my fortune are plain indeed*
> *I confess I know not how to proceed –*
>
> *"I fear that my speech is modest as well*
> *When compared to the words of your love's spell*
> *So I must speak plainly when I tell you*
> *That I, kind sir, do dare to love you too."*

Characters seem to fall in love so easily in plays. Drystan put a finger under my chin and lifted my face toward his and met his lips with mine. I tried very hard not to choke or break away. I also found myself wanting to deepen the kiss, which unleashed an avalanche of guilt. My palms dampened, and my limbs tingled. Drystan broke the kiss and stepped away from me, and his sardonic grin returned, as if he knew exactly what I was thinking and how I was feeling. I stood there, blinking.

The circus clapped. "Micah, that'll do," Bil said. "You're Iona. Zahn, you'll play the Lord at the finale. That's settled then. Come along, me lovelies, let's eat," he said, and people began to file out of the tent, a few clapping me on the shoulder as they passed.

Aenea left last and we walked out of the tent together.

"Congratulations," she said, her tone impassive.

"You're not angry with me, are you?" I asked.

She was surprised. "Why would I be angry?" She raised an eyebrow, daring me to mention my kiss with Drystan. But I could not mention it. I worried she would ask if I liked the kiss, and that was a lie I would not be able to tell.

"No reason."

"You both did very well," she said, twisting her head slightly away from me. "Have you acted before?"

I grinned, relieved she was not pushing the issue, though still remorseful. "My brother and I put on little performances growing up, and commandeered some of our friends to join in, though my brother was always the hero and I was always the heroine."

She laughed, though it sounded forced. "Your brother is older than you, then?"

"Yes." I hoped she did not ask more about my past. She did not realize that she had already met my brother, after a fashion.

"He's a little cruel, to have had you dress up as the woman all the time."

"I didn't mind. It was good fun."

She knocked her hip against mine lightly. "It'll be funny to see you dressed as a woman."

I raised my eyebrow at her. "Maybe you'll like it."

She laughed again and slapped me lightly on the shoulder. "Maybe, but I think I'll still prefer you in trousers."

We did not have enough time to do everything that needed to be done by the time we reached Imachara.

We had to arrive before the beginning of the highest point of summer, to take advantage of the warm weather and visiting nobles from all over Ellada and various colonies for the summer balls. Not only would some nobles perhaps wish to dip into the "peasantry" entertainment of the circus, but all of their servants and liverymen would definitely wish to attend. Combined with the fact that there were over four or five times as many people in Imachara as in Sicion, Bil was not about to let the opportunity for more money to go to waste.

But he should have had us leave Sicion much sooner. We were there as long as possible to eke out as much coin as we could, but now we had barely practiced, let alone learned, our new routines. In addition to their clowning, which were some of the most varied and different in the circus, some clowns also had to practice the sleight of hand needed for the "magic" in the play.

I was still trying to master the trapeze, could only do the most basic of tricks, and had to also learn far too many lines. Costumes for the pantomime were sewn as quickly as possible, and the sets had only just started to be designed, much less made. From dawn to past dusk, the entire circus was working as quickly as they could, but with speed came mistakes. And with mistakes came Bil's temper.

Bil could not admit that he had made an error, and he screamed at anyone who was, by his standards, working too slowly or not up to snuff. Threats of expelling people from the circus occurred multiple times per day, but they were empty threats. He needed us all, and disliked that we knew it.

When he realized the risk of mutiny at his rate of abuse, he become conciliatory, offering various bonuses and saying over and over again that this would be the year that R.H. Ragona's Circus of Magic would truly become the best circus in Ellada. He said that after the summer, there would be no more struggles, as if he believed it.

Nightly fights between Bil and Frit became louder and more frequent, and they would snap at each other during rehearsal, which had never happened before in all of their years at the circus, according to Bethany.

If Bil could pull off the pantomime and the various acts in Imachara, I had no doubt that it would be an extraordinary circus. It had seemed incredible the first time I had seen it months ago. But I feared what would happen if he could not keep up his delicate equilibrium.

I ducked my head and performed my own balancing act – learning my lines, learning my new trapeze routines, hoping Aenea and the rest of the circus did not discover what I was.

Bil never remembered to put someone else into my cart and I declined to remind him. Aenea would enter without a word, hang up her cloak, and visit long into the evening. I felt as though she knew me better than almost anyone – but I had still not told her my secret.

I wanted to tell her, but I was a coward.

I told myself that the time had not been right, that the moment had not presented itself yet, but it was a lie. I could have created the opportune moment. Moments had appeared, and I had let them wash over us.

It wasn't even so much that I did not trust Aenea. I did not trust secrets. Someone could overhear, Aenea could act differently around me without meaning to. Perhaps I would act differently towards her. Someone, like Frit, would notice. Secrets, once spoken, have a way of running away from you. They cannot be gathered in again.

"Do you miss your old life?" Aenea asked, once, as we were sitting together on my tiny pallet, holding hands.

"A bit," I said.

"Tell me something of your past. You so rarely mention it. Just a little detail. I'll tell you the same."

I rested on an elbow and looked at her. "I don't mention it much, do I?"

"Not really." She smiled. "I don't mind, but sometimes I am curious."

I tilted my head, considering what to say. "I miss my family, and the parents I felt I never knew. I miss my servants, who were my friends. Our maid raised me more than my mother did, in many ways."

Aenea's eyebrows shot up. "I can't imagine having a maid."

I shrugged a shoulder, knowing she did not really expect an answer. "But I also miss little things that I never thought I would. The smell of the soap we used to wash our clothing. The teacup I had my tea in every morning. The shape of the little crack in the window of my room. My books and the stray cat that lived in the alleyway by our tenements that I saw every day. Small things that I'll probably never see again."

She tucked a strand of hair behind her ear. "It must be strange. I've almost always been moving. Everything I own fits into the trunk in my cart. I can't remember the last time I was in the same place for a year."

She leaned against me, wrapped her arm around me and rested her head on my shoulder.

"Do you…" she hesitated. "Do you have a bandage about your chest?" she asked, rubbing her hand over my back. "I think I've noticed it before."

I stiffened, my mind whirring. "I have a bad spine sometimes. It's not enough to affect my tumbles, but it feels better to have the extra support." Damien's face was another reason the truth froze on my tongue. I remembered the night of the debutante ball when he realized he was partnered with me. The widened eyes, tinged with disgust, the curl of the lip, the way he backed away from me as quickly as he could, despite knowing how bad it looked.

I knew that Aenea was different from Damien. That she had grown up in the circus, with people with differing tastes. But the risk felt too great.

Aenea shifted, pressing her lips together. I did not know if she believed me. "You should be careful, then. Tell me if your back is too sore for practice."

"Of course," I said, miserable. I racked my mind for a change of subject. "You said you'd tell me something of your past."

"I did, didn't I?" She stared off into space. "It may not be a cheery thing. Is that all right?"

I focused on her face. The lines had hardened. Foreboding washed over me. "Whatever you feel like telling me."

She stayed silent a long time, and then spoke softly into the dark. "Two years ago, when I was fifteen, I met a man after the circus one night. He passed me a rose. From afar, it looked like it was real, but as I took it, I noticed that the petals were made from paper. He told me that the writing was love sonnets.

"He was a handsome man, though easily ten years my senior. But he was charming, and I was smitten. And he was every inch a gentleman. So I thought."

I cupped her hand in mine.

"This was in Imachara. He wooed me, taking me to lovely restaurants. He bought me little presents – trinkets and the like. He held me in the palm of his hand. I was ready to quit the circus for him, to leave everything. I knew I would follow him wherever he wished to take me.

"But he started to change. He'd manipulate me, subtly at first. He'd steer the conversation the way he wanted. He'd go just a little further than kissing, a little further than I wanted him to or I was ready for. And I wasn't stupid," she said, running a hand through her hair, turning her face away from me. I squeezed her hand.

"I knew he was doing it, but I thought it was perhaps what men did when they were… impatient. But he also started acting more secretive, disappearing for longer periods of time before visiting me. I wondered where he went. The circus season was closing, and I planned to go to Linde in the winter. So, when he next visited me and took his leave, I followed him."

She paused again, swallowing. The foreboding only grew. I said nothing; what could I say?

"He had a family, of course. He returned to his wife. I had suspected, but I was so heartbroken. I had thought him my knight and that soon he would propose and we would marry. He obviously came from wealth; I even imagined myself a lady – isn't that funny?" She laughed, bitterly.

"He saw me. Through the window. And he was terribly angry. He must have thought I was there to blackmail him, though I wouldn't. But he was… very cruel. The circus closed a week later, and I escaped to Linde."

There was so much more to the tale, hidden in the pauses and in the veiled meanings of her words. I did not need to know more. He had hurt her.

"Every time we go to Imachara, I worry that I'll come across him again. That he'll come to the show with his family, looking at me with that knowing smirk." She shuddered.

I drew her toward me. She had opened up so much to me. And I had left so much of myself closed to her.

"That's a terrible thing to go through," I said, my words feeling inadequate.

She tilted her head upwards and I comforted her without words, kissing her as tenderly as I knew how. She ran her hands along my back, her fingertips dancing over my bandages, twining about my ribs, to the plane of my stomach, to the waistband of my trousers–

Gently, I pushed her hand away. She pulled away, embarrassed.

"I'm sorry–" she began.

I pressed a finger to her lips. "No need," I said, and kissed her again.

We cuddled on the straw pallet.

"Micah?" Aenea asked, hesitant.

"Yes?"

"Did something happen to you?"

"What do you mean?"

"Like what happened to me. When you were younger? Is that why you're shy? I thought you were comfortable, but..." she trailed off.

I thought of my many visits to the doctors. I thought of the humiliation of disrobing and presenting myself to inspection, of being poked and invaded. I thought of how I was nearly mutilated, without a say in the matter. I remembered my mother's cutting words, always telling me that I had to hide what I was, that no one would accept me. That no one would love me. I remembered the feel of Damien's wandering hand and the look in his eyes in that tree and on the dance floor.

"I've been hurt. I don't think anywhere as much as you, but I've been hurt."

She kissed my neck. "I'll try not to hurt you."

"I'll try, too." I rested my cheek against the top of her head, wondering if it was a promise I could keep.

We drifted off to sleep.

23
SPRING: THE POLICIERS

"Under our Bow."

THE CONSTABULARY'S MOTTO

Mister Illari, after learning I had not slept the night before, urged me to rest. He brought me some brightly colored quilts and striped furs. The cyrinx fur had a purple sheen to it and was impossibly soft. Though Mister Illari and Calum seemed trustworthy enough, I still made sure that I slept with my satchel underneath my head. I slept fitfully, uncomfortable in strange surroundings, and dreamed of my parents chasing me with knives. My dreams were never cryptic.

When I awoke, it was early afternoon. "So, Micah," Mister Illari said as I stumbled into the small kitchen, rubbing sleep from my eyes. "What are you going to do now that you're in the big, wide world? How long have you been out on the streets?"

"A few days," I said, staying vague.

"Not very long at all, then."

"No, not very. And I don't know what I'm going to do. I haven't quite figured that out yet."

"You may want to have a bit of a think about that."

"I have been, believe me." I stared at the ground, brooding.

Mister Illari gave me a light slap on the upside of the head. "Come now, no moping! What are you good at? Did these noble parents teach you anything useful, or was it all horseback riding out at your country home and hunting with the hawks?"

"We didn't have horses or hawks, I'll have you know." I paused, thinking. "I can speak Byssian and read a bit of Temri." I could also read a bit of Alder, but I kept that to myself. It was a very difficult language to learn for most, but I found it easy.

"Useless. All you could do is apply to be a scribe. And then you'd come into contact with the nobility and risk discovery by someone who knows of you. They like their scribes to be illiterate, in any case, just knowing how to copy letters in the alphabet. Less chance of error if they don't know what they're writing."

They might not recognize me, but I could not risk it. My shoulders slumped. "You're right."

"Well, what else?"

What else, I thought? I could sew and embroider, though not very well. I could dance the woman's part to all of the court steps and dance passable ballet. I could play the piano badly and sing even worse. I knew a bit of history and could do my sums. Nothing my mother taught me was useful for the streets. Perhaps that was why they only taught women useless things – so that they did not run away.

"I'll find something," I said. "I'm good at climbing."

"Then there's always thievery."

I paused and considered it, imagining myself scaling walls in the dark, sliding open windows, and shimmying into houses to pluck gold and valuables from jewelry chests. Then I imagined a gas light igniting, the call of alarm, the strong arms of Policiers and the cold metal of prison bars. Pilfering food to fill my gut when I had no other option was all the stealing I was willing to do.

"I don't think I'd be comfortable with that. Wouldn't I have to steal from nobility? I would run into the same problem if I were caught. And I can't pick locks."

"You could always learn. But no matter." Mister Illari bustled about the kitchen and took out a pan and some meat, potatoes, and capsicums. "How about this?" he said, turning to me. "We'll offer you our sofa for a time and you can help with my spice business. I won't be able to pay you anything other than room and board and the odd coin or two, but at least you know that you won't have to sleep on the streets if worse comes to worse."

I was silent for a moment, stunned. "Thank you," I said quietly. "That's very kind of you."

"Don't mention it," he said gruffly. "I like children."

"I'm not a child!"

"Fiddlesticks! You are, even if you think you're wise and grown. In as little as ten years, you'll look back on your previous self with a mixture of fondness and embarrassment."

"Will not."

"Suit yourself."

Mister Illari chopped meat that looked like cow or horse. The knife made a steady thump against the stone chopping block. He lit the gas cooker and poured oil into a pan.

Once the cooking was done, he set down plates of meat and vegetables all lightly dusted with spices of red, orange, green, and brown, with a carafe of more terrible coffee. The spices made my eyes and nose run, but the meal was delicious.

"So why did you leave home?" Mister Illari asked as I wolfed down my food. "Were you striking out to find fame and fortune? Is the plan for you to dance back into your parents' home and prove you didn't need their money?"

I fiddled with the fork. "No, I don't really want either. Just a life of my own. I don't think I'll ever return. But thank you for your kindness, Mister Illari."

He waved his hand at me. "Don't mention it. You did good work. It's good business to keep you on for a time." He reached into his pocket and handed me a coin. "Here's an advance."

I pocketed the coin. "Thank you, Mister Illari."

"You might not thank me in a wee while. You'll be grinding the peppers this afternoon. I've got a mask, but you'll still sneeze something fierce."

Before I could reply, there was a knock at the door.

"Who'd be visiting me?" Mister Illari muttered as he pulled himself upright and limped toward the door.

"Who is it?" he yelled.

"Policiers," came the muffled answer behind the door. The blood drained from my face.

Mister Illari turned a keen eye on me. "Your parents might have missed you, boy," he whispered. "Or Mattos must have noticed the description of a missing child. Quick, hide in the cupboard.

"Just a minute!" he called more loudly to the door. "These old bones don't move so quickly anymore."

I darted into the pine wardrobe, filled with spare blankets and towels, sweet spices like cinnamon and vanilla tickling my nose.

Don't sneeze, I prayed.

"Sorry to bother you, Mister Illari," one said. I couldn't see what he looked like, but his voice reverberated deep in his chest. "But have you seen this young child? She's been missing for several days."

Mister Illari made a great show of huffing and hmming. "A missing girl? No, I can't say that I have. Calum, have you seen this girl?"

"No, definitely haven't seen no girl about here."

"Why do you ask, my good fellows?" Mister Illari wheezed.

"A fellow Policier sent a child to assist you who may have matched the description. Policier Mattos. He said the girl might have been dressed as a lad," the other Policier said. He had a reedy voice.

"Ah, that young fellow. He sure didn't look like a girl. He helped me carry up the spices, I tipped him, and he scampered off. That'll probably be the last I see of him, I expect. I'll be sure to let you know if he shows up."

"Be sure that you do," Deep Voice said. "Can we take a quick look around?"

"Now why would you want to do that, as I've already told you the pipsqueak ain't here. Do you have a warrant or anything?"

"No need to take that tone, Mister Illari," Reedy Voice answered.

"If that's all, boys, I'm afraid I've lots of work to be getting around to right about now."

"Fine, but we'll be checking back occasionally, to see if you remember anything else. Her family is mighty worried about her. Might be fruitful of you to remember something – they'll be thankful if she's returned safe and sound."

"I'll keep that in mind, young lad."

Their footsteps retreated down the stairs. Mister Illari waited a minute before opening the doors.

"So you're a girl, eh?" he said.

I grimaced guiltily. "I guess."

Calum gaped at me. "You don't look like a girl." He squinted. "Well, maybe a little."

"They'll keep coming back, they said. Maybe I should go. I don't want to cause a fuss."

Mister Illari shrugged. "I'm not too worried about them."

But even though they were both nice, I felt like I was intruding on their little life. I did not think Mister Illari really needed another helper, and suspected that he was digging into his retirement fund to help me.

"It's all right, Mister Illari," I said. "I think I'll leave and try and find my own way."

He scratched his balding head. "Maybe it might be best, until the dust with the Constables settles. One of 'em, Smythe, thinks I'm cheating on my dues to the Crown. And, truth be told, I do, because otherwise they'd rob me blind. He's always starting trouble. He'd love to find me harboring a young scamp like you."

I nodded, though dread settled deep within me. Just as I thought I had found a safe place, I learned that it was no such thing. And this flat was too small for three.

"But if you see yourself with a decided lack of food and face sleeping in an alleyway, you come right back, you hear?" He waggled a finger at me.

"I will," I said, relieved, though I realized I would probably never actually return. "How should I go about acting less… noble, then?" I asked, timid.

Mister Illari laughed. "It'd take too long to teach you and I'm not sure you'd catch on all that quickly. No offense," he said as I opened my mouth to protest.

"So what do I do?"

"The best advice I can give you is this: listen far more than you talk, and listen to what others say and how they say it. You'll get the noble knocked out of you in no time."

Calum plucked at my sleeve. "What?" I asked.

"Your clothes are too posh," he said, wrinkling his nose.

I held my arms out and looked down. "They're just a linen shift and trousers," I said defensively. And they were none too clean any longer.

"With no holes, no mends, and no threadbare bits?" Mister Illari shook his head. "Tut, tut, lad. You stood out a mile away. That's likely why Policier Mattos sent you over to me, and why he thought of you again when the Constabulary received your description. Give your clothes to Calum and we'll give you some proper street rat clothes."

"You're a sly merchant," I said. "You get a nice pair of clothes for some shoddy ones? That hardly seems fair."

"Calum gets something he can grow into and you don't get your throat slit one night for them to be taken off your corpse." Mister Illari shrugged. "Seems fair enough to me."

I swallowed, remembering the two moonshades who had stolen all of my money. *Be grateful we're letting you go.* "Good point."

Calum grinned as wide as his mouth would allow. "Come on," he said. "I'll let you choose any outfit of mine you like. I'll even give you an extra shirt!"

I followed him into a small bedroom. A large bed was covered with more bright quilts and furs. Books lined the shelves in haphazard order, dotted with yet more figurines.

Calum rummaged in a canvas bag and dumped a small pile of clothes onto the bed. "Here," he said. "Take your pick." He snatched at a couple. "Well, except for these."

They were all nearly identical. I grabbed two shirts and a ratty pair of mostly-brown trousers. One of the shirts was more patch than original fabric.

"Your… master seems to be fairly comfortable. Why do you wear such shabby clothes?" I asked.

He shrugged. "I'll outgrow them soon enough. Mister Illari says when I'm full-grown I'll have nice clothes. But not too nice, because then you start attracting unwanted attention."

"He seems to be a wise man."

He nodded proudly. "That's why I love him."

"Is he a relative of yours?"

"Nah. Policier Mattos chose me to help with the spices, just like you. I was the wee one of my family. Got six brothers and two sisters. When my ma fell with a babe again, I asked Mister Illari if I could come stay here instead, and he said aye. I think he was lonely, and I like it here. I'll probably take over the spice business when Mister Illari gets too old."

I nodded.

"I'll be out in a moment," I said. "I'll leave your new clothes on the bed."

"Ah, right," Calum said, coloring. "I shouldn't watch a girl change. Are you a Lady of the Sap, then?" Sap was the slang-term for nobility. It was borderline rude, but I knew Calum meant no harm.

I half-smiled. "I was, I guess. But not anymore." Calum shot me a grin and scuttled from the room. I changed quickly and slung my rucksack over my shoulders. The clothes were too small, and my bony wrists poked far out of the sleeves.

I felt suddenly awkward in the lounge. Here were two people who had shown me true generosity. I wish I did not have to leave them so soon. I gave them both handshakes. "I'll never forget your hospitality." I took the coin he had given me from my new pocket. "Here, you should keep this, as I haven't ground the chili pepper."

Mister Illari gave me a dismissive wave. "It's no bother. Keep it. I feel rotten having to throw you out so soon after inviting you into my home. And come see me at the market some time for some spices, if you end up doing well enough on your own." His tone was joking, but underneath, I could tell he did feel badly for having to turn me out. Or maybe he regretted taking me in the first place.

One side of my mouth quirked in sad imitation of a smile. "I will," I said. "Thank you." I hesitated.

"Get on with you, then," he said, waving me toward the door.

● ● ● ●

Again, I had no idea where to go. I clutched the Kedi ornament in my hand as I walked through the streets, keeping an eye out for Policiers, hiding behind the people in the crowd when I saw one. I did not know what Deep Voice and Reedy Voice looked like.

Constantly glancing over my shoulder, I made my way to the little nest in the attic of the tenement in the Pauper District. But setting foot in the attic, I realized I could not stay there any longer, either. I must have left some crumbs from my food, for between that and the weather warming, I saw a rat or two, and heard more scrabbling in the walls. Scrunching my face with distaste, I left, vowing only to return if I had no other choice.

Evening was turning to dusk as I made my way toward the beach. I had always wanted to go the beach when I was young, but we rarely went. Father was always too busy, and Mother did not exactly love the outdoors.

"You brown too easily. Besides," she had said whenever I asked. "It's not like you would be able to wear a bathing costume with your... condition." My mouth twisted at the memory.

The few times we did go to the beach, I had to be weighted down with skirts. I loved walking barefoot in the sand. So while I had swum in ponds in the summer, I had stuck little more than a toe in the ocean, and Mother had chided me for it when I had salt-stained a dark green dress.

The beach was quiet other than the soothing sounds of the waves rising and crashing, a rush and swoosh as if the ocean was breathing. The sea mist sprayed my face. I breathed in time with the waves and rolled up my trousers and waded into the ocean until it reached mid-calf. The water was beyond freezing and my feet and ankles had gone numb, but I did not care.

Life had been strange, the past few days. When I think back to that time now, I cannot believe how lucky I was. Had the moonshades seriously harmed me, had Mister Illari been a darker sort of fellow, had someone attacked me under the docks, then my time may have been cut short.

Maybe I would have never run away in the first place, had I known.

The beach was deserted but for fewer than a dozen people. I sat down, buried my frigid feet in the sand, and wished I had some food to eat. I shivered, wrapping my arms around myself, staring at the dark horizon. When the cold became too much to bear, I walked up the beach, my feet in the sea water. I remembered that tonight was the last day of spring, and that tomorrow would be the first day of summer.

I could see lights up ahead, not just the sickly amber glow of gas lamps lining the streets and the beach promenade, but lights of white, red, green, and blue. As I approached, sounds floated towards me. Bright brass instruments, a low thumping of a drum, laughter, shouting, and the throaty roar of an animal. When I realized what it was, my salt-caked face split into a grin.

The circus was in town.

24
SUMMER:
THE SCALED HERO OF A COWL

"There has been a sharp rise in birth defects in the last score of years. Many have not been live births, but sad, twisted creatures that the doctors have hidden from their mothers. Something that could never live. Some say it's a curse from Styx's Darkness. Others say it's the fault of the mother, for feeling too many lustful or vengeful emotions during pregnancy. Some say it is caused by Penglass or Vestige, or that it is the first sign of returning Chimaera. No one truly knows, but doctors are working to find a cure."

HEALTH REPORT TO THE ROYAL SNAKEWOOD
UNIVERSITY OF MEDICINE

When we put on our final show for the tiny village of Cowl, the villagers loved it.

Every man, woman, and child came. It was an annual event, the first look at the circus worthy of the great city of Imachara, which most of them had never seen. It made the villagers feel privileged, and livened up their town while we were here. They dressed in their best garments. The girls tied ribbons, little more than colored rags, in their hair and the wives twisted their hair into patterned cloth. The men wore fabric flowers in their buttonholes, for fresh flowers were too rare and dear.

Even so, we only had to erect one small stand to fit the entire population of Cowl. But we performed for them as if we were already in Imachara, as if royalty were in the stands. Many of the circus performers were from small villages like these, and they remembered how precious any bit of entertainment could be. The villagers stood up after the circus was over, and even the old men and women, whose faces seemed to have never been touched by a smile, beamed at us. I felt happier performing for them than I would have performing for the queen and princess of Ellada themselves. Well, perhaps.

And so one night, the circus came into the village square of Cowl.

We did not go into the city center more than once per visit, for the small village had trouble finding enough food to feed us. And, as much as they might enjoy our perform-ances, we were still the outlandish outsiders, ones that, as Drystan had put it, played a joke on the world.

The thatched roofs of the dilapidated buildings were greying. But although everything was third-hand, the peo-ple were responsible curators of their few possessions, and the town had no refuse in the streets. The air smelled of salt and smoked fish.

We all entered the room of the sole pub and inn of Cowl, the *Scaled Hood*. Tauro and Karg had to stoop under the low ceiling timbers. The pub smelled of paraffin and roast-ing meat. No residents of the village sat at the rough tables. They were in their homes.

The innkeepers, a husband and a wife whose family had owned the *Scaled Hood* for generations, entered and bid us welcome. As soon as we were all seated, they brought us tankards of ale, which was surprisingly good, though perhaps anything tasted wonderful compared to the swill we drank at the circus.

"Who was the scaled man?" I asked Aenea as we waited for the food.

She shrugged.

"Oh, petal, you don't know the story of Fisk? He was the hero of this little village, many, many years ago," Bethany answered, dabbing the beer foam from her moustache with a cloth. "He was a malformed weakling at birth, and very nearly left to the elements. He had red eyes and large red lips, but the strangest part was his skin. White as snow but cracked deeply into diamonds."

"Like a fool's motley," Drystan interrupted from several seats down. The whole table was listening to Bethany's tale, though most had probably heard it before.

"Don't interrupt, poppet. The poor boy looked more demon than fool. The village wanted him killed, but the parents persuaded them to wait and let the babe die of natural causes. Babies like this were, and still are, born more often in Cowl than any other town in Ellada."

"Are there any here, now?" I asked.

"Don't know. If there are, they've never come to the circus as long as we've been practicing. But stop interrupting, dove."

"Yes, Beth."

"The parents made the villagers promise that no harm would come to the boy. He was called Fisk, for as a child he looked like a fish. As you can imagine, he did not die, but grew. He swam in the sea every day, no matter the weather, to soothe his skin, and he took herbs his mother gathered or bought for him, for she was a great healer. Perhaps he was indeed part-fish, as he was the best fisherman in Cowl at the time. And because he was kind and good, the villagers loved him despite his strangeness, and any other scaled babies were left to live."

She leaned forward. "One fateful day, Northern Temnian raiders attacked the coast, planning to conquer Cowl and build a base to later attack the capital. The raiders were merciless, and no one could stop them. The townsfolk fought bravely, but the invaders were too strong. All seemed lost, and Cowl was doomed to fall.

"But Fisk knew the Temnians were a superstitious lot. He dressed in a black cowl and carried a staff topped with a glass globe to cast eerie shadows on his face. He strode amidst the battle, showing no fear, singing a song in his harsh voice that his mother had sung to him as a babe, a lullaby of loss. The raiders stopped the battle, terrified. He sung and lifted the staff, as if casting a spell. The raiders fled, never to return. Though many perished, including Fisk's own mother, the village of Cowl was saved, all because of a scaled man that had almost been left to die."

The food came, and we were silent as the platters clunked against the wood. It was a sad tale and yet it was not. Fisk did save the town and lived a long life.

The conversation turned to other topics, but the story of Fisk stayed with me, tucked into the same corner of my mind as the Kedi.

• • • •

The food was marvelous – small portions of roast pork, apple chutney, mashed potatoes, gravy, and some peas, all served with freshly baked bread cooked with oats and butter. We were paying a high price for every morsel, but to me, it was worth it. And throughout the meal, the ale flowed freely.

I had grown used to drinking ale with my meals, but not so strong, and before I knew it, the room took on a warm and pleasant glow. Everyone around me was ale-happy as well, though some more than others.

As the drink flowed, barriers lowered. The Kymri tumblers began to play their flutes and harps, dancing in place to their own music. Circus folk who rarely spoke with me clapped me on the back or swept me into a jig. I enjoyed the jocular atmosphere, and due to the copious amount of ale in my stomach, I caught myself grinning and laughing more than once. I danced with Aenea, content in this moment.

The drink made people talkative. I fell into a philosophical debate with Tin, the small man, about the merits of the monarchy.

"Fuck the Princess Royal!" Tin yelled, spilling beer.

"She's a child!" I responded. "Screwing her would mean losing a head, for her age if not her social station." I hiccupped.

"She'd like it," Tin said magnanimously.

"Why are you against her?" I had never known someone to speak against the future queen. The nobility knew better than to do such a thing openly.

"What's she done to deserve her silks and power? Naught."

I remembered my tutor's lectures. "She doesn't have any power, does she? The steward does."

"Aw, hell, she will soon enough. She's being primed for it. That wide-eyed innocence is all a ploy, so we don't care that she's robbing us blind and setting us up for war when she's of age."

Her family had avoided war for many years, but I knew better than to point this out to Tin, for war was a likely possibility.

"Doesn't seem like many in the circus are too fond of her. Funny, isn't it, considering we live outside her laws in many ways?"

"Aw, away with you, young master smart arse. We've all got problems with authority, ain't we, and you'll understand it more when you've sprouted your beard." Tin laughed at my indignant expression and took another gulp of beer. "Think I could get the innkeeper's daughter to come upstairs with me?"

"You can do whatever you set your mind to, I'm sure, Tin," I said, my mouth twisting.

"It ain't my mind I'm bothered with tonight." He jumped off of his stool and weaved his way to her. He tugged at her skirt. She looked about, brown curls swaying, and glanced down. Her expression was hostile, but at his words she broke into laughter, as if in spite of herself. I wondered what he'd said to her.

I took advantage of people's moods and spoke to nearly everyone that night. I flirted harmlessly with the contortionists, joked with the friendlier clowns, asked the Kymri tumblers to teach me a few words in their language – the curse words, naturally – and jabbered at anyone who would speak with me. Sal and Tila were on top form, finding increasingly creative ways to make me blush. Aenea watched me from across the room, highly amused, as she chatted with Bethany and Karla.

I had a mug of ale too many and the tavern began to tilt and sway. I had to grasp the table tops to make my way about. Stumbling outside for some air, I took deep breaths to settle my stomach.

I sat under the oilskin window of the pub, staring at the scaled hero of Cowl. His hood was pushed down, revealing his scaly face and wide, staring eyes.

"What had Fisk, the man behind the hero, been like?" I asked the night air, grandiose in my drunkenness. The night did not respond.

Bil stumbled out into the night from the tavern door, breathing heavily. He leant over and emptied his stomach, the sour smell causing me to gag. He did not notice me in the shadows beneath the windows.

Sal was returning from the outhouse. Bil stopped her.

"Can I interest you in a bit of business tonight, Sal?"

Sal paused, looking him up and down in his drunken state.

"You've never asked before, Bil. Trouble with Frit?"

"You don't know the half of it. Well?"

She paused, uncertain. "You don't like it much if I peddle to other circus members."

"I'm a little different now, ain't I? I only run the blooming thing." His words slurred.

She hesitated again. "I thankee kindly for your offer, Bil, but I don't think I'm of a mind to tonight."

Bil staggered toward her. "Why not?"

She backed up a step. "You and Frit, you're having some

troubles, but you'll work them out like you always do. But if Frit ever found out, she'd never forgive me, and once you sobered, I don't think you could forgive me, neither."

Bil staggered toward her, crushing her to him and kissing her roughly. One of his hands disappeared down the front of her top, the other up her skirt. Sal's arms battered against him. She was not a weak woman, and one of the blows to the side of his head caused him to let her go and lurch away.

"Stupid bitch," he snarled, tottering toward her again.

Prepared, she danced out of his reach. "You've no right, Bil Ragona," she said.

"No right to couple with a whore?" he snarled. He braced himself to rush toward her again.

I stood and started strolling unsteadily toward the outhouse, whistling merrily. At the sound, they paused and stared at me, Sal's eyes wide and Bil's red. The air seemed to deplete from Bil. He looked oddly small. He sighed. "Get back inside, Sal. Where it's warm..."

She gave me a smile, as if nothing were wrong, and returned to the tavern. Bil gave me a drunken salute and walked to the statue and rested his forehead against its cold stone. I went to the outhouse and walked inside the tavern, and after another couple of tankards of ale and more dancing, I forgot what I had seen. Mostly.

25

SUMMER: THE CLOCKWORK WOMAN

"The Moon and the Sun circled each other in their dance, warming the world. From the dust of the aether they created seeds, which they scattered. Countries grew from each seed to become large continents whose names are now lost to history, stretching for many, many miles. Forests bloomed, deserts smoldered under the hot sun, and waves lapped the sand dunes. First came the Alder, and then the humans, and then the Chimaera. But then one day, there were no more Chimaera, and then no more Alder. The waters rose, and the humans were all alone, with only a vague promise that one day, perhaps, their dreams will return."

from THE APHELION

Imachara was even larger than I remembered.

The train crested a hill and wove toward the city, which stretched from the coast to as far as I could see. The city had originally been built in vaguely labyrinthine shapes, each quarter formed into a spiral. After years of construction, the spirals had uncoiled into a maze of side streets.

The granite city's wonderful architecture was monochrome compared to the different shades of sooty limestone in Sicion. Stone was a trade Ellada did well in. The city sprawled below us like a smudged charcoal drawing.

"Haven't you been to Imachara before?" Aenea asked, noting my stare.

"Yes, but not for some time," I lied. I had been last year.

"Where did you go in Imachara, as a merchant's son?" she asked.

"Mainly we went to fetch stock and supplies for the shop in Sicion, but occasionally we would also go to a restaurant, a play at the theatre, or one of the smaller balls."

"I've always wanted to go to a ball," Aenea said a little wistfully, and I remembered her tale of the past love who had hurt her, and who she had hoped would turn her into a lady. And yet now she was with someone who had been introduced at a debutante ball as a lady. It was funny, and it was very much not.

The doors to the compartment behind us, Bil's compartment, whooshed open. Frit stormed past us on the train, her hands balled into fists. We hit a turn in the tracks, and she lost her balance, sprawling along the floor. She looked up and I met her gaze. Her hair had tumbled from her bun and eyes were rimmed red and angry as a coal in a hot fire. I flinched and she broke our gaze. Tauro helped her up. Frit brushed herself off and gathered the shreds of her dignity about her. The entire cart was quiet, pretending we had not noticed her tumble.

She glanced over her shoulder, as if she expected Bil to have followed her. Nobody was there. She limped from the cart, slamming the compartment door behind her with a sound like a gunshot.

"Poor Frit," Aenea whispered.

"It's getting worse, isn't it?"

"It is. People think she'll leave soon. And to be honest, I hope she does. She deserves better than this."

Our fingers intertwined.

"They must have loved each other, once," I said.

"They did, I know it. When I first joined, I had never seen two people more in love. People were amused as first, with Bil so large and Frit so small and thin, sort of unassuming. But they were always together, joking and laughing. Frit used to always smile. They seemed to fit together perfectly. I thought to myself, 'That's what love is'. I suppose I was wrong."

"They say love and hate are closely tied, that they can turn at a moment's notice."

She sighed.

It took over a week to construct the circus on the beach of Imachara.

Nearly every aspect of the circus had to be bigger for the capital. The big top looked like an odd cloth-draped spider puppet as it slowly emerged onto the packed sand on stone. The seating stands in the big top were stacked as closely as possible so that a few more hundred bodies could fit into the tent. A larger tent was used for the freakshow, so that more people could see its contents. The carnival would be nearly twice the size of Sicion's, with many local merchants bringing their own carts and tents of wares.

We all helped erect the circus, and practice for the pantomime lasted long into the night. After three days, we were all teetering with exhaustion.

One morning, Drystan made an announcement at breakfast. Bil was still abed, probably with a hangover from Styx, judging by how much he had quaffed the night before.

"Listen!" Drystan cried, rapping a spoon against an empty pot. "Bil has generously given us the morning off to catch our breaths." Everyone cheered.

"But it's only the morning. We're under a tight deadline, and we still have far more to do than we'd like. So be back by two hours past noon. And no drinking!" he called over the sound of many bodies returning their trays to have as much time in the city as possible.

I was bouncing with so much excitement I felt as if I had springs attached to my soles. Aenea grinned with just as much enthusiasm.

"What shall we do?" she asked. "Is there something you wanted to see the last time you were here that you did not get a chance to?"

I thought a moment, and then I kissed Aenea on the cheek. "I know just the place."

"What is it?"

"A surprise."

"I'll go gather my things."

I raced to my cart and pocketed the remains of my coins and changed from my patched practice clothes to my less-worn ones and a light summer jacket. Knowing that Aenea would be primping and preening, I polished my shoes and ran a comb through my hair with a bit of pomade Arik had left behind. Before leaving, I glanced about the cart in dismay. As soon as Arik had left, I had given up any pretense of tidiness. I shrugged into my jacket and hurried to Aenea's cart.

"My, but don't you look dapper," Aenea said when she came out of the cart she shared with Dot and the new contortionist, Ellen. She made quite a portrait herself, in the same green dress she had worn on our outing to Sicion together.

"And don't you look positively breathtaking, my lady," I said, offering her my arm. The day would be sweltering. Aenea soon opened her parasol and we strolled beneath it.

Imachara was very different from Sicion, the air more fetid and cloying, the streets packed with passersby. The Penglass ridge of Imachara dwarfed that of any other city, jutting into the air like the spinal ridge of a dragon. On a sunny day like this, the strange domes bathed large swaths of the city in blue shadow.

Imachara was a constant bustle. Every night, something would be playing in the grand amphitheater, the Crescent, or any of the various smaller theatres. In the height of the season, balls were held by each prominent noble family, three or four a week. The grandest would always be in the Beach Ballroom, which we could just see from the site of the circus. Late at night, I had crept there and listened to the music, wondering if anyone I knew was dancing inside.

Shops peddled wares from all over the world – glass and crystal from Kymri, leather and animal goods, Temri shops of jewelry, and Lindean exotic wood. The summer market was also in town, in Silvergold Square, where even more treasures could be found.

"This must be a wonderful place to be rich," Aenea said, wonder and jealousy tinting her voice as we watched a lord and lady exit a carriage, leading a toddler between them, and walk into the Kymri glass shop. By their crest on the carriage, I knew they were the Balsas – a prominent family, but nowhere near the most wealthy or powerful.

"It's probably an equally terrible place to be poor," I replied, nodding toward the dirty and pinched faces of the beggars on most corners.

"Isn't any place awful to be poor?"

"Maybe not Temne or Linde. You can eat fruit all day long and it's always warm. You could live in a tree."

Aenea laughed. "You'd like that, you monkey. And then you could be eaten alive by a snake or slowly drained of blood by insects."

"True." I went into a newsagent's and bought a map. Unfolding it, my brow furrowed as I tried to find our destination. It was not on the map.

"You don't know where we're going?" Aenea teased.

"I've only been to Imachara a handful of times, and always with my parents. Tarry a moment." I returned to the newsagent's and asked for directions. We were not far, which was lucky, as I had no fare for a hansom cab. I thanked the man and we headed toward the boundary of the Glass and Gilt quarters.

Imachara was more clearly divided by class than Sicion, out of necessity. We were wandering through the merchant section, or the Brass Quarter, which also encompassed the docks. The Glass Quarter and the Brass Quarter were where the merchant classes lived, and the Gilt Quarter housed the nobles and richest of merchants. On the side of the city furthest from the Gilt Quarter were the Nickel and Copper quarters, for the destitute. The Penny Rookeries housed the poorest of the poor. As we walked closer to the Glass and Gilt, the streets became wider, cleaner, and less crowded. The sun sparkled off the mica of the granite pavement.

"Hey," I laughed. "My name matches Imachara better than Sicion, doesn't it?"

"So it does."

The buildings grew increasingly ornate and grand. The men and women passing us wore silks and brocades. I hoped they would let us into our destination with our clean but plain muslin and cotton.

The Museum of Mechanical Antiquities was a tall, narrow building squeezed between a clothing boutique and a high-end butcher. The paint of the sign flaked, the stone was layered with decades of grit and soot, stark against the clean buildings to either side. I did not remember it being so run down. I was amazed the city of Imachara allowed it to stay open, looking as it did in such a good neighborhood.

Aenea's eyes lit with delight. "I've heard of this place and have always wanted to go. Well done, Micah!" She kissed me.

I had been to the Mechanical Museum once before, but it had been over eight years ago. One artefact in particular had been my favourite, and I hoped it was still there.

Aenea paid for both of our tickets.

"No," she held up her hand as I held out coins to her. "You paid for me last time, and I have a better wage than you." I was relieved, having few coins left to my name.

The museum had once been extraordinary, but the mirrored panels were cracked and the marble floor in need of polishing. The faded shell still housed priceless artefacts. Many people still visited the Mechanical Museum each year, and plenty were milling around that afternoon, but the money must not have stretched far enough for cosmetics. Judging by the doors and the guards, the money went to security.

"I've heard all sorts of stories of this place," I told Aenea, taking her hand. "The government once owned everything and opened the museum for the public. After a while, between the attempted break-ins and the cost of maintenance, they were going to close it down. So a private investor decided to buy the building and also showcase his artefacts, and he had enough to rival the Royal Palace.

"But the investor has been away from Ellada for years and did not leave clear instructions, so everything is slowly winding down. The government might retrieve their treasures and this place will probably close."

"So sad. This place is wonderful. It should always be open."

"Can you imagine how rich the investor must have been, to own a lot of these? I mean, look at this," I said, drawing her to the nearest display case. A monstrous gun that looked as if it should be monumentally heavy, but the placard stated weighed no more than a pistol. It once had the capability to shoot light beams that would "cut a man in twain" but had lost its power during the last Great War, over six hundred years ago.

We examined each of the weapons. A great crossbow that could shoot over a mile and had once had a tracking ability. A spear with a rotating head. Countless other guns of all shapes and sizes.

"Small wonder we blew the colonies to pieces," Aenea said, pointing at another cruel-looking crossbow with poisoned bolts.

"Never had a chance."

After the weapons came the armor, fitted on eerie, faceless mannequins made of wood. Some of the suits of armor had animal themes. A man wore armor as if made from tiny scales with the crest of a dragon on the chest. Another piece was etched as if in flames, the metal painted black, orange, and red. Untold centuries later, and there was not a chip or flake of color missing. A woman's armor had the theme of a large cat, with topaz eyes on the helm and tufted ears.

None of the objects looked crafted by men, but rather seemed organic. Metals glinted blue, green, or orange when they hit the light, like oil mixed with water. Usually artefacts did not break; they simply ran out of power.

We wandered beneath a canopy of glass globes, some small enough for fairies, others large enough for just one to light an entire ballroom.

I watched Aenea beneath the lights. She caught me looking and smiled, drawing me in for a kiss, careless of the others surrounding us. Again, we had no chaperone, and thus were causing a minor scandal.

I pushed such thoughts from my mind and concentrated on Aenea's warm lips, the feel of her breath against my skin and her hands loosely around my shoulders.

Though the kiss was chaste, my body tingled when she pulled away.

The next section held ancient clothing. The tall, blank mannequins wore a thin form-fitting fabric that covered everything but their face – their skulls, necks, bodies, limbs, and even their fingers and toes. "Would you wear these?" Aenea asked me, chuckling.

"It would probably be wonderful for the trapeze, wouldn't it?" I said, though the strange costumes made me nervous. It would be impossible to hide what I was.

"We'd probably get plenty more seats in the audience. Lord's bum, I'd look naked in it!"

"I like the sound of that," I said.

"You're terrible," she said, laughing.

I smirked and we sauntered through the remains of the clothing section, each silently thinking about the Alder – what they must have been like, why they felt the need to leave if they had not all died, and if so, where they went, and if they would ever return.

"No clothing for the Chimaera," I said, thinking of the story Mister Illari had told me of the human-animal hybrids.

"That's because they're just folklore," Aenea said, bending closer to look at the weave of one of the outfits. "It's not like anyone's found any skeletons."

"You never know," I said.

The next section held jewelry and sundry household items. The Alder liked simple lines – the jewelry were all bands for the neck, wrists, and fingers. The waist bands for the women seemed impossibly small, too small for Aenea or me. The household items' intended use was at best ambiguous. Aenea and I made progressively out-landish guesses.

"That must be for trimming nose hair," Aenea said, playing the rube, pointing at a tiny, evil-looking pair of scissors.

"The Alder would never have anything as base as nose hair. They were pristine and hairless."

"What about brushing their hair?"

"As I said, they had no hair."

"And they never needed to brush their teeth?"

"Their teeth were impervious to decay."

"So what's this?" she said, pointing at an implement covered in spikes and brushes.

"Tickling device?"

We dissolved into giggles.

The last section of the museum was the one I had most been looking forward to showing Aenea. It held children's toys and other oddities that did not fit into the other areas. A large glass display held an empty puppet stage but for a small figurine of a female centaur.

The placard called it the "Chimaera Dance." If coins were put into it, a show would perform. Aenea and I blanched at the price it cost and were about to turn away. An obviously noble young boy of about six or seven vis-iting with his parents began pointing at the display case and making puppy eyes. The father chuckled and put in the coins. Gold coins.

Jaunty music, which was definitely not Vestige, began to play. And then the centaur pranced. A crowd gathered and we all watched the little automaton dance. She reared and spun about, waving as if beckoning. More little automatons paraded onto the stage, emerging from their hiding places. A fairy man and woman spun together, gazing into each other's eyes. A man with snakes for hair and scales on his limbs flipped well enough to rival our Kymri tumblers. After another minute the other automatons danced off the stage and the centaur woman made a last twirl and returned to her previous position.

"That was incredible," Aenea breathed.

"I agree." I did not remember this from my last visit. We shadowed the noble couple, trying to be inconspicuous. The boy asked to see everything.

"You can only choose one more thing to see, my darling," the mother said. "Look at everything and then choose the one that seems the most interesting."

"You're no fun, Mummy," the boy pouted.

"I know, darling," she said, smiling down at him. "But you'll thank me later. Now, hurry along." She watched him run to the next display case. She had that plain, interbred look about her that some noblewomen had, but she had a kind face and gentle manner of speaking. I wondered which family they were. The little boy could very well be my adopted third cousin thrice removed.

At the far end of the section was the artefact I remembered from my last visit. The boy had discovered it as well and turned to his parents, triumphant.

"I wanna see this one, please?" he asked his father, though the polite cadence seemed forced and practiced. I squeezed Aenea's hand. "This one is my favorite," I whispered into her ear.

It was a clockwork woman's head. She was life-sized, and her proportions were Alder – large eyes, high cheekbones and eyebrows, long neck. Even at rest, a muffled ticking could be heard through the glass. Her face had a strange skin, realistic in every way but for the fact it was transparent. The gears and pulleys of her face visible underneath looked to be made of brass. Her eyes were uncannily real, the irises a strange mixture of blue, green, hazel, and topaz, the eyelashes copper. The eyelids blinked occasionally. The father put the coins into the slot. Everyone else who had been following the noble couple gathered around again.

The clockwork woman awoke. She shook her head, blinked rapidly, and twitched her pale pink lips. She yawned, and her tongue was as mechanical as the rest of her, the teeth impossibly even and white. Her face settled into a pleasant smile and she stared straight ahead, almost expectant.

Below the glass of the display were ten brass knobs that could be pulled. Each was labeled with an emotion: happy, sad, scared, angry, bored, sleepy, surprised, mocking, impatient, and lusty.

"You can't pull this one," the mother said hurriedly, standing in front of the last lever. "But any of the others."

The boy giggled and tugged on "happy." The woman's face laughed, though no sound emerged. She looked positively joyful – eyes shining, enthusiasm radiating from every line. Most of the crowd could not help but smile in response. Her face relaxed into its earlier repose when the boy let go.

He pulled "sad." The woman's face became heartbreaking. Her eyes somehow grew bigger, and a tear of oil slid down one cheek, rolling off of the strange skin without leaving a mark. Her face collapsed into grief and she sobbed, again silent. The boy let go of the knob in surprise. Her face became serene.

The boy worked through the emotions, and each was perfectly executed. If the disembodied woman had not had translucent skin, I would have taken her for a real Alder woman. Her anger made us wince and recoil, her fear made us wish to comfort her, when she looked as if she were about to doze off, I half-expected someone to start singing her a lullaby. Her surprise made us jump, her mocking look and the twist of her lips as she mouthed presumed obscenities made us cower, and her boredom and impatience made us wish to entertain her. I could only imagine how her lust would have affected us. We would all have blushed to the roots of our hair. The Alder could not have been that different from us, to have such similar emotions.

The boy made her happy again, and then the time ran out and she returned to her normal state, ticking softly. The crowd dissipated, their faces pensive, leaving us alone by the glass display of the clockwork woman.

"Excuse me," Aenea said, clasping a hand over her mouth and left the room. I wasn't sure if she was frightened of the head or just needed a moment to herself. I was about to follow her, but then I heard it.

"Kedi," a voice whispered. I whipped my head around, my stomach dropping to my knees, my skin instantly clammy.

"Kedi," I heard again. The clockwork woman's head had not moved. Or had it? Her face had turned. She was looking right at me.

"Kedi." Her mouth formed the words, her gaze bored into mine. There was intelligence there, and hunger, and a fierce hope.

"Two Hands. Penmoon. Penglass. Copper," she said, still staring right at me. "Kedi."

What did that mean?

I felt a touch on my shoulder. I yelled and twirled.

Aenea jumped away from me. "Micah!" she said.

I rested a hand on my chest, willing my heartbeat to stop galloping.

"Are you all right?" she asked.

"I'm fine. You startled me. I'm sorry."

"Did she frighten you, too?" she whispered, her eyes darting to the clockwork woman.

I snuck a glance at the head. She was as she had been before, staring straight ahead, ticking softly.

"It's too real." Aenea's voice was husky. "How could they make something that real?"

"I don't know," I said, taking her hand. "I really don't."

"It was as if she had been guillotined and then imprisoned."

"It does." I wondered what had happened to the rest of her body.

Aenea pressed a finger against the glass, leaving a fingerprint.

Before we left her, I read the placard of the clockwork woman. She had been found in a deep cave just outside of the city. The head had rested perfectly on a small mound of Penglass, staring at the explorers as if waiting for them. Different pressure points at the base of her neck triggered the different emotions, and when one of the explorers picked her up, he triggered anger, which caused him to drop into a faint, and she almost toppled into a crevice. The image was an arresting one, but it would have probably been odder if he had triggered lust, or boredom.

But the small print at the bottom of the plaque caused a rushing in my ears. I rested a hand against the glass to steady myself.

From the private collection of Doctor Samuel Pozzi.

We left the museum and blinked in the bright light of day. I felt miles away, my mind reeling from that small engraved name, and from the whispered words from a mechanical mouth. What did it mean? Who was Doctor Pozzi, the man who gave me to my parents, and why had a relic from his collection spoken to me? Had the Damselfly once been his as well? These thoughts floated through my mind until I felt as though I would drown in question marks.

Aenea let me wander in silence before poking me in the shoulder, drawing me back to myself.

"Thank you for taking me there today," she said.

"Did you enjoy yourself?" I asked, remembering how the clockwork woman had affected her. Though not as much as she had affected me.

"It was wonderful. Beyond wonderful," she said. "The woman's head frightened me something fierce, I won't lie, but everything else was just... beyond words. The 'Chimaera Dance' was my favorite."

"Mine, too."

She smiled at me. "I'm hungry."

"Me, too." I said, though the thought of food twisted my stomach.

"You're always hungry."

"Ravenous!" I said, pushing the thoughts of the clockwork woman and her plaque firmly from my mind. I drew the human woman I cared for into a hug and nibbled her neck. She laughed and batted me away.

"The big summer market is on. Dot and Ellen were planning to go there this morning. It's a bit of a walk, but the food will be interesting and cheaper than a restaurant or coffeehouse."

"Excellent idea, my fairy of the trapeze." I held out my arm.

She took it and made a face at me, and the expression reminded me of the mechanical woman. I swallowed and took her arm.

Sicion's marketplace was a dwarf compared to the Imacharan's giant. Like Sicion, it was divided into levels, but each level was as large as a tenement building. Merchants were packed as tightly as they could be, the shoppers jostling and pushing each other to make their way through the throngs.

The press of the crowd was almost too much for me, and I took deep breaths. I held a hand over my coin purse. Cutpurses would be everywhere.

We followed our noses to the small stalls with sizzling meats and vegetables. We bought two Byssian dishes, a wrap made of a grain so dark it was almost black, filled with piping hot pork, peppers, onions, courgettes, and a spicy red sauce. Our eyes watered as we ate standing, and we washed down the fare with cold, tart lemonade.

"My mouth is still aflame," I gasped when we were finished.

"Mine too," Aenea said, fanning her fingertips in front of her pink face.

We found the sweets and purchased pastries. Aenea had one stuffed with almond paste and cherries, and I had one with chocolate and coffee mixed into the dough. We shared bites with each other, each proclaiming that ours was tastier. Aenea's laugh and banter distracted me from the cold pit of fear in my stomach that even the spicy food could not warm.

We explored the marketplace, and we jostled among the crowd, our ears battered by people yelling and bartering, the call of caged birds, and the sounds of the carriages driving over the cobblestones.

"Looking for anything in particular?" I asked Aenea as we battled our way to the clothing section.

"I'd like to buy a new dressing gown. My current robe has ripped and is badly faded."

We found a Lindean shop and Aenea selected a dressing gown similar to the one she had before, but with fish instead of birds.

"You'll have to model it for me later," I said.

"If you're nice."

"I'm always nice."

She snorted, eyes twinkling.

A garment caught my eye; a Lindean chest binder. The shop woman to this stall wore one, and her chest was flat as any boy's. Lindean woman abhorred large breasts, thinking them immoral and too tempting to men. My bandages itched beneath my shirt, and I knew I would return for the binder. The scabs on my chest would turn to scars before too much longer.

We wandered throughout the clothing shops, marveling at the strange pantaloons of the Kymri, the scandalous female garb of Temnian women, who, in total polarity to Lindean women, walked about bare-breasted in the sweltering heat of the jungles. A man stopped and stared at the mannequin's proud wooden bust in amazement, and then crudely asked the saleswoman why her chest was covered.

"Too cold and too crass here," she replied with a wink and a heavy accent. I suspected it was a well-rehearsed answer.

The marketplace sold everything except for Vestige. They were too valuable to sell in a stall, where nimble fingers could spirit them away. My eyes drank in the sights, my nose the smells, my fingers slyly touched the wares. I did not think I would ever be able to walk through a market without being in awe of how many coins' worth of products surrounded me.

The spice floor brought back memories of Mister Illari. I began to ask the vendors if any of them knew a Mister Illari in Sicion. They shook their heads. Aenea followed me, puzzled. Finally, I found one who knew him. He was also elderly, his face as brown and wrinkled as a walnut hull.

"Aye, I know him well. Good man. Heard tell he took ill, has been staying at home and his boy going to market for him."

"Do you go to Sicion often?" I asked eagerly.

"Aye, most every month or so."

"If you see Calum or Mister Illari, can you tell them that Micah has found his way? Please?"

The man nodded. "Sure enough. How you know him?"

"They were both very kind to me when I needed it

most. I wanted to thank them, but I don't think I'll be returning to Sicion for some time."

"I'll pass it along for you. Keen on any o' my spices? They're far better than Illari's." He winked.

"I'm not so sure, but I'll take some cinnamon, please. Would you like anything?" I asked Aenea. She bought some dried lavender.

I thanked him and pocketed the paper-wrapped cinnamon sticks, a smile on my face.

"So who's this Mister Illari, then?" Aenea asked as we made our way back to the circus.

"Not long after I ran away, I went to the Sicion market and watched people all morning, not sure what else to do. A Policier pointed me to Mister Illari, who hired me to carry his chests of spices to his cart. He was nice to me. Fed me, gave me a bit of money, and gave me a place to sleep for a few hours. Told me stories. He's the man who gave me the Kedi figurine."

"That's sweet, though I still don't see why you'd want that thing," she laughed.

"I'll tell you someday," I said, meaning it.

"Aye, sure you will," she said, taking my arm in hers. "Come along, we better hurry or we'll be late."

26
SUMMER: LEANDER & IONA

"I primp and prep, but what is it all for?
I met all my suitors: each I abhor.
This one snivels and that one cruelly sneers –
How can my father think these men my peers?

I wear my costume and make up my face,
Weighted down head to toe in jewels and lace.
With these grooms I dread my own wedding day,
But I must play my part in this world's play."
                    LEANDER & IONA, Godric Ash-Oak

After the circus was set up, we had a week to practice and make sure that the spacing for the equipment was just so. But on the first morning, neither Bil nor Frit arrived. The performers stood around the ring and looked at each other nervously.

"Should we go fetch them?" Dot asked.

"I don't know," Rian said. "Perchance they made up after the rather noisy fight last night and it was… exhausting." He waggled his eyebrows. We all made faces of disgust.

The fight had been terrible, with screeching from Frit and roars from Bil. From the few words I had heard, I knew far more about their crumbling marriage than I wanted to. Several of the circus folk had knocked on the door to Bil's cart, timidly asking if all was well, and Bil had screamed at them to stay away if they valued their jobs.

The sounds stopped past midnight, but it had taken me a long time to fall asleep.

This morning had been subdued, but now we all felt the stirrings of unease. Some of the performers stretched half-heartedly, but no one wanted to begin until we knew where Bil was. He always started the practice of the morning, no matter how bitter, or hungover, or busy, swinging his cane aloft and shouting "Fly, me lovelies!"

"Bethany, go see where Bil and Frit are, would you, my dear?" Drystan drawled, studying his nails.

Bethany, who was only lounging in the stands to watch, heaved herself up and went to investigate. The clowns and the acrobats stretched, and Tym and Karla warmed up Saitha the elephant, but we were all waiting.

Bethany returned a quarter of an hour later, pale.

"Frit's gone," she said as we clustered around her.

"Gone? What do you mean?" Dot asked.

Bethany blinked rapidly at her. "He struck her last night I'm guessing, and badly, and so she's left Bil, and left us." People made sounds of dismay. Frit had been well-liked by all in the circus. I had even liked her, as much as I had been frightened of her and what she had pieced together. I wondered how much she had taken out of the safe when she left. Pride and gratitude in equal measures surged through me – though she might have stolen, she did what she had to do to survive, and she had not shared my secret. At least, I did not think she had.

"How is Bil handling it?" Jive asked.

"Not well. He nearly brained me with a candlestick when I asked after him. I don't think he'll be coming out today. I think it is best we get on without him, and make this circus the best show we can."

We practiced all day, with Drystan leading us. He was quite a good taskmaster; harsh but fair, telling us when we did something that was not right but praising us when we did something well. What was more surprising was that everyone followed him without complaint. He was a natural leader. I hid a smile as I flipped around the trapeze bar and Drystan called out encouragement below. Bil would have to watch out for Drystan.

Bil appeared for practice three days later. He looked terrible and quite obviously had not bathed, eaten, or drunk anything other than whisky since Frit had left. That day, he sat in the stands and watched Drystan lead us in practice. He did not speak a word. The next day, he stood next to Drystan, still silent. The day after that, he hoarsely led us again in practice, with Drystan assisting when Bil floundered. Bil took over the last day, but the fire seemed smothered. There was no swinging of the cane, and no triumphant shout of "Fly, me lovelies." Our next lump of pay came as promised, but of course without the bonus.

The circus was as ready as it was going to be. The doors opened for the first show of the season.

I dressed for the pantomime performance in the privacy

of my cart. It felt very strange to have a full skirt swish against my legs for the first time since early spring. I had snuck into the market and bought the Lindean chest binder, spending almost all of my money. It took barely any time to step into the stretchy yet stiff fabric, pulling laces at the front to hold down my small breasts with ease. I stuffed the bodice of my gown with cotton. Looking into the tarnished mirror, I plaited my hair away from my face at either temple and piled the rest onto my head in an elegant bun, leaving one curl to frame my face. Anna had taught me how to style my hair in this way, and it worked well enough even though my hair was much shorter now.

I applied the cosmetics I used as an aerialist, but stained my lips and applied rouge to my cheeks. After clipping earrings onto my lobes and draping a cheap necklace around my neck, the familiar face of Iphigenia Laurus looked at me. This Gene was different; her face was leaner and more determined, but it was her.

The princess dress was made of a cheap cotton velvet in dark green. I covered my elaborate hair with a scarf. I would wear another cap when I performed on the trapeze, as there would not be time to do anything but quick touchups before the final act of the pantomime. Disguises upon disguises.

I pulled my thin coat and made my way to the big top. It was half an hour before the show was due to begin, but already a crowd queued outside of the tent, and many others milled along the beach, their small faces turning to look at the tent as they passed. The warm weather had chased away the grey clouds.

I slipped into the rear entrance of the tent and entered pandemonium. Everyone rushed about, rummaging through the spare costume chest, painting their faces, stretching, and practicing lines. The dimly lit changing area offered some privacy for the performers, and I set out my all my costumes in a particularly dark corner.

The atmosphere of the tent had been transformed for the cultured and more affluent city of Imachara. Glass globes wrapped in gold, blue, and green scarves softened the light around the stage. The air was hot and muggy with so many bodies in such a small space. No one was immune to the heat; the noblewomen had servants to flap fans for them, the merchant women flapped their own fans, and the poor wiped their faces with kerchiefs.

Bil strode into the center of the ring in a new waistcoat and top hat and his cane polished to a high shine. He introduced the audience to the circus with the same vigor I had always seen. I would never know that this was a man broken, who cried loudly in his tent at night while everyone pretended not to hear.

The Vestige machine filled the tent with fog, lightning and stars, undercut by the scent of dried rose petals.

When the fog cleared, the king was in his castle, counting coins on a desk decorated with a globe of the Archipelago in his study. He chuckled as he clinked the coins together, occasionally twirling the globe.

Drystan, who played Leander, our hero and fair Prince of Kymri, tiptoed onto the stage, making an elaborate shushing motion. In a stage whisper that carried about the tent, he said:

"The King doth count his golden coins with glee
But 'tis never enough for his fine Tree
To his left, to his right – all are his foes:
Until he rules the Archipelago."

I stood in the wings, awaiting my cue, smiling as Drystan, as Leander, charmed the audience, describing the heinous crimes of the king throughout his long reign. He instructed the audience to hiss whenever they saw the king appear in a new scene. Leander found an adorable boy in the front row about ten years of age.

"What is your name, young sir?" he asked.

"Eddie," the boy said, nervously. "Your Highness." He clutched his mother's hand.

"Well, brave Eddie, can you hiss as loud as you can, to show the others how it should be done?"

The boy hissed – a whisper nearly lost in the big top.

Leander clapped. "Most excellent, my young sir. Perhaps I shall turn you into one of my knights when you are grown. But until then – how do you feel about a sword?"

The boy crinkled his brow. "A sword?"

With perfectly timed sleight-of-hand, Leander produced a wooden practice sword and handed it to the boy, who took it with delight. I smiled in turn as I peeked out at the stage. This was why I loved the circus: those looks of wonder, of shocked pleasure and delight at watching the fantastic.

The boy "sheathed" his new sword in his belt and gave Leander a little bow. Drystan had chosen his volunteer well.

The king, oblivious to the talk of princes and swords,

finished counting his gold, sweeping it into a chest and laughing. Leander motioned frantically at the king. The audience hissed. The king glanced around, as if he had heard the wind blowing.

"Iona?" he called, stroking his gigantic false beard and moustache. "Iona, child, where are you?"

That was my cue. As Iona, I entered the stage, somber and nervous, curtseying. "My lord father," I said.

"Hello, my daughter. You must wed soon," he declared. "We have known the time must come, my sweet." He rested a hand on my head.

The gesture reminded me of my father's hand on mine, the only sign of affection he ever gave me. I pushed the memory away and focused on the role of Iona.

"The princes of the colonies will be coming to compete for your hand," the king said. "You may choose whichever one your heart desires most."

I raised my head. "Thank you, Father."

"I only wish for your happiness." He tucked the chest of gold underneath his arm and sauntered from the stage.

I spat on the ground, shocking the audience into laughter.

"I can choose between a child, an old man, a man who treats his citizens badly, or the one who pinched me when I was little until I cried. How will I ever find love among them?" I ran off the stage in tears.

The tumblers performed their opening act, shirtless and oiled. I heard a scandalized gasp for every appreciative one from the women in the audience.

The pantomime returned. A line of men stood waiting to be presented to Princess Iona. The clowns wore finery of sequins and large crowns. They were noblemen of the highest order, or figurehead princes from the colonies that the king already ruled. They introduced themselves, flattering me with gifts. The prince of Linde, stooped with age, gave her a carved wooden box and said her eyes were brighter than all the stars in the heavens. The prince of Girit, a local boy of four, gave the princess a flower and simply called her pretty. Another swaggered and thrust cloth-of-gold into her arms, listing the various reasons why he was the perfect man to marry.

I turned aside from the princes. "Perhaps I should choose the child!" I exclaimed to the crowd. "So far he was definitely the nicest."

Only one prince remained. The foreign prince of Kymri, Leander. He bowed low, the false jewels and gold of his historically inaccurate doublet catching in the light.

My face filled with awe, a hand covering my mouth. Drystan came to me, grasping my hands in his. He spoke Leander's words of love, but in the magic of the stage and the costume, the words seemed charged:

"How is it that I dare to speak to thee?
Some spirit of love has o'er taken me
Oh, strike me, stone me, good Lady and Lord
I am too base to call her my adored."

All of the other characters faded off the stage, leaving Leander and Iona alone. Drystan kissed me deeply in front of the audience. The tips of his fingers grazed my cheekbone, his stubble scratched my skin. He smelled of greasepaint and a faint but not unpleasant musk. My faithless lips responded, and I glared at him guiltily when we broke away. He only smirked as he bent over my hand and bid me a saccharine rhymed farewell.

The clowns performed next, chasing each other around the ring, hitting one another and yelling rude jokes to tease laughter from the audience. Just as it seemed that they would leave the ring, they ran through the crowd, throwing bright confetti, flipping down the narrow aisles. I only paid half a mind to them, my thoughts lingering on the feel of Drystan's lips on mine, and the drop of my stomach, almost like swinging from the trapeze.

The pantomime continued.

"Whom did you prefer, of the suitors you met yesterday, my daughter?" The king asked, scribbling on a bit of parchment.

"I... quite liked the Kymri prince," I answered, bobbing my head shyly.

The king set aside his quill. "The Kymri prince? Are you sure?"

"More than anything!"

"The Kymri colony has the least dowry to pay..." Around the time the play was originally written, Kymri and Northern Temne were the only colonies that had successfully avoided the Elladan regime. While the king wanted to add to his rule, Kymri was little more than sun-baked golden sand, and not worth the effort to dominate. That all changed when the black gold of oil was discovered beneath the sand.

"The Kymri prince? Has he made you an offer, my daughter?" the king asked.

"He... he has told me he loves me, Your Highness."

The king laughed. "Love? Love is like holding water in your hands. You might have it for a time, but it escapes, leaving you with nothing."

I crossed my arms over my chest. "You said that I could choose whomever I wished. Do you honor your promise, my lord?"

"All right, all right," the king said, holding his hands in supplication. "I will think on it. But I have already decided that the chosen beau must prove his worth."

I gasped. "You can't mean..."

The king leaned in so close to me I could see the cotton balls of Fedir's false beard.

"Yes, my dear, I do." He stepped back and threw his arms wide, the glass globes bathing him in light.

"He must defeat three of my beasts to prove that the Lord and Lady bless the union."

"The beasts..." I moaned, falling to the floor. "Please don't do this, Father. I love him!"

The king grasped me by the upper arm, dragging me upright. "You know nothing of love yet, my little bird."

I fought from his grasp. "You cannot do this! You'll kill him!"

"Aha," the king said, waving a hand in front of my face. "Only if the Lord and Lady wish it."

"If you wish it, you mean!"

"That's blasphemy, my child. Watch your tongue. I hope your lover wins and brings you happiness." The king laughed. The audience hissed. He left.

I paced the stage, wringing my hands.

"I must warn him!" I muttered. "I must tell him that he can never hope to defeat the beasts, and that he must return to Kymri, to never see me again. It's the only way to save him." I wrapped a cloak about myself, leaving the palace and "fighting" my way through the prop trees to the side of the circus ring.

But the king, watching from a window of the set, saw me leave.

"Fool! Come here!" he cried.

Jive, who played the part of the Fool, bounded onto the stage. "What is your wish, Your Highness?" he asked, bowing so low his nose nearly touched the floor.

"First, return my daughter to me," he commanded.

The Fool raced across the stage. I saw him coming and ran about, hiding behind the trees to the chasing music. The Fool laughed as he hunted and grabbed me, throwing me over his shoulder. I kicked my feet and banged my fists against his back, but he dragged me to the king as if I weighed no more than a sack of potatoes.

"Thank you, my most faithful servant. Now, throw her into the Penglass tower, for… safekeeping."

More hisses from the audience.

"The Penglass Prison!" I cried. "Help! Father! Please!"

Jive threw me into the Penglass tower, which was no more than a pen of cheap bubbled glass painted blue. He waggled his fingers at me and I stuck my tongue out at him. He laughed and returned to his master.

"Now, I am sending you forth to deal with a little… problem of mine, brave Fool."

The audience hissed again.

I gasped. "Not the beasts, Father!" I cried, pounding my fists – gently – against the walls of my prison.

He grinned and laughed, an evil sound that echoed about the tent.

"Oh yes, my daughter. The beasts."

He muttered an incantation, and the tent filled with smoke and stars once again.

When the smoke cleared, the contortionists and acrobats twisted their bodies into knots, balancing on balls or ladders. Several men catcalled and threw coins into the ring in appreciation, which the contortionists picked up with their toes.

In the sidelines again, I wondered if the pantomime was taking too much away from the circus. The audience whispered amongst themselves as Dot and the new contortionist, Ellen, performed.

A painted backdrop of a forest replaced the castle. Leander read the note of his challenge from the king aloud to the audience, visibly distraught.

"Beasts!" he cried. "The king himself shall set beasts on me. However shall I survive? For I have no magic, and no protection but this sword." He unsheathed it, holding it aloft, the metal catching the light.

Drystan returned to the little boy he had spoken to at the beginning of the pantomime.

"Eddie, my young knight-in-training, do you think I should battle for love?"

Eddie puffed himself up. "Will you die?" he asked.

"I hope not, but it is a very real possibility. Most of what is worth fighting for is worth dying for, many say."

Eddie bit his lip. "You should fight, but don't die. Otherwise, I'll never be a knight."

Laughter rippled through the audience. The circus

should hire this boy for all of our shows in Imachara. Drystan saluted Eddie. "I shall do my best, young sir." The boy sat back in his seat, beaming from ear to ear.

But despite the comforting words of the young boy, Leander prayed. The light outlined the fine planes of his face and turned his white hair into a golden halo. My breath caught in my throat. I looked away from him to the backstage area, my gaze resting on Aenea. She was looking right at me, her eyes sad, as if she knew exactly what I had been thinking. I clasped my hands together tight, my fingernails digging into my palms.

High above us, the workers swapped several of the scarves around the glass globes, so that the colors shifted to sunset. More workers held a painted setting sun and a rising moon from behind the set.

"Lord and Lady, share your wisdom and light,
Beasts and other demons come soon to fight,
Born of the King's wicked greed and rancor,
Will I live to see her whom I adore?"

For a moment, nothing happened. Sad strings played from the gramophone. I snuck a look at the stage. Leander bowed his head, defeated. Yet before him, a column of smoke swirled. My throat closed tight as I watched from the Penglass prison.

The Phantom Damselfly appeared. The audience recoiled in their seats, some hastily muttering prayers of their own. Leander gazed up at the Damselfly in awe.

"What magic is this? A Chimaera fairy has come to visit me. I am unworthy."

The Damselfly only flapped her wings in response, as ever. She lingered, her upturned face looking at something far away, and faded. She glanced over her shoulder at me just before she disappeared from sight, her eyes locking with mine.

But no one else would have seen that.

I shivered, my fingertips pressing so hard against the cheap glass I thought I might break it.

Where the Damselfly had been, a shiny new sword was stuck into the sand and sawdust of the circus ring.

"A gift from the Lord and Lady!" Leander exclaimed, circling the sword, which had a sun and moon stylized on the hilt. He pulled it from the sand, and sparks flew in all directions. The audience clapped wildly.

"Let the king send his beasts!" Leander called. "I am ready for them."

Intermission was called and Bil urged the audience to pay special attention to the lovely girls selling sweets and treats making their way along the stands. In the darkened light, the circus workers took advantage of the break, lowering hoops from the ceiling and pushing jumping blocks onto the ring.

A few horse riders began the start of the animal section of the circus. The horses jumped through hoops and over the posts and the riders stood on their hands and flipped and landed on the saddles of cantering beasts, the tent filling with the sounds of hoof beats.

"I cannot let him perish for me," I cried as Iona, wringing my hands in distress. "Perhaps I should free myself from this mortal coil." I raised my hands to the heavens in supplication, and said the words I had said so many times before:

"Oh, moon and stars, lord and lady on high –
Shine your light on a wretch whose end is nigh.
Leander, my love, is in danger so true.
My cheek's petals are now heavy with dew.

"Please, moon and stars, lord and lady, free me
From this life full of lonesome agony
If no more my lips will his fingers trace
I'll trade him for sable death's sweet embrace."

But there was no answer, and I lost my nerve and collapsed into tears as the limelight faded from my prison. In darkness, I sat up, glowering. After playing Iona so many times, I thoroughly hated her character. Though she tried to escape once, she did not try again, and mewled and cried and hoped for someone else to take her fate in hand.

"Fool!" the king cried. "I summon thee."

The fool bowed low before him again. The king took out a magic wand from his robes. He muttered incantations under his breath, made up words that changed from practice to practice and show to show. Smoke covered the fool's form, and a loud *crack* sounded. The smoke cleared and the fool was gone. A Naga replaced him – Nina the snake charmer – wearing a dress that left her arms and midriff bare, every bit of skin painted with green scales, a green snake twined about her waist. She hissed.

"Go and find the Kymri Prince Leander, and finish him," the king commanded. "I have protected you from death, but it will only work thrice." The Naga bowed, her nose almost touching the floor.

Leander appeared on the stage, brandishing his magic sword. "Lord and Lady, guide my blade!" he cried. The Naga raised her hands, gathering her evil snake magic, but Leander flipped out of the way, dancing about her. The fight continued for some time with choreographed moves, until Leander stabbed her with the sword. She let out a shriek and disappeared in smoke and sparks.

Leander chuckled. "That wasn't too hard, now, was it?"

He sauntered off the ring, and the play paused for the circus act of the strong man, Karg.

Afterward, Leander sauntered about the stage, smug at his defeat of the beast.

"Behind you! Behind you!" The audience cried.

Leander turned with exaggerated slowness. A gargoyle demon – Sayid – approached, his skin slathered in grey-and-black greasepaint, blood dripping from his fangs, his wings made of paper and cloth-wrapped wire.

Leander held his sword aloft and they fought, the demon dancing about Leander, throwing insults and taunts at him. Leander swung wildly, his sword flashing. The demon flew above him, cackling, the thin rope holding him aloft barely visible. He circled Leander.

The Kymri Prince back flipped and attacked the flying gargoyle, and Sayid fell to the floor, false blood spurting from a wound in his side. He, too, disappeared in a puff of smoke.

Next came the otters, who stood on their haunches

and swayed back and forth in unison to a tune played by the gramophone. Then came Karla with her particularly well-trained horse, who could "count" to any number the audience demanded as long as Karla never released the reins. Saitha also made an appearance. One lucky child in the crowd was chosen at random and the elephant picked him up in her trunk and deposited him onto her back and walked about the ring to great applause and cheers.

Leander had barely recovered from the demon before the last of the beasts attacked. Tauro, the fearsome Minotaur, held a double-edged battle-axe and roared. Several members of the audience screamed. Tauro the Minotaur charged Drystan, who danced nimbly away. They circled each other in their fighting dance – Tauro rushing him with brute strength and Drystan showcasing his acrobatics. Like the others, Tauro fell beneath the blade and disappeared, replaced by the Fool.

The king rushed to the body of his fallen servant.

"What fool am I, to waste my faithful Fool,
For my own, selfish pride. Am I a ghoul,
My soul too haunted by dreams of power?
Iona's love – I'll not disallow her."

Freed from the prison, I rested my head on his shoulder. "Let not your greed control you any longer, my king," I said.

He rose and nodded, taking my hand and Drystan's. "I hereby abdicate, after the wedding. Long may Leander and Iona rule Ellada in peace and glory."

The tumblers and clowns reappeared for a slightly longer interlude while I dashed backstage, found my corner shrouded in darkness where I had laid out the wedding dress for the final scene. It would have been far easier to have my acrobat costume on underneath already, but the collar was too high and showed under both dresses.

I slid on my aerialist's costume, looked behind me and tried not to jump in shock. Aenea was no more than two meters away and staring in my general direction, her face expressionless. I did not know how long she had been there or how much she had seen. *She could not have seen anything*, I comforted myself. *My back was turned to her and it's too dark*. I smoothed my hands along the front of my costume, feeling the stiff fabric of the Linde garment.

I put a blue cap over my plaited hair and took Aenea's hand. We had no time to speak before our act, though I squeezed her hand and she squeezed back.

We performed the final trapeze act without flaw, and the usual feeling of *right*ness bled through me. I counted internally, matching my breath, holding out my hands to catch Aenea at just the right moment.

After the last bow, I scurried to my corner and peeled off the damp trapeze costume, wiped off the sweat with a cloth, and shimmied into Iona's wedding gown. It was a ridiculous cake of a dress, a garment of pale pink satin, festooned with cloth roses, false pearls, and glass cut jewels. Its bodice was as low as it could be without the false cotton breasts peeking out.

I untied my scarf and tidied my hair, adding touches of paint to my face in the mirror. I inspected myself in satisfaction. The arms poking out of the capped sleeves were a bit too muscular for a woman's, and I had a small bump in my throat when I swallowed, but aside from that, I was convincing enough.

Aenea found me again. She was wearing her costume as the Lady of the Moon, and looked radiant to me. The long silver robe caught the light, and she wore a crescent moon made of tin nestled into her hair.

Her gaze slid past me and she blinked and whipped her head back to me again. No one had seen me in the final dress as it had only just been finished the night before. Frit was meant to have sewn it, but when she left, the other precious few people in the circus who knew how to stitch had to take turns on completing all of the costumes. "*Micah?*"

I gave her my best court curtsey. "My lady?" I said in my old feminine tones, ones that felt unfamiliar to my throat now.

Her eyes were wide. She circled me slowly, taking in the tight fit of my mostly-false bosom, the narrow waist above the flared petticoats and skirts. "You're a prettier girl than I am!" she said, indignant.

I snorted. "Hardly." I had never thought I was much to look at as a woman.

The other circus performers waiting backstage cat-called and whistled at me softly, and I batted my eyelashes at them, reveling in every drop of affection they poured for me. Rian squeezed one of my semi-false breasts and complimented how lovely they were and I blushed and turned my face away from him. I was surprised to realize that even though I had resented being forced to wear dresses my whole life, now that it was a choice I quite liked it.

Drystan made a show of kissing my hand and looking me up and down appreciatively before he went onstage to publicly proclaim his love for Iona and thank the Lord and Lady for bringing her into his life. The gesture made me uncomfortable, for he believed me to be truly a woman.

"Small wonder Drystan is so keen to ravish you on-stage," Bethany said.

I glanced at Aenea. Her mouth was pressed into a thin line.

"Don't be silly," I said, peering out to see if it was my cue yet. "Drystan prefers boys in trousers, not ladies in skirts."

"He's been known to not turn down a lady a time or two since he's joined us. I imagine a boy in a skirt is the best of both worlds, in his mind," Bethany continued blithely.

I felt my face go hot. "Stop infuriating Aenea, Bethany," I chided, more nonchalantly than I felt. "Time to marry!" I said. I gave Aenea a quick kiss on the cheek, leaving a red smudge, and she gave me a smile as she wiped it away. I darted onto the stage and under the glass globes of the circus.

Leander, my groom, was waiting in front of the painted backdrop of the Penglass castle, beaming in his elaborate doublet and coronet. Because Leander and Iona's love was so pure, so true, and had overcome so much, the Lord and Lady gave them their personal blessing.

Iano read aloud the traditional marriage vows, and Leander pledged his undying love to Iona and she to him, and so we kissed once again as the trumpet blared and the audience stood to clap and cheer. Aenea stood in front of Drystan and me as we kissed, but she was looking towards the audience and smiling, even if the smile was a little forced.

We stood and bowed, and the other performers came out to wave and beam at the audience. The spectators filed out to explore the funfair, and the performers retired and looked forward to the early morning when the carnival would had finished. Our first show at Imachara had gone according to plan, and we deserved a celebration.

27
SUMMER: SHADOW ON THE SEASON

"There's a sense of community in the circus. They were my family, with certain members all at one time or another playing the roles of a mother, a father, a loveable uncle, an errant child. Through the good times and the bad, and even with old members left and new members joined, we knew that we could count on each other. Oh, we fought and we argued, but to this day if I saw a former member of my circus walking down the streets of Imachara, I would trot up to them and throw my arms around them, as if greeting one of my dearest friends."

from THE MEMOIRS OF THE SPARROW,
Aerialist Diane Albright

The show went on.

The tumblers flipped, the otters posed on their hind legs, and the contortionists bent over and kissed the floor. The freaks stared over the audience's heads as they gaped. Leander and Iona fell in love again each night.

The summer cooked us, the sweat trickling down our backs and temples. We sat well away from the nightly bonfire as it crackled and sparked. Full darkness did not fall until almost midnight, and even then the sky turned a deep violet. Aenea and I held hands, murmuring softly to each other as we drank awful beer and ate leftover sugar floss.

I hoped it would never end, even as the nights grew shorter and colder, the promise of autumn on the wind.

And then on the last day of the season, a Shadow fell over the circus.

I saw him in the carnival, the wide brim of his hat obscuring his face. I darted behind a tent, my heartbeat echoing in my throat as I peeked around the canvas. The Shadow tapped Jive on the shoulder. He flashed identification, and Jive looked impressed.

"What do you want, Shadow-man?"

"Where can I find the ringmaster?" The man had a polite voice, carefully articulated.

"He's in his office. That cart over there." He pointed, and the Shadow's eyes lingered on the red varnish of Jive's fingernail. "What you want with him? He in trouble?"

"No. I'm looking for someone. Many thanks for your help," he said, and I darted into the tent when I saw him come my way. I took deep breaths, watching the retreating back after he passed and then sprinting to the only person in the circus who knew who I had once been.

"Micah?" Drystan asked as he saw me, his brow furrowed. I had never once visited his cart. "Come in."

I saw Rian and Iano behind him on their bunks, playing cards and smoking cigarillos, the remnants of last night's clown makeup still on their faces.

"I need to speak with you," I said, holding my gaze with his.

He nodded, just once, and we went to my cart. My eyes darted about, searching for the Shadow's wide hat.

"Micah, what is it?" he asked once we were inside. "You're twitchy."

"A Shadow is here."

He did not say anything, and waited for me to say more.

"Said he was looking for someone. I think he was the one hired to find me. And I don't know who else read that article. Frit did. I think she suspected. Maybe she sold me out after she left."

Drystan shook his head. "She won't have."

"How can you be sure?"

"I just am." He shifted his weight. "You're sure it's the Shadow hired by your family to find you?"

"Fairly sure," I said, my voice cracking.

"Then you have to leave," he said.

I stared at him, the words echoing in my skull. *Then you have to leave. You have to leave.*

"I can't leave."

He shook his head. "Micah, I don't think you have a choice."

I fell against Arik's empty trunk, running a hand through my hair. "If you didn't know me to be Iphigenia already, would you have recognized me?" The image of the surly girl in the newspaper floated in my memory – the lace at her throat, the curls, the flat eyes. "I've changed a lot in the last half a year. I barely recognize myself in the mirror anymore."

"Plenty of people will hazard a guess for the chance of money. Who else has the Shadow talked to?"

"No one. He only asked Jive for directions."

"And what did he tell Jive?"

"That... that he was looking for someone."

"That means that soon everyone will know that a Shadow is looking for someone. Lord and Lady knows we all have our secrets to hide, but tongues will wag. People will wonder which of us he wants."

"Maybe they'll think it's someone else," I muttered without conviction.

Pity flitted across his face. "Everyone knows you can read and that you came from money, Micah. You are still one of the newest members. The people you work with are uneducated, not stupid. Eventually, they will remember the fact that you have never been seen without clothes on because you bathe in your cart, and that you look and sound a little too believable as a woman in the pantomime."

Hot tears slid down my face. I did not sob. Drystan's hand hovered above my shoulder, and then he slid his arms around me. I rested my forehead against the points of his collarbone, too upset to feel guilty at the embrace.

I sniffled. "I don't want to leave the circus."

"I know."

"What will they do if they find me? Send me back to my parents?"

"Hmm. I'm not sure. Your parents did keep your disappearance quiet for several weeks. They've probably been fined quite a few marks."

I leaned away. "Fined... Serves them right. They only moved forward two titles because the person who gave me to them also gave them a sum of money. It's a shame for my brother Cyril, though. This will darken his prospects." The words were acrid on my tongue.

Drystan's interest piqued. "They were given money?" He tapped a finger against his lips. "Now that I think on it, there had been rumors about the Laurus family for years. No one moves up two titles that quickly, unless it's direct royal favor."

"Sometimes the truth is stranger than the rumors." Dread settled in my chest like a stone.

"Quite the mystery, little Gene. You must wonder where you came from all the time."

Strange to hear my old name on his tongue, though he had called me by it once before. "You have no idea. I can't leave the circus, though, Drystan. I have nowhere to go." There was Mister Illari, perhaps, but he was ailing and returning to Sicion seemed dangerous.

"That didn't stop you before, did it?" Drystan asked.

"No, but this is different. I fit here. I belong and I've found what I'm good at."

Drystan shook his head. "You probably would not have been able to stay here forever. Eventually, someone would have noticed, or you would have tired of it."

"How long have you been in the circus?"

Drystan stared off into the distance. "Nearly five years."

"And you've tired of it."

His eyes were dull. He rubbed a hand against the stubble of his cheek. "I've grown restless, more like."

"That's surprising. With Bil faltering, you could be running the circus ere long."

At the mention of Bil's name, Drystan's gaze darkened. "I've thought about it. More than a time or two. But it does not feel like what I am meant to be doing with my life."

"You're meant to be grooming yourself to be a noble and a member of parliament, or advising the queen."

He laughed hollowly. "Perchance I can apply to be her fool."

"I'm the lead of the pantomime and half of the final act..." I began.

"And it's the last show of the circus. An aerialist can be found. An actor can be found. Don't make the mistake of thinking that you're irreplaceable to the circus. The show will go on with or without you."

I thought of Frit's hands clutching gold coins. "Are you so certain the circus will always survive?"

He waved his hands dismissively. "I suppose I was being poetic. Bil's circus may not survive next season. I do the books – I know how little there is in the safe. Bil's also crafty, though, so he may find a way. But life is a circus, and one player is rarely missed. You should bear that in mind."

Drystan had reverted to the white clown from the night I joined the circus, all cryptic riddles and wide, staring eyes. I wondered if I knew him at all.

"I'll leave after tonight's show, then," I said, the words feeling like a life's sentence. "Aenea and I were thinking of going to Byssia. Perhaps if we leave and return in four months, the Shadow will have moved on and forgotten me. And I can come back."

We both knew this was a lie.

Drystan backed away. At the door, he turned to me.

"Be careful and keep your eyes sharp, Micah. And leave just after the last pantomime has finished."

He drummed his fingers against the door frame, as if he would say something else. But he left without another word.

That night before the last pantomime and the last circus, I took a long look at myself in the mirror behind the stage. The face was very different from the face of the surly-looking girl in the newspaper. I was no longer that unhappy girl.

And why would anyone think that the daughter of a noble would join a circus? She would be pampered and soft, not capable of swinging from a trapeze or gallivanting about a stage and kissing strange and uncouth men. I did not think it was as dire as Drystan stated. Though I had no illusions that those I had worked with for a season would feel any sense of loyalty to me if they did fit the puzzle pieces together.

Aenea and I had enough money saved for the passage to Byssia. Just. But we shouldn't go unless I told her what I was. We had kissed, and a little more. I had stopped her wandering hand once or twice. There had been so many times I could have told her, and so many times I almost did. But each time my mouth opened but the words would not come. And so she did not know what I was, and I did not know how to tell her.

But if we were travelling across the sea together and sharing a cabin, she needed to know. Before we left. Tonight. Bile rose in my throat at the thought. I had wound so many lies about myself, that if I untangled them I feared garroting myself. How could she ever forgive that much deception?

I put on the cotton velvet dress and snood, and waited for my cue to become the Princess Iona. The lines tumbled from my mouth, spoken so many times it was impossible to forget them. I kissed Drystan yet again. It felt familiar now. I might have kissed him almost as many times as Aenea.

I changed in the darkest corner of the tent, behind the bed sheet curtain I had erected. For the last time, I climbed the rope ladder to the tightrope and trapeze, stared across the distance at the girl who had enchanted me into the circus. Her green costume glinted in the light of the glass globes, her long braid falling down her back. I took a deep breath, and jumped toward the trapeze swing.

Aenea and I flew to the sounds of applause below.

I walked through the carnival, still in Iona's wedding dress, which I always changed back into for the final bow of the night, and my coat. Drystan had seen Aenea go this way, perhaps to pick up a few last items before we left for Byssia the next morning. I kept a sharp eye out for her as I passed through the carnival. Whenever anyone pressed against me, I jumped. Whenever I saw a familiar face in the crowd, I wondered where I had seen them before. My breath came in shallow spurts, and the stone in my chest would not go away.

Directly in front of me, two Policiers appeared in a gap in the crowd. It reminded me of my first night in the funfair, those months ago. I froze in the middle of the busy carnival. A man complained as he strode around me, but I barely heard him. I darted between two wooden stalls and crouched by a tent, the lights and sounds of the circus thundering in my ears, my breath hissing from my throat. They walked past me, never glancing in my direction.

I could not find Aenea. The carnival closed down, sellers packing their wares for the last time, the customers leaving the beach, some glancing at the big top as they did so. Within hours, the canvas tent would be gone, as would we. The wind whipped sand on my dress.

The entire city of Imachara must have heard the celebration at the bonfire.

I lingered, grasping a mug of beer Bethany thrust into my hands, accepting her scratchy kiss on my cheek with a smile. This was my last night at the circus. I could not leave quite yet. I memorized each of their faces, not wanting to forget them if I never saw them again. Bethany and the way she laughed, throwing back her head, shoulders heaving as she celebrated with Juliet, Poussin, and Madame Limond. Tila and Sal whispering and giggling behind their hands, flirting with a few of the Kymri tumblers. Tym idly stroking the head of his favorite otter, Needle, as he spoke with Karla. Karg the strong man reading a book of philosophy by the light of the bonfire until Tin tapped him on the elbow and told him a joke. Rag and the workers throwing pebbles toward the water, swigging from paper-wrapped bottles.

Bil swirled whisky in a glass tumbler, staring at the flames of the bonfire, lost in thought. No one else in the circus had hard spirits. He gave the glass a last swirl and downed the rest of the amber liquid. Through the flames, his eyes met mine.

It was time to go.

But not before telling the truth.

I found Aenea playing a game of cards with Drystan in her cart. I wondered if he only played with her to see if I would follow through and leave as I said I would. "Aenea?"

"Yes?" she answered, putting down the cards. Her rucksack lay on the bed, half-packed with clothes.

"Before we go, I have to tell you something."

Her brows knit together. "About what?"

"About me."

"What's wrong?" she asked.

"Everything," I said.

Drystan hovered uncertainly. "Should I go?"

"You might as well stay," I said. "May as well air all my secrets at once."

I peered out of the door before closing it and throwing the bolt, and it *clunk*ed shut.

"What is it?" she asked.

My throat closed. The time had come, and I did not know what to say. I looked between them beseechingly.

I took a deep breath and forced the words through my throat. "The Shadow who came around asking questions… he was asking about me."

Aenea frowned. "Bethany thought he was looking for that noble girl who ran away months ago? What does that have to do with anything?"

"You don't know?" Drystan's surprise was genuine –

he must have assumed that she and I had been sleeping together for months, that I had confided everything to her. Not quite everything. Here was the moment I had been dreading.

Aenea turned to me, and I wished the ground would open beneath my feet and swallow me whole. "Explain, please," she said, fighting to remain calm.

I gaped at her, mute.

"Come on, Micah. Tell her. And then you need to leave the circus before that Shadow comes back." Drystan peeked through the window at the top of the door.

I took a deep breath, tried to force my way through the shock and be somewhat coherent. "I have not been truthful to you about my background."

Aenea now played the mute. She must have guessed that, but not the extent of it.

"My true name is Iphigenia Laurus," I continued, grating the words through my throat. "I am technically ninety-sixth in line to the throne, and my family is in the Third Ring of nobility."

"But you're not a woman," she said, fear in her voice.

"She is–" Drystan started.

She shook her head. "I know he's not. Micah?" she looked at me, and so did Drystan. Neither of them knew the truth. The vice wound tight around my throat. I could not tell them.

I would have to show them.

My numb fingers scrabbled at the few remaining buttons at the side of my dress. I slid the bodice down, my false breasts tumbling to the floor, my Lindean corset on full display. I unlaced the stays and pulled the garment down, baring my small breasts. Aenea looked at them as if I had an extra head sprouting from my chest. Drystan's eyes darted at them, and then away.

I swallowed again.

Turning my head to the side and trying not to sob, I pulled down my petticoats and undergarments. Though I did not see their faces, I knew they were staring at me in horror. After the longest moment of my life, I pulled the skirts up, redid the Lindean binder, and shrugged my shoulders back into the bodice of the dress.

That was it. It was done. The mere act of pushing aside some fabric, and they knew everything.

"What are you?" Aenea asked, and she sounded so fearful that it broke my heart.

"A Kedi," I said hoarsely. I rummaged in my pack and held out the soapstone figurine.

"A Kedi." Drystan looked at me in wonder. "The Byssian demi-god?"

"I'm not magical, or mythical. I'm a freak. Had Bil known, I could have been the star of the freakshow." I laughed, though it was more of a choking noise.

Aenea was looking at me as if I were a stranger. "I am still confused." Her voice fell flat and broke.

I cleared my throat. "I was raised as a girl. I didn't feel particularly feminine, much to my mother's dismay. My entire life, I was dragged to doctor after doctor, specialist after specialist. Eventually, my mother found a doctor who decided he could make me fully female, by slicing me with a surgeon's knife."

They both winced.

"I could not face it, and so I left, and you know the

rest." I reached for Aenea's hand, but she stepped away from me. It took everything within me not to disintegrate right there. I was held together by the thinnest of fraying ropes.

"Why didn't you tell me?" she said.

"I wanted to. So many times. There never seemed to be a proper time to do so."

"You could have made a time," she said.

"I know," I said. "I know. I'm sorry. One other person in my past life found out about me. He was disgusted. I was too afraid."

Her eyes filled with tears.

I did not know what to say.

Drystan shook off his own shock. "We need to leave. The sooner the better."

"We?" Aenea said.

"We?" I echoed.

"Aenea can come with us if she wishes. There's no longer a circus. We can be a merry trio, frolicking through Imachara and making our own way." His mouth twisted.

"But Drystan, you and Aenea, you have good lives here… You could take over the circus, save it from itself and from Bil."

Drystan waved his hand. "The circus is too far gone. And in any case, it's not for me. This period of my life is over."

"I'm not leaving," Aenea said. I could not bring myself to look at her.

"I'm sorry, Micah, but I can't." She turned her head away from me. "I just… I feel as if I don't know you. I told you more of myself than I'd told anyone, and all you told me were lies. My life is here. In the ring, and on the ropes."

Her words stung. "I tried to tell you the truth as much as I could." As the words tumbled from my mouth, I knew they were not enough.

"No, you haven't. If you had told me months ago…"
Then maybe things would be different.

Her next words were so soft I could barely hear them. "I feel like… you've made a fool of me."

The words hung in the air. I closed my eyes. She was not Damien. I had not given her the choice to make up her own mind.

Drystan was filling my pack with what little foodstuff I had in the cart. He had barely glanced in my direction since I had shown him what was under my petticoats. Did he hate me too, for keeping the truth from him? I was losing everything important to me.

I listened to the beating of my heart and the muted noises of the funfair drifting up the beach. "I understand," I said. "I am the fool, not you. Never you. And I am sorry for it, Aenea. Truly sorry."

She did not say anything. She gave me one long, searching look, and then her eyes shuttered to me and she walked out the door.

"I'm sorry, Micah," Drystan said.

"Me, too." I looked at him. "Are you sure you want to come with me? Wherever we end up going?"

"Of course I am." He winked, trying for levity. "It'll be an adventure."

He passed me an empty sack. "Here, go steal us some food while I go get my things from my cart. I'll meet you back here in a quarter of an hour, and we'll make our way."

"No goodbyes?"

"No. Best to sneak away and leave fewer ripples."

I took the empty bag. "See you soon." And I crept from my former home in the circus, cursing all the withheld truths that had turned to barbed lies that cut deep.

On the way to the food cart, someone seized my shoulder. I twirled and raised my fist. Before I could register their face, a rough cloth smelling of chemicals was pressed to mine. My scream was dampened by the fabric. The hand behind the cloth pushed harder onto my mouth and I choked.

The world dimmed and darkened and then I was gone.

28
AUTUMN: THE RINGMASTER'S CANE

"There once was a troll quick to anger. He had no friends, and lived by himself by a crucial pass through the Fang Mountains. People would bring him gifts and stories to try and barter passage. Sometimes it worked. Often it didn't, and their bones would scatter the rocks as a warning to others. One day, the troll hurt himself falling down a ledge. He called to a man hiking through the pass for help, but the man only hurried along, grateful that he was safe. The troll withered away, until his bones mingled with his victims'. His anger was his undoing."

"Troll Pass," HESTIA'S FABLES

I awoke, my head still in the grips of a chemical fog. The gag chafed the corners of my mouth and the cotton dried my tongue. I groaned and resisted the urge to vomit as the world came into focus. I stared at the ceiling of Bil's cart, still in Iona's wedding dress, prone and tied fast to the bedposts. The false pearls of my skirt glinted in the low light. I whimpered, each breath a struggle. Outside,

I could hear the gramophone's tinny music and the subdued mumble and laughter of the circus folk as they celebrated the last show of the season.

Time dripped past. I shivered, tears sliding down my cheeks. I yelled, the scream absorbed by the cotton in my mouth. I struggled against my bonds, chafing my wrists raw. All was futile. Eventually, the sounds of merriment faded but for the moaning witch of the wind.

The door unlocked and Bil's silhouette darkened the doorway. Even from here, I could smell the alcohol on his breath. He slid in and locked the door behind him.

"A Shadow was lookin' for you, *boy*," Bil said, closing and re-bolting the door behind him. "Policiers, too."

I said nothing, for I could not. I did not doubt the Shadow might have been looking for me, but the Policiers I saw might have merely been keeping the peace in a place where they could have a little fun of their own.

"Well, I say he was looking for you, but he wasn't looking for someone by the name of Micah Grey, now, was he?" He took a full bottle of whisky from a cupboard, unstopped it, and poured himself another glass. I would never be able to smell whisky again without the memory of fear.

"He was looking," Bil slurred, "for a girl with a funny name. Iffy… something. Last name o' Laurus."

I swallowed behind the gag.

"Iphigenia Laurus. That's what it was. Little noble girl who ran away from her perfect little life."

I glared at him over my gag.

"The Shadow asked some innocent questions, but then I remembered that newspaper article Frit told me about, few months back. That missin' girl. Frit wondered where a noble girl would run, how she'd hide what she was. You know what I said to her? I said, 'Not well, that's how. Stick out like a sore thumb, she would.'" He gulped some more whisky. "But you hid a little better than I thought. Might not a noticed, you know, if you hadn't been Iona in the panto. Too convincing a girl by half, you was." His gaze lingered on my dress before he drained the glass.

"After that Shadow left, I remembered. Remembered the Policiers were offering a reward for you, see."

My nostrils flared. I felt like a cornered rabbit looking into the eyes of a fox. I managed to make a sarcastic grunt through my gag.

"Yea, you'd think the circus would be doing all right, now, wouldn't you? I work hard so the circus folk think that. We've been selling seats, fair enough, but we've been limping along on promises. When Frit left, she took everything. D'you hear me? Every. Little. Thing. All I worked for, to support her, all gone." More whisky sloshed into the glass tumbler.

I stared at him, hatred blazing in my eyes. Again, I thought he was lying. Frit would have taken a lot, but she loved the people in the circus. She did the books. She knew exactly how much Bil could afford to lose. Or had she grown to hate Bil so much that the rest of us did not matter?

"I didn't say nothing to the Shadow because I'm not stupid. He gets you, he gives you to the Constabulary – money's all his. So, you see, *girl*, you got a couple options. One, I give you over ta the Policiers, get the money from them direct, see.

"But I'm not an unfair man. You can buy your freedom.

You grew up noble. You probably got a lot of noble friends. Rich, noble friends. You contact the ones you know and trust, get 'em to give you a little more than the reward; you can go on your merry way. I don't care. Can't say ol' Bil ain't fair then, now can you?" His words slurred. He patted me on the shoulder and I flinched. "Shame, as you're a good performer, but I don't need no more Shadows or Policiers in my circus. Think of the circus. Think of your friends. Can't leave them without a job come winter, now, can you? Not as many circuses these days."

I swallowed again, my mouth still dry and tasting of chemicals.

Bil shook his head. "Still can't believe you tricked us for all this time. Lied to us all, you have. Little Aenea fooling about with another girl, wouldn't have thought it of her." Bil's hand slid down to my stomach. I glared at him and started tugging against the bonds again. If his hand slid much further, he would have far more grounds for blackmail.

Bil's hand left my stomach, sliding up towards the neckline of my dress. His hand snaked down the front of the bodice, pushing aside the false breasts and feeling the corset over my true ones. One finger wiggled under the corset. I struggled against him as much as I could, the ropes burning my arms, my scream of rage little more than a pathetic squeak behind the gag.

He pulled his hand away, patted my cheek. "Just checking, girl," he said, and he touched the gag. "I'm going to take this off so you can speak, but you're not to scream, you hear? If you do, I'll crush your throat." His big, meaty hand slid around my windpipe.

"Understand?" he said, eyes boring into mine, hand squeezing for emphasis.

All I could do was nod.

He took out the gag and I ran my tongue around my mouth, trying to dampen it. I coughed.

"What's your decision then, little miss?"

My mind was scrambling about in circles. "If you turn me in, then you won't get your reward," I said, my voice rough.

Bil guffawed. "Oh, and why's that, pet?"

"They may give you the money, but the officials hate the circus," I bluffed, trying to make my voice sound as female as possible. It was harder to do, now – my voice had lowered. "You may get the money, but you'd have the tax men pounding at your door, with rules and bans on where you can set up. It's not worth it."

Bil perched on the bed, the ropes creaking beneath his substantial weight. I squirmed against my bonds again.

I paused.

Bil had not tied the bonds well. It had been years since he had tied the strong knots to secure the big top. I had almost managed to work one of the ropes far enough up my hand that I could pop the thumb over. Almost.

"I knew you'd say something like that. And you see, I thought of that. Which is why I would prefer the money from your rich noble friends. If you can't get it from them, your family will pay up, and I can deliver them their precious daughter, safe and sound. They get what they want without the Policiers taking a commission." He laughed, hard and harsh.

I made a show of struggling again. I braced myself and *pulled*. My thumb dislocated and popped over the rope in a burst of pain. I gasped.

"I can't go back to them," I said. "I won't. Please, don't do this, Bil. *Please*." Tears of pain slid down my face as I unworked the bonds behind my back.

Bil looked at me, regret and pity in his bloodshot eyes. He swayed softly, the stench of alcohol and stale breath washing over me. "I ain't got a choice, Micah, or whoever you are. This circus is mine, and I'll do anything to save it. Anything."

"I know," I said, and punched him in the face.

My thumb exploded with further pain. I recoiled at the meaty sound of my fist against his cheek. I had hit true, and Bil roared. I kicked him again, and, unbalanced by the punch, he staggered to the other side of the room.

Fingers fumbling, I untied my bonds from my ankles and leapt from the bed and made a dash for the door. I tripped over the long fabric of my dress. Bil grabbed my skirt, ripping it. False pearls scattered. Kicking at him, I grabbed the door handle with one hand and thumped the door loudly with the other.

"Help!" I screamed.

"Shut your trap. I'm saving my circus, girl. I won't lose sleep over sending one little brat back home for a bit of dosh," Bil grunted. He banged my head against the door of the cart and my vision swam. I wriggled wildly.

Bil's grip around my waist slipped and his hand slithered between my legs. He froze. I know what he had felt, beneath the layers of fabric. And he knew what I had under my bodice. I kicked him hard in the stomach and pulled free from his grasp. He stumbled backwards, winded but not injured. His face flushed, his eyes darkened. Bil grasped his ringmaster's cane, raising it as if about to strike me. His face showed no mercy. Only anger.

He swung, and I rolled. The cane thumped hard into the planks of the cart where my head had been moments before. Bil staggered, unbalanced by the swing and his drink. I kicked him again, but his hand grasped my leg and I crashed to the floor. I was too winded to scream.

And Bil hit me over and over again, the blows from his cane raining down. I covered my head as best I could with my arms, the pain bursting into flames on my shoulder, my arms, my back. A blow struck the side of my head and my vision wobbled. Another hit my upper left arm with a sickening crack, pain radiating through my shoulder. Through a gap in my arm I saw Bil's purple face contorted with rage, spittle flying from his mouth. He had lost it, I realized through the haze of agony.

And he was going to kill me.

The door unbolted. Hope surged in me when the blows stopped. Bil crouched over me, one hand formed in a fist, the other still clutching his cane, breathing heavily. I had a bump growing on my forehead and the beginnings of deep bruises on my arms and neck, and the remains of my bonds dangled about my wrists.

Drystan poked his head into the cart. My heart leapt in my chest. With his stage makeup cracked and his pale motley and hair, he looked like an avenging ghost.

Behind him, Aenea also peered in. They glanced between the two of us and froze.

"This isn't what it looks like," Bil slurred.

"Oh really? Looks to me like you're about to kill poor Micah, here." Drystan said.

"Micah… are you alright?"

I managed to moan.

"This is a… business meeting," he grated. "And it ain't got nothing to do with you."

"Bil, you're the one who dragged me into your mess," Drystan said. "And you didn't give me a choice in the matter. I'd say it has everything to do with me."

The words slid through me. I did not understand.

"You're drunk. Sober up, have some water, and calm down. Let Micah go. Don't punish him for your misdeeds."

"Yes, Bil, please. Just let him go." Aenea said, creeping toward him and holding her hands out.

"Him?" Bil sneered. "You don't know nothin', and you never did." Bil raised his cane again.

"Were you going to turn Micah in?" Aenea asked.

"Like I said, you don't know nothin'. The both of you." Bil's chest heaved like a bellows, his white-knuckled fists against his side.

"I know more than you, it would seem. Policiers won't give you your cut, you know. They'll hold it from the thousands of marks of taxes you owe them and then fine you for the rest." Aenea's eyes would not leave Bil's face. I was touched – she did not want me anymore, and she did not forgive me, but she wanted what was right.

Bil shook his head, mutely. "I know that. But this girl

has noble friends with deep pockets who'll pay. They'll have to. The circus needs it."

"The circus is dead, Bil," Drystan said. "It's been dying a long time. You just haven't accepted it yet. There will be no R.H. Ragona's Circus of Magic next season, or ever again. You've dug yourself a hole you can't possibly get out of, long before what happened to Frit."

What happened to Frit?

Bil's face purpled. "Don't you mention her to me. You hear? Don't you dare!"

"Haunted by the memory of your murdered wife, Bil? Regret and guilt keeping you up at night?"

Aenea gasped.

The pieces fell into place with horrible certainty.

Bil roared, lurching to his feet. His hands balled into fists as he glared at Drystan, with me forgotten in the corner.

"Let it go, Bil," Drystan said, holding his fists at the ready. "I don't want to hurt you."

"You do," Bil growled. "You both hate me and have for a long time now."

Aenea's gaze met mine, and she nodded, as if confirming something.

Lightning quick, Aenea rushed Bil and jumped onto his back, her strong arms closing about his neck. Bil sputtered and tried to shake her off, but she held on like a limpet. I forced air into my lungs, struggling to my feet. Bil pried Aenea off his neck. Drystan darted toward him but Bil backhanded him with his other hand and sent him sprawling. While Drystan recovered, Bil drew back his fist and punched Aenea full in the face. Her head snapped back like a doll's and she went limp. With a growl, Bil tossed her across the room. Aenea's head hit the bedpost and I heard a sickening crack. She fell to the floor. Her open, glassy eyes stared at me, seeing nothing.

For a moment, time stopped. None of us moved. None of us breathed. My mind could not register what had happened. And then Drystan attacked Bil. Like me, he was strong from his time in the circus, but it was his agility, honed from chasing the other clowns around the ring, that was frightening. Drystan stooped down and picked up the discarded teak cane.

He pressed it against Bil's throat.

I struggled upright, staggering over to Aenea's motionless body. Bil had ripped the bodice of the dress in our struggle. I pulled the scraps of fabric uselessly about a bare shoulder and I pressed two fingers to her neck. There was no pulse. I let out a wounded cry.

It happened in an instant. A fraction of an instant.

Drystan swung the cane at Bil's head. I must believe that he only wished to knock Bil out. But Drystan's thumb pressed against the ruby eye of the carved ram at the head of the cane. Just at the moment of impact, a long, thin blade emerged from the end, sliding sickeningly across Bil's throat.

Bil sputtered. The acrid tang of blood filled the air. The color fled his face as scarlet rivulets of blood slid down his neck. He looked at me with an accusatory stare as his eyes dimmed.

I covered my face with my hands and shuddered. In less than a day my entire world had changed. I had gone from star attraction at a circus to a fugitive, and now two people were dead – one I had loved and one I had feared.

I had never seen a dead body before. I hoped I would never have to see one again.

The sound of retching made me look up. Drystan had dropped the cane in horror, its blade stained red with blood.

"I... I didn't mean to," Drystan said, his voice flat.

"I know," I said, though I could not be completely sure. What if he knew of the hidden blade? I pushed the thought from my mind. "He was going to kill you. Kill both of us. Like he killed–" I could not say her name. My throat closed tight as I stroked her hair.

"I know, Micah. I know."

The wall within me broke and the tears started, which turned into loud, ugly sobs. Tears fell onto Aenea's head. With trembling fingers, I closed her eyes. All my fault.

Drystan helped me up and I gasped in pain. My upper arm bone was definitely fractured, if not outright broken, and I had more bruises than the Leopard Lady had spots. The pain coursed through me and my mind was fuzzy from shock and several blows to the head. I shook my head from side to side, as if that could erase all that I had just witnessed. If only I could go back in time and run away sooner – leave it all behind before it went wrong.

"We should go," Drystan said, staring at the body. He looked deflated; his shoulders slumped, the smeared clown makeup of his face garish. A parody of a sad clown. I fought down a hysterical giggle.

"Should we... do anything for them?" I asked.

"There is nothing for them we can do," he said, and I knew it was true. Blood soaked into the floorboards, giving Bil a crimson halo. With her eyes closed, Aenea looked as though she were sleeping. The floor was littered with overturned circus props and the remnants of my rope bonds and the pearls from my dress. I knelt and began picking them up.

"They link me to here, don't they?" I said, my hands shaking so badly I could barely pick up the pearls. Some were scattered in the blood. I reached for them–

Drystan's hand clasped mine, drew it away. His hand was cold and dry.

"Don't bother, Micah. They'll know it was us," Drystan said. He gave my hand a squeeze, mindful of my swollen thumb, and I knew that we were linked in this. Our ears strained for sounds of approach. The bonfire celebrations must have drowned the noise of our struggle.

I let the pearls scatter to the floor.

"What will happen to the circus?" I asked, already knowing the answer.

"The circus is over. The collectors will prey on it the moment they know Bil is gone. Everything will be broken down and sold off. The performers and workers will scatter to other shows and other circuses. There is no more Circus of Magic." Drystan's voice was still horribly flat, devoid of any emotion or inflection. Mine did not sound much better.

"Did he really kill Frit?" I said, refusing to look at what had once been Bil Ragona.

"He did. The night of her so-called disappearance. He hit… He hit her too hard." Drystan's voice cracked and he avoided looking at Aenea. "He panicked. He called on me to help him get rid of her body." He gestured toward the ocean. He shook his head, trying to forget the images that lurked beneath his eyes.

I opened my mouth, but he shook his head and my mouth snapped shut.

"I didn't want to. But he knew my secrets. And I had no choice."

What secrets did Drystan have?

I sniffed and rubbed at my nose, turning from him. My gaze fell on the safe where I had seen Frit, her hands filled with gold coins and her eyes filled with pain.

"Do you know the combination?" I asked.

He nodded.

"Open it."

He nodded again and moved to the safe, his long fingers turning the lock. I went to the door, listening for any sounds of approach. A sea shanty floated up the beach. Sayid had begun to play his sitar, and another tumbler, probably Amir, played the drums. Juliet sang the tune, her strong voice dancing over the notes. The sounds of merriment clashed with the horror surrounding me. The performers, the workers, my friends and my enemies. None of them knew what was coming tomorrow.

The safe clicked open. Drystan shoved coins in his pockets.

"Only take what we need. Leave the rest for the others," I said. "They'll check it before the creditors come." Drystan hesitated, but nodded.

In a daze, I went to the safe and took out the flat, Vestige disc.

Drystan's face asked the question.

"This does not belong to the creditors," was all I said in response. I felt a hum when I touched the metal. I dropped it into my pocket, as though it had burned me.

I wrapped my coat around myself. We crept from Bil's cart, keeping to the shadows.

29
AUTUMN: LAID BARE

"...none are missed as much as the Kedi..."
FRAGMENT OF TRANSLATED ALDER SCRIPT

We darted to Drystan's cart, and I hid behind one of the wheels as the former white clown snuck in to grab his belongings. I felt like we had wasted so much time already, and any little sound set my heart thumping. I clutched the spokes of the wheel with the hand of my unhurt arm, my knuckles white, shivering in shock and fear. I had taken all I had seen and tried to push it into the deepest, darkest corner of my mind. If I did not, then I would start crying and never stop.

Drystan crept down the stairs and joined me under the cart. He passed me a blanket and wrapped another one around his head and body, hiding the pink and white motley from view.

We began walking up the beach arm and arm. Drystan made a great show of stooping and leaning on me like he was an old woman. The sand rocked beneath us as we walked. With each step, I hoped that we were closer to safety.

But we heard a muffled yell and the sound of people running.

We dared a glance over our shoulders. Jive and the other clowns were racing up the beach, and though their faces were blurry, I knew they would be twisted with rage. They had found Bil and Aenea. They suspected Drystan and me now, and betrayal makes for anger. With a sickening start, I realized they probably thought that we had killed Aenea as well.

"Run!" I cried.

Drystan straightened and grabbed my unhurt arm, dragging me across the sand so quickly my feet barely touched the ground. My cracked arm burned with every step, but I had to ignore it. Soon I was leading Drystan, though I had no idea where we were going. I was too afraid to look behind us.

We raced along the promenade, knocking into people and spilling their drink, causing them to duck out of the way.

"Left!" Drystan yelled. We darted into a side alley and ran, startling the street rats who had burrowed under trash for the night.

"Left again!" Drystan yelled, and we turned, shocking a man nuzzling the neck of a moonshade. The whore screeched at us as we ran past, and her shrieks would bring the carnies right on our trail.

"Right!" Drystan continued to holler directions at me as we navigated our way through the labyrinthine streets of Imachara. The thin slice of the moon barely silvered the edges of buildings. We stumbled a time or two over missing cobblestones.

But they were gaining on us. We were in the Copper

district, a bad part of town. We had run into a dead end: a Penglass dome blocked our way. It glowed softly, for it was the night of the Penmoon.

Two Hands. Penmoon. Penglass. Copper.

I heard the clockwork woman's voice in my head, as if she whispered the words in my ear. The Phantom Damselfly disc burned in my coat pocket.

Two Hands. Penmoon. Penglass. Copper.

I had no time to think, or to wonder if this was a terrible idea. I grabbed Drystan's hand and ran straight for the Penglass dome.

"What are you doing?" he said. "We're trapped."

"Close your eyes!"

"What?"

"Just close them!" I yelled, and I held both palms flat against the dome, squeezing my own eyes shut.

Even behind my eyelids, the light was blinding. The clowns, close enough to touch us, screamed. I took my hands off of the Penglass and waited a moment for the light to fade enough to open my eyes. When I did, I still had to squint at the scene of horror.

Jive, Ianio, Rian, and all the rest of the clowns – they were blinded. Impossible, newly formed cataracts had turned their eyes milky, and they cried tears of blood. Jive clawed at his face. Rian waved a hand in front of his own. They were screaming in pain and fear. I retched, but there was nothing to bring up. I had no idea what would happen when I touched the glass. I had done this – blinded men who only thought they were chasing murderers to justice. I stared at my hands, which did not seem to be my own.

The clowns, some of whom had been friends, were still screaming.

Drystan stared at me in fear as well. I could not meet his eyes. People leaned out of their windows, and from far off I could hear footsteps approaching the Penglass I had touched, which still shone twice as brightly as any other dome in the city.

"Come on," he said, taking my hand hesitantly, as though he feared it would burn him. "We don't have much time."

We ran. We ignored our pain and our wounds, running until the screaming faded and the only sound we heard were our own footfalls, our heartbeats in our ears, our ragged breathing. When we could run no longer, we slowed. I had no idea where we were. I glanced behind us. Empty. We walked, hoping to draw less attention, though our frightened panting still drew suspicious looks from anyone we came across.

My breathing calmed, though the enormity of what had happened that night still had not settled upon me. Everything had a dream-like quality about the edges. Adrenaline thrummed through my veins. The grief and sadness would come later.

"Iphigenia Laurus," a voice said.

I twirled around, my heart clamoring in my ears.

It was the Shadow. He breathed heavily from following us. He wore a wide-brimmed hat, and brown stubble shadowed a handsome face lined with time.

Another glowing Penglass was to my right. I inched toward it. "What do you want, Shadow?"

"You've gotten yourself into more trouble than you

know how to handle, little girl," the Shadow said. "You know how this looks, don't you? Like you've killed your girl, your employer, and run off with gold and your new boy."

"That's not how it happened," I said. "Bil killed Aenea and tried to kill us both. It was self-defense."

"And the money? There was barely anything in that safe."

I swallowed. "There wasn't much to begin with. Bil spent most of it. It'd all go to the creditors anyway." I wondered if he had taken the rest. Something about him seemed off.

"It's still stealing." His smile transformed his face, and he looked as cunning as a fox.

"Stealing isn't the same as murder," I said.

"Your parents hired me. It's time to come along home and give up the charade. They'll find a way to clear up this mess and you can go back to your old life."

"They're not my parents. And that's not my life," I said, my voice shaking as I inched even closer to the Penglass. I did not want to touch it again – I did not want to hurt this man, even if I did not like him.

"How many more people are you going to hurt because you don't want to live a perfectly comfortable life, Iphigenia?"

"Don't listen to him, Micah," Drystan whispered behind me.

"Your girlfriend is dead," the man said, relishing the cruel words. "Were you the one to kill the ringmaster, or was it your other little friend here who struck the blow? One of you will have to take the fall for it."

I did not answer. I reached out with my hand, my fingers hovering scant inches above the glowing dome of Penglass. But his words made me feel very small and very selfish. If I had not been so dead set against my life as Iphigenia Laurus, Aenea would still be alive. Drystan was now a wanted man because of me. Perhaps I should go with him, back to my old life.

I let my hand fall.

"Will you vouch that we didn't kill anyone? That it was Bil, so that Drystan's name is cleared?" I asked.

"Micah…" Drystan whispered. "Don't listen to him." I ignored him.

The Shadow sensed my faltering. "Of course I will, Iphigenia. Of course. All will go back to how it was. Your parents will make sure you're healthy and life will be grand. Come on, now. Let's take you home."

"Make sure I'm healthy?" I echoed.

The Shadow nodded. "I was at your house giving a report. A doctor came. I heard him say you were sick. They're going to give you some medicine, and fix you, and you'll be right as rain."

"Fix me?" So even after all of this, they would still perform the surgery? My fingers rose again toward the glass.

"I think they said something like that. Don't really know. Said it would be simple and not painful, so don't you worry, Iphigenia. Come along, now. Time to go." He held his arm out to me.

My muscles tensed. "I don't think so—" I began.

But the Shadow realized the tide had turned. He rushed me as I spoke, grabbing a pair of handcuffs from his pocket. Before I could react, he had one of the handcuffs around my injured arm. He barely tugged it, but a scream of agony still tore from my throat. Drystan started to dance away from his reach, but the Shadow tripped him with his foot and sent him sprawling, pinning him down with his other foot. He still held my injured arm and absolute agony pulsed through my body. I couldn't breathe. Red stars danced in my vision.

"You can come willingly or not at all," the Shadow said. "But you're going back to your family tonight, and that's the end of it."

"Not... the... end..." I gasped, and twisted with a scream, putting both my hands on the Penglass. I squeezed my eyes shut, the handcuff dangling from my wrist. The Shadow gave a cry and I heard him stumble back. Lashing out blindly, I felt the swinging handcuff hit him with a solid *thwack*. Twisting away from the Penglass, I peeked at him. He had his arms over his eyes. With my good arm, I grabbed Drystan and we ran again, as fast as we could. We heard the Shadow give chase, but his movements were slower. I do not think I blinded him as I had with the clowns – my stomach still clenched at the thought of what I had done – but I had temporarily removed his sight, at least.

Drystan took the lead, and I staggered along as well as I could as he took us even deeper into the labyrinth of Imachara.

Eventually, we could not run any longer, and Drystan lead me to a thin alleyway that stank of rotting trash. We hid behind a bin, trying to slow our loud breathing.

"Do you know where we are?" I asked Drystan when I could speak again.

"Deep in the heart of the Copper District. Not the best place to be."

I looked about and shivered, acutely aware that I was wearing ripped petticoats and a loose tunic.

"Are you sure about this?" I asked.

"About what?"

"Throwing your dice in with a monster?" I asked, and I hated the petulant tone of my voice. "You've seen what I am. You've seen what I can do. You don't have to. I could make my own way just fine. I've done it before."

He drew me to an empty alleyway, peeking out into the street to see if anyone was coming. The smell of the dying leaves of autumn, coal chimney smoke, and putrefying trash overwhelmed me. "You're not a monster, Micah," he said.

"You're not... disturbed by what I am?"

He kept a wary eye on our surroundings before turning to me. "No. You're strange, and there's no denying that. But I'm strange as well, and most certainly more monstrous than you." He said the words so sadly. I rested a hand on his shoulder, my dislocated thumb throbbing.

And then I drew him into a hug, mindful of my arm, and we clung to each other, the full impact of what had happened finally hitting us. It was one of the few times we had really touched outside of the pantomime. Both of our bodies shook with sobs. Drystan held me so tightly it hurt my injuries, but I did not pull away. I refused to let the image of Drystan accidentally stabbing Bil enter my mind. He did not mean to. He could not have. We held each other until our sobs quieted and we were shivering with the cold.

I opened my eyes "What do we do now?"

"I don't know. Do you know anyone in Imachara?"

I shook my head. "We could go to an inn?"

"Inns won't be safe for us. It's the first place the Policiers will look for us. We're far too conspicuous."

More Policiers after me. But now for very different reasons.

"Where can we go?"

"I have a friend."

"And what type of friend is he?"

"He's a magician."

I sucked in a breath. I knew little of magicians. Mother had called them charlatans and tricksters. But she had said the same of the circus, where I had never felt more at home. I had also heard stories of magicians who had done impossible things. Some say they performed true magic, not simply illusions.

"Is he a… real magician? Or a sorcerer?"

Drystan leaned back from me. "His magic shows were beyond compare. Some said they could only be true magic." Drystan was dancing about my questions.

"What's his name? Will I have heard of him?"

"Unlikely. He last performed before you were born. He's a magician in disgrace."

"Disgrace?" My stomach twisted. What had he done?

Drystan stared into space, resting his hands on his chin, the light of the lamps catching the gold in his hair. He looked achingly beautiful. "It's a long story and I haven't the heart to tell it, but he lost a duel with a rival magician, and he hasn't been allowed to perform since. He performs séances, now."

"He raises the dead?" My stomach dropped.

Drystan's mouth twisted. "So some say."

I rubbed my face with my hands.

"Can we trust him?"

"He owes me a life debt."

I stared at him. A life debt was no small matter. It meant that anything Drystan asked, the magician had agreed to do.

"Do… do you think we'll be safe there?"

"As safe as we can be." Drystan's mouth tightened.

He took my hand and led me through the streets of Imachara, and I had no choice but to follow.

30

ALMOST WINTER: THE FUGITIVES

THE DEATH OF A CIRCUS

Correspondence by Arianna Gilbert

It has been one week since the tragedy of R.H. Ragona's Circus of Magic on the Imacharan beach. Unfortunately for circus lovers, Ellada now has one less. Due to financial problems with creditors, the circus has gone into liquidation. An auction for circus paraphernalia will be held tomorrow at half past two at Thomson & Farquhar's Auction House.

The ringmaster, William Hakan Ragona, was found murdered in his cart, the safe open and money missing. A young woman and aerialist, Aenea Harper, was also found dead in the cart, and officials believe it may be a crime of passion, as one of the fugitives was romantically involved with the aerialist.

The two suspects are missing and wanted for immediate questioning. One is a Micah Grey, a newcomer to the circus, who was the other half of the aerialist act and an actor. Micah is around seventeen with auburn hair and green eyes. The other is Drystan, surname unknown, who was a clown and actor. He is in his early twenties, with flaxen hair dyed white.

There is a substantial reward for information leading to the capture of these two men. They may be armed and dangerous – their pursuers the night of the attack are in critical condition. Do not approach directly, and proceed with extreme caution.

Authorities have high hopes that they will bring these two fugitives to justice before the next Penmoon.

FROM THE DAILY IMACHARAN

Acknowledgments

There are so many people who supported me in the making of *Pantomime*. First of all, to my mother for being my rock my entire life and showing me how to be a strong woman who works for her dreams. Thank you to my best friend, Erica, for reading this book many, many times and being wonderfully picky. To my husband, Craig, for his endless love, support and patience with my ceaseless questions and fears. To my father for his encouragement.

Many people helped me after the draft of the book was written. Endless thanks to Amanda Rutter (and everyone at Angry Robot), who plucked me from the slush pile and saw the promise in my manuscript and gave me another chance to make it shine. To Juliet Mushens, the Leopard Lady, for loving my book and being the best agent and advocate I could ask for.

I owe Anne Lyle many favors for telling me in one sentence how to fix the pacing. So much thanks to Wesley Chu for being my partner in angst and literary best friend. To the other two-thirds of the Three Amigos:

Kim Curran and Adam Christopher. To the rest of the Anxious Appliances writers' group and to Write Club and the Cabal. All of my beta readers have my sincere gratitude.

Lastly, to my teachers and professors for fostering a life-long love of learning and the importance of craft. To the authors I read that left their mark upon me and my writing.

And to you, readers, for picking up my book and spending some time in this circus: thank you.

"Weird, wise and witty, Blackwood is great fun."
– *Marcus Sedgwick*

EXPERIMENTING WITH YOUR IMAGINATION

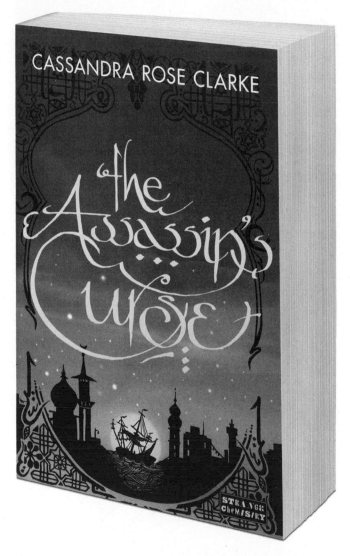

CASSANDRA ROSE CLARKE

the Assassin's Curse

STRANGE Chemistry

"Unique, heart-wrenching, full of mysteries and twists!"
– *Tamora Pierce, author of* Alanna: The First Adventure

"A really well-imagined world, a great mix of technical detail and breathless action."
– *Charlie Higson, author of the Young Bond series*

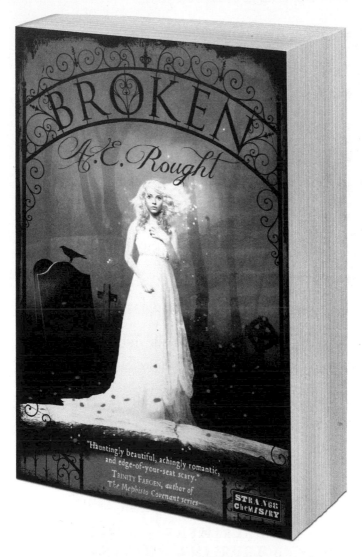

"Death, kissing and a smoking hot mystery boy: what more could you ask for?"
– *Amy Plum, author of* Die for Me

MORE WONDERS IN STORE FOR YOU...

- Gwenda Bond / BLACKWOOD
- ◆ Kim Curran / SHIFT
- ◆ Sean Cummings / POLTERGEEKS
- Cassandra Rose Clarke / THE ASSASSIN'S CURSE
- ◆ Jonathan L Howard / KATYA'S WORLD
- A E Rought / BROKEN
- ◆ Julianna Scott / THE HOLDERS
- Martha Wells / EMILIE & THE HOLLOW WORLD
- Christian Schoon / ZENN SCARLETT
- Cassandra Rose Clarke / THE PIRATE'S WISH
- Bryony Pearce / THE WEIGHT OF SOULS
- TL Costa / PLAYING TYLER
- ◆ Ingrid Jonach / WHEN THE WORLD WAS FLAT (AND WE WERE IN LOVE)

**EXPERIMENTING WITH
YOUR IMAGINATION**

strangechemistrybooks.com
facebook.com/strangechemistry
twitter.com/strangechem